INVASION OF

PRIVACY

Other John Cuddy novels by Jeremiah Healy

Blunt Darts
The Staked Goat
So Like Sleep
Swan Dive
Yesterday's News
Right to Die
Shallow Graves
Foursome
Act of God
Rescue

Published by POCKET BOOKS

INVASION OF PRIVACY

A John Francis Cuddy Mystery

J.F. (JEREMIAH HEALY, 1948-

POCKET BOOKS

New York   London   Toronto   Sydney   Tokyo   Singapore

This book is a work of fiction. Names, characters, places and incidents are products of the author's imagination or are used fictitiously. Any resemblance to actual events or locales or persons, living or dead, is entirely coincidental.

POCKET BOOKS, a division of Simon & Schuster Inc.
1230 Avenue of the Americas, New York, NY 10020

Library of Congress Cataloging-in-Publication Data

Healy, J. F. (Jeremiah F.), 1948–
  Invasion of privacy : a John Francis Cuddy Mystery / Jeremiah
Healy.
    p. cm.
  ISBN: 0-671-89876-0 (HC)
  I. Title.
PS3558.E2347I58   1996
813'.54—dc20   96-1196
                                                            CIP

First Pocket Books hardcover printing July 1996

10 9 8 7 6 5 4 3 2 1

POCKET and colophon are registered trademarks of
Simon & Schuster Inc.

Printed in the U.S.A.

For Bonnie, still the best

INVASION OF
PRIVACY

1

The woman choosing one of the client chairs in front of my desk was attractive without being beautiful or even pretty. Wearing a gray herringbone business suit, carefully tailored, over a white blouse and Christmas-ribbon bow tie, she seemed around forty. At maybe five-five and one-ten, her body looked trim but not athletic. The hair was a lustrous brown, curling upward and inward just above the shoulders. High cheekbones slanted slightly toward her nose while pale blue eyes slanted slightly toward her temples. Everything about the woman suggested sophisticated but foreign, and I wasn't surprised when she spoke English with a faint, precise accent.

"I am sorry to come here without an appointment, Mr. Cuddy."

I pushed a legal pad and pen to the side of my desk. "That's all right," I said, placing the accent as Eastern European or—

"My name is Olga Evorova." She pronounced it "Ee-*vor*-oh-va." "I obtained your name from a computer search of recent newspaper articles."

1

There are worse ways. "Which ones?"

Evorova told me, then glanced away toward one of the windows behind me, the chair she'd taken giving her a view of the Boston Common as it sweeps up to the golden dome of the Massachusetts Statehouse. The trees were barely turning, the early October air on that Tuesday afternoon as mild as Labor Day weekend. When I'd come in, tourists were mobbing the guy who sold tickets to a sight-seeing trolley from his carny stand across the street.

Without looking back toward me, Evorova said, "I have never before needed the help of a private investigator."

My office door has pebbled glass in the upper half, and I noticed that the reverse stenciling of "JOHN FRANCIS CUDDY, CONFIDENTIAL INVESTIGATIONS" bowed over her head like the arch of a medieval church. "Why do you feel you need one now?"

The pale blue eyes returned to me. "This June past, I met a man. I soon grew to care for him very much, and our relationship has . . . progressed to the point that I would very much like to marry him if he should ask."

I nodded and waited.

She moved her tongue around inside her mouth, as though trying to dissipate a bad taste. "I am, however, concerned about his background."

"In what way?"

More hesitation. "What we discuss, it remains confidential, yes?"

"Unless a court orders me to talk, and maybe even then, depending."

"Depending upon what?"

"On how much I like you as a client."

That brought a shy smile. "You are very easy to talk with, Mr. Cuddy."

"It's a useful quality."

"Useful?"

2

"People who come to see me often have difficult things to talk about."

A dip of the chin as she seemed to reach a decision. "Originally, I am from Moscow. It was nearly impossible, but I was able to immigrate to the United States for my master's degree in finance. After graduation, I obtained a job with Harborside Bank. When the Soviet Union began to break apart, I was promoted several times rapidly as someone who might bring to the bank a certain advantage in business dealings with the 'new' country of Russia. Even though the dealings have not come so far so fast, I am very well compensated for my work." Another hesitation. "I am talking too much?"

"No. Go on, please."

Evorova looked down at my desk. "You will not take notes?"

"Not right away. I'd rather hear you describe things first."

The chin dip. "In Moscow, my family is all gone, just one uncle here I am able to help. Many died from the Nazis in the Great Patriotic War. So, except for my Uncle Vanya—Ivan—I am alone."

"And you're concerned that . . . ?"

The pale eyes glanced toward her lap, then fixed me with an executive stare. "I am concerned that I seem a 'fat cat,' a potential target."

"For someone like this man you've grown to care for?"

"Exactly, yes. His name is Andrew Dees. He is a wonderful person, Mr. Cuddy. Andrew owns his own business and a condominium in the town of Plymouth Mills on the South Shore. He is romantic and intelligent and . . ." Evorova blushed. "Soon I will be blushing."

"Then what worries you about Mr. Dees?"

"As I said, his background. Or that he has *no* 'background.' I ask Andrew where he is from, and he says Chicago, but does not talk about it. I ask him about his family, and he says they are all dead, but does not talk of them. I ask him about his schooling, and he says he graduated from the University of Central Vermont, but does not talk about his time there or . . . anything."

Evorova seemed to run down a little, like a wind-up toy after a long spurt. I gave her a moment, then said, "Have you done any investigating on your own?"

She looked out my window again. "Some. I ran a D&B on Andrew. You know what this is?"

"A Dun & Bradstreet credit report?"

"Exactly, yes." A small sigh. "Nothing."

"Nothing?"

Evorova came back to me. "Oh, Andrew has a personal checking account, and a business checking account, and a business credit card, which he never uses. But there is no personal credit card, no prior loan history, not even a current line of credit for the business."

"What business is it?"

"A photocopy shop in the town center near his condominium."

"That would mean some capital investment to get started, right?"

"Exactly, yes. But he paid cash for everything that is not leased."

Cash. "And the condo?"

"It is in a complex called Plymouth Willows."

"But how did Mr. Dees pay for it?"

"Oh. By cash also. Well, certified check, actually. Andrew purchased from a realty trust—do you wish the details in a banking sense?"

"I don't think so."

"Then just assume that he paid the deposit for his unit by certified check and the balance the same. Andrew also filed a homestead exemption. You know what this is, too?"

4

"A protection of so much equity in his condo from any future creditors?"

"Exactly, yes."

"Did Mr. Dees have an attorney represent him?"

"In the purchase, do you mean?"

I nodded.

"No," said Evorova. "Andrew told me he did not."

I'd had a year of evening law school, and the homestead exemption in Massachusetts was a pretty advanced device for a layman from Chicago to know about. "Mr. Dees is willing to talk about that transaction, then?"

"But only a little. And when we were reading in bed . . . One Sunday morning, casually I pointed to him a newspaper article in the *Globe* about ante-nuptial agreements. Andrew laughed and said he did not believe in those things and very quickly changed the subject to something else."

"Do you know his Social Security number?"

"Yes."

"Do you also know there are other sources you can check by running that number through some computers?"

"Yes. And I have done that." The executive stare again. "Nothing."

"No prior employment?"

"No."

"Military service?"

"No."

"Divorce?"

"No, no, and no."

I stopped. A bit of what it must feel like to sit across a negotiating table from Evorova came through to me.

She waved her hand in a way I found both alien and expressive. "I am sorry, but this is quite . . . upsetting, even just to discuss."

Understandable. "Where did you meet Mr. Dees?"

"In a bar, but not as you would think."

"Tell me about it."

"I was driving back from Cape Cod—my best friend at the bank, she has a summer house there. My car is a Porsche, the 911 Carrera six-speed. Do you know it?"

"Only by price tag."

The blushing again. "One of my few indulgences, Mr. Cuddy. I even had the car custom-painted my favorite shade of orange, and I permit no one else to drive it."

"Not even Mr. Dees?"

"No. But I have digressed. That day, when I am coming back from the Cape, I hear a noise in the engine which I do not like. So, I exit Route 3 at Plymouth Mills, where the Porsche manual says there is a dealership, and while my car is being examined, I cross the street and go into a bar, to wait."

"And?"

"I am sitting at the bar, reading _Forbes_—the business magazine?—when this man on a stool nearby says to me, 'He died on a motorcycle, like James Dean.' At first I would not have talked to him, but Andrew's voice is wonderful. I do not have a perfect sense for American accents, but I have developed some ear for them, and he sounded from the Midwest. So I did."

"Talk to him."

Evorova dipped her chin once more. "For an hour, two. Andrew has very dark hair, and a very strong face. I almost forgot about my car. But when he asked me for my telephone number, I said, 'No, give to me yours, and I will call you.'"

"And then you started going out?"

"Yes. Andrew does not like to come to Boston much because of his business—to leave it alone?—but he enjoys the ballet, and the symphony, especially chamber music. And we go to restaurants. Andrew does not like Italian or Indian food, but he very much enjoys the Chinese and . . ." Another blush. "Again, I am sorry."

It wasn't hard to see why Evorova was so troubled. She suspected the guy was a little off, but she was nuts about him too.

I said, "From the way you met, it doesn't sound like a set-up."

"A . . . you mean that Andrew arranged that we would meet?"

"Right."

Evorova shook her head vigorously. "No. No, I think that would be quite impossible. The bar is one near his business, one he goes to very often, I think. But Andrew could not know I would be driving back from the Cape that day and develop engine trouble."

I picked up my pen for the first time. "The name of the bar?"

"The Tides, in the town center, also." She tensed a bit. "You will go there?"

"That depends on what you want me to do."

Evorova seemed relieved. "What I want you to do is . . . find out things. Perhaps to watch Andrew, to . . ." She admired the Statehouse again. "Find out things."

"But without Mr. Dees knowing I'm doing it."

Back to me. "Exactly, yes. I do not wish to threaten our relationship by committing an invasion of privacy."

I put down the pen. "Ms. Evorova, that won't be easy, and it may not even be possible."

"Why so?"

"It's difficult to do more than what you've done already without Mr. Dees hearing from other people that I've been asking around about him."

"You could perhaps follow Andrew, yes? With discretion?"

"Do you have a photo of him?"

7

Evorova looked toward her lap once more, speaking almost to herself. "He does not like the camera very much, my Andrew."

My Andrew. I brought both hands onto the blotter, folding them. "Ms. Evorova, even with a photo, following somebody isn't quite as easy as it looks on television."

"Why so?"

"Everyone can tell after a while that they're being tailed unless the followers use a team approach, like the police or FBI could mount."

She seemed to digest that.

I said, "Is there anybody you know who I could talk to about Mr. Dees without it getting back to him?"

A slow shake of the head. "My uncle has met Andrew, and likes him very much. If you talk to Vanya, it would . . . get back."

"How about people from work?"

"Andrew has only one employee, and she is loyal to him, I believe."

"No, I meant at your bank. Has anyone met Mr. Dees?"

"Only my friend, Clude, who owns the house on the Cape."

"Clude?"

"She is French-Canadian, but born here. The spelling is C-L-A-U-D-E."

I wrote it down. "Last name?"

"Wah-*zell*, L-O-I-S-E-L-L-E." Evorova seemed troubled. "I would prefer you not speak with her."

I placed the pen back on the blotter. "It might help if you could tell me why."

The troubled look grew deeper. "Probably I will talk to Claude about coming to see you. However, she has had dinner with us—with Andrew and me—twice. I think she made up her mind about him the first time, but she agreed to meet him again."

"And?"

"Claude is a very . . . instinctive person, Mr. Cuddy. She believes Andrew is hiding something from me."

"Did Ms. Loiselle suggest you see a private investigator?"

"No." The executive stare again. "She suggested I stop seeing Andrew."

I'd already heard enough not to contest Evorova on that one, but she kept going anyway. "You see, I have not had a very . . . secure life. Before I am born, my mother was pregnant with twins, another baby girl and me. When she reached her sixth month, my mother was passenger on a bus in Moscow that collided with a truck. Afterward, she felt sick, so she went to the doctor. He said to her, 'I am sorry, but one of your babies is dead.' He said also that it would be safer for the other baby—me—if my mother carried both babies . . . to term. She did what the doctor advised, and so I lay in the womb three months next to my dead sister." A tear trickled over the corner of Evorova's left eye. "I never met her, but I . . . I still miss her."

A moment. Then, "As my other family, the ones who survived the Great Patriotic War, began dying, I dreamed of the United States, and a different life here. A secure one. And now I have that. But for me, life has been only study and work. All my time, all my energy, all my . . . heart. Until I met Andrew. And my heart tells me I cannot lose him just because my banker head—or my banker friend—tells me some things are perhaps not quite right. Do you see this?"

I thought about my wife, Beth, before the cancer took her, and about Nancy Meagher, who'd very nearly come to replace her. "I think so."

Evorova suddenly shrugged heavily. "I am sorry. I am one professional coming to consult with another, and instead, I . . ." The expressive wave again.

I picked up my pen. "We need to talk about my retainer and how you want me to stay in touch with you."

She looked at me. "You will try to help, yes?"

9

"I'll try."

A sense of relief came into her voice. "Thank you so much."

Evorova thought my usual rate was fine, giving me her home number but asking that I use her voice-mail at the bank, "just in case Andrew is . . . might be at my apartment."

"And where do you live?"

She reeled off the street address. "A condominium of my own, on Beacon Hill."

Which triggered an idea. I said, "You told me Mr. Dees lives in a condominium too."

"Yes. Unit number 42 at Plymouth Willows in—"

"Plymouth Mills."

Evorova seemed pleased that I'd remembered the name of her Andrew's town.

I said, "He has neighbors close by, then?"

"Exactly, yes. Townhouses on either side. In little 'clusters,' he calls them."

"How big a complex is it?"

"Plymouth Willows? A total of perhaps fifty units, sixty?"

Good. "So there's some kind of property company that manages it?"

"I believe so." Evorova's eyes seemed to search inside for a moment. "Yes. I remember Andrew saying once the name of it, when he was writing his monthly maintenance check."

"Do you remember the name?"

More searching. "No, I am sorry."

I put down the pen and smiled at her. "Can you find out?"

Olga Evorova smiled back, but I could tell she wasn't sure why.

2

Knocking lightly on the jamb of the open door, I said, "Mo, got a minute?"

Mo Katzen glanced up at me. He was sitting behind a desk that looked roughly like the Charles River Esplanade after the July Fourth fireworks' concert. Pieces of waxy sandwich paper jockeyed for position with empty soda cans, the straws still bent at the angle Mo preferred while drinking from them. Discarded stories were scattered around the old manual typewriter he wouldn't consign to the junk heap despite the fact that every other reporter at the Boston *Herald* had computerized years ago. A half-smoked, unlit cigar was jammed in the corner of his mouth, the eyes sad beneath an unruly wave of snow-white hair. Seventy-something and looking every day of it, the man himself was in his standard uniform, the vest and pants of a three-piece suit, the jacket nowhere to be found. Only this time, the suit was black instead of the usual gray.

"John, John." Mo motioned listlessly. "Come on in."

I took the seat across his desk. "Something wrong, Mo?"

He shrugged, the cigar doing a sit-up. "Nothing much. Just the passing of a generation, that's all."

"Somebody died?"

"Of course somebody died. People die every day, John. Every minute, probably every second, you want to stretch the net wide enough. Why do you think I'm in this outfit?"

"Sorry, Mo. Someone close?"

A smaller shrug, the cigar rising only halfway. "Close enough. Guy I went to school with, back in Chelsea."

The city north of Boston. "How did it happen?"

"How? How. I'll tell you how." Mo came forward, some animation flowing back into him. "Freddie—that was his name, Freddie Norton—Freddie was walking by the McCormack Building downtown. He was trying to figure out where the feds had hidden the Social Security offices so he could ask them a question, since of course trying to get them on the phone is just this side of establishing radio contact with Mars. Well, Freddie looks the wrong way stepping off the curb and gets pasted by this truck, pedal to the metal in third gear trying to pass a police car on the right. I mean, what kind of jerk does that? Pass a cruiser, and in the slow lane, yet. Anyway, Freddie gets thrown fifty feet—he was always just a little guy, and he hadn't grown any lately— and despite the cops already being there and calling for an ambulance and all, he's DOA at Mass General, like seven blocks away."

"I'm sorry for your troubles, Mo."

"Huh, tell me about it. People dwell on how they're afraid to ride planes or even cars in this city. You know how dangerous it is just to walk around here?"

"I have some idea—"

He pulled the cigar out of his mouth and gestured with it. "I called this guy I know over in the Transportation Department—those guys you *can* reach by phone, account of nobody ever makes calls about safety, you know?—and he told me that pedestrian deaths dropped from over thirty to just eleven in four years."

"Impressive."

"Impressive? What, are you kidding me? That eleven was something like forty percent of the total motor-vehicle fatalities in the entire city for the year. Which puts us just behind New York. Can you imagine that? We're killing our pedestrians at almost the same rate as the Big Apple."

"Mo, I'm not sure your figures support—"

"Plus, after that drop to 'only' eleven, the toll jumped back near twenty last year. I'm telling you, John, it's like open season out there." Mo laughed silently. "The kind of thing Freddie would've liked to hear."

"I don't get you, Mo."

He looked up at me, waving the cigar impatiently. "Freddie was an undertaker, didn't you know that?"

"I guess not."

"He had some great experiences in that line of work too, more than you'd think. I remember a couple of times I had to cover the funerals of people laid out at his home—pols mostly, hacks all—and Freddie'd take me aside, ask with that undertaker's dirge if I could use them in one of my columns."

"Use what, Mo?"

"His experiences, what do you think? You got to pay closer attention, John."

"Sorry, Mo."

"I mean, it's like you're losing the whole thread of the conversation here."

"Won't happen again."

Mo shuffled through the mess on his desk till he came up with a war-memorial lighter the size of a softball. He flicked it three times, no results. Then he examined it more closely, the thing no more than six inches from his eyes. "Bastards!"

"What's the matter, Mo?"

"The ASNs. They stole my wick again."

"The who?"

"Not 'who,' John, 'what.' My wick, the little thing in there, lets the flame come out. What college did you go to, anyway?"

"Holy Cross, Mo. But—"

"And you don't know what a wick is? The priests didn't have candles in the chapels there and all?"

"They had candles. What I meant was, who are the 'Ay-Ess-Ens'?"

"The initials, of course. The Anti-Smoking Nazis."

"First I've heard of them, Mo."

"They steamrolled some kind of 'secondhand smoke' policy through the powers that be, and now we're supposed to go outside every time we want to light up."

"That's becoming pretty typical of—"

"Only I won't go along with it, so they sneak in here and steal my wick." He hefted the lighter for me to appreciate. "You have any idea how hard it is to replace one, an antique like this is?"

"None."

Mo shook his head. "And to think my favorite was the one about this paper."

"Your favorite?"

He fixed me with a baleful eye. "My favorite of the experiences that Freddie told me about in his funeral home."

"Oh."

"You gonna be all right now?"

"Just a momentary lapse, Mo."

"I hope so." He put down the lighter and stuck the dead cigar back in his mouth. "Freddie had some great ones, like the time this lifelong rival of the decedent comes into the viewing room, walks up to the corpse, and spits in his face. Spits in it. Or this other time, a nickel-and-dime loanshark comes in, pays his respects to the surviving family, then goes to the prayer rail. Only instead of kneeling down, the shark leans in and grabs the corpse by the lapels—grabs him, John—and starts banging the decedent's head against the side of the coffin, yelling, 'You deadbeat, where's my five hundred? Where is it?' "

I didn't see where the newspaper fit in, but I wasn't about to ask.

Mo took a deep breath. "But my favorite, all time—all *world*—was this widow, comes up to Freddie straight from the hospital to make the arrangements for her husband, and she says to him, 'Freddie, my Gerry spent every blessed night of his life sitting on one of our kitchen chairs, reading the *Herald*'—it wasn't the '*Herald*' for all those years, John, but you get the picture—and Freddie says to her, 'There, there,' or something like that, and she says back, 'No, Freddie, you don't understand. That's the way I want Gerry laid out, sitting on one of our chairs at the front of your viewing room here, his legs crossed and the *Herald* open in his hands.' Freddie tried to talk her out of it, but she wouldn't budge, so he swallowed kind of hard and the next evening, there was Gerry, like any other night, in one of those chairs, upright and edifying himself with the day's well-recounted news."

"A lovely image, Mo."

"I think so. In fact, it's kind of lifted my spirits some too. Now, what brings you here?"

"I'd like to run a few names through your computer, see if anything useful pops up."

"Sure thing." Mo reached for his telephone. "I'll get one of the ASNs to help you out—keep their fingers on the keyboard and away from other people's harmless vices."

The young man who appeared at the door a few minutes later led me back through a rabbit warren of cubicles to his own, more a library study carrel than an office like Mo's. I gave him "Olga Evorova" first, and he typed her name after some sort of search command. The screen showed two articles that referred to her participation in deals underwritten by Harborside Bank as well as a couple of "Executives in the News" blurbs, one with photo, announcing her promotions within the bank. My client appeared to be who she claimed to be, a nice reassurance.

The young guy did another search, for "Andrew Dees." I was disappointed but not surprised when the computer came up empty.

I got back to my office in time to gather the afternoon mail from the floor under the horizontal, flap-covered slot in my door and open most of the envelopes before the phone rang.

Cradling the receiver against my ear, I said, "John Cuddy."

"Mr. Cuddy, this is Olga Evorova."

"Yes, Ms. Evorova."

"I have for you the name of the company which manages the Plymouth Willows condominiums."

"That was fast."

"I told my friend, Claude, about hiring you. She thinks it was a good idea. Claude then telephoned a banker she knows on the South Shore, and he obtained the name and address of the company for me."

"So Mr. Dees wouldn't be tipped off."

"Exactly, yes. The name of the company is Hendrix Property Management." Evorova gave me an address in Marshfield, a few towns north of Plymouth Mills. "Is there anything more you need?"

"Not just now. I'll contact you if I've made any progress."

"Thank you so much."

Nancy Meagher had suggested I meet her that night for dinner and "something different," as she described it, which was her way of saying she'd be driving and taking care of the tab. After locking my office and going downstairs, I crossed Tremont Street and walked north, politely dodging hordes of office workers. The gainfully employed formed a high tide swelling toward the Park Street subway stop, washing away clutches of bewildered people in vacation clothes, cameras around their necks and folded maps in their hands, trying in vain to find that trolley ticket stand. I passed the Old Granary burial ground on the left and King's Chapel on the right, turning at One Center Plaza for an escalator to the Pemberton Square level.

The still-called "New Courthouse" was attached to the "Old Courthouse" in the thirties, surviving a terrorist bombing of the probation department in the seventies and the failure of most major internal systems like electricity and plumbing through the eighties and nineties. The scaffolding now rising up the exterior walls had something to do with waterproofing, the building creaking and therefore leaking at every joint and seam. They're about to break ground on a new site, the budgetary crunch on the old structure so severe the judges have been reduced to bringing their own light bulbs and toilet paper from home.

I cleared the sheriff's metal detectors inside the revolving door on the first floor and took the elevator to six for the Suffolk County District Attorney's Office. I was making small talk with the two blazered security men at the half-moon desk out front when Nancy emerged from the labyrinth in back.

She wore full battle gear: pale gray suit, white blouse with a small ruffle and faint blue piping, no tie, and only sensible heels. The crow-black hair just brushed her shoulders, framing the bright Irish face with widely spaced eyes and bat-wings of freckles crossing the nose. Then she smiled, and I felt my heart do the same little jig it had the first time I'd seen her, arguing in an arraignment session a year and a half before.

Nancy said, "Not carrying?"

I smiled back at her, tapping the hollow over my right hip. "They're very conscientious downstairs." I gestured toward her arms, themselves empty except for a compact leather handbag. "And you?"

"Meaning the conspicuous absence of my briefcase?"

"That's what I meant."

"I have an attempted murder starting tomorrow, but the remaining pretrial motions and impaneling the jury will kill the whole day. So, tonight, no work for a change."

"Just 'something different.' "

"That's right. Come on."

We stayed quiet in the elevator, Nancy slipping her arm into mine once we were outside again. A mime wearing chalky makeup and a black costume trudged toward us, parodying the walk of the tired commuter in front of him.

Nancy said, "Never liked mimes."

"Leave me speechless too."

We walked to her car, a red Honda Civic, and she began driving, the traffic worse than ever because of the "Big Dig."

Nancy said, "You think they'll ever finish it?"

"Not in our lifetimes."

The Big Dig was what Boston called the attempt to drop the elevated "Central Artery" (which separates downtown from the waterfront) and to add a third harbor tunnel to Logan Airport. The project, thanks to something the late Tip O'Neill worked out with then-President Ron, began as a two-billion-dollar effort; I'd stopped reading about the cost overruns when they'd hit $10 billion the prior summer. The demolition and reconstruction already had transformed rush "hour" into a 6:00 A.M. to 10:00 P.M. phenomenon, and the predictions were for round-the-clock problems and helicopter shuttles as the city slouched toward the new millennium.

When Nancy swung into the North End, I said, "We're not headed for Harvard Square."

"You know anybody who'd *drive* to the Square when the Red Line's almost door-to-door by subway?"

"Only you."

A measured pause. "I did that just once, and I'll never do it again."

"Glad to hear it. So, where then?"

"Be patient, John. Enjoy the scenery."

I looked out the window. Pile drivers, cement dust, and tarring crews. "No wonder we're knee-deep in tourists this time of year."

"You've just become blind to the city's charms."

The Civic crossed the Charlestown Bridge by North Station and another construction site, this one for the new Boston Garden, the stonework crowding one of the ramps not so far changed by the Dig. On the other side of the bridge, Nancy turned left and then right onto the Monsignor McGrath Highway before turning left again for Cambridge Street.

I said, "Busman's holiday."

"What?"

"We're going to the Middlesex Courthouse."

"Negative."

Continuing west on Cambridge Street, we passed the Middlesex County jail and court building. A mile or so later, Nancy parked across from a bright stucco restaurant.

The sign read CASA PORTUGAL. "I hope I know what this means."

"Only the beginning."

" 'Only just the start,' " I sang softly.

Nancy canted her head. She's a lot younger than I am, and sometimes it shows.

"Old Chicago tune, Nance."

"Chicago being a band?"

I cleared my throat. "Right."

We crossed the street and stepped up into the restaurant,

a cozy, low-ceilinged room that seats maybe forty people. The tables are small and comfortably separated, the walls covered with colorful frescoes of what I've always taken to be Portugal. The former owner sometimes had guitar players and singers perform in front of the fireplace, but the establishment was always more restaurant than cabaret, and the music was too much sound. His successor has members of his own family waiting on tables, the place pretty successful since it's changed hands only once in the twenty-some years I've been going there.

The current owner welcomed us at the door and provided escort to the candlelit table for two in the window looking onto Cambridge Street. We opened the big menus, but really only for something to do, since we always have the same entrées there: the marinated pork cubes for Nancy, the veal marsala for me, both accompanied by the house's kale soup, homemade bread, and Portuguese french fries, the last like thick, deep-fried potato chips.

Nancy asked me to pick a wine. After the owner left us, I said, "You were kidding, right?"

"Kidding about what?"

"About not recognizing the name of the band."

A smile tweaked the corners of her mouth. "I don't know what you mean, John."

"Nance, everybody's heard of Chicago. I mean, they had a dozen hits in the—"

"John, John, I *was* kidding, all right? What's got you so touchy?"

The owner arrived with our wine, a dry red called Imperial Dao. Sampling it, I approved, and he poured for both of us before leaving with our meal orders.

Nancy looked at me over her wineglass.

I said, "I'm not touchy."

"Is it age or aging or what?"

I told her about Mo and Freddie Norton.

She nodded. "And my kidding around just reminded you of the . . . differences between the generations?"

"I sometimes have trouble following Mo's train of thought, Nance, maybe because he's so much older than I am. And I guess I don't like to think that people close to me are having the same trouble with what I say."

Nancy took a polite sip. "We're not."

"Thanks."

"Most of the time."

"Drink your wine."

The bread and the kale soup arrived, nearly constituting a meal in themselves.

Between spoonfuls, Nancy said, "So, how was your day?"

"Interesting, I think."

"You don't know if it was interesting or not?"

Nancy and I have developed an uneasy truce about my obligations as a private investigator to keep client matters confidential and her obligations as an assistant DA to prosecute crimes, but I didn't see any problem with an abstract outline. "A woman came to see me. She wants a confidential investigation of her boyfriend-*cum*-fiancé."

"To see if he's on the level," Nancy said, very matter-of-factly.

I looked at her. "Yes. That doesn't surprise you?"

"These days? Uh-uh. One of the other prosecutors was dating this professor at her old college—somebody she met again going back for a reunion?—and they became intimate. Of course she took precautions, but when the relationship became more serious, she asked one of the state troopers attached to our office to just check him out. And guess what?"

"The professor was married."

"No."

"Not really a professor?"

"He'd been her teacher, John."

"Okay, I give up."

"Be a little more imaginative."

I'm slow about some things. "Bisexual?"

A nod before another sip. "Kind of chilling, huh?"

I had some of my wine. "You ever have me 'checked out'?"

"Yes, but not that far."

"How come?"

A self-satisfied smile. "You'd been on the shelf a while."

"And out of circulation means safe?"

"John, you just have a feeling about some people, you know?"

An image of Olga Evorova came into my head, her shy blushing showing her love but not stemming her concerns about the man she wanted me to investigate. I didn't envy my client that feeling.

"John?"

"Sorry."

The entrées arrived in hand-turned pottery bowls, hot and fragrant and just spicy enough on the tongue. And, as always, too much food.

When we finished, I said, "Doggie bags?"

Nancy shook her head. "Leftovers wouldn't keep where we're going." Checking her watch, she brought out the wallet from her handbag. "And we should be going."

As we arrived in Davis Square, I said, "The Somerville Theatre."

"The same." After parking a block away, Nancy bought us tickets at a window on the side of the building. A small line accumulated behind us as she got her change and the stubs, handing me one. When we got to the front of the theater, the marquee read: SCOTTISH FIDDLE RALLY.

I looked from it to Nancy. "A coming attraction, right?"

"Wrong. Come on."

On the right side of the lobby was an old-fashioned counter for popcorn and soda and the usual overpriced cavity-creators in brightly colored boxes. On the left side were tables displaying cassette tapes and compact discs with names on them I didn't recognize. As we reached the doorways leading to the seating, a teenaged girl in a tartan skirt handed us yellow programs.

I said, "The Boston Scottish Fiddle Club."

"Yes."

"Nance, we're Irish."

"The cross-pollination will be good for you."

I flipped through the program. "They've got fifteen, twenty entries on this. 'Reels' and 'airs' and 'marches.' "

"So we'll get our money's worth."

"We'll be here till dawn, too."

"A friend of mine saw this last year and said it was terrific. Let's find our seats."

Inside the theater proper, the orchestra level sloped down toward the stage, somebody having impromptu-marked the chairs with letters and numbers on taped pieces of cardboard. We got to our row, the red velvet cushions flat and worn as I sat down. The two couples behind us were comparing culinary experiences from ocean cruises.

After ten minutes of their small talk, I whispered to Nancy, "This is what siege warfare must have been like."

She was about to reply—something cutting, from the cast of her lips—when the lights went down over the seats and came up on the stage, showing twenty or so fiddlers, sitting concert-style on chairs with music stands, other instruments like guitar, cello, and piano sprinkled in their midst. The music started immediately, reminding me at first of the soundtrack to a John Ford western. Then the playing stopped for a few minutes, the director introducing the club and its purposes to us before bringing on four teenaged girls from Cape Breton, one of them our program aide, I thought.

2 3

They step-danced through a loud, lively song—not a "march," but the theater too dark to read whether it was a "reel" or an "air." About midway through their performance, I found myself tapping my foot on the floor.

Nancy leaned over and nearly shouted in my ear, "See?"

The director next presented a Cape Breton fiddle soloist, his style a cross between folk and bluegrass music. While he was good, the next performer was incredible. Introduced as Alasdair Fraser, the bearded, bearish guy addressed the audience in a thick Scottish burr, every other word going right by me. But then Fraser began to play, his foot keeping time, his body weaving and bobbing as the bow made the fiddle laugh, scream, and weep. I found myself stomping my own foot against the floor, and after he finished, the man received from all of us the kind of ovation given when the best in the world has done his best for you.

This time Nancy just smiled.

"Why do I ever doubt you?" I said.

"Don't ask me."

We enjoyed another half an hour before intermission, then a rousing second set with the step-dancers and the soloists and a remarkable Highland dancer, noticeably past her teens, who literally flew around the stage. After the second encore, we moved out into the lobby, me stopping at one of the tables and picking up a cassette tape of Alasdair Fraser.

Nancy said, "And why are we buying that?"

"Because I don't have a CD-player."

The smile that always reminds me, for no good reason, of Loni Anderson scoring points against the males on the old *WKRP in Cincinnati.*

"Don't gloat, Nance."

She tuned the smile down but not off, leading me into the crowd moving outside.

* * *

We drove to the place Nancy rents in South Boston, the top floor of a three-decker owned by a police family. As we climbed the interior stairs, Drew Lynch, the son in the family, quietly opened and closed the door on his landing, nodding to us in between.

I said, "It's nice that they still check on your visitors."

"They're the best landlords an assistant DA could have."

On the third floor, Nancy opened the door into her apartment, her cat scurrying out to meet us. Renfield had needed surgery on his rear legs a while back, and he's managed only a gimpy, crablike way of moving ever since. But there seems to be no pain, and because I was the one who picked him up from the animal hospital, the vet thought Renfield had "imprinted" on me as a kind of surrogate parent.

Right then, though, he was chewing on my right shoe-laces, his clawless front paws trying to burrow down past the leather to sock and flesh below. "Well named."

Over her shoulder Nancy said, "Sorry?"

"Renfield. After the guy in *Dracula* who eats small mammals."

She turned, smiling down at him. "He's a toughie, but you know he loves you, John."

"Pity he shows it through a foot fetish."

Nancy said the word "Yummies," and Renfield immediately forgot about me, scurrying back into the kitchen and watching intently as Nancy took down a small can, popped the top, and mashed the contents into the remains of his cereal food from the morning.

Laying the Alasdair Fraser tape on the shelf near her telephone, I said, "What's he having tonight?"

"Savory Salmon."

"Why not Chunky Chicken or Tender Beef?"

"He had those last week. I don't want him developing gastronomic ennui."

"Not exactly marinated pork and veal marsala."

She set the bowl on the floor, then came over to me, wrapping her arms around my neck and aiming a saucy smile roughly at my collarbone. "A certain prosecutor was thinking about Irish sausage for dessert."

With the knuckles of my right hand, I tilted her chin up. "She's in luck."

Afterward, we lay in bed, cuddling front to front, the door closed to keep Renfield out until we were ready to fall asleep. Nancy's right side was toward the ceiling, and I stroked it slowly from shoulder to hip with the tip of my left index finger.

In a purry voice, she said, "That should tickle, but it doesn't."

"Only because I'm going slowly. If I speed up—"

"John, don't."

"—or use the fingernail—"

"Please."

"Okay."

"It's just so nice like this," she said.

"I'm glad we both think so."

The purry voice. "Being with you is like being with nobody else."

I stopped the stroking. 'Kind of an odd way to phrase it, don't you think?"

A giggle muffled by the pillow. "You know what I mean."

Starting over at the right shoulder, I said, "I hope so."

Nancy shifted a little, causing my hand to stray onto the base of her breast. I stopped again but this time sat up.

"John, what's the matter?"

"Hold still a minute."

"What are you doing?"

I touched and pushed and probed.

"John?"

"Nance, I feel something here."

"Something?"

"I don't . . . it's like a small lump."

"Oh, that's nothing."

"Nancy, it's the size of a cherry pit."

"Sebaceous cyst."

"A what?"

"It's just a cyst from the oil in my skin. My mom had them all the time, and I've had a few already."

"I've never seen one on you. Or felt it before."

"That's because the last time was years ago. They form pretty quickly, and you can either have them cut out or just leave them."

"Leave them?"

"Yes. They usually kind of wax and wane on their own."

I stayed sitting up, images of Beth flooding into me. The hospital room's mechanical bed and tiled walls, the smell of disinfectant, the sound of hushed voices. And too many tubes connected at too many places, her head on a pillow, the white turban wrapped in an unbalanced way around where her hair used to—

Nancy said, "John, what's the matter?"

I let out the breath I was holding. "It just took me back."

"What did?"

"Finding something like that lump."

"How would . . . oh." Nancy drew herself up to her knees, her arms around my neck again, but differently than in the kitchen. "Oh, I'm sorry. This reminds you of Beth."

"Yes."

"John, believe me. The lump is nothing. I—"

"You've had it looked at?"

"Like I said, the doctors have always—"

"This particular one?"

A pause. "No."

I searched for the right words. "Nancy, I know you're

trying to make me feel better, but I'm not completely rational on this, and I really wish you'd go to the doctor."

"Soon as I can."

"Name the day, Nance."

"I'll call you."

"Now."

She broke off the embrace. "John, I told you outside the office, I have an attempted murder—"

"Nancy, that's your job. This is your life. Not to mention mine, if I'm lucky."

A quieter voice. "And ours, if I'm lucky too." Another pause. "I'll call her tomorrow before court."

"Thank you."

We hugged and kissed. Rolled over and stayed still. But I don't think either of us got much sleep.

he next morning, I woke up when Renfield licked my eyelids open. Nancy wasn't next to me in her bed. I felt the sheets where she'd been lying. Cold.

Swinging my legs to the floor, I stood with that dull fatigue that comes from getting only half as much rest as you need. I used the bathroom, then went into the kitchen. There was a handwritten note propped up against the sugar bowl.

John,
     I didn't have the heart to wake you this morning when I knew you hadn't slept well. Thanks for pushing me last night. I'll call my doctor today.

                                        Love,
                                        Nancy

Today. Not "before court," as she'd promised.

Crumpling the note and pitching it into the wastebasket, I went to see if I had some clean clothes in her dresser.

*   *   *

I didn't. Have any clean clothes at Nancy's, I mean.

After riding the bus to South Station, I took the Red Line to Park Street Under. I seemed rank enough to myself that instead of walking to the office across Tremont, I turned west and moved through the brisk morning air toward Back Bay. It being a Wednesday, most of the people with real jobs were already at them. While the Common therefore wasn't crowded, the grass wasn't empty, either.

The nice fall weather brought out the decrepit homeless, the crazy homeless, and the enterprising homeless. Interspersed with them were others, like a young mom and her toddler playing Frisbee with a Heinz-57 mutt, the dog able to leap nearly two of its own body lengths into the air from a standing start, the child squealing in delight. Farther along the winding walkway, separate benches held African-American teenagers necking chastely, a middle-aged Asian-American man in a business suit working on a notebook computer, and an elderly white couple, apparently having an argument, each angled away from the other but speaking alternately in grumbles and hisses.

Across Charles Street, Parks Department employees lovingly tended the flower beds in the Public Garden, their supervisor the bearded man with the headband who seems to have replaced the tanned man in the hiking shorts. I nodded at the bearded supervisor the way everybody does, meaning thanks for making the effort. He nodded back, a little sadly, I thought, maybe thinking how little more time was left for the blossoms this year.

Which after last night with Nancy was the wrong way for me to be thinking. I shook it off and continued over the bridge above the Swan Pond. The red and green pontoons for the boats were moored in the center of the pond next to a skiff, the white swan figureheads and bench seating already removed and sent somewhere else till spring. I walked around the equestrian statue of George Washington, saber drawn but broken off at the hilt, and then up the Commonwealth Avenue mall under the century-old Dutch elms that were also reaching the autumn of their days.

Jesus.

I picked up my pace, breaking a little sweat under the second-day shirt. At Fairfield, I turned right, shortly hitting Beacon and going up the steps of the brownstone on the corner. I was renting a one-bedroom unit from a doctor doing a two-year residency in Chicago, and when I opened the apartment door, the morning sun slanting through the violet stained-glass windows across the rear wall of the living room reminded me briefly of a church service.

I felt tight enough inside that I postponed the shower and change to pull on my running gear and go back downstairs. Crossing Beacon, I went over the pedestrian ramp straddling Storrow Drive and started upstream on the macadam path into a northwest wind that would have spent yesterday blowing newspapers along the streets of Montreal.

I forced myself to watch the river. Ducks playing tag near the docks, cormorants diving for the fish making a comeback against the receding pollution, a lone night heron looking a little lost in the crotch of a maple tree. College freshmen learned to sail in the tricky, skyscraper-skewed winds, their sunny sails dazzling against the blue-black water. A women's scull surged downriver in eight-oared spurts, Harvard colors on the crew shirts. A State Police launch drew alongside a *Miami Vice* motorboat, checking some kind of paperwork.

After two miles, I turned back at the Western Avenue Bridge, using the pace to force my thoughts toward managing my breathing, a deep breath drawn in for six strides, then blown out with three short bursts to follow. Six-three, six-three, over and over. It bought me fifteen minutes of focused, empty peace.

Warming down against the trunk of a poplar at the Fairfield ramp, I noticed a golden retriever swimming along the opposite shore of the lagoon. On the grassy perimeter, two terriers, a cairn and a Scottie, scampered point and drag to the retriever. An older woman waved leashes at the dogs, whistling for them. The terriers responded but the retriever didn't, just plugging along in the water, jaws open, drinking in the day—and I hoped not too much of the lagoon water.

Finishing my stretching, I walked back over the ramp, looking forward to a little professional deception to get my mind off my own reality for a while.

"Let me get this straight," said the young woman at the copy center, twisting a hank of frosted hair around her index finger. "You want me to type this up like a questionnaire?"

"Word process it," I said.

"All's we do anymore. We just say 'type' because it's easier, you know?"

Elbows on the counter, I nodded as a disheartened yuppie asked a male near an enormous Xerox machine to print his résumé on "the ivory stock again, same as last time."

My helper read my writing, twisting a different hank of hair. Either she'd been awfully active that way or she'd had a perm recently. "Now, you want lines next to the questions?"

"Lines?" I said.

"Yeah, like for the people to write on. Their answers, I mean."

"No. Just some vertical spaces between the questions."

"Even the simple ones, like MAIDEN NAME and EDUCATION, that stuff?"

"Yes."

A frown. "Gonna make it more than a page."

"That's okay."

"We get paid by the page here, typing and copying both."

"I understand."

"I took a course in school, too, on public-opinion polling?

Lots of people, they won't fill out forms longer than one page."

"I'll risk it."

"Your call." She walked toward a desktop computer, a third hank twisting around her finger.

Carrying the duplicated questionnaires back to my condo, I put them in a portfolio with some of my business cards. Then I brought the portfolio and a camera down to my silver Prelude, the last year of the original model, but still holding up pretty well. The camera could be hidden nicely under an old newspaper on the passenger's seat.

Driving south out of the city, I refined my strategy. A pretty simple one, actually. Olga Evorova wanted me to investigate Andrew Dees as discreetly as possible, and that would require a credible cover story. So, first stop, Hendrix Property Management in Marshfield, to lay a little groundwork for the story: that I'd been hired by an undisclosed condo complex to check out potential management companies for it, Hendrix being on my "shopping list." After Marshfield, I'd continue on to Plymouth Mills, interviewing Dees and his neighbors at Plymouth Willows. Ostensibly about Hendrix, but really using the questionnaires to profile everybody's background equally, so Dees wouldn't suspect he alone was my target.

The more I thought about the cover story, the more I liked it.

It took me thirty minutes to reach the Route 128 split. Once on Route 3 toward Cape Cod, the traffic began to thin, becoming downright manageable by the time I passed Weymouth. Another nine miles and I saw the exit for Marshfield coming up. I took it, the ramp dumping me eastbound on a two-lane highway with a third, middle, lane meant as a temporary sanctuary for left-hand turns. It was almost twelve, and rather than gamble on when the Hendrix folks took lunch, I pulled into their parking lot before looking for food myself.

The building was beige brick and two stories tall, the center section of an otherwise one-story strip mall with bakery, florist, dog groomer, two dentists, and eight or ten others. The sugary scent from the bakery's ovens made my stomach growl but probably made the dentists happy. The signs over the doors were all done in curlicue lettering on wooden plaques, rendering them hard to read. Maybe that explained why the lot was only a third full, at least half of those vehicles probably belonging to people working for the businesses themselves.

I left my car in one of the slots outside the dog groomer and went up to a plaque with the Hendrix name on it. Opening the door, I came into a small reception area with two leatherette sling chairs flanking a coffee table, the magazines on it a bit tattered. The indoor-outdoor carpeting was institutional green, the paneling that stuff you can buy in three-foot sheets and glue to the studs if a hammer isn't your favorite tool. The desk to the right of the door was unoccupied, a bodice-ripper romance opened face down at the halfway point of the paperback book. Other than a phone, pink message pad, and some pencils, there wasn't much to see.

Then an inner door opened, and a short woman with thick calves came through it. About fifty, she wore a simple wool dress that clung unflatteringly around the thighs. Her hair was graying, probably naturally, since I didn't think anyone would use salt-and-pepper dye on theirs. The face was alert but pleasant, like a career bureaucrat who knows her way around the agency.

"May I help you?"

"Ms. Hendrix?"

"Me . . . ? Oh, no." The pleasant face treated me to a pleasant smile. "No, I'm Mrs. Jelks. Did you want to see Mr. Hendrix?"

"Please. My name's John Cuddy."

"Will he know what this is in regard to?"

Awkward, if polite. "I'm here about a condominium that's seeking new management."

The smile seemed to waver. "Certainly. Please have a seat, and I'll see if he's available."

I thought, "Like you hadn't just left him alone in there," but kept it to myself.

She disappeared through the same door, coming back twenty seconds later. "Mr. Hendrix will see you now."

I moved past her and through the doorway.

The inner office was bigger than the reception area, but that was the most you could say about it, the only window giving a panoramic view of the strip mall's Dempster Dumpster. There was another door to the left, and a desk with relatively little on it tucked into the right corner. A credenza matched the desk, sort of, holding an IBM clone, fax machine, and multi-buttoned phone.

A man of about forty with sandy hair and tortoiseshell, round-lensed glasses rose from a swivel desk chair to greet me. "Boyce Hendrix, Mr. Cuddy." A mellow voice.

Apparently Hendrix believed in "Dress-down *Every*day." From the soles up, he wore old Adidas tennis shoes with no socks, stone-washed blue jeans, and a buff-colored safari shirt with flap pockets. His handshake was firm and decisive, though.

He gestured toward another black leatherette sling chair that seemed to be pining for its twins outside. I took it.

Easing himself back down, Hendrix said, "Mrs. Jelks tells me you're interested in our help?"

Only slightly confused. "Perhaps. I'm representing a condominium complex that's considering a change in its management company."

"Representing?" A judicious look. "You're an attorney, then?"

"No." I handed him a business card.

After reading it, Hendrix snapped it down on his desktop as though he were dealing blackjack. "Private investigator." He looked at the card a while longer, then to me, more judiciously. A careful one, Mr. Hendrix. "Go on."

"The board of trustees has asked me to inquire for them, since they obviously wouldn't want their current company to be . . . offended."

"Obviously. Which complex is it?"

I just smiled.

His smile was judicious, too. "And naturally the complex involved therefore wishes to remain anonymous."

"Naturally."

"I'm not sure where that leaves us, Mr. Cuddy."

"Maybe if I could have some brochures for my clients to review?"

A measured nod, then a very methodical search through a desk drawer, more as though Hendrix were buying time than hunting for something. Which made me realize something else: I hadn't seen any brochures in the reception area, not even a holder for business cards. If you were a management company, and potential clients were waiting to see you, wouldn't you at least want them to have—

"Here we go," passing a glossy piece of paper over to me. A grainy, black-and-white photo showed a couple standing in front of a six-paneled door, beaming at the lens. Their hair styles and clothes looked out-of-date, and given the cropping at the borders, the picture could have been taken anywhere. Just skimming the brochure's widely spaced paragraphs of text, I found two obvious typos.

"How long have you been in business?" I said.

"At this location, only five years."

The photo looked older. "And how long have you been in the profession, yourself?"

"Around ten."

"That should be about right for my clients."

Hendrix frowned. "Can you tell me how big their complex is?"

"Let's just say over fifty units."

"And how far from Marshfield?"

"Oh, within fifteen miles."

I was intentionally dangling the bait, and Hendrix seemed intentionally not to take it, making no effort to sell me on his company.

"Well," he said finally, the tone still mellow, "that certainly sounds like it's in our ballpark. Unfortunately, though, we're pretty heavily booked at the moment."

"You are."

"Yes. A lot of our clients prefer a more hands-on but low-key approach to property management, especially in this economy. We're not expensive, and that matters, so we tend to hold the complexes we attract."

I wanted to keep this going, find out why he was now trying to gently discourage new business. "That's good."

Hendrix just watched me.

I said, "You see, that's why the complex hired a private investigator instead of a lawyer. I'm cheaper, and a lot more 'hands-on.' "

Another measured nod.

"Well, I guess that brings us to references." I gestured toward the brochure drawer. "And maybe a sample contract?"

Hendrix used his feet to rock just a little in the swivel chair. "We don't really have a 'sample contract,' Mr. Cuddy."

"Not even a form you use as a model?"

"I kind of negotiate each one individually."

"On behalf of the corporation."

"Corporation?"

"Your management company here."

The rocking stopped. I was setting off a lot of bells for him, and I couldn't see why.

He said, "I'm a sole proprietorship."

"Ah. 'Boyce Hendrix, doing business as' ... ?"

"Hendrix Property Management Company."

I gave it a beat. "In addition to you and Mrs. Jelks, how many employees do you have?"

"Some resident supers."

"Superintendents?"

"That's right."

Hoping to hear "Plymouth Willows," I went back to an earlier request. "Maybe just the references, then."

"The references."

"Yes. Other complexes you currently manage, so my clients can get a sense of how they might be treated."

"Tell you what," said Hendrix, coming forward in the chair, his voice steady but his feet planted for standing. "Why don't you take our brochure there with you back to your clients? They like what they see, we can go on to those other things."

I held the brochure in my palm, making a weighing motion with my hand. "Kind of skimpy, compared to the competition."

Hendrix rose, flexing his shoulders back. "Each management company has its own personality, Mr. Cuddy." The mellow tone still. "I think you've gotten a pretty good sense of ours. Let your clients decide, huh?"

As I went out through the reception area, Mrs. Jelks nodded pleasantly to me over the romance novel.

4

Back in the Prelude, I drove east, almost to the ocean. I couldn't see why Boyce Hendrix hadn't really pitched for "my" complex's business. Also, a little enthusiasm on his part would have been nice toward greasing the skids for my cover story at Plymouth Willows itself.

Nice, but not essential, I hoped.

Turning south, I followed the narrow, twisting roads that used to be the only routes between Boston and the summer communities. I passed a forlorn shopping mall and at least a dozen condominium developments, mostly weathered shingle, trying hard for the quaint island look of Nantucket but coming up just a bit cramped and sad. After about twenty minutes, I reached the outskirts of Plymouth Mills.

At first glance, the town center seemed picturesque, its buildings extending five or six blocks in each direction from a four-way intersection. The architectural style alternated between clapboard and red brick, the clapboard mostly white with black or green shutters, the brick sandblasted at some point after the dingy mills it covered had closed down. The retail stores were more likely to be called "shoppes" than the places in the strip mall back in Marshfield, with some specializing entirely in woven baskets or stuffed animals or wine and cheese. Look a little closer, though, and you could see the peeling paint and missing bricks, the cracked sidewalks and unfixed potholes. Since the demise of the "Massachusetts Miracle," most of the state had gone from recession to depression, despite the optimism in the newspapers, and Plymouth Mills, like the towns to the north, seemed not to have been spared. Even the Porsche dealership struck me as dreary.

The police station came up just after the dealership, which I'm sure made the Porsche people sleep better at night. The department occupied one of the brick buildings, and ordinarily I'd have stopped in, letting the desk officers know I'd be working the town they were paid to serve and protect. However, I didn't want to risk my license by extending the cover story about nonexistent condo clients to the local uniforms.

Just before the intersection, the photocopy shop appeared on the right, but from the low lighting inside, it wasn't open. I'd intended to ask about Dees first at Plymouth Willows anyway, but why wouldn't an independent businessman have his place up and running by noontime?

Beyond the crossroads was The Tides, where Olga Evorova told me she'd first met Dees. Pretty hungry by now, I had to have lunch somewhere, and I found a parking space next to it.

The interior of The Tides was pretty generic: an oblong pub bar in the back, burled walnut veneer on both the walls and the booths against them. Benches for the booths stood high, with brass coat hooks screwed into the wood and cream-colored Formica covering the tables. Paint-by-numbers beach prints were framed and almost centered under brass wall sconces. The midday-meal crowd seemed mostly retirees lounging in the booths and people who drank their lunches lounging at the bar, which wasn't tended just now.

I took a stool across from a booth that held the only teenagers in the place, a pair of girls wearing the kinds of outfits, hairdos, and jewelry you'd find on the cover of a science fiction magazine. The Tides was quiet enough that I could hear their conversation, even though they weren't trying to project.

One had purple hair, purple rouge, and purple lipstick, her yellow-and-green-striped sweatshirt torn at the shoulder, the matching athletic pants torn at the knee. "God, it is *such* a bummer about your dad."

The second girl—metallic platinum with dark roots but dressed in a long-sleeved black T-shirt, ankle-length black skirt, and black combat boots—pushed the remains of a garden salad around on her plate. "Hey, like tell me about it, awright?"

"But it's just *so* wicked unfair, Kira. I mean, you are seventeen years young, you know? This is supposed to be *the* most awesome time of your life."

"So. I'm gonna have to wait a while."

"But all the school you're missing—"

Putting down her fork, Kira said, "Look, Jude, I have to get back, and you got class in like ten minutes."

"Awright. Where's our check?"

A brunette waitress in a frilly white blouse and pink stirrup pants came out from what I guessed to be the kitchen, Jude paying cash for both meals. As the girls left, the waitress moved behind the bar. Oyster and clam shells were sticking up from a bed of crushed ice garnished with some lemon wedges and parsley sprigs. She smiled at me from the far side of thirty. "What'll you have?"

The nametag on the blouse read "Edie." Glancing toward the booths, I said, "Double duty?"

A shrug, but she kept the smile shining, maybe because

it was her best feature. "Used to do it on the airplanes, I can do it here. Drink?"

I nodded at the draft pulls. "Harpoon."

"You got it."

Edie sidled over to the freezer and pulled out a ten-ounce mug with frost coating its sides. Curling her lower lip under her front teeth, she concentrated on drawing the ale, reminding me of a kindergarten kid with finger paint. After topping the mug, then spilling some off and topping it again, she brought the drink over to me, first slapping a napkin down on the wood.

"Menu, or would you like something from the raw bar?"

I looked toward the bed of ice. "They fresh?"

"Hey, they're not just fresh, they're still alive in there. That's what makes it so hard to shuck them." She picked up a short, sturdy knife. "When I stick this in, they're still holding on to the insides of the shell. If they were dead, the shells'd be open, like you see on the beach by the tideline."

"And since they're still alive in there . . ."

"I'm really breaking their grip by cutting their heads off at the neck."

"Glad I asked."

Edie laughed. "So, the raw bar's out?"

"For today, anyway. How are your burgers?"

"Dead. Definitely dead."

"Medium, then. No fries, green salad."

"Watching your weight?"

I decided to establish a little more of my cover story. "Have a long afternoon ahead of me."

"This town, all the afternoons are long."

Given the inflection, I thought Edie might be floating an invitation. Liking the way she did it, I still didn't want to mislead her. "I'm checking out how a management company runs one of the condos around here."

"Checking out?"

"I'm a private investigator."

"No kidding?"

"Here's my identification."

Edie unfolded the little leather holder, her lip under the front teeth again, reading the laminated card before handing it back to me. "Which complex you interested in?"

"Plymouth Willows."

The remains of Edie's smile froze. "Don't know much about how that's going."

"You don't."

"No. I live the other way."

One of the retirees motioned for another round, and Edie moved stiffly to fill his glass before taking my food order to the kitchen. It was a while before she came back out, busying herself rearranging shells on the bed of ice that had looked fine as they were.

I said, "How about just directions, then?"

Edit kept her eyes on the ice. "Directions?"

"To Plymouth Willows."

She spoke mechanically, toward the shells. "We're on Main Street here. Take Main south to the little bridge over the river. About a mile after the bridge, just past the . . ." Something was giving her trouble. "Just past the bluff on the left, you'll hang a right and go down maybe another mile and a half to the Willows sign on your left."

"Sounds easy enough."

"You miss the turn and keep going straight, you'll get to the gore."

"What's the gore?"

"It's a blip on the survey maps that . . . somebody did for all the development down here in the eighties. The gore's like a bog with swampy water around it."

Another customer called out her name. To me, Edie said, "Sorry, but I'm going to be kind of busy here." She didn't sound sorry.

I nursed the ale, and Edie circulated, studiously avoiding my end of the bar until a lighted bell chimed above the liquor bottles, causing her to go back into the kitchen and reappear with a hamburger plate.

As she set it in front of me, I lowered my voice. "Did I push the wrong button or something?"

"No," a little too quickly. "I'm just busy, like I said."

"You wouldn't happen to know anybody who lives at Plymouth Willows, would you?"

Edie looked up, guarded. "You mean, like for you to talk to?"

"Yes."

"Maybe Andy Dees. He runs the photocopy up the street."

Perfect. "Thanks, I'll try him."

I thought she wanted to say something else, but another customer got her attention, and I finished my drink and meal without speaking to her again.

The southern tip of downtown ended at the bridge Edie mentioned, which arced over a dry riverbed and a stagnant harbor. Fishing and lobster boats were beached at peculiar angles on the sandbars by the low tide. No one was on the docks, and I had the feeling that the boats hadn't been anywhere recently, even when the water level was more cooperative.

I drove over the bridge and south another mile or so, the road curving left to create a "scenic overlook." I pulled the Prelude into the small parking area but left the engine running. Getting out and walking to the railing, I looked down a bluff perhaps forty feet high onto rocks the size of Buicks. Given the tide, most of the rocks were exposed, scumlines around their middles. There was a freshening sea breeze, the smell of salt heavy and bracing in the air. A couple of long-haul barges were sloughing toward Boston, but no pleasure craft, motor or sail, despite the nice weather.

Back in the car, I left the lot and continued south. Taking the next right, I measured off two miles before realizing I must have missed the Plymouth Willows sign that should have been on my left. I came instead to the "gore," as Edie had called it, a deep swamp surrounded by cattails and reeds, the road hooking left over an old wooden bridge spanning it. There were tire tracks at the edge of the mocha water, cars probably parking there at night as boys with new driver's licenses tried to practice their manhood on girls like the pair back at The Tides. Following the road left and over the bridge, I wasn't sorry to see the gore fade in the rearview mirror.

The macadam rose to climb a bowl-like hill, and I entered Plymouth Willows from what was functionally its back door, near the tennis courts (nets up) and pool (water drained). The hill I'd climbed provided a postcard backdrop to the complex, the trees mostly hardwoods, here and there a pine or two. A small prefab house sat between the courts and the pool, but otherwise Plymouth Willows seemed to be laid out like a giant shamrock. The roads were looping cul-de-sacs with clusters of townhouse units distributed around each leaf of the shamrock. I counted four townhouses per cluster, four clusters per leaf. Symmetry *über alles*.

The architecture was all gray, weathered shingles, striving also for that Nantucket motif. The only variations were the color of the doors and window trim, which went from red to yellow to blue to white, depending on which cluster in the leaf you were passing. I drove around all the cul-de-sacs, spotting the address Olga Evorova had given me in one of the yellow-trimmed clusters with a nice view of the opposite hillside. There were only a few ornamental willows on the grounds, but everything looked well kept, shrubbery trimmed and grass mowed. While I realized Hendrix Management should most likely be thanked for that, what struck me was how few of the units seemed to be occupied. There were no garages, yet only a handful of cars. Most people might be at work, but many windows had no drapes or curtains in them. And no FOR SALE signs on the front lawns, either.

Then, driving back toward unit number 42, I caught a break.

A man came out the townhouse's front door, juggling a box and some paperwork as he pulled the knob closed behind him. He roughly fit the description my client had given me, and the burden of the box and paperwork slowed his walk down the path to a crawl.

Pulling over and reaching under the newspaper on the passenger's seat, I retrieved my camera. I'm not a terrific photographer, and the man I took for Andrew Dees was some distance away, but with a Pentax K-frame long lens, I can do simple, candid stuff well enough. I rolled down my window, the air much warmer again now that I was a few miles from the ocean.

Dees showed clearly through the viewfinder: dark hair and prominent brow, straight nose and strong chin. I snapped off three head-and-shoulders portraits before he reached his car, a brown Toyota Corolla hatchback. Dees lifted the hatch, dropping the box and paperwork inside, then closed it and walked to the driver's door. He turned once in my direction, and I got a fourth shot of him before he climbed behind the wheel and drove off toward the front of the complex.

I was leaning down to slide the camera back under the newspaper when a male voice next to my window said, "You like to take pixtures?"

If the voice had been normal, I probably would have jumped. But it was squeaky and shy, and somehow it didn't startle me, despite being so close by. I looked up into the sort of face we'd have casually called "retarded" when I was growing up, the compressed features and crimped ears and hanging jaw of a Down's syndrome child.

Only the person standing next to my door wasn't a child. At least thirty, on a stumpy frame of five-six or so, he had a few strands of gray in the brown hair that lay flat along the ears. I couldn't see the rest of his hair because he wore a red, white, and blue New England Patriots ballcap down tight, almost to the eyebrows. The rest of his outfit was a one-piece maintenance jumpsuit in faded green, the name "PAULIE" stitched in yellow thread over the left top pocket. He had a rake in his hands, and I realized he was gripping the handle tightly, nervously.

"Well, do you?"

I said, "Do I like to take pictures?"

A blink and a nod.

"Yes, I do."

"Me too."

"Paulie?"

"That's me." He let go of the rake with his right hand and traced over the embroidery. "My last name's Fogerty, but that's not on there."

"You work here?"

A blink and a nod again. "I'm the super."

Fogerty said it proudly, and I remembered Boyce Hendrix telling me he ran a lean ship except for the superintendents.

"Mr. Eh-men-dor showed me."

"Who?"

Paulie gestured toward the cluster of townhouses where I'd seen Andrew Dees. "Mr. Eh-men-dor."

"What did he show you?"

A puzzled look. "How to take pixtures. With the camera."

He pointed at the newspaper on the passenger seat. "How come you hide your camera?"

"I can't always trust people to be honest."

He gave me a troubled look this time. "I'm honest. I don't steal anything from anybody."

"I wasn't worried about you, Paulie."

A hang-jaw smile. "Good. I'm not worried about you too."

I said, "Was that Mr. Dees who just left?"

The blink and nod. "Why do you want pixtures of Mr. Dees?"

"I don't, actually. I'm just taking photos of the condos here. I spoke to Mr. Hendrix this morning."

That seemed to sit well. "Mr. Hend'ix hired me. I'm the super."

I swung my head around. "You do a fine job, too. The grass and bushes look great."

Another blink and nod. "I spend the whole week cutting and mowing and raking, and you know what?"

"No, what?"

"By next week, I got to start all over again."

"Well, if I had a place like this to run, I'd sure hire you."

The troubled look again. "Oh, no. No, you can't. I work for Mr. Hend'ix. I'm the super."

"And you're so good at it, I'll bet you'll be here a long time."

A more troubled look, as though Fogerty had never thought of not being there until I'd planted the idea. To get him off that, I said, "Mr. Dees lives in the cluster over there?"

Now the look went back to puzzled. "Cluster?"

"Those four houses with the yellow doors."

"Oh, yeah. He lives in the second one. But they're *units*, not houses."

"Who else lives there?"

"Mr. Dees lives by himself."

"I mean in the other hou—units around him."

"Oh. There's Mr. and Mrs. Stepanian, Mrs. Robinette and Jamey, and Mr. Eh-men-dor and Kira."

Kira. Unusual enough name that. . . . "What does Kira look like, Paulie?"

"She's pretty." Fogerty looked down, his cheeks flushing, his hands moving nervously on the rake again. "She's very pretty."

"Does she wear black clothes?"

Blink and nod. "Black, yeah. Lots of them."

"Do you think Kira's home now?"

"Yeah. Mr. Eh-men-dor is sick, and she takes care of him."

What the other girl, Jude, must have meant in The Tides about Kira's father. "How about the Stepanians?"

"They're not sick."

"Are they home, though, do you think?"

"Mrs. Stepanian, maybe. Mr. Stepanian goes to work. She does too, sometimes."

I was feeling a little guilty pumping Fogerty, but at least I couldn't see it getting back to Hendrix. "How about Mrs. Robinette?"

"She's home a lot."

"And Jamey?"

"He's not home yet. He goes to school. Special bus, like me."

"Like you?"

"Like when I went to school. This special bus came to my old house and picked me up."

"Where do you live now, Paulie?"

He pointed at the prefab building near the tennis courts. "My new house. Mr. Hend'ix hired me. I'm the super."

"Well, listen, you've helped a lot. Thank you."

"You going to see Mr. Eh-men-dor?"

"Probably."

The hang-jaw smile. "Good. He can show you how to use your camera to take pixtures right."

Paulie Fogerty walked off to tend his greenery, bouncing the tine end of the rake off the ground every other step, like he was counting cadence for himself.

5

I drove toward the four-unit cluster I'd seen Andrew Dees leaving. His number 42 was second from the left. Given what Paulie had told me about the other residents, I figured Kira and her father were the most likely to be home and the Stepanians the least, with Mrs. Robinette in the middle. Taking my portfolio briefcase with the questionnaires in it, I walked up the path to number 41, the end unit next to Dees. Since STEPANIAN appeared under the button, I tried it first.

Perhaps twenty seconds after an electronic bong, a woman opened the yellow front door. She was about thirty and slim, maybe five-five in flat shoes. Her black, shiny hair crept just slightly into sideburns, a faint duskiness above her upper lip as well. She wore a plaid skirt, the blouse red and picking up one of the minor colors in the skirt, the pantyhose blue and picking up one of the others. I had the immediate impression of someone who was all dressed up with no place to go.

"Yes?"

"Mrs. Stepanian?"

"Yes."

"My name's John Cuddy." I took out the identification holder and held it up for her to read.

"Private investigator?" Her face, shaped like an inverted teardrop with a dainty chin, clouded over. "What's this about?"

"I've been asked by another condo complex to look into how well the Hendrix company manages yours."

"How well?"

"Yes. My clients are thinking about perhaps changing companies, but they'd like a discreet rundown on the possible alternatives."

"Oh." Stepanian seemed to relax a little. "Well, that certainly is prudent of them, isn't it?"

She spoke the sentence neutrally, without any sarcasm.

I put the ID holder back in my pocket. "Could I come in, ask you a few questions?"

"I suppose that would be all right."

Stepanian ushered me through the little entrance alcove into her unit. In front of us was a living room that segued without walls into a dining area. To the right of the dining area was a squarish kitchen, behind it a sliding glass door leading to a rear deck. The space above the living room part was open air, the second floor overhanging only the dinner table and kitchen. A set of stairs with picketed balustrade rose to a catwalk above the first level. The catwalk provided access to a pair of doors fifteen feet apart, an indentation between them that I took for the upstairs bath. Most of the wall area was plasterboard painted a matte white, wainscoting in naturally stained oak covering the three feet from the bottom of the plasterboard down to the wall-to-wall carpeting.

I said, "Very nice place," meaning it.

Stepanian moved to the center of the first floor and looked up and around, as though she were seeing the unit for the first time. "Yes, it's just perfect for Steven and me."

"Steven is your husband?"

"Oh, yes." She walked me around the plushy, khaki-colored furniture to an entertainment center that occupied one wall with television, VCR, CD-player, and so on. Pointing to a posed family portrait of her and a tall, slim man, she said, "We've been very happy here."

I made a show of admiring the photo in the stand-up frame. Mrs. Stepanian was smiling, and I realized that I hadn't yet seen her teeth, because in the photo they were tiny, with little gaps between them. Steven Stepanian seemed a man who smiled reluctantly, only grinning with a slight strain noticeable around the corners of his mouth. He had the same dark, shiny hair and dainty chin as his wife. Whoever contended that opposites attract had never met the Stepanians.

I said, "Have you lived here long?"

"Nearly six years."

Which meant they would have bought at the top of the market, back before the crash in real estate prices. "In that case, you'll be an ideal person for me to interview. If you have the time."

She seemed to consider that, almost solemnly. "Well, yes, I guess so. I'm also on the condominium board of trustees, so I deal with Boyce more than most."

"Terrific. I saw him this morning at the office in Marshfield."

Stepanian paused. "Boyce didn't tell you who was on our board of trustees?"

Uh-oh. "I told him I wanted to just visit the complexes he manages on my own, get kind of a random sampling. Once I was here, I would have asked about who was on your board, partly to see how well Hendrix keeps residents informed, but you happen to be my first stop."

"Oh." Again the relaxation. "Well, you haven't seen any of our units, then?"

"Just from the street."

She glanced around, frowning. "I'm afraid our place is a mess, as usual."

I glanced around with her. Everything seemed to be in perfect order, and I wanted to be able to picture the interior of Dees' unit next door. "How about just a quick tour?"

The frown relented. "All right. And then you can ask me your questions."

"That would be a real help."

Stepanian gestured. "All of the townhouses here at the Willows follow this same basic design, though the unit next door would be the mirror image of this one. That's so the plumbing for the kitchens and the downstairs half-baths share a common wall. I guess you can tell this is the living room and dining area?"

"Functional."

"Yes, it's really easy to prepare and serve meals without being cut off from conversation with Steven in the living room." She pointed to one door. "Closet." And another. "Half-bath."

Then Stepanian led me farther back. "This is the rear deck. I was reading when you rang the bell."

Or bong. The deck was wood-planked, about fifteen feet square with a low railing around its perimeter. I could see two webbed lounge chairs, a white resin table between them and a kettle grill with barbecue utensils off to the side. On one of the chairs lay a hardcover Joyce Carol Oates, a bookmark stuck near the end of it.

Stepanian gestured again. "Every unit has a deck like this, though where the kitchen is kind of dictates which side the sliding glass doors will be on." My guide turned and took an extra step to pass well away from me. "The second floor is the master bedroom and the guest bedroom."

I followed her up the stairs. The catwalk was wider than it appeared from below, though the Stepanians had left it bare except for the carpeting. She opened the door closest to the top of the staircase.

"Master bedroom." Big and rectangular, a sloping ceiling toward the back wall. "That door's the master bath, the other a walk-in closet." Stepanian came out past me, taking that extra wide step again. At the indentation, she said, "Second bath, and"—beyond to the other door on the catwalk— "guest bedroom, though we use it as a study." Smaller, square, filled with desktop computer stuff and some peripheral gadgetry. Like the first floor, there wasn't so much as a knickknack out of place.

I gave her the extra margin this time as she came out and went down the stairs and around to the kitchen. "This door leads to the basement. Just workspace for Steven and the utility closet."

"Washer-dryer?"

"And the rest of the 'guts,' like heating, air-conditioning, and so on."

Stepanian brought me back to the living room. "Please, sit down and be comfortable."

I took one of the plushy easy chairs, thinking as I sank into its cushions that "plushy" wasn't quite generous enough. The thing nearly swallowed me, as though there were room for another person underneath the cushions. Stepanian seemed unable to take advantage of her own hospitality, instead perching on the edge of the matching sofa like a seventh-grader attending her first coed dance.

I unzipped the portfolio and handed a questionnaire to her, putting another on top of the portfolio as a writing surface.

The clouded look again. "What's this?"

"I want to be able to have a consistent interview with each person I visit in each complex, so I figured my working from a form and writing on it would make more sense. That copy's so you can see what the questions will be, and maybe save us both some time in answering the earlier ones. If you notice anything on there that troubles you, please let me know."

She scanned the questionnaire.

I said, "Okay?"

Her eyes came up from the paper. "I suppose so."

"FULL NAME?"

"Lana L. Stepanian."

"HOMETOWN?"

"Do you really need that?"

Stepanian was proving to be good dress rehearsal for using the questionnaire on Andrew Dees. "My clients thought it would help them to judge how people from different parts of the country might view their condo management company."

I wasn't completely convinced myself, but Stepanian said, "Solvang, California."

"Can you spell that for me?"

"S-O-L-V-A-N-G. It means 'sunny field' in Danish."

"You're from Denmark?"

A small smile, showing me the smaller teeth. "No. Mexican-American. Solvang is northeast of Santa Barbara."

"MAIDEN NAME?"

"Lopez, with a Z."

"EDUCATION?"

"Boston University."

"SPOUSE?"

She glanced down at the form. "Steven, as I said. With a V, not a P-H."

"And his HOMETOWN?"

A pause, as though these details seemed increasingly strange to her. "Idaho, somewhere."

A little vague, but I didn't want to push my luck. "EDUCATION?"

"University of Idaho."

Smiling as warmly as I could, I looked up at her. "How did you two meet?"

"A party, when I was at BU." A cocking of the head, as though she thought that was the strangest question yet. "Mr. Cuddy, why do you—"

Move to firmer ground. "Now, you said you've lived here for six years?"

"Almost six, yes."

"Did you PURCHASE outright OR RENT?"

"Purchased, from the first developer."

"The first?"

"Yes." Stepanian seemed to redirect herself. "Well, I guess the only developer, technically. We were buying at a bad time, when it looked as though everything was going up and up and what we had in the bank was shrinking from about ten percent of a purchase price to more like five. Steven and I had almost given up hope on a normal life."

"Normal?"

"Owning our own home." The neutral voice again. "Then we saw Plymouth Willows, and really liked it, and so we offered the asking price on this unit and just beat two other couples to it. Or so we thought."

"I don't get you."

"Well, the project was in trouble. The developer had kind of squirreled away some of the bills, getting people to buy in the hope that he could pay them off. But in the end, he had to sell at a discount to a lot of investor-owners, not owner-occupants."

"So the absentee owners began to rent out to tenants."

"And the developer did too. Which wouldn't have been so bad, except it got to be more than fifty percent of the units."

"At which point . . . ?"

"The banks didn't want to lend to new buyers if the current owners weren't occupying, so the banks made the new buyers come up with twenty, even twenty-five percent down payments."

"Which was tough."

"And got worse. Once the real estate market went into a spin, the prices started tumbling, and the investor-owners couldn't rent the places for what they were paying to carry them. We had trouble getting those owners to send in their monthly maintenance fees for the grounds and all, and once the foreclosures started, we had even more trouble getting our money."

"The banks that foreclosed wouldn't contribute the monthly maintenance?"

Stepanian wagged her head. "It was the developer who did most of the foreclosing, because he'd taken back mortgages from a lot of the original purchasers who were perhaps a bit . . . shaky on their financial statements? Then the owner-occupants we did have started losing their jobs to the recession, and that meant more foreclosures, and—oh, it was terrible."

I looked around. "You and your husband came through it well."

"Oh, yes," she said in the neutral voice. "The unit may never be worth what we paid for it, which kind of ties us to Plymouth Willows. And I do just temporary work, because I like to be in charge of my own schedule. But Steven is a research chemist, and fortunately, his job is quite secure. We get along nicely."

A "normal" life, as she'd said before. I went back to the form. "Have you ever had any FAMILY MEMBERS come visit you here?"

The cocking of the head. "What difference would that make?"

"My clients want to know how the complex seems to outsiders so they can judge how potential purchasers would see their places toward resale."

A pause as she considered something. "I wouldn't be able to help you there."

"No?"

"Steven's parents are dead. And when we got married, him being Armenian-American, and me Mexican, as I said . . . well, let's just say my folks back home didn't approve."

"I'm sorry."

"Not your fault."

Stepanian again said it in her neutral way, without sarcasm or even irony.

I put my pen on the next question. "We've already covered OCCUPATION, SPOUSE. How about your DEALINGS WITH THE HENDRIX COMPANY?"

"Well, when the developer finally went broke, the units he still owned—either because he hadn't sold them or he'd had to foreclose on them—got auctioned somehow. I'm not quite sure how all that worked in the technical, legal sense— I wasn't on the board then—but I had the impression that the FDIC or some other federal bank agency had them and then auctioned them off, with a realty trust buying most of them."

Olga Evorova had mentioned that, and I thought I ought be solidify my cover story with Stepanian toward asking her about Andrew Dees. "Which realty trust?"

"I just know the name on the checks they send in for their monthly maintenance."

"Don't those go to Hendrix?"

"Yes, but we on the board kind of . . . informally audit the financial statements Boyce prepares for us."

"You have any reason to think those statements need to be audited?"

"Oh. Oh, no, not in that sense. I think every condominium association that's big enough to need a management company kind of keeps an eye on that company. Doesn't yours?"

"I rent."

"I mean, doesn't the complex you're working for do that with their current manager?"

"Well, yes. In fact . . ." I shrugged.

"Oh. Oh, I see. Is that one of the reasons they're thinking of changing companies?"

"You're very astute, Mrs. Stepanian."

The small teeth. "Thank you, Mr. Cuddy."

"How have you found working with Mr. Hendrix?"

"Oh, very pleasant. He's always available by telephone, and visits the complex regularly."

"How does he treat you when you visit him?"

"Visit him?" The clouded look. "I don't think I ever have. Why would I, when Boyce is always happy to come here?"

So a trustee has never seen Hendrix's office. "Does he produce or process the documentation on time?"

"There's really just the annual meeting notices, and the monthly maintenance bills, but he also does a good job of analyzing things like 'reserve for replacement,' and advising us on insurance rates and so forth."

"How does he handle complaints?"

"Well, there are very few, actually. The developer here might have gotten into trouble financially, but he made sure the buildings and systems were done right structurally. And our superintendent does a wonderful job of maintaining the grounds and pool."

"I might have seen him on my way in. Baseball cap, rake?"

The small smile, but with a tinge of sadness to it. "Yes. Paulie Fogerty. When Boyce first hired him for us, I was a little . . . well, I suppose it's 'politically incorrect,' but I was a little concerned about Paulie being up to the task. However, I have to say, he's really turned out well, and even does the extra things."

"Extra things?"

"Yes, like helping you in with groceries if he sees you

struggling at all, or accepting packages when you're not home. He can sign his name and everything."

I wasn't quite sure how Stepanian meant that, but, again, she spoke without sarcasm, just that hollow sound to the words, as though she'd memorized them and trotted out a given phrase when she thought it might fit the occasion. "Has Mr. Hendrix's company always been the manager here?"

"No. The developer did the 'managing' while he owned the majority of the units. He then stayed on as manager, but once the foreclosures and all started, we were kind of 'self-managing,' which is very hard in a complex this size. Fortunately, when that realty trust took over, they brought in Boyce to run things for us."

"And what's the name of this realty trust?"

"The C.W. Realty Trust."

"Which stands for?"

The small teeth peeked out at me. "Nobody knows."

"I'm sorry?"

"You know how these realty trusts work. They're anonymous—no, that's not the right word. Confidential. They don't have to disclose who they are, not even at the Registry of Deeds. I even went there once to look them up. Zero."

"So you don't know who stands behind the C.W. Realty Trust."

"No, but I do know one thing."

"What's that?"

"Their checks always clear."

"For the monthly maintenance on the units the trust still owns."

"That's right."

Back to the form. "Do you and your husband have any CHILDREN?"

"No. Actually, I can't have any."

That same neutral voice. I looked up.

"But, as a result, we can afford to live here because we don't have to try to clothe, feed, and educate anybody else. Also, Steven's on the school committee, and I do the condo work, and I guess that's how we . . . compensate."

There was something hollow about that comment too, but I had other things I wanted to cover with her. "NEIGHBORS is next. I promise whatever you say will remain strictly confidential, but it would be a help if you could describe your neighbors for me, to give my clients a sense of how comparable your complex's situation is to theirs."

"Our neighbors. You mean here in our cluster?"

"Yes."

"All right. First, there's Mr. Dees next door."

I sat as far forward in the marshmallow chair as I could. "Spelling?"

"D-E-E-S."

"And where is he from?"

"From? You mean like 'hometown' again?"

"Yes."

"The Midwest somewhere. Chicago?" She looked away, to the wall her townhouse shared with his. "Yes. I'm pretty sure he said that to Steven once."

"EDUCATION?"

"I don't know. He certainly seems like he went to college, if that's what matters to you, but I don't remember ever talking with him about it."

"OCCUPATION?"

"He owns the photocopy store in town."

"Owns or just manages?"

"Owns, I think." The cocking of the head. "Why don't you just ask him?"

"I plan to, but I saw him leaving just as I was arriving."

"Oh. Oh, that would be late for him, but I was on the deck, reading, so I might not have heard him."

"Does Mr. Dees have any family?"

"That lives with him here, you mean?"

"Or that visits."

"Well, he lives alone, and he's never introduced me to anyone."

"To any family, you mean."

"Anyone, period. He stays pretty much to himself. I believe he's kind of dating a . . ."

Stepanian stopped.

"What's the matter."

She looked at me. "I just realized I was starting to sound like a gossip. I don't think it's right to invade his privacy."

Olga Evorova had used the same phrase with me, and I realized I'd have to watch how deeply my "condo clients" would be interested in the personal life of Andrew Dees. "I understand, and I certainly don't mean to pry. It would just help my clients to know this general 'census' information."

Stepanian nodded, but more in wariness than agreement, I thought.

To protect my cover story, I said, "How about the other two townhouses here?"

"Well, next to Mr. Dees is Mrs. Robinette. And her son, Jamey."

"Do you know where they're from?"

"I'm pretty sure Jamey was born in the states, but she has a little bit of an accent, so maybe from the islands."

"The Caribbean, you mean?"

"Yes, she's . . . well, if she's from there, I'm not sure whether you'd call her African-American or whatever-American, but she and Jamey are black."

"How old is he?"

"Fifteen, sixteen."

"What does Mrs. Robinette do?"

"I don't know. I've never seen her going off to work anywhere. Her husband died, so maybe there's some kind of pension or death benefits, because she can afford a car and those baggy clothes for Jamey that you see all the kids wearing now."

"Do you socialize with them much?"

"No." A pensive pause. "I'm not sure how to put this, but everybody here at the Willows pretty much stays to themselves except around the pool in the summer, and the Robinettes aren't 'pool people.' " She gave me the cocked head look. "Don't you want to know how long they've lived here?"

I hadn't thought of it, but Stepanian was right, I "should" want to know that. "You said almost six years for you and your husband, right?"

"Right. Well, Mrs. Robinette and Jamey moved in just, oh, two years ago, maybe. And Mr. Dees about a year after that, so only the Elmendorfs have been here as long as Steven and me."

Guessing "Elmendorf" was Paulie's "Eh-men-dor," I tried to stay on track. "Did Mr. Robinette die before they moved here, then?"

"Oh, yes. Sometime before that. I'm not sure when, though."

"And now, how about the Elmendorfs?"

"That's Norman, and his daughter, Kira. K-I-R-A."

"Wife?"

Stepanian looked away, a pained expression on her face this time. "Norman's wife left him. After he got sick."

"Sick?"

"Yes, he . . . it has to do with the war."

"Which one?"

"The Persian Gulf." Stepanian came back to me. "I mean, can you imagine, just abandoning your husband, and child, and . . . taking off?"

"Any idea why she did that?"

"None. It's so . . . abnormal to me," looking to the framed

photo on the shelf. "But I'm starting to sound like a gossip again."

Okay. "How old is his daughter?"

"Kira? About the same as Jamey Robinette, only . . . I don't know, I guess I have this feeling that she's a year older than he is? I'm not sure why."

Lana Stepanian had given me more than I thought she would, but I didn't want to overdo the questionnaire on its maiden voyage. I also had the feeling that Stepanian was running out of information on her neighbors. "Last point, then. Where are the Elmendorfs from?"

"His wife was from the South, somewhere. I never knew her well." A bitter laugh. "I guess that's obvious, isn't it? Anyway, Norman's originally from Massachusetts. He did photography for the Brockton newspaper until—well, you can ask him yourself."

Brockton was a small city, also in Plymouth County, and a number of reserve units from the South Shore had been mobilized for Desert Storm. "I wonder if you could just review and sign this form I've filled out."

Stepanian looked at it, then to me. "Is this really necessary?"

"It just shows I spoke with you and have a basis for my eventual recommendation on the Hendrix Company."

More hesitation, but she finally picked up the pen. When Stepanian gave the form back to me, "Lana Stepanian" was scripted in a precise hand at the bottom.

I said, "Do you think Mrs. Robinette would be home now?"

"I wouldn't know."

"How about Norman Elmendorf?"

Lana Stepanian smiled sadly, without showing any of the tiny teeth. "Mr. Cuddy, Norman's always home."

6

Leaving the Stepanians' townhouse, I felt pretty good about the cover story I'd given Hendrix and the way the questionnaire had "tested" with the first neighbor, especially how Lana Stepanian's reactions tipped me to some of the more "questionable" parts of it. However, I really hadn't learned anything about Andrew Dees beyond what Olga Evorova already had told me.

I walked down the Stepanians' path to the sidewalk and past the Dees unit. At the next path I went up to the door with number 43 on it and ROBINETTE under the button. When I pushed, another bong sounded inside, but nobody answered. After trying the button twice more without success, I tracked back down their path and over to the Elmendorfs at number 44.

Their bong was answered by Kira's muffled voice saying "Just a second," and then she herself at the door. Up close, the eyes under the platinum hair were brown, some silver glitterdust sparkling at the corners. A stainless steel ring pierced her left nostril, its triplets through her left ear but an inch above the lobe. She carried a Sony Walkman in her right hand, the headpiece to it down around her throat like a necklace.

Kira looked at me oddly, as though aware that she ought to know me. "Can I help with something?"

I introduced myself and gave her my ID. There's no photo on the license, but she still compared what was written on it with my face, saying, "You were in The Tides today, right?"

"Right."

Kira handed my holder back to me, with a little flourish I took to be her idea of coy. "So how come you're following me?"

"I'm not. I represent another condominium association that's thinking of hiring the Hendrix company to run their complex, and I'm just checking on how well people who live here think Hendrix performs for them."

"Well, I don't know much about it, but come in anyway."

I'm not sure what I expected after the Stepanians' place. In terms of structural layout, the Elmendorf unit had exactly the same design, but mirror-imaged, so the kitchen was on the left and the staircase to the catwalk on the right. While the Stepanians had overstuffed furniture and carefully selected knickknacks, this place seemed more cluttered than decorated. Magazines covered all the horizontal planes. *Teen, Outdoor Life, Elle, Popular Mechanics.* Some technical photographic journals were sprinkled into the general mess. The couch, chairs, and table in the living room looked twenty years old, used pizza boxes and Chinese food cartons stacked on the counter separating kitchen from dining area. No sign of Norman Elmendorf.

But some sound of him.

A gravelly male voice called out from the upstairs. "Kira, who is it?"

"No problem, Dad. Just a man wanting to know about the condo management."

Kira said the words sweetly, no condescension toward him or me in her manner.

"Well, send him up."

She looked at me, spoke very quietly. "If you don't go up to see him I'll, like, hear about it for a week. Do me a favor, though?"

"What?"

Kira bit her lip once and let out a breath. "Be gentle and patient with him, okay?"

Watching her, I said, "Okay."

She sat down on the old print couch, putting the head-piece to the Walkman back on and picking up a magazine.

Climbing the stairs, I noticed only two chairs at the dining room table. Looking down at the staircase itself, I saw a number of indentations on the wooden steps. The marks were round and roughly the circumference of a half-dollar. As though somebody on crutches had been making this journey for a while.

When I arrived at the threshold to what I predicted would be the master bedroom, the door was half open, but I knocked anyway. The gravelly voice said, "Come on in."

Entering the room, I saw a man of six feet or so lying in bed, propped up by two pillows behind him, a pair of metal braces like polio victims might use leaning against the night table next to him. The bedclothes covered his body up to the waist, but on top he wore a hooded, navy-blue sweatshirt which I would have thought too warm for the mild temperature on the second floor. Elmendorf's smiling face was cheery, but the rosy cheeks, bulbous nose, and crooked teeth caricatured him like an engraved portrait out of Dickens. He was about my age with homecut hair, the rosy color of his cheeks extending in blotches down his neck and onto his chest along the zipper of the sweatshirt. I could see why Kira had asked me to be gentle with him.

A liter bottle of Jim Beam was nearly dead on the night

table, two fingers of the bourbon in a glass next to the bottle. Probably why his daughter had asked me to be patient as well.

"Pull up that chair. Kira uses it to watch over me when I have nightmares, but they're hours away yet."

I tugged over a wooden armchair that might once have stood at the head of the dining table downstairs. A print on its seat cushion matched the one on the living room couch.

"Nightmares from what?" I said.

A tolerant laugh, though it came out more a grunt, like he had phlegm in his throat. "The war, what else? Desert Storm." Taking a swig of his booze, Elmendorf squinted at me. "You?"

"Vietnam."

"Army?"

"Yes."

"Where?"

"I was MP, so mostly Saigon, occasionally the bush."

"The 'bush.' God, what we would have given for some 'bush' where old Bushie sent us. Even a branch or a twig, anything to throw a little shade."

"How did you get sent over?"

"My own stupid fault." Another gulp of bourbon. "I went into the Reserves after college. Make a little extra money, you know? Then I got married and Kira came along, and the extra money looked even better, so I re-upped each time. Never thought I'd ever go anywhere, just weekends at Fort Devens or wherever we did our training for two weeks in the summer. Kind of fun, actually, be with the guys away from home every once in a while."

"Until."

"*Until* is right. Should have known better." Elmendorf set down his glass. "My father was in WW II, the 45th Infantry. He's from Lowell here, but he gets stuck in the 45th with all these National Guard guys from Colorado and Oklahoma, he can barely understand how they talk. And where do they send him first? Martha's Vineyard, to practice amphibious landings. Then he ships out for Sicily somewhere. Here he is, this son of a German immigrant himself, trying to take Italy back from the Italians and the Germans. Crazy, huh?"

I wanted to be patient, for Kira and for me, so I said, "Crazy."

"And that's not all of it, either. When he's in Sicily, my dad gets to see the first Bob Hope USO show, the very first ever. There's Dorothy Lamour, Jerry Colonna, and Hope himself, coming out on stage and telling jokes and dancing some, then comedy skits. The show had to be held during the daytime, account of they were afraid the German bombers'd see the lights at night. All that and wounded at Palermo to boot, and he still gets called up for Korea seven years later. Which is why I should have known better than to stay in the Reserves."

"Where were you in the Gulf?"

"Oh, here, there, and everywhere."

Which seemed a peculiar answer, as vague as Lana Stepanian had been about her husband's hometown.

Reaching for the glass, Elmendorf shook his head, then downed the remaining liquor like a shot of tequila. "They talk about Desert Storm as a war, and I guess it was, I don't have anything to compare it to, myself. But you know how long the actual shooting lasted? I don't mean those air raids in January and all, just the actual ground war."

"Not long, as I recall."

"Not long is right. A hundred hours. Saturday, twenty-four February, to Wednesday, twenty-eight February. I heard one guy call it 'the Andy Warhol War,' account of it was like somebody being famous for fifteen minutes, you know? Well, all I know is I saw enough death and destruction to last me a lifetime. It wasn't war so much as slaughter. A video game where you just racked up points from planes or tanks or even the little bit of house-to-house there was.

The Iraqi Republican Guards, they were well-armed enough, with nice green uniforms and these scarves around their heads and necks, fishnet pattern, like desert chieftains or something. But the poor regular soldiers? Shit, we just plowed them under, right under the sand. The ones that surrendered, the EPWs—Enemy Prisoners of War?—you could see them miles away, like long lines of ants, marching across the horizon with their hands up, praying to Allah because they were going through a minefield. I swear, I was on guard duty one night, and there was a windstorm, and by morning you could see all these mines the Iraqis had laid, a whole line of them, forty or fifty, maybe five meters apart. And I looked down at my LPCs and—"

"Your what?"

He motioned with the empty glass toward his feet. "My boots. LPC, that stands for 'Leather Personnel Carrier.' Get it?"

"Got it."

"Like the Hummers, the desert jeeps we had? You run them on asphalt, that's 'hardball.' You run them on sand, that's 'softball.' I read in a magazine that this car dealer in New Jersey's selling them for winter driving, get through the snow like we did the sand over in the Saud."

"What happened to you there?"

"You mean, how come I'm in this bed?"

"Yes."

Another tolerant laugh as he reached for the bottle and poured a few more ounces without offering me any. "I used to say it was from the MREs. You know what that stands for?"

"I heard it as 'Meals Ready to Eat.' "

"Yeah, well, I called them 'Meals Rejected by Ethiopians.' Like, even starving Africans wouldn't touch them, get it?"

A poor joke, but I let him have it.

"Only thing is," said Elmendorf, "it's not the food that

got me, though I had to eat those MREs anytime the supply sergeant couldn't come up with better through his 'General Store.' Scrounging and trading, you know?"

"I don't think that part ever changes."

A nod, then another toward the Jim Beam. "No booze, though. Jesus, they were strict about that. A Moslem country, we couldn't disrespect our hosts by drinking liquor before we went off to die for them."

"That where you got hit?"

"Hit? I didn't. Least, not by something you could see." Elmendorf unzipped the sweatshirt and spread it open with each hand. The rosy blotch grew darker and uglier as it swept toward his waist. "I was exposed. Lots of us were."

"Exposed to what?"

"The Army doesn't know, or at least it isn't saying. Guys started getting sick over there, but because most of us weren't there long, the thing didn't hit us till we got back. Headaches, nerves, rashes like this here. Plus aches in the joints so bad you'd think they were engines running without oil, just seizing up on you. How come I have to use the braces most of the time. And how come I can't go back to photography. Man, there are days when I can't even hold a newspaper much less adjust the settings on a camera."

"What about the VA?"

"The Department of Veterans Affairs? They're a joke. They had all of us register, we had any symptoms. But the Defense Department's saying there isn't any 'syndrome,' and without a 'syndrome' they can't treat us and won't pay us. Thousands of soldiers now, but they say they aren't responsible because we didn't really get infected, or whatever, over there."

I thought about Agent Orange, and how long it took those vets to receive any—and meager—satisfaction through the courts. Good Luck, Norman. I said, "So you can't work at all?"

"Not with the aches, man. They just dominate the day, you know?"

I didn't like the feeling I was getting about Elmendorf, that big-talk, no-action sense you develop about some troopers in bars. I took out two of the interview forms and handed one to him.

"What's this?"

"As I told your daughter, I'm looking into whether another condo complex should switch to the Hendrix company for its management, and I've been asking your neighbors a few questions to assess your satisfaction with how Hendrix is managing Plymouth Willows."

"Okay by me. I don't exactly have anything else to do."

"NAME?"

"Elmendorf, Norman, NMI."

"For 'No Middle Initial.' "

"Right. Guess that didn't change, either."

"Change?"

"From your war, I mean."

I nodded. "HOMETOWN?"

"Lowell, like I said."

"EDUCATION?"

"Lowell Tech. They call it 'University of Massachusetts—Lowell' now, but it was just Lowell Tech when I went there."

"Your wife?"

"We're divorced. She took off when I got back from the Saud. Basically abandoned Kira, the cunt."

I decided to skip the rest of the SPOUSE questions. "How long ago did you move here?"

"About six years. Pioneers, like. First purchasers from the guy who developed Plymouth Willows."

As with Lana Stepanian, I wanted to ease slowly toward the Andrew Dees questions, hiding them among the others. "One of your neighbors told me about the problems he had."

"Which neighbor was that?"

I couldn't see it did any harm, but . . . "I'm telling everybody I talk to that their answers will stay confidential."

"Doesn't matter. Lana's the only one here long enough to really fill you in. She's a nice girl, only kind of uptight about life. You know, a place for everything and everything in its place? I don't see how you can live that way, myself."

Explained his living room. "I understand the Hendrix company was brought in by the C.W. Realty Trust."

"If that's the name of the people who bailed out Quentin's estate, yeah."

"Quentin?"

"Yale Quentin, the guy who built Plymouth Willows."

"And he's dead now?"

"Four, five years. There was some kind of stink about fraud, him supposedly making up dummy buyers to fool the banks he borrowed off. I even remember him coming to the paper I worked for, checking me out with the editor so he could show the banks he was legit. Guess he wasn't, though."

"How come?"

"Well, he killed himself over the mess."

Lana Stepanian would probably classify suicide as "gossip." "That's too bad."

"Yeah, brand-new Caddy, too."

"I'm sorry?"

"Quentin. He took his car over that ocean bluff you pass on the left just before our turn. Smashed the Caddy and himself on the rocks down by the water."

I nodded, bringing Elmendorf back to the form. "Any FAMILY MEMBERS visit you here?"

Elmendorf looked up from his copy. "If you mean overnighters, no. I got a brother comes by for dinner once in a blue moon."

"Has he always been treated well by the Hendrix people?"

"I doubt he's met any, except for maybe running into Paulie. He's the retarded kid does the lawns and all."

"How about your DEALINGS WITH THE HENDRIX COMPANY?"

"They've been fine, only they want to be paid."

"Paid?"

"Yeah. After I couldn't work at the paper anymore, I got unemployment. You ever had to live on that?"

"Years ago."

"Well, let me tell you, it still isn't much. I can barely cover the mortgage, bread, and water. I'm in hock up to my ears, and I don't know how long we can hold on."

Elmendorf said it awfully matter-of-factly. "I'm sorry to hear that."

"Yeah, well, for your form and all, the Hendrix guy has been pretty good, considering how much Kira and me owe. He hasn't been pounding on the door with the sheriff, anyway, and all his letters and calls are pretty decent."

That didn't square with my impression of him, but you never know where people's hearts lie. "Have they been helpful in accommodating your disability?"

"I can't get the VA to recognize I'm disabled, I don't see Hendrix having to, but I've never asked them, other than to explain how come we're not current on the bills."

"Ever visited the Hendrix offices?"

"No."

"How does Hendrix handle COMPLAINTS?"

"You mean, like from me if there's a leak or something?"

"Yes."

"We haven't called him recently. I mean, we're so far behind in our monthly maintenance, I figure, don't kick the sleeping dog, right?"

I could see his point. "NEIGHBORS is the next entry, and, as I said, I'll keep whatever you say confidential."

"Look, buddy, I worked on a newspaper, okay? I know how the reporters I'd go out with felt about confidential sources and all. Even if you're as good about it as they were, I got to tell you, I could care less what my neighbors think of me or think I said to you. They want to sue me, they can sue me. I got diddly squat for them to come after."

Good. Work toward Andrew Dees gradually. "How about the Stepanians?"

"Nice, like I said. The husband, Steve, he's kind of uptight too, but it seems to me they try to be good citizens. School committee, condo board, and Lana spells Kira once in a while so the poor kid can have something resembling a life for herself instead of having to look after me all the time."

Glancing toward the braces, I said, "Can you make it up and down stairs?"

"Barely. And I try it more than twice a day, I'm dogshit the next morning. Like I'm not puppy shit now, you know?"

"How about Andrew Dees?"

"Christ, you'd just about have to describe him to me. I mean, these windows look out the back, but I can't see his deck, and I haven't been out front for months. I shook hands with him once, saw him another time with a good-looking woman, something foreign about her. But I can't see where that helps you with your condo association any."

It wouldn't. "So you don't know HOMETOWN?"

"No. Wait a minute . . . No, I got the feeling Midwest somewheres, but that's probably from his accent."

"What about EDUCATION?"

"We never got to talking about that. Like I said, it was just a handshake kind of thing. 'Welcome to the Willows,' you know?"

"And other than the woman, nobody visiting him?"

Elmendorf seemed taken aback. "What does that have to do with how Hendrix manages the complex?"

"Just toward the FAMILY VISITING angle."

"Well, I don't see it, but you'd have to ask him."

I didn't want Elmendorf thinking I was focusing on Dees. "How about the Robinettes?"

"Depends on whether you like rap music."

"I'm sorry?"

"The Afro music Jamey plays on his ghetto blaster. Account of my nerves, Kira uses that Walkman thing so I can't hear it, but she's always having to go next door, pound on the door to get him to turn his shit the fuck down."

I didn't like the racist undertones from Elmendorf. "You don't know anything more about them?"

"The woman doesn't seem to work, but they've got a pretty new car, so maybe she's figured out a way for the government to recognize some disability of hers. What do *you* think?"

"Haven't met her yet," I said quietly. "I wonder if you'd mind signing this."

"What is it?"

I gave him my filled-in form. "The questionnaire we've been going over. Just so I can show I spoke to you."

"Sure, sure. I'm kind of shaky, though, so you might not be able to read my signature."

"That's okay."

Scratching along the dotted line, Elmendorf said, "Her kid goes to some private school on top of it."

"Jamey Robinette?"

"Who else? He'll have my job someday."

"Your job?"

"Yeah. He'll be a photographer or better, the degree he'll have." Norman Elmendorf gave me back the form and my pen. " 'Upwardly mobile,' they call it."

*   *   *

Coming back down the stairs, I saw Kira catch my movement from the corner of her eye. She sat up and slid the earphones onto her neck again. "You get what you wanted?"

"Yes," stretching the truth some. "I wonder if I could talk to you for a while?"

A shrug that made her hands flap a little on the wrists. "Sure. Let me, like, clear away the junk first."

Kira Elmendorf gathered up the magazines that covered an old easy chair. Instead of carrying them off somewhere, she just dropped them onto the floor. The carpet looked to be original equipment, but unlike the Stepanians', this one showed dirt and stains.

I sat as Kira took the couch again and, despite the combat boots, did a yoga crossover with her ankles.

"So," she said, "what do you want to know?"

I gave her a questionnaire and waited while she read through it.

"What's this for?"

"It would help me with my clients if I could ask you some of the stuff on there. I already got most of it from your dad."

Another shrug, the form in her hand flapping. "So, sure."

"How do you feel the Hendrix company does in managing the place?"

"Oh, wow." A hand went through the platinum hair, causing neither damage nor improvement. "They do what they're supposed to, I guess. The heat's on, the road's plowed in winter, the grass is cut in spring—thanks to Paulie, anyway, he's just *so* extremely cute in his little uniform—and he does the pool right in summer, no bugs or leaves or other disgusting uck in it."

"You never had any trouble with Mr. Hendrix, then?"

"No. Wait." Kira ran her hand through her hair again. "Do you mean like, did Boyce ever hit on me?"

Boyce. "Any kind of trouble at all."

7 8

"No. I mean, he's cute too, in a sort of older mode, with good buns."

"Buns?"

"For sure. Whenever he's over checking in with Lana—that's Mrs. Stepanian?"

Boyce and Lana. "I've met her."

"Yeah, well, she's like one of the presidents of the condo somehow, and when he visits her, Boyce is always dressed real cazh."

"Hendrix dresses real casual."

"So you can scope the buns."

Scope the . . . "Kira, have you ever heard any complaints from the other neighbors about Mr. Hendrix?"

"No. Just does a totally fine job, I guess."

"Nothing from Mr. Dees, either?"

The shrug. "He's kind of a quiet dude. I guess staring at a machine that makes copies kind of flattens the brain waves."

I sat forward. "How do you mean?"

"Well, like, the man doesn't ever get to do anything creative, right? All day long, it's just put the original in, push the button, take the original out. I mean, a chimp could do that and stay ecstatic, maybe, but a real human person? Give it up."

Kira seemed to be my best bet so far. "You've talked with Mr. Dees some, then?"

"Some. He's kind of quiet. Nobody around here is exactly into partying hard, you understand. But he never seems to do much except get up, go to work, and come home. I figure he could use some *Short Attention Span Theater*, you know?"

"*Short Attention* . . ."

". . . *Span Theater*. It was on the cable, until we couldn't afford that anymore. This coolest dude, Marc Maron, he looks kind of like a photo I saw of one of the Beatles guys. Not Paul—the guy who got assassinated, you know?"

"John Lennon?"

"Yeah, like this old photo I saw from somewhere in the seventies of John Lennon, with the hair and the glasses. Anyways, this show was *so* cool, it had these little clips, couple minutes each, of Gary Shandling—I think he is just a-*dor*-able—and then *Saturday Night Live* with a bunch of dudes I didn't know, and then this British thing, *Monty Python*–something, and then this soap called *Soap*, but I didn't get it because it was supposed to be funny and soaps are, like, a scream, but they're not *trying* to be funny, you know?"

I was losing ground. "And you thought Andrew Dees would benefit from that kind of show."

"Or something, *any*-thing, just to get his heart started. Then he started showing up with this executive-fox type, and I think his heart's not the only thing pumping, you know what I mean?"

"He ever talk with you about where he was from?"

"From? Like, who *cares*?"

"How about where he might have worked before the photocopy shop?"

Kira frowned, the nostril ring doing something that made her nose itself wiggle. "What does that have to do with Boyce's company doing a righteous job?"

Good question. "I got the impression from your father that you have to go next door sometimes about the Robinettes' music noise."

A shrug, but this time with some theatricality to it. "Oh, that's totally nothing. Daddy, he's super hypersensitive to noise. So when Jamey cranks it up on the boom box, I go over and tell him to, like, cool it. No problem. He's a good kid, and his mom's nice too."

"They don't mind you telling them to turn things down?"

"From never. They understand, and they know that even I got to hear my sounds over this thing," jiggling the Walkman, "which is just as well, now that we don't have a stereo rack anymore."

8 0

"What happened to it?"

"The sound system? My friend Jude—you saw her with me at the pub today?—Jude took me down to this extremely disgusto pawnshop, and we got money for it."

"You hocked the stereo?"

Kira seemed to bristle. "Hey, man, ever try to eat a cassette? Daddy's been out of work, like, unto years, and things are pretty tight."

"I'm sorry."

She eased off a bit. "Used to be, I'd go to the mall and actually *buy* something? These days, only time I'm there is to earn some bread, handing out fliers and stuff, like 'Three for two, How about you, come to Papa Gino's'—you know?"

I nodded. "Back in high school, I had to work part-time jobs. Not an easy way to get through."

"Hey, it could be worse. I could be on drugs, or, like, virtually married the way Jude and some of the other juniors are. Or even flunking out, I suppose. But I'm not really a junior because I'm not in school this year, and I'm not in danger of flunking out because I already *am* out, you know? My dad's sick, and he needs me. I know he can get around better than he lets on, with the braces and all, but he still needs me. And after my mom pulled the ripcord, I needed him so bad, I can give him some time now. Besides, it's like I told Jude today when she drove me back."

"What did you say?"

"Well, Jude's doing this dance on me, how I shouldn't be letting my father run my life, he's the one who's sick. So I say to her, 'Hey, Jude'—wait." Kira stared at me. "That's just *so* totally weird. Here we're talking about the Beatles like two seconds ago, and I know that's one of their old songs, right?"

"Right."

"Wow. The powers of the occult." The flapping shrug. "Anyways, I say to Jude, 'You really want me to trip you out, here's my view of life to-*tal*. You got to live for the moment, because tomorrow's only hours away, and it's bound to be so much worse.' "

"Not very optimistic."

Kira Elmendorf made a gesture with her hands that took in all around her. "Hey, man, you can tell me about it as they're throwing us out of here and onto the street, okay?"

7

As Kira Elmendorf closed up behind me, I could hear rap music coming faintly from the Robinette unit. I walked over, thinking I still hadn't learned very much about Andrew Dees, even with his neighbors telling me what they knew of him. Hope springing eternal, I pushed the button at number 43. The voice of the rapper jumped a few decibels, though still not very loud, when a young black guy swung open the door.

He looked to be a little over both sixteen and six feet, in baggy basketball shorts, a baggy T-shirt, and a Miami Dolphins cap worn Yogi-style. A proud, handsome face framed steady brown eyes, not much hair showing under the cap. It would be a while before the flesh filled in the spaces around all the angular bones, though, and in the outfit he was wearing, a strong wind might have given him some difficulty.

"Help you with something?"

"My name's John Cuddy. I'd like to speak to your mother if she's around."

Just the steady eyes before over the shoulder with a loud, "Yo, Mom?"

"What is it?"

"Man here to see you."

"Jamey, I cannot hear you."

He punched his own voice above the rapper's. "I said there's a man here to see you."

"One minute."

I smiled politely at Jamey Robinette, but evidently he didn't think that merited an invitation to enter.

Ten seconds later a woman came to the door. About five-seven and slightly overweight, it was as though she were hoarding a dozen extra pounds in case her son decided he could use them. She wore aquamarine pants and a white blouse with a small scarf tied under the collar, like a cowboy's bandanna. Her skin was a few shades lighter than Jamey's, and you could see where he got his features. But her most striking aspect was the hair, almost an orange, yet somehow not unnatural.

"Yes? Can I help you with something?"

Reduced to a conversational level, her voice had a lilt and accent to it, maybe Caribbean, as Lana Stepanian had ventured. I introduced myself and showed her my identification.

She looked up from the holder. "What is this about?"

"I'm representing a condominium complex that's thinking of retaining the Hendrix company as its manager, and I wondered if I could ask you a few questions about how you've found their services here?"

A very slight flaring of her nostrils without taking a breath. "Yes. Yes, I believe I can do that. Please, come in."

I followed her, Jamey closing the door behind us. As we got to the now-familiar first-floor layout, he said, "So, Mom, okay if I disappear for a while?"

"If you turn off that music first."

Jamey went by her, an affectionate hand on her shoulder. At the home entertainment center, he toggled a key, and the rapper stopped in mid-syllable. Over the shoulder again with, "You want something soothing?"

"No, thank you."

Jamey turned to me. "Drink, maybe? We got iced tea and Coke that I know of."

"Iced tea would be great, thanks."

"Mom?"

"Coke, please."

When Jamey moved toward the kitchen, I could see a rubber Halloween mask lying near the sound system. Pretty good likeness of the actor Tom Cruise.

Mrs. Robinette noticed me looking at the mask. "For a party at his school."

I nodded.

She said, "One of his Jewish friends is going as Denzel Washington." Then a parental shrug, like a silent "Who can understand these kids today?"

I shrugged back.

Mrs. Robinette motioned me toward one of two tweedy chairs that matched a couch, she taking the middle of it. A dining room set bought for a larger space stood in front of the sliding glass doors, but I didn't see any furniture on their deck. Bookcases held a couple of framed photos showing a younger version of Mrs. Robinette with a broad-shouldered, dark-skinned black man. One was a casual candid, the other a posed portrait from some formal occasion. Between them was a triptych of photos showing Jamey at roughly five-year intervals from ages three to thirteen or so. I looked back at the broad-shouldered man.

"My husband."

I nodded.

She said, "He died, some years ago."

I turned to her. "My wife too. I'm sorry."

The beginning of a nod from Mrs. Robinette, a pause, then the continuation of it as Jamey brought us our drinks and went toward the front door with the words, "Back for dinner, don't worry."

"Your jacket."

"It's hot out, Mom."

"Then just take it, even if you will not wear it."

"Okay, okay."

I could hear a closet open and close before the front door did the same.

Lifting my glass, I said, "From the little I know about it, I'd say you've done a pretty fair job raising Jamey on your own."

That slight flaring of the nostrils again. "You did not have any children, then?"

The iced tea was laced with lemon and just enough sugar. "No."

"They make a difference." She regarded me a bit differently. "Since you know I am still alone, I assume you have been talking to some of my neighbors."

Sharp lady. "Yes." Putting my glass down, I took out one of the forms. "I'll be writing your responses on a copy here, but it's sometimes helpful to have the questions in front of you too. I can assure you that all your responses will remain confidential with me."

Robinette looked up from her form. "Go ahead."

"FULL NAME?"

"Robinette, Tángela."

"T-A-N-G-E-L-A?"

A sip of her coke. "That is correct. My father was from Jamaica, and when he saw my hair, he said, 'Why, she looks just like a tangerine.'"

"You were born in Jamaica, then?"

"No. Haiti, Port-au-Prince."

I stopped writing. "Still have family there?"

"Some. I left so long ago, I stay informed from CNN more than anything else, but I was glad President Clinton finally sent in our troops. The attachés and the Fraph—that is the 'Front for Advancement and Progress?'—are the younger brothers and older sons of the Duvaliers' Tonton Macoutes, and I saw enough of them while I still lived there."

"How long have you been in the States?"

"Since I was ten years old."

I went back to the form. "MAIDEN NAME."

"Ste. Hilaire. That's S-T-E and H-I-L-A-I-R-E."

"EDUCATION?"

"Bachelor's degree from UMass Boston, some graduate credits but no degree from Northeastern."

"I'm sorry to have to ask this, but ... your husband?"

Robinette placed her glass carefully on a side table. "He died before Jamey and I moved to the Willows."

We looked at each other for a second before she said, "And therefore he could not have known anything about Hendrix Management."

"Right, of course. How long have you lived here?"

"About two years."

Again from the questionnaire, "PURCHASE OR RENT?"

"Purchase."

"Based on what I've learned so far, I understand the original developer had some problems?"

"Yes, or rather that is what I heard too. But I bought directly from the new owners."

"The C.W. Realty Trust?"

A hesitation. "I believe that was the name. I just send the monthly maintenance checks to the Hendrix people."

"Have any FAMILY MEMBERS visited you here?"

"Well, Jamey lives here, he does not 'visit.' But no, no family otherwise."

"OCCUPATION?"

"Jamey is still in school."

"Here in Plymouth Mills?"

"No. He commutes as a day student to Tabor Academy."

I'd heard of it, an expensive boarding school maybe half an hour away, in Marion. "Impressive."

"He has always been a fine student."

I wrote on my paper. "And you?"

"I am no longer a student."

"Sorry. That next question stands for your occupation."

"I do not work."

When I looked up at her, Robinette seemed prepared to wait me out. No job, but she purchased a condo, pays monthly maintenance, and covers tuition at Tabor. However, my "clients" wouldn't be interested in how she handled all that.

Back to the form. "How have your DEALINGS been WITH the HENDRIX COMPANY?"

"No complaints."

"None?"

"When there is something wrong, I call them, and it gets fixed. We have a resident superintendent, Paulie."

"I've met him."

"Well, he takes care of the grounds just fine, and the only thing I can think of that has gone wrong was the mosquitoes from the bog, and when a number of us complained about that, I believe the company had the town go in and spray."

"And that took care of things?"

"Or knocked them back some, which was enough."

"And no other problems that Hendrix didn't fix?"

Robinette shifted a little on the couch. "Not that I know of."

"NEIGHBORS is the next item. Again I want to stress the confidence in which I'll hold your answers."

She shifted some more. "I do not quite see what my neighbors have to do with your interviewing me. You have talked—or will talk—to them too, correct?"

"Yes, but it's helpful for me to get a sense of how everyone in your cluster here sees everyone else, so my clients can judge whether your responses correlate with their situation."

The flaring of the nostrils again. "Then it does not sound as though my answers are going to be 'held' very 'confidentially.' "

I shook my head. "What I meant, Mrs. Robinette, is that I'll know who said what, and that will remain confidential with me. I'll summarize those individual answers, in an identity-blind way, for my clients. That's how they want it, too."

A slow blink. "Ask your questions."

I was afraid of losing her, so I cut to the car chase. "Let's start with next door. Andrew Dees. That's D-E-E-S, I believe?"

"Correct."

"HOMETOWN?"

"I do not know."

"EDUCATION?"

"I do not know that, either."

"Okay. OCCUPATION?"

"Andrew runs the photocopy store in the town center."

"Owns it or just manages it?"

"I am not sure, but he refers to it as 'his shop.' "

"FAMILY?"

"Of Andrew?"

"Yes."

"Why would you not just ask him?"

"I plan to, but I haven't caught up with Mr. Dees yet."

More shifting on her cushion. "He has never introduced me to any relatives."

"Any PROBLEMS with him?"

"Problems?"

"Yes. Any difficulties you've had with Mr. Dees as a neighbor?"

"No."

"Loud parties, that sort of thing?"

Robinette stared at me, then the slow blink. "Mr. Cuddy, why would your clients be interested in Andrew's social life?"

"Well, they're not, really. It's more if there've been any difficulties, and the Hendrix people had to be called in—"

"They have not."

"You're sure?"

"At least not by me."

"Anything else you can think of about Mr. Dees that might help me?"

"Help you with what?"

Her voice had some steel in it, the kind of command/demand tone you get from being in charge of others at some point in your life.

"With my job here," I said.

"Mr. Cuddy, I am not quite sure I still understand what your job is."

"How about the Elmendorfs?"

"I think you should go."

"Mrs. Robinette, I'm sorry if—"

"Or would you like to be able to tell your clients how well the Hendrix company can call the police for me?"

The steel was back in her voice, and I decided that I might be overstaying my welcome just a tad.

Walking to the car, I also decided my cover story was wearing thin quicker than it was producing much new information on Andrew Dees. Once behind the wheel, I drove around the other clusters, thinking I might spot Paulie Fogerty again. I even checked in the rear, by the pool, the tennis courts, and his little house. No rake, no Fogerty.

To head back toward town, I went down the front driveway this time. At the intersection with the road was Paulie, facing away from me, at a white, vertical post with a crossbar. Balanced awkwardly in his hands was a rustic PLYMOUTH WILLOWS sign I'd missed on my way in, maybe because it had fallen. Fogerty was trying to hang it back on hooks screwed into the crossbar.

I stopped and got out. "Give you a hand?"

"No."

"You sure?"

He half-turned, tears in his eyes. His palms were red with little streaks of blood—from the rough edges of the sign, I guessed.

Paulie shrieked at me. "I can do my job! I can do my job! I'm the super!"

Then he began to cry, and I apologized for interrupting him before getting back into the Prelude.

eaching the shore road again, I turned north, passing on the right the "scenic overlook" where the developer of Plymouth Willows had ended his problems the hard way. After the bridge, I entered the downtown section of Plymouth Mills and slowed to fifteen miles an hour. Sliding past the photocopy shop on my left, I could see the lights on and a person behind the counter helping a customer. I found a parking space against the opposite curb.

Crossing Main Street, I walked to the shop's door, holding it open for the man coming out. Inside, the counter occupied the rear of a shallow front room, a door beyond the counter closed. There was no visible furniture, the paneling reminding me of the cheap stuff in Boyce Hendrix's office back in Marshfield.

As the shop door closed behind me, an Asian woman looked up from the cash register on the counter and smiled. She was perhaps early thirties, in a blue oxford shirt with some designer's squiggle on the pocket. Her hair was pulled behind her head in a simple ponytail, her nails short but polished, her makeup modest. She also wore a wedding band on the left ring finger.

"May I help you?"

A slight, singsong accent. "Yes. I'd like to speak with Mr. Dees, if he's available."

She glanced at the telephone next to the register, a tiny red light glowing through a clear button. "He's still on the phone, but if you don't mind waiting, I'm sure he'll be done shortly."

I said, "My name's John Cuddy, by the way."

The woman just nodded. "Fee."

"Fee?"

"F-I."

"Short for . . . ?"

A gracious smile. "Filomena, but I could never stand that name. 'Filomena the Filipina,' you see what I mean?"

"Manila?"

"Just outside." Filomena reached under the counter for some forms that she began counting. "Met my husband there." She waggled the ring finger at me. "He's in the service here, the South Weymouth Naval Air Station."

I liked the way Filomena answered my question by also answering one I hadn't asked. "I came by before lunch, but you seemed to be closed."

Still counting the forms, she shook her head. "Sorry about that. Andrew was working at home this morning, and I was supposed to open up when the car blew some kind of belt on the way. I'm just part-time here, but I hate to let Andrew down."

"I didn't see any competition to worry about."

Filomena looked up. "Do you mean here in town?"

"Yes."

She went back to the count. "No, but that doesn't mean you can take customers for granted, either. Andrew says that if you have a shop in the suburbs, you make your mark by giving 'personalized service.' "

I decided to nudge things a little. "Sounds like the voice of experience."

"Who, Andrew?"

"Yes. He's done this kind of thing before?"

"Not that he ever said."

Best not to nudge too much. "Have you worked here long?"

"Almost since the place opened. I'd been in the market for a part-time job. Cover when the kids are at school, you know? I was lucky to stop in just when Andrew needed somebody to help out."

I heard a faint click, and Filomena glanced again at the phone. The red light was off, but as she reached for the receiver, the light came back on again. "Sorry, I didn't catch him in time."

"That's okay." I gave it a beat I hoped seemed natural. "Ever work in a photocopy shop before?"

"No."

"How do you like it?"

"What's not to like? The work isn't exactly challenging, but at least you don't go home worrying about it afterwards. And the closest thing there is to danger on the job is a paper cut."

"Danger?"

Filomena looked up from the telephone before going back to her forms. "Like an industrial accident, or getting robbed. Plymouth Mills is a pretty quiet town, but a liquor store or even a convenience mart can be a target. Who's going to hold up a place that charges eight cents a copy?"

I grinned, and she showed me the gracious smile as she finished her count. "Is there anything I can do for you while you're waiting for Andrew?"

I was about to risk another background question on Dees,

when the faint click sounded again. Filomena grabbed the receiver immediately and pushed a button that made a buzzing noise. "There's a gentleman here who'd like to . . . Good." Hanging up, she said to me, "He'll be right with you."

The door behind her opened, and the man I'd seen leaving unit 42 at Plymouth Willows came out. Up close, Andrew Dees was about six feet tall on a medium build, the thick, curly hair barely speckled with gray at the temples. His prominent eyebrows almost knit over a perfect nose, the strong chin jutting out nervously as he spoke.

"Who are you?"

I thought it was an odd reaction, given the little that Filomena had told him about me. "My name's John Cuddy, Mr. Dees." I offered him my ID holder. "I'd like to ask you some questions about the Plymouth Willows condominium."

He didn't take the holder, hardly even looked at it. "Why?"

"I represent another complex that's thinking of changing management companies, and I'm talking with people about how they like Hendrix as—"

"I don't have time for that."

The voice was strained, and from over by the cash register Filomena shot Dees a concerned look.

I reached into the portfolio to get one of my forms. "It would only take—"

"I said I don't have time."

His voice nearly cracked, and Filomena's lips parted briefly, as though she'd never heard him speak to someone this way before.

I withdrew my hand from the portfolio empty. "Maybe if I came back—"

"The answer is no, Mr. Cuddy. I don't have time for you or your questionnaire. Is that clear enough?"

Dees turned and stalked back into the inner office, closing the door just this side of slamming it.

Filomena's eyes went from the door to me. "I'm really . . . sorry. Something . . . something must have . . ."

"That's okay, don't worry about it. Probably just hit him at a bad moment."

She gave me a very weak version of the gracious smile, and I left the shop. Carrying the portfolio back to the Prelude, I wondered how Andrew Dees knew I had a questionnaire to work from before he'd ever seen me bring it out.

9

I drove north, sailing along Route 3 until the merge at 128, then getting mired in afternoon traffic on the Southeast Expressway just before the Dorchester gas facility. In the early seventies, an artist had painted one of the giant tanks with bold slashes of red, blue, green, and other colors. She'd since died, and a couple of years ago Bostongas tore the tank down, pleading obsolescence. There was enough cultural outcry that the company let another artist painstakingly re-create the pattern on a new tank, which from the highway looks pretty good, especially compared to the skeletons of grandiose office and residential towers that ran out of development money before anything but the structural steel got erected.

Back in the city, I double-parked by a one-hour photo place long enough to drop off the film I'd shot at Plymouth Willows, asking in advance for a dozen copies of the fourth frame on the roll, which I figured to be the best one of Andrew Dees. Leaving the car in the slanted space near the dumpster behind my office's building, I went upstairs and dialed the district attorney's office. A secretary said Ms. Meagher was "on trial." Probably the attempted murder case she'd told me about the night before. I asked the secretary to let Nancy know I'd called.

Then I tried Olga Evorova's number at the bank to bring her up to date on how little I'd found out and to ask her how far she wanted me to push an already upset Andrew Dees. I drew a very formal secretary who advised me that Ms. Evorova was attending a meeting out of the office. I left basically the same message with her that I had at the DA's.

After organizing the questionnaires from Plymouth Willows into a simple file, I did some other paperwork for an hour or so, involuntarily thinking of Nancy and glancing at the telephone from time to time. Following that, I signed my name to reports a nice woman at the accountants' office down the corridor word processes "under the desk" for ten bucks a throw. Then I looked at the Plymouth Willows file again. I was about to start counting the turning leaves on the Common's trees when the phone finally did ring.

"John Cuddy."

"John, it's Nancy."

Just hearing her voice made my heart settle when I hadn't been aware it was stuck too high in the chest. "You got my message?"

"At the office, but I'm calling from a bar thing."

Her voice sounded stilted. " 'Bar thing'?"

"You know, a Bar Association event, cocktails and then dinner. Boring, but appropriate for a lawyer of my acumen."

More stilted. "Nance, is everything all right?"

"Fine. I guess I forgot to mention the bar thing, huh?"

Now over-casual. "Yeah, I think you must have."

"Well, I'm sorry. I've got this trial still tomorrow, so I'm just going to head home tonight."

"Right."

A silence between us.

Then Nancy said, "John, are you okay?"

"Only if you are."

Another silence. "You mean, did I call the doctor?"

"That's what I mean."

"I called her but didn't get a chance to speak with her. I have an appointment for tomorrow morning."

"What time?"

"John, it's nothing. Don't worry."

"I do worry, Nance. What time?"

"The appointment?"

"Yes."

"Ten o'clock."

"That won't foul up your trial?"

"The judge will let me work around it."

"I'll drive you."

"Where?"

"To the doctor's."

"No."

"Why not?"

Her voice became a little sharp. "Because I'm a big girl, and I can make it to the doctor for a simple checkup on my own."

"Nance, do me a favor. Don't turn my concern for you into some kind of insult to you, okay?"

"John, I'm not in a position where I can discuss this very well."

"Call me tomorrow, then, after the doctor's."

"If I can. I've got to be back on trial for the afternoon."

"I love you, Nancy."

A softening. "Same here, squared."

Then she rang off.

I hung up the phone with a bad feeling. I tried to shake it off, then thought about burning it off at the Nautilus club back near the condo. Downstairs, the traffic on Tremont

Street was gridlocked, so I walked to the photo place before getting my car. The pictures were ready, and the dozen extras of Andrew Dees at the driver's door came out beautifully. Small triumph.

Putting the envelope of prints and negatives in a jacket pocket, I walked back toward the office, my mind on Nancy and whether I should have pressed more or less in talking with her. Coming around the corner of my building to the parking area, I registered only the forearm coming up, clotheslining me just under the throat.

I went down backwards, a pair of strong hands on each of my arms as soon as I hit the ground. The hands brought me back up, face against the wall, my wrists twisted behind my spine as one hand on each side frisked me quickly.

"I'm not carrying," I said.

One of the frisking hands rapped at my left kidney. The pain and nausea broke over me like a wave, my knees buckling a little.

A man's gruff voice spoke into my left ear. "And if you was?"

I managed to say, "Then you'd be dead, and somebody else would be asking me these questions."

The one on my right arm spun me around. I braced my stomach muscles for the shot I expected from his partner, but the punch, with fingers stiffened at the second knuckle like a striking cobra, still penetrated deep, taking my breath away as it doubled me over. Then the other guy used the heel of his left hand to smack my forehead, whiplashing my skull back against the brick. One hand from each gripped my lapels while the other hands pinned my arms against the wall. I was fighting the gag reflex and seeing stars, but I could also make out the two men.

Both had dark hair, slicked back in a way that looked wrong, like they didn't have the right cut for wearing it that way. Each wore a suit jacket, with fly-away-collar shirt open to the third button and a gold chain instead of a necktie. Olive-skinned, burly, and a few inches shorter than my six-two-plus, one guy had coarse features, the other fine.

Fine said, "You been asking around about Hendrix Management, Cuddy. Why?"

"You guys . . . have condos too?"

Coarse tightened his grip on my lapel and pushed me against the wall harder but didn't hit me. "You were fucking asked why, asshole."

"I'm representing . . . another complex. They—"

Fine pushed me too. "That's bullshit. Why?"

"—they want to know how . . . good a company Hendrix—"

Coarse pushed me again. We'd gone from a solid working-over to the schoolyard at recess, and I couldn't see why. "Which complex we talking about here, asshole?"

The line didn't sound right coming from him, like Nancy on the phone. "Confidential."

Fine said, "You got any idea the pain we can cause you?"

Coarse grinned at me. Nice teeth. "My associate here, he likes to kill people."

"Loves to kill," said Fine.

"Lives to kill." Coarse grinning broader.

Fine moved his lips to within three inches of my face. "We got a message for you, Cuddy."

"Simple message," said Coarse.

"Yeah, but real important," said Fine.

Coarse brought his lips to the same distance from me as his partner's. I could smell the mint on his breath. "You tell your clients, Hendrix ain't interested in their business."

Fine said, "You don't fuck around with Hendrix Management or its properties, *capisce?*"

Coarse almost kissed me. "You don't go see them, you don't call them, you don't even fucking think about them."

"Seems clear enough," I said.

Fine feinted, as if to give me another shot with the cobra hand. I tensed as best I could before he pulled his punch. "Don't make us fucking deliver the message again, huh?"

They both let go of me at the same time, Coarse hunching his shoulders, Fine shooting his cuffs like he'd just learned how that morning.

Coarse said, "You stay right here."

Fine gestured toward the dumpster. "Enjoy the garbage, like we had to, fucking waiting for you."

"And don't start up or anything before we're ten minutes gone." Coarse flicked his fingertips at me. *"Capisce?"*

I watched them walk out, Fine forward, Coarse backward, watching me. When they reached the side street, they turned left and disappeared.

I rubbed my stomach, coughing up some remnants of lunch that didn't have any blood in them. As the adrenaline wore down, I shook a little too. The guys had come on hard, then backed off. They didn't feel right to me, like they'd seen somebody else do this kind of routine and were trying to copy the model.

So, maybe they were mob-connected and maybe they weren't. I wasn't sure, but I thought of one person who might be able to shed some light on the subject.

10

"Hey-ey-ey, Cuddy, how you doing."

A greeting, not a question. His right hand returning a car phone to its cradle on the console, Primo Zuppone looked up at me from the wheel of his Lincoln Continental, the same one he'd had when I first met him. Mid-forties, he wore a double-breasted blue suit that didn't do much to hide his blocky body. The hair was still black and slicked over the ears, duck's-ass style. His complexion hadn't changed, either, ravaged by the pits and scars of teenage acne. The brown eyes glittered happily above his half-smile, a trademark toothpick stuck in the corner of his mouth.

"Primo, it's been a while."

"Get in, get in." He leaned over, opening the passenger's side door. "We'll drive around, listen to some music."

I slid onto the front seat gingerly, the buttery leather creating almost no friction against my suit pants. I noticed Zuppone checking his rearview and sideview mirrors, and then me. A leather coat the same color as the upholstery was folded carefully on the back seat, an audio cassette partway into a dashboard slot next to the radio.

Primo pushed the cassette the rest of the way into the player. "Tim Story. Solo piano mostly. You ever hear him?"

"I don't think so. I have some Liz Story tapes. They related?"

A tick-tocking of his head, left to right and back again, as we moved into traffic. "Beats me. I just listen to the shit, I don't study it."

I'd first met Zuppone working a case that involved the Danucci crime family from Boston's North End. Primo had been the "situation guy" assigned by them to "coordinate" with me. A mobster who loved New Age music.

The cassette began to play, a mournful piano accompanied by something acoustical.

I said, "That Wim Mertens album you gave me still sounds great."

He rolled the toothpick from one corner of his mouth to the other. "Glad to hear it. That was *Close Cover*, am I right?"

"I think so. It was a bootlegged tape, so there isn't a lot of information on the cassette holder."

"Yeah, yeah. It's a homemade jobbie, that was *Close Cover* all right. They love him in Europe—he's Dutch or some fucking thing—but it's tough to get the guy's stuff over here. I'll dupe one of the other albums for you."

"Thanks."

Zuppone nodded. "How do you like old Timmie so far?"

"Reminds me of old Wimmie."

Primo glanced over. "That's pretty fucking good, Cuddy, just off the top of your head and all."

My turn to nod. "Hope you'll understand if I don't ask after the family."

"Tell you the truth, they probably wouldn't be so hurt about that. You're not exactly on the Christmas list from the last thing, you know?"

A killing I was part of had been cleaned up by a friendly funeral home and covered up by a doctor beholden to the Danuccis.

"So, how have you been, Primo?"

"Pretty good. All things considered, anyways. Just got back from A.C."

"Atlantic City?"

"Yeah." The toothpick rolled to the other corner. "I go down there a couple, three times a year. This friend of ours comps me to the charter flight and hotel. You oughta see their idea of a fucking honeymoon suite, it'd look great in a Madonna movie. Best part, though, I met this guy named Enrico, used to be a POW in World War II."

"Prisoner of war?"

"Yeah, but one of ours."

"I don't get you."

"I'm standing around the casino, taking a break, and I overhear this little old guy talking in Italian to a little old lady, looks like she's gotta be his wife. So I say something to the guy, and it turns out this Enrico served his home country in the Italian army and was one of our prisoners, way out in the desert, Arizona someplace."

"And he came back after the war?"

"And got made a citizen some fucking way, don't ask me how. Anyways, Enrico starts telling me what it was like to be a POW, and it was fascinating. I mean, he remembers being in the middle of Indiana, and then they get told by this MP—that's what you used to be, right?"

"I was Military Police, but a lot later on the time line."

"Right, right. Vietnam, I remember. But this little old guy, he's telling me about the MP captain who's moving them by some kind of convoy—like fifty trucks, ten Italian soldiers to a truck, all lying down on the floor of the thing, with guards and a canvas stretched over slats above them. Like a fucking olive-drab covered wagon, get it? And the MPs, I guess they bought these prisoners box lunches along the way when they stopped for gas or whatever."

"Anyone try to escape?"

"No. Enrico said the captain told them through an interpreter that if anybody lifted his head, the guards would shoot it off. Then, after they drive around the clock, they get to this camp in the desert, godforsaken fucking place with chain-link fences and barbed wire, like five hundred of the guys per compound. And one day, there's an attack."

"Attack?"

"Yeah. Must have been locusts or grasshoppers or something, but I guess the prisoners just went nuts, account of they thought it was like the plague from the Bible and the fucking bugs were gonna eat them. So apparently this same MP captain—he wasn't their commandant like that Klink guy from *Hogan's Heroes*, he had to come from somewhere else—he yells at them through an interpreter again to get back, get back into the center of the compound. And then the captain, he takes a flamethrower—a fucking *flame-thrower*—and starts frying these bugs, on the wire, in the air, you name it."

"Sounds wild."

"It gets better. After the bugs incident, I guess the real commandant decided he ought to do something for the prisoners, they been scared out of their fucking wits and all. So he asks them, 'What do you guys want to do?'—as kind of a break, you know? And they tell him, 'We want to go see Hollywood.' They've been captured in a fucking world war, but everybody knows about Hollywood, right? So the commandant, he tells them, 'I'll take you out there a couple, three busloads at a time.' "

"You've got to be kidding."

"Uh-unh. Enrico says the prisoners were real well-behaved in the camp, and Hollywood turned out to be only a few hours away from where they were. I guess the com-

mandant got all these Italian prisoners GI American uniforms, but no insignia on them. Enrico said he thought
there'd be some kind of 'shoot-us-like-we-was-spies' problem if the commandant gave them patches and stuff. So,
they troop onto these busses, in American uniforms, and go
to Hollywood, where—get this—the guards let them leave
the buses and fucking walk around, see where the actors
had their stars in the cement and all."

"This really happened?"

"Hey-ey-ey, Cuddy, what do I know? I wasn't there, but
Enrico says he was, and the way he described things, I'm
inclined to believe him. Well, anyways, they're walking
around Hollywood when this same MP captain—the one
who moved them from Indiana and fried all the bugs?—
comes roaring up in a jeep to the bunch of guys Enrico's
with and just goes bullshit on them. In English, of course,
but Enrico said you could kind of catch the guy's drift in
any language. And then they all had to get on the buses
again and back to the compound. The rest of the prisoners
never got to see Hollywood, and Enrico says he never saw
the camp commandant again."

"Great story, Primo, but how was the gambling?"

"Huh?"

"In Atlantic City. You went there to gamble, right?"

"Oh. Oh, yeah. Picked up almost four thousand on one
of the tables."

"Roulette?"

"Right, right. But I gotta tell you, I like watching the suckers play the slots almost as much as gambling myself. The
machines, they've changed most of them over to a computer
thing now. Totes up your money, keeps track of it like a
bank account, all you got to do is look at the screen."

"Sounds like expensive equipment."

"Yeah, but you know why they did the changeover?"

I thought about it. "So the suckers don't have to waste gambling time by feeding in the quarters."

"You got it. Good example of what can happen when higher technology falls into the wrong hands. Of course, there's a row or two of the old-fashioned machines, too, the jobbies with the big handles? They keep those for the illiterates, I guess, the ones get scared off by anything like a computer. Anyways, I'm walking along, and this rickety broad—had to be eighty she was a day—is pulling the lever on one of the old machines so hard and so fast, you'd have thought she got paid by the quarter herself. Only thing is, she all of a sudden lets go of the handle and grabs her chest, like she's having a heart attack. The rickety broad hits the floor, and there's at least three other old people rushing to take her place at the machine, thinking, 'It's *gotta* pay off now, right?' Then this young broad next to me says, 'What do you suppose happened to her?' And I say, 'Maybe all the blood rushed to her wrist.' "

A laugh from Primo. "Get it?"

"I got it."

"You just don't think it's funny, am I right?"

"That's right."

The toothpick rolled from port to starboard this time. "Good thing the young broad did. We had ourselves a hell of a weekend." Zuppone glanced over again. "Climbing in the car here, you looked a little tender."

"Actually, that's what I wanted to talk about."

The half-smile faded. "Maybe you oughta get to it, then."

"I had some visitors an hour ago. Two guys, starting rough then tapering off."

The smile disappeared altogether. "Let me guess. Italian-looking, am I right?"

"Could have been."

"Could have been? You didn't see them?"

"Dark hair, slicked back, only I don't think it was cut to wear that way. Olive-skinned."

A nod. "What about clothes?"

"Long-point collars, open buttons, gold chains."

"And that's what makes you think they're connected?"

"They tried to play the role, Primo. Only they overplayed it, like out of the movies."

"How?"

"They said *'capisce.'*"

Zuppone winced.

"Twice," I said.

We made a left turn. "These guys, they were the first people talked to you?"

"And they didn't start out by talking."

Zuppone shook his head. "It don't sound right to me. You stepped in something, we'd send like an emissary first, you know?"

"Like you."

The half-smile came back. "Yeah, like the way I handled it with you the first time. Nice-nice till nice-nice don't work no more."

"That's what I thought."

"You got any idea what you might have stepped in?"

"They were pretty clear on that. I'd been asking questions about a real estate management company, and they told me to butt out."

"What kind of questions?"

"How good a company it was, as though I had a client that was interested in hiring them."

"You were doing like a reference check?"

"That's right."

Another shake of the head. "What's the name of this outfit?"

"Hendrix Property Management, out of Marshfield."

"Marshfield, down on the South Shore there?"

"Right."

Zuppone said, "It don't ring a bell, but then that's No Man's Land."

"Sorry?"

After making another turn, Primo checked his mirrors. "You know how that guy Sammy 'the Bull' Gravano turned rat down in New York there?"

"Testifying against John Gotti?"

"Right, right. It's happening every-fucking-where, but that cocksucker Gravano, he gets a reduced sentence of five years—five fucking years, now—for being involved in nineteen killings he admits to, and even then, the feds'll give him the witness protection thing when he gets out. Meanwhile, he's nearly destroyed three of the Five Families down there with his testimony."

"And?"

"And that's kind of what's happened up here too. The destroying part, anyways. Back when the Feebs—the FB-fucking-I—wired the Angiulos' place and put them all away, things around Boston were kind of up for grabs, you know what I mean? One family, it runs most of the operations for twenty, twenty-five years, then it gets brought down, the operations, they have to be . . . 'redistributed' would be a good word for it."

"And Marshfield didn't get 'redistributed' to anybody in particular."

"Not much there to work with, kind of a summer resort that's going year-round. Still . . ." A shrug.

"Still?"

"Maybe somebody's trying to establish some kind of presence there. But it don't have to be from the North End, you know."

"Meaning they could have come up from Providence."

"Maybe. Or to tell you the truth, the La Strada guys from

East Boston or some of your Irish friends from the Winter Hill Gang. That's assuming, of course, that it's us."

"Us?"

"White people. You got the Jamaicans, or the fucking Dominicans, now, Christ knows what the hell they're doing."

Tángela Robinette said she was born in Haiti of a father from Jamaica, but that seemed a pretty slender thread. "Go on."

"Only those crazy bastards'd make more sense in Rox."

Roxbury, a substantial minority neighborhood of Boston. "Actually, Primo, I was thinking that part of the Danucci family lives on the South Shore not so far from Marshfield."

Zuppone chewed on the toothpick. "One of the brothers lives down there, he ain't gonna piss in his own soup."

"How about if he just lives close?"

"No. No, it don't feel right, even to you. The family sent me to talk with you the first time when I didn't know you. Now I know you, if they're in this, they'd for sure send me to talk with you, am I right?"

"Probably."

The half-smile. "You're a piece of work, Cuddy. Don't you trust nobody?"

"I trust you, mostly." I decided to take a chance. "My asking around about the management company was just a cover. I'm really looking into the background of a guy."

"What's his name?"

"I'd like to keep my own counsel on that for now."

Another shrug. "Hey-ey-ey, you're the one called me, remember?"

"I remember." Reaching into the pocket of my suit jacket, I took out one of the Andrew Dees photos. "This is him."

Zuppone checked all three mirrors again before bringing up the interior lights and looking at the photo I held. Then he doused the lights and rechecked the mirrors. Ever the careful driver, and even more the perfect poker player. I couldn't tell by his expression whether he'd recognized the man in the photo or not.

Primo made a left. "You let me see the guy's picture, but won't tell me his name?"

"I just want to know if you recognize him."

"Why?"

A reasonable question. "If I got paid my visit because somebody's interested in Hendrix Management, so be it. I'd want to know, though, if the man in this photo is the real reason the two guys came to see me."

"Because he's connected himself."

"Right."

Another glance at the photo. "I gotta admit, there's something rings a bell about him, but he's a pretty ordinary-looking fuck, so what can I tell you? Could be he's just somebody I passed on the street some time."

"Can you check around?"

"What, I'm supposed to describe your guy to my friends, see if one of them makes a match? Come on, Cuddy, this fuck could be anybody."

Zuppone had a point. "How about if I give you his picture, and you show it around discreetly, ask if anybody knows him."

The tick-tocking head again. "I guess I can do that." He took the photo from me. "You got any other information on this guy?"

"Not for sharing."

Half a laugh. "Christ, Cuddy, you gotta have trust in something, you know?"

"What do you trust, Primo?"

"Me?" Zuppone got serious. "I trust the organization. Back in school the nuns treated me like a dunce, far as I went. I try to get a job in the straight world, the citizens'd treat me like a bum. I don't talk so good, I don't spell so

112

good, I don't fit in so good. With the organization, I'm in my element, you might say. A made member, blood oath and everything. They know they can trust what I do for them, and that makes me want to trust them too. Understand?"

"I do. But that's why you should understand the reason I can't entirely trust you."

Primo turned left again, bringing me back to where he'd picked me up. "You got that right. You got brains for thinking of it and heart for saying it to me, man to man. But I like you, Cuddy, and that can make all the difference in the world." A glance. "All the fucking difference, you know what I'm saying here?"

The toothpick rolled one last time.

After Zuppone dropped me off, I walked randomly for a while, just in case anybody who might have been interested in him decided to be interested in his passenger as well. I didn't spot anybody following me, so I found a pay phone and dialed Olga Evorova's home number on Beacon Hill.

"Yes?"

"Ms. Evorova, John Cuddy."

"Ah, you have something to report?"

"Yes, but it would be easier in person."

"Well . . ."

"Is Andrew Dees with you?"

"No, no. But . . . how long would it take for you to come see me now?"

"I'm five minutes away."

"Then come, please."

I hung up and started walking.

Beacon Hill is the neighborhood around the gold-domed Statehouse that I can see from my office widow. The Beacon Street side overlooks the Common on the downslope and the Public Garden on the flat. The major thoroughfare that divides the slope from the flat is Charles, home to antique shops and trendy restaurants. Unlike Back Bay, much of the Hill remains single-family homes, though there aren't very many single families that can pony up the nearly two million required to own one. Condominium development was slower to catch on here, the narrow floor plans of the Federalist townhouses being less amenable to internal division that the Victorian architecture elsewhere. As I climbed the red-brick sidewalks to reach Evorova's address, however, I realized her building was plenty wide enough for condos.

There was a keypad mounted on the wall outside the front door, another glass-paneled, inner door visible before the foyer. A typed list under a clear plastic cover next to the pad gave directions and two-digit telephone numbers for the occupants, listed in alphabetical order. I assumed the order was a security measure, scrambling unit number and owner name so a browsing burglar couldn't figure out which apartment had nobody home at any given time.

I pressed the DIAL TONE button, then Evorova's number. I heard a telephone ringing through the speaker in the pad, and then a pickup and Evorova's voice saying, "Yes?"

"John Cuddy."

"Good. I can buzz you through the first door, but someone must come down to let you in the second."

I got out the first syllable of "Someone?" before the dial tone told me that Evorova had cut the connection. I pressed the HANG UP button, and the tone stopped as a bumblebee noise came from the outer door's jamb. I opened it, went inside, and waited. Through the glass panel, the foyer had burgundy carpeting leading up a broad staircase and a small, tasteful chandelier suspended three feet from a fake mantelpiece with a mirror over it.

About a minute later a fortyish woman in high heels walked deliberately down the foyer's stairs, carefully holding the railing. She was dressed elegantly in the sort of eveningwear you don't usually see on a weekday, workaday night. The green gown appeared to be buff velvet, a broach at the throat and spaghetti straps crossing both shoulders. If the gown was the first thing you noticed, the upswept auburn hair was the second, and I bet myself that her eyes would be somewhere around the green of her gown.

As the woman opened the inner door for me, I won the bet.

Extending her hand, she said, "Mr. Cuddy, Claude Loiselle."

I shook politely. "Not exactly what I expected."

A lopsided grin that made me think of Audrey Hepburn as Holly Golightly. "What *did* you expect, something from the Women Seeking Women section of the personals? 'White professional bull dyke seeks femme for roller derby, beer blasts, and possible relationship'?"

Loiselle slurred some of the words, and I realized she'd had a few pops of something. "Ms. Evorova just said you were a banker, like her. And I was referring to your gown."

"Oh." Loiselle looked down at herself, then back up to me. "We're going to the opera, Verdi's *Rigoletto*. Even bankers dress up when they do that." Teetering a little on the heels, she turned and beckoned me with a single, crooked index finger. "Hope you don't mind the stairs. The elevator's no bigger than a dumbwaiter and gives me claustrophobia."

"The stairs are fine."

Loiselle had to hitch up her gown a little at the hips to negotiate the first few steps. "Claustrophobic Claude. Kind of 'sings,' don't you think?"

"I give it an eighty-five. Good melody, but tough to dance to."

Her laugh was almost a gargling sound. "Too bad Olga didn't meet you instead of the Horse's Ass."

As we reached the first landing, I didn't see any open doors, so I said, "Andrew Dees?"

"The same. I mentioned 'relationship' before? His idea of a deep and lasting relationship is about six inches 'deep' and 'lasting' twenty minutes."

We started the next flight. "You know him well, then?"

"Met him twice. The second time wasn't necessary, if you take my point."

"Bad first impression?"

"No first impression."

"I don't get you."

"The man's not really there . . . what do I call you, anyway?"

"John is fine with me if Claude is fine with you."

"Dear God, a private investigator who speaks in parallel structure? I can't find a fucking assistant who even knows what parallel structure *is*."

"It's just the generation. Reading and writing isn't what they were focused on."

"Now, that's a dangling participle, right?"

"Preposition, I think."

Second landing. "Right, right. Preposition."

We kept climbing. "Back to Mr. Dees. You were saying . . . ?"

"Saying what?"

"Something about his not really being there."

"Oh. *An*-drew doesn't talk about himself. I mean, have you ever *met* a man who didn't drone on about how he starred at quarterback in high school, or what a screwing he took from his bitch of an ex-wife, or *some*-thing?"

"And Dees doesn't."

"Not a word. You get the impression that he's an actor, not entirely comfortable with a new role he's playing."

We reached a door that stood ajar, what sounded like chamber music coming from behind it. Loiselle bumped the door open with her right buttock. "Welcome to the Dosto-yevsky Museum."

Inside the unit, a short corridor had a carpet runner of a design I'd never seen before, brocades of red and gold. The corridor walls had been scooped out, shelved in, and glassed over, with indirect lighting above exotic bric-a-brac that I didn't have time to catalogue.

Loiselle led me into a living room decorated from top to bottom in the most striking taste I'd ever seen. Orange drapery over the windows, pulled and tucked in a sequence that drew your eyes first upward then outward to the antique prints of armored warriors and dancing women and the not-quite-Catholic icons on the walls. There were delicate chairs and heavy tables, some with marble tops. Festive, folkish dolls sat or stood on open shelves around a magnificent fireplace, other shelves holding books, spine out, with Cyrillic lettering on them.

Two loveseats opposed each other in front of the fireplace, a hand-carved, black wood coffee table between them. On the table stood a fluted glass, white wine filling a third of the bulb. The fireplace wall was painted a deep green that matched my guide's gown so well she looked like a floating face and shoulders in front of it.

Loiselle gestured toward one of the loveseats. As I went to sit, she said, "Drink?"

"How close are you and Ms. Evorova on time?"

"Time?"

"For the opera."

"Oh. An hour yet. Olga's still getting dressed, but I've hired a car."

"Then yes to the drink, whatever's easiest."

"We have a nice chardonnay open."

"Half a glass would be great."

"Done."

Loiselle moved to a linoleum area, the kitchen visible

through a pass-through hole in that wall. The loveseats were upholstered in silk, strands of shining red and gold thread embroidered into the fabric, reminding me of the carpet runner in the hall. The music sounded like a crying piano, and I thought I recognized the piece.

Loiselle returned with my glass, a little more than half full, but close enough. After setting the wine on the coffee table, she sat down across from me.

Raising her own glass in a mock toast, Loiselle said, "To whatever you've discovered about the Horse's Ass."

I tried the chardonnay. Vanilla and oak, nicely blended and not so cold the flavor couldn't come through. "Excellent."

"Ought to be. That Bonny Doon's thirty dollars a bottle."

"I'll sip it slowly."

The lopsided grin again. "I didn't realize private investigators were so easily offended."

"We've gotten more sensitive over the years."

"I could tell right away," said Loiselle.

"Tell what?"

"That you weren't a clod."

"How?"

"From the way you reacted downstairs." She tilted her glass, allowing the wine to slide around and coat the inside, then sniffed it without drinking from it. "When I mistook your 'not what I expected' remark and came on like a chip-on-the-shoulder lesbo, as one of my dear departed colleagues used to call me."

"Departed."

"After he said that to me once, I dedicated the next month to undermining him, and he was gone two more after that."

I nodded.

"Anyway," said Loiselle, "you took my shot in stride and just turned it around on me. I do the same thing to others often enough myself."

"What kind of banking are you in?"

"Commercial lending, and deadly serious stuff it is, too. Say you want to develop a shopping center or office building, but you need a hundred million or so in construction financing. I'm the one you have to make happy."

"And does it make you happy?"

"Sometimes." Another nip at the wine. "Not often, actually. But it lets me own a house down in Provincetown and my version of this place, with Melissa Etheridge instead of Tchaikovsky on the stereo."

"I think it's Rachmaninoff."

Loiselle stopped. Then she stood up and moved to the stereo stack in the corner, reaching under something to pull out a compact disk cover. Coming back to the loveseat, she said, "You didn't look at this, did you?"

"The CD case?"

"Right."

"No, I didn't."

"Then how did you know . . . ?"

"Took a music appreciation course back in college. You happened to be playing the one piece I could have gotten right, that's all."

Lifting her wineglass, Loiselle said, "Olga was playing, actually."

Speaking of whom. "Before she joins us, anything else you can tell me about Andrew Dees?"

Loiselle put the glass down again, spreading her hands on her thighs as though she were wiping the palms. In a serious tone, she said, "I'm sorry . . . John, right?"

"Right."

"I know you're trying to help Olga—and God knows, I think she needs it—but I've been flip as hell with you because I skipped lunch and had two glasses of Bonny here when I should have stopped at one."

"That's all right."

119

A sniffing that had nothing to do with the wine. "Andrew Dees. He wants to be with Olga, but not enjoy some things with her. Take tonight, for instance. He'll go to the ballet, or even a folk concert. But while Olga loves opera—especially Puccini and Verdi—he won't budge on it. Listening to a CD of the Three Tenors? Fine. Going to see Pavarotti live? Not a chance."

"There has to be something more than that."

"No, there isn't, and that's my point. It's like I said on the stairs before. *An*-drew's a cipher, an android. He—"

"I am so sorry to keep you waiting."

I stood up at the sound of Olga Evorova's voice. She came into the room, dressed in a black gown with silver sequins at the shoulders and holding a sequined handbag in the shape of a dinosaur egg. Wearing more makeup, she now looked glamorous rather than merely attractive, and I began to wonder why Andrew Dees wouldn't want to be out and about with her, appreciating the attention she'd garner.

Claude Loiselle rose from her loveseat. "I'll just go powder my nose while you two talk."

"No," said Evorova. "I would like you to be here, Claude." She turned to me. "Unless it would destroy some of the confidentiality we discussed, yes?"

I said, "As a client, you usually can have a confidante with you. If you want Ms. Loiselle—"

"Claude," said Loiselle.

"And I am Olga, please."

"Olga," I said, "if you'd like Claude to be here too, that's fine with me."

Sitting back down, Loiselle shoved over a little, and Evorova joined her on the loveseat.

I sat so that I was facing my client directly. "I went to Plymouth Willows, acting like I was representing another condo complex interested in hiring Hendrix Management."

Evorova only watched me, but Loiselle nodded in quick bobs, like she'd already known that.

"I spoke to Hendrix himself before the neighbors, just to make it look right, and then to Mr. Dees afterward. However, about three hours later, a couple of guys roughed me up behind my office building."

Evorova's jaw dropped as she sucked in an audible breath. Loiselle leaned forward, elbows on her knees, concentration cutting through the wine haze.

I said, "They warned me off Hendrix Management, saying it wouldn't be a good idea for me to investigate the company or the projects it handles."

The two women exchanged looks.

Then Evorova spoke to me. "Hendrix and Plymouth Willows, but nothing about Andrew?"

"That's right. Hendrix wasn't nuts about seeing me, but the other neighbors were more or less cooperative."

Loiselle said, "And *An*-drew?"

I spoke to Evorova. "Not cooperative at all."

My client dipped her chin, as she had back in my office. "So you think maybe it is the Hendrix company that is the problem, or maybe it is the condo complex, or maybe it is Andrew."

"Right, and no real way of telling which, since everybody in those three hours would have had time to sic the goons."

"I am sorry?" said Evorova.

Loiselle patted her friend's forearm. "Call for the bad guys."

Evorova looked to me. "What do you recommend?"

"If there's something sour about Hendrix's operation, maybe the complex should get rid of him. If it's the complex, maybe Mr. Dees should move."

Evorova let out a breath. "And if it is Andrew, maybe I should know, yes?"

"I think so."

"Me too, Olga," said Loiselle.

Evorova closed her eyes for a moment. Opening them again, she stared at me hard. "How can you do this?"

"I'd like to try tracing Mr. Dees backward, and the only sure thing we have is him telling you he graduated from the University of Central Vermont. That means a trip up there, and it would be a help if I could have a sample of his signature."

"His signature?"

"Yes. For me to get a look at the school records, I'd need some kind of authorization signed by him."

Loiselle showed me the lopsided grin. "Or at least apparently signed by him."

"Right."

Evorova said, "I do not know. Forging Andrew's signature?"

Loiselle patted her forearm again. "In a good cause, Olga."

"What cause?"

"You," said her friend.

Evorova closed and opened her eyes once more, then gave me another long stare. "When we are first going out together, I was at Andrew's house one night, and I was short of cash for the next day. He drove me to the ATM machine in Plymouth Mills, but it was broken. Andrew thought that was funny, a banker who could not get money for herself. So he loaned me fifty dollars, but this was early in our relationship, as I told you, and I wanted to give him a check. He was reluctant, but I insisted."

"And Mr. Dees endorsed and deposited it," I said.

"Exactly, yes."

"Do you have it here?"

My client consulted her watch.

Loiselle said, "Plenty of time, Olga."

Evorova rose, the gown shadowing her figure nicely in the process. "I will get the check."

Loiselle watched Olga walk back the way she'd come, then picked up her own wineglass. Speaking to me over the rim, Claude said, "Blinded by love."

"It happens."

She gave me a harder look than Evorova had. "Yeah, tell me about it."

Then Claude Loiselle drained the last of her Bonny Doon.

11

After leaving Olga Evorova's condo carrying the check Andrew Dees had endorsed, I went back to my apartment. There was no message from Nancy with my answering service or on my telephone tape machine. I thought about trying her, but after the way we'd left it that afternoon, I decided to wait. Besides, she could always call me, right?

I fell asleep without hearing from her.

Thursday dawned bright and clear, the kind of brilliant October morning that brings the tourists back year after year for foliage season. Even the northwest wind was doing its part, a steady ten miles an hour pushing all the smog out to the harbor and beyond as it brought high, patchy clouds over the city.

I waited until eight, then dialed Nancy at home, getting just the outgoing tape announcement. Figuring she might have gone into work before the doctor's, I tried the DA's office too, the secretary telling me that Ms. Meagher wasn't expected until after lunch. I left the message that

I'd be gone most of the day but would still appreciate a return call.

Hanging up, I sat down and composed, in longhand, the letter I intended to bring with me to Vermont.

"Okay, now you want me to do this letter, right?"

Leaning an elbow on the counter of the copy center, I watched the woman twist her frosted hair around an index finger. "Just like last time."

"Yeah, but last time you wanted that questionnaire."

"Right."

"So, what'd the people say?"

"Say?"

"Yeah, about it going two pages and all."

I nodded. "They weren't very helpful."

"See," she said, twisting another hank of her hair. "I told you. Keep it to one page, you're better off."

"Which is why I'm taking your advice on this letter."

She looked at it again. "What's that word there?"

" 'Authorization.' "

"And you want it centered?"

"Right. And all caps."

She made her way down to the signature line, then the return address in the upper-right-hand corner. "And you're Andrew Dees?"

"No, I'm just getting this typed for him."

"Word processed. We don't actually 'type' things anymore."

"I'd forgotten."

She said, "Five minutes."

"And I'll need three originals, please."

"Not an original and two photocopies?"

"No. Three originals right off the printer."

"It'll take longer."

"How much?"

"Two minutes, maybe."

"Fine," I said.

"And it'll cost more, too."

I tried to keep the impatience out of my voice. "How much more?"

"Another fifty cents per original."

"I'll take the plunge."

Torturing a different hank of the frosted hair, the woman moved slowly toward her desktop computer.

Back in my condo, I practiced copying the endorsement signature on the back of Olga Evorova's check until it felt natural. Then I signed the three originals of the authorization letter, gathered some other papers, and went down to my car.

Used to be, driving north out of Boston was simple, if not easy. Either you took the Sumner Tunnel, completed in 1934, under the harbor and past Logan Airport, or you took the Mystic River Bridge, completed in 1950 and renamed the Tobin Bridge in the mid-sixties. You could die from the fumes in the tunnel or the crosswinds on the bridge, but at least your choices were clear. Then in sixty-one, they opened a second tunnel, the Callahan, which seemed to multiply both the traffic and the fumes by a factor of four. Now, another aspect of the Big Dig is the revamping of all the ramps that lead onto and off the funneling highways, like the Central Artery, Storrow Drive, Route 1—enough. The point is, now the drive's still not easy but no longer simple.

I thought keeping the Prelude's moonroof back and heater on might take my mind off both Nancy and the traffic. It didn't, but it helped.

Once into New Hampshire, the miles on interstates 93 and 89 rolled by, me keeping the speedometer between fifty-five and sixty without cruise control, the roadside foliage going from not-quite-peak to peak to past-peak. About a hundred miles northwest of Boston and through the second range of mountains, things went from past-peak to pretty bleak. The trees had lost most of their leaves, the varied colors now checkerboarding the ground like the French Quarter after Mardi Gras. It was depressing, and I found my finger on the button that closes the moonroof even though I didn't think the air had turned that much colder.

Crossing over into Vermont, I went another thirty miles before seeing the exit for the university. At the bottom of the ramp, I took a right, slowly climbing a switchback road up a mountain. Cresting it, I looked down into the valley and on alternate curves got better and better views of the town and campus, which seemed to join each other at the narrow point in a geographic hourglass.

The town had a quaint main street, tall—if bare—oaks, maples, and poplars lining the curbs. Broad, clapboard houses, built at a time when ten kids in the family put you somewhere near the middle of the pack, stood a little too close to the road. The houses gave way to a small commercial center, with a postage-stamp movie theater, an old-fashioned ice cream parlor, and the Towne Restaurant, where the soup and half-sandwich special probably would go for half what the soup alone costs in Boston. Across the street was a small department store, a Chinese take-out place, and a photocopy closet that would be pleased to type any résumé "professionally." At the edge of town stood a flat-faced taphouse with a "C&W Dancing, Th–Sat" sign next to a video store next to a gun-shop advertising "Re-load Ammo, Cheap." One-stop shopping for all your weekend entertainment.

I drove through a glade of evergreens that formed the waist of the hourglass I'd seen from the crest of the mountain, the gates of the University of Central Vermont just past it. Beyond the gates, I came onto a narrow macadam road with yellow speedbumps every two hundred feet. Around me spread a tree-and-lawn campus, the cement sidewalks narrow, the hedges near the Colonial-era buildings trimmed lovingly and blending into the ivy climbing the outside walls. I found myself thinking that Paulie Fogerty, the superintendent at Plymouth Willows, would like this place.

The combination football-soccer field appeared on my left, the portable goal nets pushed to the sides at the moment so the football team could run no-pads drills. Off in the corner, the cheerleading squad—five females and one male—was practicing a gymnastics routine in shorts and sweatshirts. The grandstands were all steel-and-board bleachers, the capacity more befitting a high school than a college. Bordering the field was an elliptical gravel track, stringy men and women alternating in windsprints from a crouching start. A campus cop in blue shirt and slacks leaned against the front fender of a yellow Ford Explorer. His tires on the edge of the gravel, he watched all the activity around him, giving special attention to the cheerleaders.

After a curve in the road, I found the Administration Building and a parking lot. Leaving my car in a VISITOR slot with a meter on it, I fed the meter two dimes before I realized the first had bought me an hour. I went up the sidewalk, taking in the scattered clatches of students. Almost all impossibly young, the hair styles ranging from New Wave butcherings to No Wave butch cuts, the clothes spandex or L.L. Bean or oversized flannel shirts over tees, the buttons on the flannel ones all open, shirttails out over jeans with intentional slashes. Everybody in uniform, just different branches of the service.

Look a little closer, though, and you could see a stout thirty-year-old woman, maybe a young mother, coming back to school and maybe not with a lot of friends her own age, sitting on a threadbare jacket and nibbling a peanut-butter-and-jelly sandwich while she poured over what looked like an English lit text. A trio of African-American students, sitting by themselves and eating ice cream cones, Chicago Bulls and Philadelphia Eagles colors on the two boys, one looking around every once in a while, watching the street in a different kind of neighborhood. A studious Latino, wearing black tie-shoes and a white dress shirt, his back against the stoop of the Administration Building, tapping the keys of a notebook computer he balanced on his knees.

I climbed the stoop and went in the main entrance, taking the corridor toward the registrar's office as two of the L.L. Beaners came out, knapsacks on their backs. Inside the door was a rectangular waiting area, probably designed to accommodate long lines of students, a couple of molded-plastic scoop chairs against the wall. I could see two women behind the open counter, one in her late fifties and severe, the other in her early twenties and fresh-scrubbed.

The older woman shrugged stiffly into a coat, saying in a clipped New England accent, "Be back by one, Zina."

The younger woman sat at a desk bracketed by tall file cabinets, scanning some computer printouts on green-and-cream spreadsheet paper in front of her. "Take your time, Harriet. I'm just meeting Lyle for lunch at the Towne."

Harriet fussed with her coat as she strode past me, never even looking at my face. After she was gone, I went to the counter.

Zina smiled up from the printouts. "Help you?"

"Please." I took out one of my forged authorization letters. "I need a transcript and whatever else you can show me on a former student."

Zina nodded and rose, lifting one form from a sheaf of them on her desk. She came up to the counter and turned the paper around for me to see. "We just need you to fill this out and get it signed by the graduate involved."

I glanced down at the form. At the top over a couple of detailed paragraphs, it had spaces for FULL NAME, DATE OF BIRTH, and YEAR OF GRADUATION. Since I didn't know the last two, I positioned my letter the same way she held her sheet. "I already have an authorization."

Zina read it. "Hey, Plymouth Mills, that's, like, south of Boston, right?"

"Right."

"We don't get many grads going all the way down there."

"You don't?"

"Uh-unh. Most of our students are state residents when they come here, and they already know Vermont's the best place to live you could ever find."

I smiled with her. "Well, after I get a look at his records, maybe I can persuade Mr. Dees to move back."

Zina shook her head. "I'm real sorry, but you have to use our form."

"But I'm only going to be here for today."

"Sorry."

I read the two paragraphs of fine print on her piece of paper. "Look, I know my letter isn't worded quite the same way, but it's pretty clearly the same thought. Andrew Dees here is authorizing you to release all his records to me."

"Uh-huh, but your letter there doesn't have the disclaimer clause or the hold-harmless clause, and the university counsel says we have to have both to cover ourselves from liability."

Zina said the legal phrases correctly, but she pronounced them slowly, as though she didn't know for sure what they meant. In a bureaucracy of any kind, that usually means the person you're dealing with isn't going to yield. I thought about asking to see her superior, then remembered Harriet's demeanor and had a better idea.

"Could I have a couple of those forms, then?"

Zina seemed relieved. "Sure."

*　　*　　*

"Hi, can I help you?"

"It's not exactly a résumé, but I was wondering if you could type this up for me?"

The young guy in the photocopy place across from the Towne Restaurant looked at the registrar's form and said, "Why don't you just use the form itself, mister?"

"I don't want all that stuff about DATE OF BIRTH at the top."

He ran his hand over hair too short to twist around a finger. "Okay, but it's still going to be five dollars a page."

"A steal at twice the price."

He took it to a desktop computer and got to work.

I sat in my car outside the Towne, enjoying the soup and half-sandwich the waitress inside had put up for me in take-out fashion. Homemade vegetable beef in the cardboard cup, deviled ham on toasted wheat in the waxed paper. Two bucks. The fifties aren't dead everywhere.

A few minutes later, I was finishing my soup when Zina bicycled down the street from the direction of campus. No helmet, though, and she just leaned her bicycle against the wall outside the restaurant, not bothering to lock it when she went inside. I thought about Primo and the concept of trust.

Then I ate the rest of the half-sandwich before turning my key in the ignition.

"Yes?"

"I'd like to see the records of a former student here?"

Harriet sighed deeply, then stood stiffly, plucking another form from the sheaf on her desk like she was pulling a weed in her garden. At the counter she managed not to slap the thing in front of me.

"Have this completed and signed, then bring it back to us. There'll be a three-dollar charge for copying the transcript."

I looked at the form and frowned. "Gee, I'm really sorry, but the former student typed up his own version of this."

"We insist upon that form, sir."

"Yes, I can certainly understand that, but . . ." I took out the résumé shop letter I'd forged and gave the impression of comparing the two. ". . . but, fortunately it looks as though he got all the magic words right, just left off the stuff at the top."

I turned the form and the letter so Harriet could read them. She took her time, then flinched a little at the end. Looking up at me, Harriet smiled sweetly. "Well, you're certainly right. However, without YEAR OF GRADUATION, it will take me a few minutes."

"I can wait." Patience and deference, the keys to success. "I'd say he's in his early forties, if that helps at all."

"Certainly does. Please," waving toward one of the scoop chairs, "sit down, make yourself comfortable."

Harriet disappeared into the bowels of the office. Five minutes later, the door to the corridor opened and three campus police officers—a big male, a medium female, and a small male—came in, hands on their still-holstered sidearms. Harriet materialized at the counter, as though she'd been hiding behind one of the file cabinets. She used a manila folder to point in my direction. "That's him."

The medium female said to me, "You want to stand, please? Slowly."

I looked at them. "Let me guess. Poppa Bear, Mama Bear, and Baby Bear, right?"

The small male said, "Just one more word, jerk-off."

I stood, slowly.

12

I'd driven by the campus police headquarters on the way in without realizing it, since their operation looked like one of the old, ivy-covered classroom buildings. After the big male officer had frisked me for weapons and the medium female had taken the file folder from Harriet, all three cops walked me out to another yellow Ford Explorer. Momma Bear got behind the wheel, mumbling into a radio mike held too close to her mouth for me to hear what she was saying. I rode in the back seat between Poppa Bear and Baby Bear. Even with the small man to my right, it was a tight enough fit that I was glad no one had decided to cuff me.

The female officer pulled us into the curb, taking a POLICE VEHICLES ONLY slot. She got out first, followed by the big male officer, then me and the small one. We went through the high doors, a blue-on-yellow plaque reading CAMPUS SECURITY.

Inside, the floor was old grooved wood, the walls covered by bulletin boards so covered themselves with notices that you almost had to take the existence of the boards beneath as an article of faith. A woman in civilian clothes behind the counter might have been Harriet's older sister, but we weren't introduced. She just nodded to us, and we all moved through the swinging gate in the counter, past a few unstaffed desks and to a door stenciled DIRECTOR.

As the female officer opened the door, I said, "Action, camera . . ." and the big male officer nudged me into the office.

A woman about my age in a maize blouse and the skirt to a suit stood from behind a desk with computer and fax on one corner and an elaborate telephone on the other. She was medium height, with even features, a milkmaid's complexion, and brown hair brushed back the way Primo Zuppone's would look if he kept it dry. The jacket to her suit hung on a multi-pronged brass fixture next to a framed diploma from some company that made parking meters. The woman wore the blouse with the cuffs unbuttoned and the sleeves rolled twice up her forearms. When she smiled, I got the feeling she'd been doing this kind of work a long time.

"I'm Gail Tasker." Both hands flicked out, like the woman was shooing flies. "Sit down, please."

She sounded like a classmate of mine at Holy Cross who'd come from the Bronx. As the female officer handed Tasker the manila file Harriet had given her, the big male officer pushed a chair over for me. It was institutional gray, with black, punctured pads on the seat and back.

I said, "Only if there's room for everyone."

Baby Bear started to growl something, but Tasker cut him off with a shake of her head. "There are two ways we can do this, my friend. The modern, polite way, and the old-fashioned, hard way. So far, you've been on the fringe of polite, so we try that a little longer. It doesn't work, we regress."

"Maybe if you regress enough, I institute a civil rights suit."

"I'm not worried."

And she wasn't, either, which meant Tasker thought she had something on what I'd been doing at the registrar's office.

I sat down.

Tasker nodded, once to me, then to the officers behind me. "Dave, if you'd stay. Trish, Garth, you can return to patrol."

Dave was the big male. The other two left, closing the door behind them.

Tasker dropped back into her desk chair, elbows on the blotter, hands joined to prop up her chin. "How about we start with some ID?"

I took out my holder and extended it to her.

She opened it, read a moment, then looked up at me. "Mr. Cuddy, you have one of these for Vermont too?"

"No."

Tasker picked up a pen, jotted down some information, then closed my holder and tossed it—politely—back to my side of her desk.

As I put it away, she opened Harriet's file folder. "What's a private investigator from Boston, unlicensed in the Green Mountain State, doing at our registrar's office?"

"Trying to get a copy of that file."

Tasker looked up again, then went back to the folder. "Haven't seen one of these in a long time. Back before we had computers, individually typed courses, *hand*written entries for grades. God, it must have taken forever for them to get things done."

I waited patiently while she turned pages, flipping back and forth a few times. "While you're browsing, mind if I ask you a question?"

Tasker looked up a third time. "Go ahead."

I glanced toward the diploma. "You really go to Parking Meter School?"

Officer Dave coughed behind me, but Tasker threw back

her head and laughed out loud. My mother would have called it a good, healthy woman's laugh. "Given where we are, Mr. Cuddy, just about everybody on this campus has a car. You have any idea what that means for us?"

"None."

"Well, first you've got faculty members, who think it's their God-given right to have a dedicated space reserved for them personally every day of the week, even if they're in their offices only Monday, Wednesday, and Friday. Second, all the students think the tuition they pay ought at least to include a spot for their car, since it sure doesn't guarantee them a job when they graduate. Then you've got administrators, and visiting parents with their teenage kids 'shopping' for colleges, and—"

"I get the picture."

Tasker paused. "So the only way you can possibly manage this mess is by economic self-determination."

"Meaning making them all feed meters."

"Or most of them, at least. The meters are really pretty good, and not just as moneymakers, either. They're very well-made, mechanically speaking. Only problem is, they *are* mechanical, so they're going to break down, and it costs us twenty-nine ninety-five each time we send one back to the factory. So I took one of my PSA's down—"

"Pee-Ess-Ays?"

Dave shuffled his feet on the floor. Tasker said, "Parking-Service Attendants. I took one of them with me to this school the manufacturer runs down in Arkansas. You fly into Springfield, Missouri, home of Bass Pro Shops. You ever been to L.L. Bean in Freeport?"

"Yes."

"Well, this is the same idea, only bigger. Five-story waterfall, trout stream, aquarium. Two different places to eat, a zoo full of stuffed animals."

"A zoo . . . ?"

"Full of stuffed animals. Then we drove south to the factory. And guess what you pass along the way?"

"Bill Clinton's hometown?"

"No. Branson, Missouri, home to the performance theaters of country stars, has-been sixties' singers, and you name it. Zillions of buses and RVs filled with retired people hitting the theaters and shops and restaurants. And let me tell you, they really pack those theaters."

"To see . . . ?"

"Bobby Vinton, Tony Orlando, Pat Boone—"

"Stop, you're making me giddy."

Officer Dave coughed a little louder, and Tasker paused again. Then, "Mr. Cuddy, Trish said over the radio you were a wiseass. Didn't anybody ever tell you that first impressions were the most important?"

"Sorry."

Tasker flicked her hands again. "The road south from Branson goes through mostly rural areas, with homemade signs advertising quilts and fenced-in yards full of cement lawn ornaments."

"Lawn ornaments?"

"Miniature deer, full-sized swans, even a lawn pig, with colored rocks."

"Colored rocks too."

"Painted, to serve as border markers. And we saw, I forget exactly where, this sign for maintaining the highways. You know, volunteer your group to do roadside cleanup?"

"We have those in New England too."

"Yeah, only down there, the sign said, 'Adopt a Highway. This Mile Maintained by the Ku Klux Klan.' "

Tasker shook her head. I checked my watch.

She said, "You have an appointment somewhere?"

"No. I was just wondering how long we were going to kick around the Wonders of the Ozarks before whoever it is you're stalling for gets here."

A very slow nod. "I must be slipping."

"Not by much. I brought up the diploma, remember? All you did was build on it."

Another nod.

I said, "You want to tell me why I'm being held at all?"

The nodding stopped. "You don't know."

Tasker hadn't spoken it as a question. "No, I don't."

"Somebody—I'm guessing you—forged a signature on a letter to fraudulently obtain a former student's records, seemingly with his permission."

"How about if I promise not to do it again?"

"You've probably violated a federal student privacy act."

"Can you give me chapter and verse?"

Tasker said, "No."

"Then who are we waiting for, the FBI?"

"No. Our locals."

I leaned forward in my chair slowly, so as not to excite Officer Dave. "Ms. Tasker, don't you think this is a little excessive, given the circumstances?"

"Maybe you don't know all the circumstances."

"Like for instance?"

Tasker tapped the folder in front of her. "This file belongs to Andrew Dees, class of 1973. Harriet's been in the registrar's forever and remembered his name. He was killed in a car accident two days after graduation. My first 'for instance' would be why you're forging the signature of a boy dead twenty-odd years."

I sat back in my chair, thinking Gail Tasker had a pretty good question there.

"Gail, what's up?"

We'd sat—Tasker and I, anyway, Officer Dave still standing behind me—silently for another ten minutes, her studying the file like she had a final exam coming up on it. Dave shifted position just enough to open the door when we heard a knock. The man entering the room was around fifty, with a beer belly over brown pants cinched with a cracked leather belt. His broad shoulders had outgrown the green sports jacket two sizes ago, and he was the first male I'd seen wearing a porkpie hat in probably a decade. What hair the hat didn't hide had stayed black, and his walk was more a waddle as he took up space against the wall near Tasker's diploma.

She said, "This is John Cuddy. Cuddy, Pete Braverman."

"Detective Braverman?"

The man smiled, cruel and somehow familiar. "Chief Braverman, if it matters to you."

I looked from one to the other. "Director of Campus Security, Chief of Police. All the big guns, rolled out just for me."

Braverman crossed his arms in front of his chest, seriously threatening the seams of the jacket. "And just what did you do, Mr. Cuddy?"

"Maybe you'd best ask the director here."

Braverman kept his eyes in my direction long enough to let me know he didn't like his questions answered that way, then glanced toward Tasker.

She summed up what had happened so far.

When Tasker got to the part about Andrew Dees being the student I was after, Braverman didn't look at all happy. Then he came back to me. "You got anything to add?"

"No."

"Why are you checking into things at the university?"

"Confidential."

"That doesn't count for shit here, Cuddy," said Braverman. "You're not licensed in Vermont."

"All I did was try to get a record. I don't need a license for that."

"Then you don't need to keep it confidential, either."

"I'm not. I told you what I was doing, just not why I was doing it."

"That doesn't explain you trying to beat the registrar out of a record with a forged letter."

"I wasn't trying to beat anything. I'd have been happy to pay a reasonable copy charge."

The cruel smile. "Pity this isn't thirty years ago. We'd save ourselves a lot of time."

I said, "Chief, Ms. Tasker already mentioned the old-fashioned way. Living in the past wouldn't be good tactics for either of you."

The smile died a little. Braverman brought one hand up to rub his chin. He blinked twice, then turned to the desk. "Gail, I got a bad feeling about this gentleman, but I don't see what all we can do about it."

Tasker reddened a bit. "Pete, he forged a request on a dead man."

Braverman said, "Yeah, but that just means Cuddy here didn't know the boy—shit, he'd be what, in his forties now?—was dead. That doesn't sound like much ground for prosecution to me."

Tasker reddened a bit more. "So, what, we just let him walk?"

"It's either that, or we're up to our mutual asses in paperwork only to see him get less of a slap on the wrist than a jaywalker down on Main."

Tasker didn't seem to like the way Braverman was handling the situation. Frankly, I didn't blame her. In his shoes, I'd have put me someplace while they had this talk, then come back to me with a united front. Maybe the "don't-you-ever-again-on-my-beat" sort of warning from both of them, even if they'd decided to cut me loose.

Tasker heard him out, though, before saying evenly, "It's your call, Pete."

Braverman turned back to me with a cruel smile. "Well, now, since I've got my car out front, why don't I save Gail and Dave here the trouble of giving you a lift back to yours?"

"Major reason I'm the chief here, nobody could stand to partner up with me. Can you guess why?"

As soon as we'd gotten in his older, unmarked sedan, I nearly gagged. The stale cigar smoke was as much a part of the car as the upholstery it'd invaded. The sensation was like Mo Katzen's office being reduced to a five-foot cube of tainted air.

Braverman took a thick, half-gone one about three inches long from the ashtray and used a Bic lighter to coax it back to life, the smoke puffs almost covering his face. Then he turned the ignition key and started off.

"Major reason I keep this junker is the headroom for my hat. Only one I've—"

"There a 'major reason' you let me watch back there too?"

Braverman seemed to bite down hard on the cigar. "Let you watch what?"

"You pulling rank on Tasker. She thought she smelled a skunk, and you made a show of kicking the woodpile, but it seemed to me you didn't really want to find out what might be in with the logs."

A heavy drag this time, and a cloud of smoke as we turned. "Gail called me, only told me her people were bringing over some wiseass—her expression—who was making a fuss at the registrar's and would I swing by, have a look. After she explained the problem back in her office just now, it doesn't seem exactly like capital murder, somehow."

When Braverman didn't continue, I said, "And so I'm free to go."

A variation on the cruel smile, lip winching over the cigar. "Unless you'd rather be booked. I could still arrange it."

"I don't think so."

"Good."

"I mean, I don't think you'd book me."

Braverman made another turn, wagging his head. "And you seemed so smart earlier."

"I get the feeling, Chief, that you want me the hell out of Dodge instead of in it, defending myself on Tasker's idea of charges."

"And why would I want that, Cuddy?"

"I honestly don't know."

We arrived at the Administration Building. "Which one's yours?"

"The silver Prelude."

Braverman came to a stop behind my rear bumper. "You like the older ones, too, eh?"

I just looked at him.

"Cuddy, there something still eating you?"

"Curiosity."

"Bad emotion, curiosity. Remember what it did for the cat."

"You see lots of us cats around, Chief."

Braverman drew heavily on the cigar again. "Just the live ones. Could be like icebergs, you know? Ten percent you can see, the other ninety percent under the surface."

I got out of the car. As I closed the door, Chief Pete Braverman said, "Deep under," before motoring slowly away.

13

From the lot of the Administration Building, I drove back through the gates, searching for a pay phone. I found one near the Towne Restaurant and started dialing.

I tried my office answering service first. No message from Nancy, but a Mr. Zuppone had called three times. Next my home telephone tape, tapping in the remote code and getting three additional messages from Primo, each a little more desperate, telling me to meet him at "the condo," which I took to be my place. Still nothing from Nancy.

I thought Primo was better dealt with face-to-face in Boston, after I knew a little more about "Andrew Dees," but I tried the DA's office, a secretary saying Ms. Meagher was back on trial. I left what I hoped sounded like a calm message: "Call me at home tonight." Given the way the secretary asked if there was anything else, I'm not so sure I pulled off the "calm" part.

Then I stopped back in the restaurant to find out where the local newspaper was located.

* * *

"Hi. Interested in a subscription?"

"Afraid not. I'd like to take a look at some of your old editions."

"How old?"

"Nineteen-seventy-three."

"*Seventy*-three?"

The young man on the other side of the veneered counter said the year as though it belonged to ancient history, which for him it probably did. Maybe eighteen or nineteen, he had hair cropped short as a shorn lamb's, so that it looked like acrylic fuzz. With two steel rings through his left ear and one through his right eyebrow, I almost asked if he'd like an introduction to Kira Elmendorf back at Plymouth Willows.

"Seventy-three," I repeated. "The issues from around graduation time."

"For the university, you mean?"

"Yes."

"We're just a weekly, you know, but I think I can find them. So you want all of May, right?"

"And June."

He frowned. "June?"

"Yeah."

"The university graduates in May, man."

"Back then it might have been later."

"You mean going to school all the way into June?"

"Times were tough."

"Tough? Try terrifying, man."

"Terrifying."

"Totally. I mean, like, strapped to a desk until . . . ? Beyond my ability to comprehend, you know?"

I was afraid I did.

The front-page story from the June 19th edition was consistent with Gail Tasker's summary. Andrew Dees, born in Chicago twenty-two years before, went off the highway and rolled his car three times in a "one-vehicle accident," breaking his neck. Two of his fraternity brothers said he'd had a "a little too much suds at this party that's been 'happening' since graduation." The article concluded with, "According to university records, Mr. Dees has no immediate family surviving him."

"Tragic, man."

I looked up to the boy helping me. "At any age."

"Huh?"

"This guy getting killed, driving drunk."

"Oh, that's not what I meant." He pointed to the paper's masthead. "I mean, like, the date."

"The date?"

"Yeah, man. It's just the way you told me. They had to stick with school all the way into June. Tragic, right?"

"Totally," I said.

"Harborside Bank. Ms. Evorova's line."

The very formal secretary. "Can I speak to her, please?"

"And who may I say is calling?"

"John Cuddy. She's expecting to hear from me."

A couple of clicks, then, "John, you have some news for me, yes?"

"I do. Are you alone?"

A pause, then a lower tone. "Your news, it is . . . bad?"

"I'm calling from Vermont, near the university. I tried to check Andrew Dees' college records here."

Some weakness crept into her voice. "And?"

"The campus police came for me because it turns out that the student whose authorization letter I supposedly had was dead."

"What?"

"Andrew Dees died in a car accident over twenty years ago."

"No. There must be a mistake, yes?"

"I don't think so. I went to the local newspaper, and I have a copy of the article on the accident. It's consistent with what the campus police told me, and anyway I don't see why they would have lied about it."

Another pause.

"Olga?"

"I am trying to think, but I cannot."

It hurt to hear her say the words. "Is Claude Loiselle there?"

"I am not sure."

"Maybe it'd be a good idea for you to speak with her. I can keep looking into this, but I'm afraid that what I've found suggests Mr. Dees is involved in something very wrong."

No response.

"Olga, are you still there?"

"I think you must be right about—'Andrew,' can that even be his real name?"

"I don't know. If you want, I can approach him directly, and maybe—"

"No. No, please, do nothing further until I speak with you, yes?"

"Okay."

A very sad sigh. "Thank you so much."

Somehow that was even harder to hear.

After hanging up, I tried Nancy again, but got the same secretary with the same information about her being on trial, so I left the same message. I considered checking my answering service and telephone tape machine one more time, but figured if Primo was on them again, I'd be back in Boston sooner if I just started driving.

I pulled the Prelude into the night-darkened space on Fairfield Street behind the condo building. I was thinking about Nancy, about the reassuring message I hoped was waiting for me, and so I missed spotting the car until I heard the voice.

"Cuddy!"

I ducked, and my empty hand told me I wasn't carrying a weapon just a split second before I recognized the voice and face.

"Primo."

Zuppone had started to duck himself, still standing at the open, driver's side door of the Lincoln when he saw me reach behind my back. "Christ, the fuck were you gonna do, shoot me?"

"Sorry. I was thinking about something else."

"Something else, huh? Let me tell you about something else." Primo slammed his door. "What's the matter, you don't return your fucking phone calls no more?"

It was the first time I'd seen Zuppone do anything but baby the Lincoln, and there was an edge to his voice I'd heard only once before. When I'd been in a lot of trouble with his employers.

"What's going on, Primo?"

He came up the sidewalk toward me, taking the toothpick from his mouth and throwing it violently to the ground. "What's going on is I been calling you non-fucking-stop at your office, at the condo here, I even thought about leaving a message for your girlfriend the DA, asking her to pretty please get you the fuck in touch with me."

We were almost nose-to-nose. "Don't ever call her, Primo."

"I didn't."

"Ever."

Zuppone drew in a deep breath. "All right, all right. Let's both calm down a little, huh?"

The "situation guy" was rattled, and I didn't like that at all. "Primo, what do we have to calm down from?"

He let out the breath with a whooshing sound. "You and me got a problem."

"Where're we going?" I said.

The Lincoln turned soundlessly onto Storrow Drive, the potholes and speedbumps we'd hit on Back Road barely noticeable through the land yacht's suspension system. Zuppone was thumping his right thumb against the cradled car phone, and I didn't like the fact that no New Age music was coming from the speakers.

"Primo, where?"

"Logan."

"Why the airport?"

Zuppone glanced over, then checked all his mirrors before focusing on the traffic ahead of him. "That picture you gave me. Of your guy, remember?"

"I remember."

A fresh toothpick moved from one corner of his mouth to the other. "Yeah, well, I said I thought something rang a bell somewheres, but I wasn't sure?"

"Go on."

"So I show his photo to some friends of ours, including this one friend, does some coordination work between us and Providence, us and the Outfit."

"The Chicago organization?"

"Yeah, that's what they call themselves in the Windy fucking City. And I even went out there with this coordinator once, kind of show the flag a couple, three years ago. But you told me your guy was South Shore or some fucking thing, right?"

"That's right."

"I mean, that's where the property company and all was from."

"Yes."

A reverse migration of the toothpick as Zuppone drove

past the exit for Government Center. "Okay, so that's what I'm thinking when I show his picture to our friend the coordinator this morning. Only thing is, the friend takes one look at the photo and another at me, then says, 'Primo, keep an eye on this guy, understand?' "

"Keep an eye on him?"

"Yeah, and the coordinator basically—the fuck would you call it, 'outranks' me like—so I gotta say, 'Hey-ey-ey, I'd be glad to, only I don't know where he is.' And this friend of our says, 'Well, you better fucking hope you can find him again.' And I don't like the sound of that, so I don't say nothing else, and lo and fucking behold, the coordinator's on the phone, wants to call Milwaukee— "

"I thought you said Chicago?"

Zuppone shot me a look. "You wanna let me fucking finish?"

"All right."

"You let me finish, then you'll fucking know."

"Sorry, Primo."

He shook his head, spoke more deliberately. "This friend of ours gets on the horn, and he asks me what the fucking area code is for Milwaukee, like I'm Nynex or something, then all of a sudden it hits me."

I said, "What hits you?"

"Why your guy's picture rang that bell with me, why I thought I knew the fuck."

"And?"

We stopped for the traffic light at Leverett Circle. "It's from when I'm in the Midwest there with this coordinator, visiting the Outfit."

"In Chicago."

"Right, right. Only he wants to take a little side trip, over to Milwaukee, see this other friend—a gentleman named Mr. Ianella."

I didn't like that Primo was telling me the name of a mobster from another organization.

"This Mr. Ianella," said Zuppone, "he did us a favor one time, and we wanted to pay our respects, understand?"

"I think so."

"Okay. We drive to Milwaukee, and we meet Mr. Ianella at his house—big fucking place on this cliff overlooking the lake, only it looks like a fucking ocean to me, seagulls and everything. We're just sitting down to lunch with this gentleman when his bookkeeper comes in the room, carrying some papers that gotta be signed that day, otherwise the IRS is gonna have a coronary."

The Lincoln started to climb the ramp for the Central Artery. "So?"

"So the bookkeeper's your guy from the photo there."

Swell. "You're sure, Primo?"

"Yeah, I'm sure. Oh, he looked a little different back then. More gray in the hair, and I think his nose's been fixed or something, that's why I got thrown off when you showed me the picture. I mean, three years ago, and I'm not paying a lot of fucking attention to the bean counter in Milwaukee, you get me?"

I just nodded.

Zuppone glanced over. "Be helpful you kind of said something, I'm supposed to be keeping my eyes on the road and all."

"Sorry, Primo."

Another head shake. "So, anyways, our friend the coordinator is on the phone to Milwaukee today, and he tells the Ianella family that we found DiRienzi for them."

"DiRienzi is the bookkeeper?"

"Yeah, Alfonso DiRienzi."

Andrew Dees, keeping the same initials. When Zuppone didn't continue, I said, "What do you mean, we 'found' him?"

A shorter glance. "That's the problem part."

"Go on."

"Seems this DiRienzi got a whiff of something coming down the pike from the IRS out in Milwaukee there. Something they could indict on and send him away for a long time to the wrong kind of cellblock, spend his nights choking on foot-long dicks, black in color."

I had to hear the rest of it. "And so DiRienzi flips."

"Like a fucking pancake. You remember what I was telling you last time, about Sammy the Bull down in New York there? Well, your guy the bookkeeper, he goes to the feds, cuts a deal like Gravano did, and rats out Mr. Ianella."

"Testifies, you mean?"

"Secret grand jury, evidence out the wazoo, trial's over so fast it'd make your fucking head spin. The gentleman we owe the favor to finds himself in federal stir a thousand miles from Milwaukee. And nobody in the family's very fucking happy about any of it."

I tried to think things through. Olga Evorova's boyfriend picking a town in "No Man's Land," between the Boston and Providence mobs, an area where grads of Central Vermont who might have known the real "Andrew Dees" tend not to settle. Camera-shy, living in a nondescript suburban condo complex, running a low-profile and very local business. Never talking about his background with neighbors or even his almost-fiancée. Being willing to eat at most kinds of restaurants but not Italian, being willing to attend most kinds of musical events with Olga except her favorite, Italian opera—like Verdi's *Rigoletto*. Because of who he might run into?

I said, "This DiRienzi's in the Witness Protection Program."

"Yeah, that's my guess. I'm thinking the feds sent the bookkeeper east, as far from fucking Milwaukee as they could. They dye his hair, change his nose, and put him some place you happen to find him."

"But what about the two guys who came to see me?"

"Not ours, like I told you. This friend, the coordinator—who recognized DiRienzi from the photo?—he thinks they must be freelancers, maybe something to do with the property management people."

I filed that as Zuppone took the exit for the Callahan Tunnel. "So why are we going to the airport?"

Zuppone rolled the toothpick. "Usually, one of our people rats somebody out and goes underground, we catch up to him pretty quick. He doesn't know how to live without the old neighborhood, the family—his relatives, I mean. He's gotta stay in touch, telephone, postcard, that kind of shit. Sooner or later he fucks up, and somebody figures out where he is, and that's the ball game."

"Primo, I'm—"

"Or, the rat goes into the Witness Protection thing there, but he can't break his other habits, you know? The guy's got a thing for the ponies, he goes to the racetrack. Somebody spots him, thinks he looks familiar from somewhere, and after a while remembers where. Or maybe the guy likes cards, so he goes to a casino, though I gotta tell you, with all the Indians opening up on their reservations and the states having all these boat games, it's getting pretty fucking hard to cover them all with enough soldiers, you're gonna be sure to spot somebody, he shows up."

"Primo."

Another glance over as Zuppone merged into the traffic entering the tunnel. "What?"

"I'm not setting this DiRienzi up for a hit."

"That's something else we gotta talk about."

"We just did."

"I mean we gotta talk about it with some other people."

"Primo, I'm also not going to Milwaukee."

"You don't have to." Zuppone took a breath. "Milwaukee is coming to us."

The traffic in front of the Lincoln made Primo stand on his brakes, and through the windshield I noticed again how being stopped in the tunnel could remind you of lying in a big, beige coffin, lid closed.

"So, you ever been there, Cuddy?"

"Where?"

"Where? Milwaukee where."

"Not that comes to mind."

We were waiting in the arrival lounge of the Northwest Airlines terminal, the only people around except for a weary gate agent. Before parking the car, Primo had asked me if I was really carrying, and I said no. Then he drew a Beretta semiautomatic from a shoulder holster and slid it under the driver's seat.

In the terminal, Zuppone sweet-talked the security people into letting us meet our party at the gate, even though we didn't have any tickets ourselves. In the ten minutes we'd been sitting in the black-and-chrome chairs near a bank of telephones, he'd gotten up to check the video monitor three times.

Now Primo stretched some, rocking his heels on the purplish carpet, trying to relax. "I was out there just the once I told you about, but it was enough."

To help pass the time, I said, "How come?"

"Well, first off, Mr. Ianella sends some of his associates to pick us up in Chicago, and we drive north through some of the worst fucking traffic I ever seen. You think the Southeast Expressway is bad? I'm talking eight, ten lanes across, jammed in the middle of the fucking day. Then maybe eighty, ninety miles later, you get up to Milwaukee itself. And the city's clean as a fucking whistle, only there's this smell."

"Smell?"

"Yeah. I can't understand it. The air looks clean—the

streets, you could fucking eat off—but there's this smell. Guy told me later it was probably one of the breweries, the wind was right."

"I've heard they like their beer."

"You kidding? We're out to dinner with these people, they take us to the one Italian restaurant they say can really do the food justice, and it's just, like, mediocre. Mediocre at best. Then, instead of wine, they order beer with it. I mean, it was fucking disgusting, they're drinking beer with pasta. You give them a bottle of wine, I think they would've poured it on the fucking salad."

I laughed. Zuppone did too, a little looser now.

"And the hotel, Cuddy. I forget the name of the place, but you should have seen it. Usually when we're out of town, we stay with some of the people we're seeing, kind of a home away from home, you know? But this gentleman we're paying our respects to—Mr. Ianella, the one gets rattled out by your guy there?—he wants us to stay in the best place in the city. So we're at the check-in desk, and there's some convention or other going on. The clerk tries to tell one of our Milwaukee people—this gentleman's son, got a scar through his eyebrow and a look that'd scare Tyranno-saurus fucking rex—that there's no rooms available. So the son leans over the counter, and says something real quiet like, and you'd have thought the clerk grew fucking wings, he moved so fast for us. And I get this a-*part*-ment, it's got a living room and a bathroom with a Jacuzzi the size of a fucking regular room. And the bed? Let's just say you would've thought you were in the Wilt Chamberlain Suite.

"Anyways, I get settled in the room, figuring it might be nice to pick something up at the bar, show her the Jacuzzi, you know? And when I get down there, I see ten, fifteen broads standing around, all sipping wine and club sodas, and they're even pretty young. And I say, 'Great, they must be here for the convention'—not pros hustling, you understand, just like attending it. Then I notice the hotel has this computer bulletin board in the lobby right by the bar, and they've got what the convention events are, rolling over the screen. And guess what the convention turns out to be?"

"I give up."

"It's some kind of nurses' thing, only the fucking theme or whatever you call it is 'Sexually Transmitted Diseases.' The computer screen's rolling panels with titles like 'Dysfunctional Vaginal Bleeding' and 'Canker Sores of the Male Organ,' and I say to myself, 'Fuck, the vibes this board's giving off, there ain't gonna be nobody laid in this hotel for a year.' "

Zuppone's laugh was cut short by the gate agent's announcement that our flight was just hooking up to the jetway. He rose to look and said, "Come on."

"No."

"What do you mean, no?"

"I mean I'm not setting up Alfonso DiRienzi for your hitters."

His face coloring, Zuppone sat back down. "Cuddy, they aren't 'my hitters.' They're the guys have a score to settle with a certain bean counter who betrayed them."

"I don't see the difference."

"The difference is that my people owe the Milwaukee people a favor, and the coordinator I told you about let the cat out of the fucking bag that 'we' know where the rat is. And that 'we' includes you, since it was the fucking favor you asked with the photo that got me into this situation in the first fucking place."

"And they expect you to produce me for a little talking to."

Primo shrugged. "You might say that, yeah."

"Not tonight."

"What?"

"They know who I am?"

"Cuddy, you winking out on me or what? They never fucking met you before."

"So they don't know my name."

Zuppone struggled to keep his voice down. "Of course they don't know your fucking name."

"All right, then. You tell them you've been trying to reach me. Tell them you camped out in front of my house and I never showed up."

"Your car's there now."

"Tell them it wasn't when you left."

"Cuddy," the face getting more flushed, "why should I tell them any of this fucking shit?"

I pointed to the jetway. "Because when they come through that door, I'm going to be holding one of the telephones next to us, speaking on an open line to Boston Homicide. Just to make sure nothing cute happens here."

Zuppone glanced nervously at the jetway door. "You got rocks in your head or what? These guys just flew how many fucking miles to talk to you tonight, get this thing done."

"You tell them you're working on finding me, and meanwhile you'll show them the city."

"Show them the city? Cuddy, these guys didn't come here to shop Quincy fucking Market. They came here to avenge the family honor and fly the fuck back."

The gate agent opened the doorway, putting on a yearbook smile to greet the arrivals.

I said to Zuppone, "I'm going to make the call, and then I'll try you tomorrow on your car phone."

"Tomorrow? What the fuck am I supposed—"

I stood up and walked over to the phone bank. After I picked up a receiver and dialed, Primo took a series of breaths, the color in his face finally returning to normal. Only three people—an older couple with what looked like a granddaughter—came through the doorway and into the lounge before two men appeared and nodded to Primo. Both wore suits. One was tall, stooped, and balding. The other was husky, with dark, styled hair. Neither of them looked anything like the two guys who had worked me over behind my office building, but the husky one, talking animatedly to Zuppone, was familiar in a different way.

There was an obvious scar line through his left eyebrow, a lot like the one Primo described as belonging to the son of the "gentleman" Alfonso DiRienzi had helped send to prison.

14

To allow Primo Zuppone enough head start to clear the baggage carousel area downstairs, I stayed at the arrival lounge telephones. Trying Olga Evorova's home number, I got an outgoing tape, her voice anonymously announcing, "Please, leave your message." After the beep, I said to call me at my home number as soon as possible, any hour. Then I dialed the bank number and left the same on her voice-mail.

Trying Nancy at home next, I got her machine too. After a similar beep, I said into the receiver, "Nance, if you're there, please pick up," but only static crackled back at me.

I replaced the receiver and thought about it. I could go to Nancy's in South Boston by taxi, but I'd have to make the driver wait, because if she didn't answer her door, I'd be stuck over there without a car, and hailing or calling a second cab would mean hiking to Broadway. On the other hand, I could go to Evorova's apartment on Beacon Hill by taxi. If she didn't answer her door, I'd be within walking distance of my parking space, assuming Primo and the Milwaukee contingent weren't already planted outside the condo building, watching for me to do just that. Then I could drive to Nancy's, and my car wouldn't be where I'd told Primo to tell the hitters it wasn't.

I checked my watch, sat for another five minutes trying to think of a better plan, and finally went downstairs to the revolving door marked GROUND TRANSPORTATION.

I had the cabbie drop me at Joy Street, a few blocks from Evorova's address. Then I zigzagged another two blocks around it. Given the narrow, one-way streets on the Hill, there was no way anybody in a car could follow me without tipping themselves, and nobody on foot who looked like one of Primo's "associates" stayed close.

Finally reaching Evorova's building, I saw the telephone-style keypad at the main entrance and realized that if I punched in her code, I'd only be ringing her phone, and therefore would still get just her answering machine. I tried anyway, heard the "Please, leave your message," and said it was me, waiting downstairs, and if she was there, would she please pick up or buzz the outer door. Neither happened, so I pressed the HANG UP button, then walked around the block to the back of her building.

There was a parking area tucked into what should have been the rear garden of the first floor unit, but I didn't see the orange Porsche Carrera my client had told me she owned. One slot stood empty, though, between a green Mercedes and a gray Lexus, and I figured I'd done as much as I could about warning Olga Evorova about "her Andrew," at least for the night.

Using a similar zigzag pattern, I walked down to Charles Street and over to Beacon. I went west up Marlborough to approach my building, then loitered at the corner of Fairfield for a while, watching the Prelude in its space under the streetlamp. Expanding my field of vision a few parked cars at a time, I didn't see any people obviously sitting in them.

Moving as casually as possible to my driver's side door, I opened it, slid behind the wheel, and started the engine. Nobody tried to block me in as I backed out, and no vehicle seemed to stay in my rearview mirror very long on the drive to Southie.

I left the car around the corner from the Lynches' three-decker. At their stoop, I pushed Nancy's button. No fancy phone pads or intercoms in this neighborhood, just old-fashioned bells that rang above doorways upstairs. I pictured her coming down the interior staircase, a towel over her right hand, a Smith & Wesson Bodyguard with shrouded hammer under the towel, in case a customer she'd nailed in court had somehow gotten the prosecutor's address and decided to cross the line.

I waited a minute, then forced myself to use my watch to wait a full minute more. I tried her button again. Same lapse of time, same lack of response.

Mrs. Lynch, in her sixties, lived alone on the first floor. Her son, Drew, shared the second with his wife and baby. I pushed the middle button.

When the front door opened a foot, Drew stood inside wearing a hooded gray sweatshirt over red sweatpants, his right arm hanging straight down from the shoulder, the hand hidden behind his thigh. As he recognized me, the right hand came out, relaxing its grip on a long-barreled revolver.

"Drew, I'm really sorry to disturb you, but Nancy's not answering her phone or the bell, and I'm kind of worried."

A nod. "I heard her walking around the kitchen above us, so she's there."

I didn't ask to come in, but he swung the door wide for

me to enter. Saying thanks, I moved past him and up the stairs, trying my best not to take them two at a time.

On the third landing, I waited until I heard Drew's apartment door close below me, then knocked gently on Nancy's. I could hear Renfield pawing against the other side, but nothing else. I knocked louder, and the cat upped the ante too, now mewling a little as he couldn't get at whatever was on my side of the door.

I bent down and over the sill said, "Renfield, tell her if she doesn't open up, I'm kicking it in."

That's when the deadbolt clicked back, and the door finally cracked ajar.

Renfield scuttled out, his bent rear legs churning like a locomotive's wheel linkage, his clawless front paws trying to burrow a hole through my shoe laces. Nancy stood in front of me. She wore a cotton turtleneck under a fuzzy mauve robe, knee socks going up past the hem of the robe. Her eyes were red, and her hair was mussed, but less like she'd been lying down and more like she'd been tossing and turning.

In a hurt voice, Nancy said, "Didn't you get my message?"

"No. When did you leave me one?"

"A couple of hours ago."

Well after I'd checked in from Vermont. "What did your message say?"

Nancy closed her eyes. "That I was still on trial tomorrow, and couldn't see you tonight because I wasn't feeling well and had to make up for all the time I lost today."

The explanation sounded brittle. "Time you lost going to the doctor's?"

Opening her eyes, she started to say something, then stopped.

"Nance, how about if you let me in?"

A frown.

I said, "Maybe before Renfield tears the shoes from my feet?"

She stepped back and turned away, the cat leaving me alone as he trailed her into the apartment.

I came through the door and closed it behind me, noticing the tape from our Scottish fiddle night still on the shelf near her telephone. Then I followed Nancy and Renfield into the living room.

She plopped herself down on the couch, the cat at his station under the glass-topped coffee table, where I'd feed him scraps if we were eating. But instead of food covering the table, there was only a half-glass of white wine and a box of tissues, some soul-rending jazz piano at low volume coming from the stereo.

I sat across from her on a chair. "Nance?"

"It's just ..." She ran a hand through her hair. "It's just this stuff they're doing at the courthouse."

"What stuff?"

"Well, when you came to pick me up, you saw all the scaffolding they have against the building?"

"Yes?"

"They've been renovating, but they put some kind of waterproofing chemical on the outside last June, and when the fumes seeped into the rooms, everybody started feeling sick."

"Sick how?"

"Oh, nausea, dizziness"—Nancy gestured at her face—"itchy eyes, even migraines."

"And that's the problem?"

"Yes," unconvincingly.

"Nance?"

"What?"

"The fumes have been there since June, and they're only getting to you in October?"

"They affect different people differently. And different parts of the courthouse at different times."

I just stared at her.

She said, "The Clerk's office got the worst of it at first, and they closed the whole building four days in August while a vent system was being installed. Even the people just using the Social Law Library felt it."

I stared some more.

"The Appeals Court is way up on fifteen, John, and three of the judges had to be moved off-site—they're doing their business now from Middlesex and even Concord District Court via personal computers and fax machines."

"Nancy."

Now she stared at me.

I said, "Making it longer doesn't make it better."

"Doesn't make what better?"

"Your story about the fumes."

Her expression hardened.

I ignored it. "Now, what's really going on?"

Her face turned harder still, then cracked in a way I'd seen only once before. When she'd had to kill someone trying to kill me.

"Oh, John . . ." She brought her face down to her hands, and began to shudder. "Jesus Mary, I didn't want this."

In one motion, I shifted over to the couch and closed my arms around her. All the muscles felt clenched, and she began rocking, like her stomach hurt.

"Nance?" I lowered my voice to a whisper. "Nance, please tell me. Whatever it is."

She kept rocking and began crying. I stroked her back with my right hand, deeply, almost like a massage.

Nancy lifted her face a notch, glancing at me rather than turning. "I saw my doctor, and she . . . examined my breast, and she said I ought to go for a . . . tissue sample."

I felt a little part of me die inside. "When are you scheduled?"

Now Nancy turned toward me. "It's already happened. The doctor sent me immediately, this morning right after the examination."

"And?"

"It'll be a while before we have any results. She told me she'd try to get the lab to rush it, but then ..." A weak smile as Nancy looked away. "I guess she probably says that to all the women she treats, because we'd all want to know as soon as possible."

"What else did the doctor say?"

"Oh, she was very good, John, very reassuring. She asked me if there was any history of breast ... of it in my family, and I said no. But, Jesus, back then, I'm not sure I would have known if one of my aunts ever had something like that. I mean, nobody talked about it, and my mom sure never mentioned anything before she died."

I didn't want to interrupt.

"And then the doctor asked me when I first noticed the lump myself, and I had to tell her, I wasn't sure." Nancy turned to me. "And she tried, John, she really tried not to let the look show on her face, the look I try not to show the cops when I know they've been procedurally stupid in handling a suspect, and the officer involved begins to realize he or she may have blown the case."

"Nance—"

"The doctor told me that given my age, it's probably just a cyst, like I said when you found it. But I could tell she was doing the same thing I do with the cops, trying to re-store their confidence about testifying—hell, about *being* cops, about doing their job, when they have screwed up royally. And then she said even if there was a problem, it might be just cancer *in situ*, not cancer *per se*."

"What's the difference?"

"The way she described it, cancer *in situ* is kind of precancerous."

I said, "Which would be . . . good, right?"

"Not exactly." Nancy looked down at her hands, moving one then the other, as though she were weighing things in them. "The traditional treatment for that is mastectomy."

I tried not to react. "What else did the doctor say?"

"She wanted to make me feel better about not having . . . examined myself, that the lump was probably growing there for years before I would have felt it by self-examination. But I could tell she was just saying that, the way I talk to the cops."

Nancy's voice grew deeper, slower. "And then I went down to where they take the biopsy—the tissue sample, John—with this . . ." She faltered. "And after it was over, I had to get dressed again and go back to the office and back to the trial and back in front of the jury, in my nice suit and two-inch heels. Because that's what the jury expects every female lawyer to wear, John, high heels, at least if she's still . . . I was going to say attractive, but . . ."

Nancy dropped her face again into her hands.

I said, "Is that why you wouldn't return my calls?"

She looked up. "What?"

"Is the tissue sample and all the reason why you wouldn't tell me what was going on?"

A deep breath. "Partly. But mostly it was . . ." Nancy searched my eyes, curling her lips like someone without their false teeth in. "John, I know what you went through with Beth."

"Nance—"

"I'm sorry, I didn't mean it to sound that way. What I meant was, I knew that you'd been through all this once, and what it did to you, and I couldn't, I just couldn't tell you that it might be starting all over again with—"

"Nancy, stop."

She did.

I said, "I don't know much about breast cancer, but I did learn something about how you deal with the risk of cancer in general. You notice what might be a problem, like we did on Tuesday night, and you get tested, like you did this morning. And then you have to wait for the results."

A tentative nod.

I brought my hand up to her cheek, tracing my fingertips down toward her chin. "And the person who loves you does the wait with you."

She closed her eyes, the tears starting again, following after my fingers. "John, you don't understand. They took this needle, and they had to stick it in—"

"Can I see?"

Nancy opened her eyes.

I said, "Can I see where they did this?"

She shook her head. "Not yet, I'm not . . . ready."

Okay. "Then how about if I touch but don't look?"

Another weak smile. "Give me your hand."

I let her take the left one, as though she were a palm reader, about to predict my fortune.

Nancy brought my index and middle fingers toward her, then beneath the robe but outside the turtleneck, before stopping short. "It's still very tender under the bandage."

"I understand."

"It really hurt, even to have my bra on over it."

This time I just nodded.

Nancy brought me in contact. I could feel the bandage as she flinched.

"Sorry," she said, giving my hand back and shaking her head. "It didn't hurt when you touched it, I was just afraid it would."

"Tell you what, then."

"What?"

"How about if I go to the kitchen and get that Alasdair

Fraser tape and put it on? Then we might have some wine and kind of cuddle up here until you fall asleep."

Nancy swiped at her tears, once with the forehand, then with the back. "I think that would be the bestest couple of hours I've had in two days."

"It's going to be more than a couple of hours, Nance." I took both of her hands in mine. "It's going to be all night, every night."

"What comes after . . . 'bestest'?"

We both laughed, but as I stood and walked toward the kitchen, I heard the faint rustling sound of tissues being torn from their box. And I tried to close the door in my heart on what I remembered from years before, with the only other woman I'd ever loved.

15

While Nancy was in the bathroom the next morning, I picked up the phone to check with my answering service. No message from Olga Evorova, but "Mr. Zuppone" had called twice, the service operator telling me she thought somebody was yelling at him in the background and did that sound right? When I tried my telephone tape at the condo, another, or the same, two messages from Primo. Nothing from Evorova. Again. Same when I called her at work (voice-mail) and at home (answering machine).

After Nancy and I had a quiet breakfast, talking around the things we'd talked through the night before, she left for work. Killing time until I figured the bank would be functioning, I took the Scottish fiddle album from the cassette player. The music had carried just the right "normality" echo for us on Nancy's couch, and now reading the quaint titles of the pieces somehow seemed doubly reassuring.

At 9:00 A.M., I slipped the cassette into my jacket pocket and tried my client again at the bank. Her very formal secretary said Ms. Evorova was in conference and could not be disturbed. When I asked for a transfer to Claude Loiselle, I drew a very brusque male secretary who said Ms. Loiselle was in conference and could not be disturbed as well. When I asked the second secretary if Ms. Loiselle was in conference with Ms. Evorova, I got a firm "I'm not at liberty to say."

That's when I hung up. Whenever you're waiting for something, including test results, it's a good idea to do something else. Nancy had her trial, I had Evorova. If I could see her.

But first, a visit with someone I didn't have to look for.

The breeze blowing down her hillside toward the harbor was warm, that Indian Summer tease still in the air. Carrying the dozen tulips wrapped in clear plastic, I walked the rows of stones until I reached hers, the engraving somehow looking less sharp now, the freeze-thaw of winters rounding the letters of ELIZABETH MARY DEVLIN CUDDY to the point they truly seemed only a memory.

John, I wasn't . . . expecting you.

"It's been a while, Beth." I went to one knee, laying the flowers diagonally on the grave. "Mrs. Feeney had only a couple of roses, but these just arrived."

Tulips in October?

"She said they were from France."

Well, it's her business, she ought to know.

Which was Beth's way of giving me an opening to talk about my business, if I was ready. Instead, I looked at the harbor. The low sun slanted off the dark chop, creating a latticework pattern, the barges and fishing boats and sloops appearing to stand still as the water flashed around them.

John—

"Nancy's afraid she might have cancer," the last word not coming out quite right.

A pause. *What kind?*

169

"Breast."

Has she had tests?

"Yes. We're waiting to hear from her doctor."

Another pause. *And in the meantime?*

"I guess I was hoping for some advice."

John, I don't think I learned anything back then that you didn't learn with me.

I nodded.

So maybe you ought to think about what you already know.

"How do you mean?"

Remember the first time with us, when we were waiting for my test results?

"I try not to, actually."

A third pause. *You brought me a single rose, still closed up like a bud. It pointed to the future.*

I cleared my throat. "It didn't point very far."

That wasn't the rose's fault. And it helped.

I nodded some more.

John?

"What?"

Have you ever brought Nancy flowers?

I couldn't recall an occasion when I had, not one.

Why not?

"It was something I did with you, for you. And nobody else."

John, Nancy is the somebody else now. And she has been, for more than a while.

Nodding one last time, I took in the sun and the water and all the stones around Beth before moving back to the car. Starting the engine, I thought, Mrs. Feeney's going to believe I'm getting senile.

I left the Prelude, and a rose for Nancy, in an illegal space under the still-elevated Central Artery and walked three blocks to the financial district. The Harborside Bank had its offices in a building the board of directors would like you to think they'd hewn themselves from pink, virgin granite. The floors in the lobby were pink too, but marble, a security/information counter curving like a scimitar in front of three banks of elevators, each serving a different twenty floors of the structure. The security guard pointed toward the last group of them, telling me to get off at fifty-four to see Ms. Evorova.

After an ear-popping ride, the elevator opened on an office suite done in wall-to-wall carpeting the same shade as all the stonework. A woman wearing a pilot's headset sat behind a teak desk so highly polished it reflected like a mirror. The prints hanging above the matching loveseats surprised me, though. Instead of seascapes or foxhunts, they were abstract geometries of yellow, orange, and purple.

The woman in the headset looked up from a computer board in front of her. "May I help you, sir?"

"I'd like to see Olga Evorova, please."

A slight hesitation, then a smoothing over. "I'm fairly certain she's in conference right now, but let me try for you. Please be seated."

I took one of the loveseats. Stiffer than I'd guessed, more a football bench than a piece of furniture.

The woman clacked out a concerto on the keys in front of her, then frowned, as though she were playing to the balcony. "I'm so sorry, but it's as I feared. She's in conference and simply—"

"—cannot be disturbed."

A little frost heaved under the smoothness. "Correct."

"Claude Loiselle, then. Please. And tell her John Cuddy needs to see her."

Another concerto on the board, shorter this time. "No, I'm afraid Ms. Loiselle—"

"Tell me, are there names on the doors here?"

"I beg your pardon?'

"Names. If I walk past you and start down one of the hallways, will I see names that'll help me know which office is whose, or do I just barge in, a door at a time, until I find the people I've asked for?"

Her left hand moved almost imperceptibly on the board, and I figured she'd pushed, quite reasonably, a panic button connected to a monitored security panel somewhere.

I said, "How long do I have before the cavalry arrives?"

No answer.

"The reason I ask is, those women, if they're here, would really rather see me than have you and the rent-a-cops throw me on the sidewalk."

To her credit, the receptionist showed teeth that bespoke more snarl than smile, but hit some different buttons and said into her mouthpiece, "Ms. Loiselle? I'm terribly sorry, but ..."

It was a green tweed suit with reddish nubs today, a pattern that highlighted her eyes and her hair, both of which could use some highlighting, as she wore no make-up and had the hair pulled back in a severe bun. There was a pie-wedge of harbor and airport runway visible through the window, if you craned your neck a little. Loiselle gave the impression that it wasn't worth the effort.

Sitting behind her desk, a utilitarian metal job that would have looked just right on the movie set of *1984*, she gestured at her computer in a way that made me feel stupid for not understanding exactly what I'd interrupted. "This had better be good, Mr. Detective."

"Private investigator."

"What's the difference?"

"Detectives are confused police officers. I'm just confused."

A studiously blank stare. "About what?"

"About why all of a sudden I can't reach my client and your friend, either at home or at work."

Loiselle dropped the stare. "To be frank with you, John, I can't either."

Leaning forward in my chair, I said, "When's the last time you saw or heard from her?"

"Yesterday afternoon."

"What time?"

"Around three."

About when I'd phoned Evorova from Vermont, telling her what I'd discovered at the university and newspaper. "She say anything to you?"

"I didn't talk with her directly. She just left a message with Craig."

"Your secretary?"

"Yes. The message was that she had to go out, think something through toward making a decision."

"About what?"

"She didn't say."

I shook my head.

Loiselle said, "But you have some idea, don't you?"

I looked at her. "You a mind reader, Claude?"

She gave me one of the lopsided smiles. "You know what my nickname is around here?"

"No."

"It's a play on Helen of Troy."

" 'The face that launched a thousand ships.' "

"Very good. Only mine's 'the face that launched a thousand shits.' "

"Intimidation."

"It works, John."

"Not on me."

Loiselle stopped. Then, her voice quieter, "What's happened to Olga?"

"I honestly don't know. Can you think of anything else?"

"Only what I've told you, and the fact that her secretary said she had two things on for this morning and she's blown off both of them."

I processed that. "Anybody seen her?"

"Today? No. I called Olga—at home, I mean—and got just her tape. Left a message."

"Behind the ones on there from me."

Loiselle closed her eyes.

I said, "Can you try her at Dees' place for me?"

"Already did. No answer at his condo, and some woman at his shop said he was out and she didn't know when he'd be back."

"Can you try Olga at home one more time?"

Loiselle opened her eyes. "Now?"

"Now."

She dialed. After a moment, "Olga, this is Claude again. If you're there, please pick up." Another moment. "Olga, please!" A shorter wait before Loiselle slammed the receiver back into its console. Rubbing her eyes with the heels of her hands, she said, "Goddammit. What's going on?"

"I can't tell you without Olga's permission, but it could be bad. Can you get me into her office?"

Loiselle looked left-right-left in quick succession. "Why?"

"I'd like to see whether there's anything there that could help us."

Loiselle seemed to consider that. Then she stood up and walked past me in a way I remembered from the Army, a way that said I was supposed to follow.

"Have you heard from Olga?"

The secretary looked up at Claude Loiselle. When the seated woman spoke, I recognized the formal voice from my earlier calls. "No, not since the last time you asked me."

The secretary sounded more frightened than insubordinate, and Loiselle blew by her and through an inner door that showed a nicer view of the harbor than Loiselle's own. The furniture was exotic, reminding me of the stuff in Evorova's apartment and making me appreciate that bankers of her rank probably bought—or at least got to pick out—their own office decor.

Loiselle closed the door. "All right, how many rules do you want me to break?"

"You know her routine better than I do. Where would we look for where she might be?"

Loiselle moved past me to the desk and sat near the computer, adjusting the monitor on a kind of ball-bearing stand for her own eye level. "Olga probably didn't come in early this morning and leave early."

"Because?"

"She'd have logged on, then used a screen-saver to avoid burning an image."

Loiselle flicked a switch on the side of the machine. After some humming and bleeping from inside it, her fingers began to hammer the keyboard. "Calendar for this morning shows just the two things her secretary mentioned. One was supposed to be a face-to-face, the other a conference call from . . . huh?"

"What's the matter?"

"The conference call. Given the time zone for one of the participants, she wouldn't have been able to match everybody up again easily till tomorrow."

"Meaning it's not likely she would have blown it off today?"

"Not likely."

"Could Olga have just forgotten about the call altogether?"

"Not possible, John. Her PDA would have it."

"Her 'Pee-Dee-Ay?' "

"Stands for 'personal digital assistant.' The PDA is a mobile modem, kind of a traveling appointments calendar and address book."

"A computerized thing?"

"Yes." Loiselle hammered some more on the keyboard. "And both items for today were entered into it. Or from it."

I glanced quickly around the office. "Do you see this PDA?"

Without looking up, she said, "No. Olga would have it with her. You never leave anywhere without . . . Shit!"

"What?"

"I'm into her voice-mail now, but I'm getting blocked. Hold on a second." She picked up a phone, smashed three buttons, then drummed her fingers. "Hello, this is Claude Loiselle. Who's this . . . Well, 'Feckinger,' I need Olga Evorova's voice-mail override. . . . Stop. Drop that and find the override. . . . No, not now, Feckinger. Twenty seconds ago, when I first asked you. . . . Good, go."

I saw what Loiselle meant about "the face that launched . . ."

Into the phone, she said, "Finally. . . . Right, bye." Then to me, "That birdbrain doesn't know the difference between CD-ROM and k.d. lang." Returning to the computer, Loiselle began hammering away again. "Here we go." She hit another button with a flourish, and from a speaker at the side of the machine flowed clear but incomprehensible messages, about faxes, accounts payable, stock quotes, etc., followed by a heavily accented voice, saying something like "*Oh*-litchka," then "It is Vanya, why do you not call me?"

I didn't recognize any of the voices. "That last one, her uncle?"

Loiselle nodded. "O-L-E-C-H-K-A is a familiar form of 'Olga' in Russian. A term of endearment."

My recorded voice came out next, sounding tinny, thanks to the airport arrival lounge behind it, from the night before. Then my voice again, this time quieter, from Nancy's apartment that morning. Finally, an electronic voice enunciating each syllable independently, saying, "End of messages."

Loiselle looked up at me.

I said, "Can you tell if Olga picked up any of those?"

"Yes. She didn't."

"When was the first?"

"I was watching the screen log them off." Loiselle rotated the monitor toward me and said, "Wiz-ee-wig."

"Sorry?"

" 'What you see is what you get.' You never heard that acronym?"

"I'm kind of an anachronism, myself."

A shake of the head.

I said, "So, when was the first message received?"

"Just after Olga left that message with Craig yesterday."

"About coming to a decision."

"Yes."

I couldn't see what else her office would tell us.

Loiselle said, "You have any more questions, John?"

"Just one."

"What?"

"Can you get me into Olga's condo too?"

After Claude Loiselle keyed the upstairs lock, I put my index finger to my lips and motioned for her to step aside so I could open the door. I only cracked it first, sniffing the air. No trace of that high, sickly smell a closed room holds when something dead is inside.

I nodded to Loiselle, and we entered Olga Evorova's apartment.

At the end of her entrance hall, the living room seemed normal, no indication of a struggle or search. I said, "Anything strike you as wrong?"

"What do you mean?"

"Anything out of place. Or missing?"

She glanced around without moving, then walked a little farther into the room. "No. It's like Olga would have left it."

"Let's look in the back."

The bathroom was clean, tub curtain closed. Opening it, I checked the liner. No beads of water. Soap stuck to its dish, towels like they'd been blown dry.

I said, "She might have used this room today, but I doubt it."

There were more of the elaborate draperies over the bedroom window, more of the exotic dolls on a mantelpiece over its fireplace. The bed was made, the closet closed. I opened the louvered door. All in order, including a matched set of luggage stacked on the floor.

"What are you looking for?" The tone Loiselle had used with her people at the bank.

"I don't know. Is this Olga's only luggage?"

Loiselle came over and stood beside me. "That's what she carried any time I had her down to my house on the Cape."

"Where's her answering machine?"

"In the den."

Loiselle led me to another room, with more of the bric-a-brac from halfway around the world. The machine, on one corner of a black, lacquered desk, was blinking.

I said, "Do you know how to work this?"

"How hard can it be?" She moved toward it, scanning the buttons for a moment before pressing one. " 'MESSAGES,' " she said.

I heard Andrew Dees' voice, a romantic murmur. "Just letting you know I love you."

Loiselle made a retching sound. "Usually takes two people to fuck up a relationship, unless one of them happens to be the Horse's Ass."

Through a couple of hang-ups, she continued. "Remember when I met you here and you asked me about him?"

"Yes."

"Well, that message sums it all up. The man's not so much transparent as translucent. The bad light shines through, even if you can't quite see where it's coming from."

Then out of the machine came another voice I'd heard before, from Olga's computer at the bank. "Olechka" again, plus something rapid fire in what I assumed to be Russian.

Loiselle said, "Did you notice?"

"What?"

"Uncle Ivan used English at work, Russian at home."

"And therefore?"

"He has nothing to hide, John. Otherwise they'd both be in Russian."

I watched her as my voice came next, first from the arrival lounge and the front door the night before, then alternating with Loiselle's own, the last message her "Olga, please!" from the bank half an hour earlier.

When the machine clicked off, I went to the window and looked down. "Can you come here a minute?"

Loiselle joined me.

I said, "Is that empty space where Olga would park her car?"

"Yes."

"Not good news."

"There's worse."

I waited for it.

Loiselle held up a toy the size of a hand calculator. "Olga's PDA."

"Where was it?"

"On the desk." Loiselle looked back to the black furniture. "She must have come home from the bank yesterday and dropped this here, then taken off in her car."

"And not on business."

"Without this baby? Never." Loiselle's expression grew dark. "What's going on, John?"

"I'm hoping you can help me find out."

Loiselle looked around the room. "How?"

I inclined my head toward the PDA. "Can you make that thing give us Uncle Ivan's last name and address?"

As she poked furiously at it, Loiselle said, "I *told* Olga."

"Sorry?"

"If I told her once, I told her a hundred times: 'This Dees character is just no good for you.' "

"I hope you get the chance to tell her again."

Claude Loiselle looked up at me, then went back to work even faster.

The address turned out to be a turn-of-the-century building on Beacon Street near Coolidge Corner in Brookline, about three miles from my place. Red brick with white cornices, the landscaping of low shrubs and postage-stamp lawn was meticulously trimmed, and the twin entry doors were oiled mahogany. Obviously cared for by someone who really cared, and I thought again of Paulie Fogerty at Plymouth Willows. Propping Nancy's rose upright against the passenger seat so the water from its little tube wouldn't run out, I left the car and walked to the main entrance.

Uncle Ivan's last name wasn't on the list of buzzers and mailboxes between the entry doors and the security door, so I pushed the one marked SUPERINTENDENT. After a short time, a bandy-legged man who looked eighty but moved spryly appeared inside the foyer. He opened the security door and stuck his head out.

"I can help you?"

It sounded like the voice from Olga Evorova's tape machine. "If you're Ivan Evorova."

"That is who I am, but it is pronounce 'Ee-*vor*-ov', no 'a' at end. Because I am man, not woman."

He spoke with a certain loopy elegance. "My name's John Cuddy, Mr. Evorov." I held out my identification holder to him. "I'm a private investigator from Boston, and your niece hired me. Now I'm trying to find her, and I'm hoping you can help."

Evorov absorbed all this without looking at my ID. "Olga, she has some kind of trouble?"

"I hope not."

His face darkened. "You will come in?"

"Thank you."

Evorov made a curious gesture with his right hand, almost like a conductor cuing the brass section, and I followed him down a sparkling, tiled corridor, the floor beneath my feet feeling freshly waxed.

"You do a fine job of maintaining the place."

"It is good job for me now. Olga, she helped me from her bank to get it." We reached the end of the corridor, and he made the same conductor's gesture toward a door just barely ajar. "Please."

I passed through a coat-closet foyer into a small living room, the furniture that puffy style of the Great Depression, the floor hardwood and as polished as the tiles outside. Instead of his niece's Russian motif, though, Evorov had framed posters on one wall. Of Carnegie Hall, the Metropolitan Opera House, and other New York institutions. On another wall were framed photos, all eight-by-ten black-and-whites, showing a 1940s version of him in a tuxedo with entertainers like Frank Sinatra and Judy Garland.

I said, "You were in show business?"

"I played the concert violin." He gestured again, this time toward a glass cube on top of a mahogany server. Inside the cube were a violin and bow, arranged like museum pieces. "Not for one orchestra only, but for many vocalists."

He walked to the wall of photos. "When I come this country—from Soviet Union, 1932—the boat lands in New York. But first I see the Statue of Liberty, and I tell you this thing: it makes me feel very good, very warm inside. I am then on the dock place, and all I have is my violin, in a leather case with handle. And a man I do not know"—Evorov touched the corner of a photo showing a man I didn't recognize, also in a tuxedo, hugging him at the shoulders, "Teddy Adolph, who is there on the dock place waiting for a relative, he sees me with my case and he says to me, 'You are musician or gangster?' And I do not know what he talks about, but Teddy laughs and tells me if I am good violinist, he can maybe get a job for me. Imagine, I am in this country five minutes, and already yet somebody is helping me with job!"

I nodded at the other photos. "And you got to work with some real celebrities."

Evorov shrugged. "Teddy, he was fine fellow and always with his camera, but he took photographs only of the ones we admire." He touched the corner of another shot. "Sinatra, he was the best male vocalist I ever work with. The quality of the voice, the showmanship on the stage. Nobody else ever come close to him."

Evorov moved to a third photo, a man who was vaguely familiar, with flowing gray hair. "This is Leopold Stokowski, the finest conductor. His hair, like the mane of a lion it was. And the hands? Stokowski, he never used a baton." Evorov made his curious gesture with both hands. "He used his fingers, so long, so graceful, and all his conducting he did with them. You play for him, and it is like watching the butterflies on the first day of spring."

Evorov touched a jaunty face I remembered from movie musicals. "And Maurice Chevalier, you see his straw hat? He made all the orchestra wear a hat like he did—a 'skimmer' is how he called it. Wonderful man, Chevalier, wonderful personality. Was only one problem for me with him. I have to wear the skimmer, and everytime I do an up-bow, I knock my hat funny. So I try to do more the down-bow, because it is the stronger motion, the exclamation point if music is literature."

And one more. "This of me with Judy Garland here, Teddy takes this photo at the old Metropolitan Opera House, where I play for her two weeks. She was the best female vocalist. Garland sang, you could hear the hurt in her voice. The only time I ever cry when I am playing for the public." Evorov's voice suddenly changed. "Mr. Cuddy, you going to make me cry about my Olga?"

"I hope not."

He turned, indicating that we should sit. "Tell me what you here for."

I took a puffy chair across from his. "Your niece didn't come to work at the bank today. I found your messages on her telephone machines there and at her apartment. Have you spoken with her since?"

"Not since I leave for her the messages. She always calls me back, unless she tells me she is going on trip."

"Trip?"

"Like for her bank or the vacation?" A small smile. "Or maybe the weekend with her boyfriend."

"Andrew Dees?"

"Yes. You know him too?"

"Not really. We met once."

"He is fine fellow. Good match for my Olga. I tell her so."

"You like him, then."

"What is not to like? He has his own business, good manners at the table."

"Then you have no idea where your niece might be?"

"No, but I tell you this thing: my Olga, she cares about other people. She does not leave without telling me where she is going, the people at her bank what she is doing." Evorov's mouth twisted a little over his next words. "Her friend there—the one who likes women—you talk to her?"

"Claude Loiselle. Yes."

"And she does not know too where my Olga is?"

"No."

The darkening came over Evorov's face again. "This is very bad, yes?"

"It's hard to say. She's been missing only since some time yesterday afternoon."

"When I am in Soviet Union, it is time of Stalin. You know what that means, Mr. Cuddy? That means missing is gone forever."

"Maybe not here, Mr. Evorov."

A head shake. "Stalin, he shot many people. Millions, even during the Great Patriotic War. I am over here already in the United States, but my friends, they tell me. All our relatives, Olga's and mine, are dead from the war or dead from the shootings or dead from the gulags. Stalin, he killed a whole country of people. Hitler was a devil, that one. But Stalin, he was the devil's devil, yes?"

When I stood to leave, Ivan Evorov made me promise to call if I found his Olga. Then he rose too, but got no farther than the photo showing him with Judy Garland, and I let myself out.

"Lieutenant, you have a minute?"

"Cuddy. Where you been keeping yourself?"

"Out of state, on a case."

I closed the office door behind me. Lieutenant Robert Murphy of Boston Homicide sat at his desk in a building off West Broadway in Southie, a flowered tie snugged tight to the collar button of a starched shirt, the points of the collar held close by a golden stay. The single gold pen from the holder in front of him contrasted, like another piece of jewelry, against the black skin of his hand. Closing a file folder, he replaced the pen in one of the holder's angled sheaths, next to the miniature American flag flying at forty-five degrees in the other.

Murphy said, "Sit."

I arranged one of the green padded armchairs for conversation, then tilted my head toward the folder he'd closed. "Am I taking you away from anything?"

"Just another dead end. Had a shooting in Charlestown last night. Seventeen-year-old Townie, three to the back of the head. Neighborhood's only a mile square, and that's the ninth hit we've had there since Fourth of July. Almost all the folks involved are yours."

Meaning Irish-American. "The victims."

"And the shooters."

"You know who they are?"

"We know it, all right, based on who the victims are. But knowing's one thing, and proving's another. Townie witnesses won't come forward, and we can't arrest, much less convict, on motive alone."

"What about the victims' families?"

"Not a word." Murphy rocked in his chair, the swivel part squeaking like a saddle. "Last night, for example. I'm watching the medical examiner's people finish up, and I spot this one woman, she lost her own son two years ago to this shit, and I ask her how long she's gonna put up with it, with seeing other kids gurneyed off a street corner like her boy was. And you know what she tells me?"

"No, what?"

"She says, 'Hey, if somebody knows who did it, the somebody'll call the family, tell them what happened. Then, the family wants to take out their grief, one of the sons or nephews'll go kill the guy.' "

"The Townie code."

Murphy let his eyelids drop to half-mast. "Every society has one. Makes me wish I worked South Portland instead of South Boston."

"South Portland. As in Maine?"

"Yeah."

"Why?"

"They got Cop Cards up there."

" 'Cop Cards'?"

"Right. Like for baseball or football, except they got these color photos of the people on their police force, from patrol officer to chief. There's information on the backs of them about the cops and their families, and antidrug stuff, and so on. I guess they release one card a week, and the department's swamped with kids on that day, all wanting the newest 'collectible.' "

"You're kidding?"

"On the level." Murphy leaned back, lacing his fingers together behind his head like he was in a hammock on a summer's day. "Can you imagine the union here letting us put information about families and hobbies and shit on a card with the cop's photo on the front?"

"Not in this century."

Murphy used both hands to move his head left to right, a very limited calisthenic. "Most popular cards are supposed to be the K-9 Unit's, account of the dogs. Never cared much for dogs myself, but maybe I should have gone with the Mounted back when I had the chance."

"You on a horse?"

"Hey, don't you remember Hopalong Cassidy and Gene Autry? Besides, it's a good gig. Friend of mine from the academy works the Mounted, he's on eight to four every day. Which really means one hour beginning at eight over by the stable in Jamaica Plain, and one hour beginning at three to take the horses back. So it's actually only a six-hour shift. And this friend says the details you get to work are the best. Events with kids, patrol alongside pedestrians, everybody liking you because of the animal and all. Usually, the only time citizens meet a cop is when they're getting a traffic ticket."

"Yeah, but what about the weather?"

"I admit, I wouldn't fancy the duty come January, but every time I draw a case like last night, I still think about my friend, everybody liking him while he—what's that word, not 'trot' or 'gallop,' but my friend uses it?"

" 'Canter,' maybe?"

"Yeah, 'canter,' that's it. Here I am, trying to break the Townie code, and there's my friend, cantering his way toward thirty years and out."

"Lieutenant?"

"Yeah?"

"I was wondering if maybe you could help me with something?"

"Oh, and here I thought you'd come by just to cheer me up."

"Seriously. You know anybody in Witness Protection?"

"You mean the federal program for cooperating witnesses?"

"If that's what they call them, that's what I mean."

Murphy rocked forward in his chair. "We talking a witness now, or a marshal?"

"The U.S. Marshals run it?"

"Last I heard. 'Office of Enforcement Operations' sticks in my head some place."

"So you do know a marshal in the program."

"One."

"Any chance I can talk with this person?"

"No."

"How come?"

"Cuddy, I don't think they even talk to each other."

"Look, Lieutenant. I'm in a real bind here. I have a female client who's involved with a guy I think's protected by the program, and I need to find her."

"You need to find *her?*"

"Yes. I know who the guy in the program is."

A confused expression. "Wait a minute. You lost your own client?"

"In a manner of speaking."

"Well," leaning back as he drew out the word, "the Witness Protection people aren't what you'd call forthcoming, like I said."

"Any suggestions, then?"

Murphy ran a hand down his tie, smoothing nonexistent wrinkles. "Might be they have a watcher on the one you think's in the program. Might also be you push on the witness, you get the marshals to come out and greet you."

Good tactic, except Olga Evorova had told me expressly not to approach Andrew Dees directly.

I stood up. "Thanks, Lieutenant."

"Just be sure that advice don't come back here with any shit on it."

Turning away, I said, "Do my best."

Behind me, Robert Murphy's voice trailed away. "A palomino. That's what I'd want." His chair squeaked rhythmically. "A big, bad-assed blond one, like Roy Rogers used to have, you know?"

16

I used a pay phone on West Broadway across from the Homicide Unit to dial my answering service. Nothing from Nancy, but then I didn't expect she'd have heard from her doctor as yet, either. The service operator also said no log entry showed for Olga Evorova, but Claude Loiselle was already on record with "Call me if you've learned anything." Primo Zuppone had left three messages, essentially, "As soon as you get back from out-of-state, I need to introduce you to some friends of mine." At least he'd come up with a good dodge to hold off his Milwaukee people.

Hanging up the phone, I went to a coffeeshop for lunch and tried to piece together what I knew so far. On Tuesday, Olga Evorova appears in my office, wanting a confidential investigation of her virtual fiancé, Andrew Dees. His past seems an empty cupboard, and her closest friend, Claude Loiselle, is suspicious of him. I think of an indirect way to interview Dees' neighbors at Plymouth Willows about him on Wednesday, but to make the cover story better, I first see Boyce Hendrix at the management company for the complex. I'm barely back to my office from the South Shore that afternoon when two sluggers come calling by the dumpster, advising me to stay away from both the company and the complex. At the University of Central Vermont on Thursday, I discover Evorova's boyfriend isn't who he claims to be, while Primo Zuppone was finding out the man's real identity. Now it's Friday afternoon, my client and her lover both unreachable in a way that scares Loiselle and Uncle Ivan, neither of whom has heard boo from Evorova for almost twenty hours.

And I've left Primo—the guy trying to do me a favor by showing the photo of "Andrew Dees" to people who might recognize him—hanging out to dry with his Milwaukee friends. Who, having flown into Logan the night before, probably aren't by now in the best of moods.

It seemed to me there were two ways to play it. One was to violate Olga Evorova's express instruction and confront Dees, as Lieutenant Murphy suggested. The other was to go innocently back to my condo or office, pretend to have just picked up Primo's many messages, and call him on his car phone, in which case the play might be taken away from me.

Leaving half my sandwich untouched, I came to a decision, choosing the office over the condo since I had less there to break.

Sitting behind my desk, as ready as possible, I timed it. Five minutes and thirty-five seconds after Primo rang off on the car phone, the three of them came through my pebbled-glass door. Without knocking first.

Zuppone was the point man, looking greatly relieved to see me actually there before he put the poker face back on and motioned the other two into the room. The balding guy walked in second, single-breasted coat unbuttoned, watching me and nodding once, his expression the one you'd wear taking the space next to a stranger on the bus. The younger man brought up the rear, looking all around my office without even glancing at me. His double-breasted suit was buttoned, which at least told me the action would come from the balding guy, if any action there'd be.

Still not looking in my direction, the younger one said, "City's a fucking shithole compared to Milwaukee, but cooling my fucking heels outside your apartment building, I'da thought the office here'd have a little more class."

The flat, midwestern "A" was lodged in his voice and pitched it a bit high, as though he were twenty pounds lighter. I said, "This part of the country, we tend to decorate down to the clientele."

Zuppone said, "Hey-ey-ey, everybody, let's not get off on the wrong foot here, huh? How about I make some introductions?"

The younger man just looked at him, still ignoring me, and moved to one of the two client chairs in front of my desk, rearranging the angle of it so that he'd be focusing past me toward the Statehouse dome. The balding guy positioned himself at the wall, shoulders against it, hands at his side, watching me and nothing else.

Primo laid a palm lightly on the back of the younger man's chair. "Rick Ianella, John Cuddy."

Nobody made to shake hands.

Sitting down next to Ianella, Zuppone thumbed toward the balding guy. "Coco Cocozzo."

To Cocozzo, I said, "Sorry there's only the two chairs."

"I want one, I can always just take yours."

Same accent, but deeper voice. Primo jumped in with, "So, Cuddy, you're back from out-of-state, and you got in touch. That's good. These gentlemen flew in last night, and they need some information."

I looked from Ianella to Cocozzo and back again.

The younger guy said, "*Now*, dickhead."

"What's the matter, Rick, you leave your manners on the plane?"

Zuppone winced.

Ianella's face grew mottled, the eyebrow with the scar through it twitching, as though maybe some nerve damage went along with the scar. Within seconds, his grip on the arm chair was so tight, you could see the man shaking and hear the wood creaking. "Now you listen, you little piece a shit, and you listen good. My father's doing a long fucking stretch, time that's gonna probably kill him, account of a fucking bean counter saved his own ass by selling us out to the fucking feds. DiRienzi wasn't family, but my father treated him that way. And my father gets rewarded not by loyalty, but fucking betrayal. So, we're here in this filthy fucking city, and it's just as easy to do two as one."

"Not necessarily."

Ianella looked to Cocozzo, but the balding man just kept watching me, which seemed to bother Junior enough to turn back in my direction. "All right, dickhead, where's DiRienzi?"

"I don't know."

"The fuck does that mean—'I don't know'? Primo here showed us the picture you took of him."

"I'm going to tell you some things, Rick. You're patient, I'll tell you some more."

Zuppone closed his eyes for a moment. Cocozzo, so far as I could tell, came from a species that didn't need to blink.

Ianella crossed his arms, bunching the fabric of the suit jacket. "Just start talking, dickhead, and don't fucking stop."

I said, "A woman asked me to look into the background of her boyfriend. I started to, finding out he wasn't what he seemed. I gave her a hint of that, and she seems to have disappeared."

Junior coughed impatiently. "Look, I don't give a shit about—"

I took a little leap. "And your bookkeeper seems to be gone, too."

Ianella stopped, the eyebrow twitching again. "Gone where?"

"Like I said before, I don't know."

"The fuck you mean, you don't know."

Old ground. "I was out of state, Rick, checking on this guy's supposed education for my client. After learning he wasn't who he claimed to be, I called her long-distance, and she said, 'Thanks, don't do anything more.' Now I'm starting to think that she contacted her boyfriend and something happened. I don't know what, and if they're really gone, I don't know where."

Cocozzo, still watching me from the wall, said, "She tells you to butt out, how come you know she's taken off somewhere?"

Damned sharp question, since it was Zuppone's information on the ride to the airport about who Dees really was that prompted me to try contacting her again. I thought Primo was holding his breath.

"One of her friends called me," I said. "Worried about her."

Cocozzo nodded. "And how did you know DiRienzi was a bookkeeper?"

"What?"

The balding man inched his right hand a little closer to his beltline. "A minute ago, you said 'And your bookkeeper seems to be gone too.' How'd you know what DiRienzi was to us?"

I looked at Cocozzo, then to Ianella. "Rick here used the word 'bean counter.' That's what makes me think bookkeeper or accountant."

Junior uncrossed his arms, waving off the cross-examination. "Look, 'bookkeeper,' 'bean counter,' whatever the fuck he was, that's none of your concern, dickhead, you hear what I'm saying to you? What your concern is, you had this fucking Judas, and now you say you can't find him, am I right?"

"That's right."

"Well, then, here's what you're gonna do for us. You're gonna get up from behind your shit-eating desk here, and out of this shithole of an office, and you're not gonna sleep till you find him. And when you do, you're gonna sit the fuck on him till we get there. I got to clarify any of that for you?"

"Maybe the part about why you think my office is a shithole."

The mottled face, with the twitching now more like jumping jacks and the grip that set the chair to groaning. "Coco, how's about you clarify that for dickhead here."

Cocozzo still hadn't taken his eyes off me. "Not a good idea, Boss."

Ianella acted as if he'd never heard the phrase before. "What the fuck are you talking about?"

The balding man said, "I'm ninety percent sure he's holding a piece in his lap."

"What?"

Cocozzo sighed just a little, like he'd had to explain a lot to the younger man over the years. "His hands, Boss."

"His hands?"

"Yeah. We been here ten, fifteen minutes, talking away. You seen his hands yet?"

"No." Junior watched me now too. "No, I haven't, now that you mention it. Show us your hands, shit-for-brains."

"Uh-unh."

"And what if I stand up and come over and look for myself?"

I said, "Then you'd maybe come between Coco there and me, in which case he's going to draw whatever he's got under his coat, and I'm going to have to shoot him."

"Shoot Coco?" said Junior.

"Yeah. I don't have to worry about you, Rick, because you're having him do the carrying."

Ianella looked at Zuppone. "The fuck you letting happen here?"

"Hey-ey-ey, Mr. Ianella—"

The younger man cuffed Primo, a heel of the hand to the jaw. Junior was quick, but, in my opinion, not very smart for doing it.

Zuppone struggled to control himself. "Mr. Ianella, please—"

Another cuff.

"Mr.—"

And another.

I saw Primo's fist get ready to come up, and I think Cocozzo saw it too, because the balding man said, "Boss," but not as a question or for permission to speak.

Ianella turned to him. "What?"

"I got a different idea. What say we have Primo talk to this guy some more while you and me go out, buy a capuccino or something, wait by the car?"

"You mean just walk the fuck out, after all the shit this dickhead's been giving us?"

Again patiently. "Boss, we want to find DiRienzi, but this ain't our turf. We'd be spending our time asking for directions, spinning our wheels, am I right? We let Primo and Cuddy here handle it for us, we're ahead of the game and back home sooner, with that rat's head on a platter."

Ianella didn't like it, but I was getting the impression that Cocozzo had been right in the past about a lot of things, and somebody, maybe the patriarch, had made Junior recognize it.

The scarred eyebrow seemed to resolve itself as the younger man rose, unbuttoning his own suit jacket. I tensed, but all Ianella did was pick up my chair and use it as a battering ram, legs first, on the door side of Cocozzo's wall. Once, twice, and a third time, the legs penetrating the fiberboard, sending dust into the air and chips of paint to the floor. A series of three, like his cuffing Primo, and a dozen jagged holes.

Junior dropped the chair so that it was standing on its feet. Then he shrugged his shoulders to get the suit jacket to drape correctly and buttoned up. "Next time, dickhead, it won't be your wall."

Cocozzo waited until the younger man was into the hall before backing up and through the door himself, closing it behind them.

Zuppone had watched all this without a word. Waiting a count of five after they left, he turned back to me. "Thanks for returning my calls, you stupid fuck."

"Look at it this way, Primo, things could be worse."

"How?"

"Well, instead of just the one section of fiberboard there, I might have to replace—"

"I don't mean about your fucking wall, Cuddy." Zuppone squared himself in the client's chair. "You got to understand something. My organization owes their organization, only it's more personal than that. We owe them for a favor they did us when we fucking needed one bad. Now they think we can, like, reciprocate, get me? And it sure looks like we can, and should, but you're playing the turd in the soup."

"Primo, I told you before, I'm not setting up this DiRienzi for those guys to kill."

"The fuck do you care, they whack him or not? The fucking guy's a rat. What's he to you?"

"Nothing. But I'm not going to be the reason they find him if I can help it. And besides, it's more complicated now."

"Complicated how?"

"My client's missing."

"On the level?" said Zuppone.

"Yes."

"That wasn't just some bullshit con you were running to stall us?"

"No. Ever since I told her that the boyfriend wasn't checking out, nobody's heard from her, and several people should have."

Primo looked down at the floor. "I guess I gotta take your word on that."

"It's the truth."

"And that's the complication."

"If she and this DiRienzi are together somewhere."

Zuppone's head snapped back up. "What, you're worried about us hitting the woman too?"

"Yes."

"I told you once, Cuddy, we don't go off on a drive-by, spray some fucking street corner with an Uzi like these kid gangs. We do a hit, it's specific."

"Primo, why do you suppose Junior there came on this trip?"

" 'Junior.' That's all you need to call—"

"Cocozzo's the executioner type, Rick's here without a gun, but when it comes to happen, I think I can picture the son avenging his father. That way on visiting day, he can go out to the prison, say to the old man, 'Hey, Poppa, I'm the one did the Judas for you. Tell him, Coco.' "

Zuppone just shrugged.

"Primo, if somebody anonymous was tapped to pull the trigger on DiRienzi, then I can see my client being okay. How's she going to identify some guy from Vegas or St. Louis, brought in for one specific contract? But Junior does the hit, and my client's anywhere near DiRienzi at the time, Cocozzo has enough brains not to leave a witness behind who can finger a member of the family."

Zuppone tsked his tongue off the roof of his mouth. "Cuddy, I won't lie to you. Yeah, she'd be cooked too. And

I can understand why you're trying to protect her. No shit, I do. But that's not the problem."

"It is from my end."

"No. No, you and me are the problem. I'm sitting in a fucking frying pan, and Rick Ianella's turning up the heat. And it's not even his fucking fault, really, on account of he's just trying to do the right thing. You're the one gave me the bookkeeper's picture, and now you're the one's got to come through somehow."

"After the way Junior treated you?"

Zuppone flicked his head, shaking something off. "Don't bring that up, okay?"

"Primo—"

"Look, the guy's under a lot of pressure. His father's in the fucking slam, and he sees us as the way to avenge the gentleman, and instead you play Lone fucking Ranger with him. What's the guy supposed to do?"

"Not knock you around in front of me."

"Nobody knocks me around, Cuddy."

"You really believe this Ianella is worth helping?"

"That's not my call. And it's not yours, either. I told you this once already, I'm not gonna say it again. The organization's been good to me. They took me in and they gave me a chance and I grew into it. Maybe with you it was the Army. Or your girlfriend there, her law school. I don't know, maybe for each person it's something different. But I do know it's all the same too. You got to be loyal to the thing that made you what you are, Cuddy. And you got to remember that about me."

"And vice-versa."

Zuppone blew out a breath. "All right, so where does that leave us?"

"How long can you stall your guests?"

"My guests." Primo shook his head. "The fuck, you saw

1 9 8

them. How long you think it'll be before they decide talking and wall-banging ain't working out too good?"

"What kind of control does Cocozzo really have over Junior?"

"I wish you wouldn't call him that."

"Sorry."

"I mean, you get used to saying an insulting nickname, it'll pop out some time, and then we'll see blood whether we had to or not. I remember this one guy from the neighborhood, he was big, huge even, but you took a leak next to him, you could tell he had this little tiny dick. Not that you'd exactly be *looking* at it, you know, but you'd just kind of notice it. And another guy kept referring to this huge guy as—"

"Primo, you're right. How much control?"

"What? Coco over Jun—Jesus Christ, now you got me doing it."

"I said I was sorry."

"Cuddy, if this ever—"

"Primo, how much control?"

The head tick-tocked. "About what you saw today, if I was betting on it. Ianella's into the grand gesture. You know, like putting the fear of God into that hotel clerk out in Milwaukee, get me my suite there, or your chair thing here. Coco's more like me, a 'situation guy.' He can handle his boss, but only up to a point, account of Ianella's still the boss, and they both got to go back home sometime."

Probably a fair assessment. "Okay. Do your best to keep them occupied, and I'll call you as soon as I can."

"With what?"

"With what I can do."

"Cuddy, let me tell you something, you don't already know it. I'm in the frying pan, like I said. These people, they start believing they can't trust me, they're gonna put you in the fire. They ain't gonna care you got friends on the cops, or your girlfriend's a DA. And there ain't gonna be a fucking thing I can do about it."

Primo Zuppone stood and left me. I thought he was pretty cool not to have asked whether I really had a gun in my lap.

17

After waiting five minutes, I tried Olga Evorova at her condo. Just the tape machine. Then I called her at the bank. The formal female secretary said Ms. Evorova was "in conference." I asked for another extension. When I gave my name to the brusque male voice, Craig said, "One moment," as though he'd been instructed to put me right through.

"Claude Loiselle."

"This is John Cuddy. I asked for Olga first and got the 'in conference' answer."

"That's just the party line. Nobody's heard from her." Loiselle hesitated, then said, "I take it you haven't learned anything either?"

"Not that helps us find Olga."

"Well, I feel small and weak just sitting here while my friend may be in trouble."

"Believe me, I know what you mean."

"Can't we file a missing-persons report or something?"

"Olga hasn't been missing very long by police standards. Also, there's no indication she didn't go off on her own."

"Oh, for God's sake! You have to believe Andrew Dees has something to do with this."

"He probably does, Claude. But my client told me not to horn in on him directly."

"An observation?"

Loiselle was using the command voice. I said, "Go ahead."

"Maybe it's about time you stopped worrying about your client's wishes and started worrying about your client's welfare."

The phone went dead in my hand.

Setting the receiver back in its cradle, I thought about what Claude Loiselle had just said. Then I thought about Primo trying to stall the Milwaukee boys. Finally I thought about what Robert Murphy had suggested.

Client's wishes, client's welfare. Maybe Loiselle was right.

Calling the DA's office, I drew the secretary who liked to tell me Nancy was still on trial. I left a message that I'd see her in South Boston that night.

Then I locked up and went down to the Prelude.

Driving south along Route 3, the moonroof was open to the warm October air, the rose in its plastic wrapper now wedged between the passenger-side seat and door. I left the highway several exits short of Plymouth Mills, just to see if a Lincoln Continental or other car followed me. None did.

Reaching Main Street in the town center, I cruised slowly past the photocopy shop. No sign of the brown Toyota Corolla I'd seen Dees using, and inside there was only Filomena, talking to a customer.

Continuing on, I parked near The Tides. From the pub's front door, the rear bar seemed nearly filled with late-afternoon, TGIFing business people. As I moved up to it, two fiftyish guys in sports jackets holding what looked like scotch/rocks were lamenting the legislature's decision to ban happy hours as a way of protecting lives on the roads.

The ban had gone into effect three years earlier.

Then one of them brought up baseball. "Hey, you get to Camden Yards last summer before the strike?"

"No. The company had me in Wichita till a couple of weeks ago."

"Man, you missed something. Baltimore really done itself proud there."

"That's what I heard."

"And not just the ballpark, either. The food you can get, Boog Powell's Barbecue, Tom Matte's Ribs—"

"Matte?" said the second guy. "He played for the old Colts, not the Orioles."

"Right, right. Remember the season both Unitas and Morrall went down, and Matte had to switch from halfback to quarterback, and they *still* won?"

"Like it was yesterday. But Matte played *foot*-ball, not *base*-ball. What's his food doing at Camden Yards?"

"Baltimore's a good city," said the first guy, taking a bite of the scotch. "They don't discriminate."

Just then, a younger man shifted toward a woman holding a beer bottle with a lime section in it, and I could see Edie, wearing that same frilly white blouse, her lower lip curled under as she concentrated on drawing somebody a Harpoon from the tap. I moved in past the new couple and said hello to her.

She glanced up once from the frosted mug in her hand, but without smiling. "You want a drink, it'll be a while. I'm kind of backed up."

"I'll pass for now. Thanks again for your directions to Plymouth Willows."

"Don't mention it."

No expression on the face or inflection in the voice. "I talked with Andrew Dees, by the way."

Edie topped off the draft. Without looking at me, "Was he any help to you?"

"Some. You seen him around today?"

"No. Try the photocopy shop."

I said, "You know, if I did something last time to—"

Edie paused with the draft long enough to fix me with hard-set eyes. "Wasn't you. Just a bad memory that got stirred up." Two different patrons called out to her by name. "Look, it's busy, and I have to go."

I watched her carry the mug down the bar, sloshing a little onto her shaking hand.

Filomena was behind the counter, her back to me when I came in the door. As she turned, the "May I help you?" smile seemed to die on her face.

I said, "I'm still looking for Mr. Dees. John Cuddy?"

The Asian features stayed somber. "I remember you."

"And you're Fi, right?" I grinned at her. "Short for Filomena."

"You upset Andrew very much."

"Not intentionally. I think you'll remember that too."

Filomena didn't reply.

I said, "I'd really like to speak with him."

"He's not here."

I looked down to the telephone she'd used on my first visit. No buttons were lit. "Any idea how I can reach him?"

Filomena chewed on the inside of her cheek. "What's going on?"

"Like I told Mr. Dees the last—"

"I mean, what's *really* going on?" in a rising voice. "You upset Andrew more than I've ever seen, and he stayed that way until . . ."

"Until when, Fi?"

More chewing on the cheek. "I wish I knew whether to trust you."

"I don't know what I can say to persuade you. Trust is something you feel. Or don't feel."

Finally the gracious smile. "You remind me of my husband, a little."

"The one from the service, that you met in the Philippines."

Filomena nodded. "He says I'm crazy, but Andrew's been so nice to me for so long, I can't just leave the place closed up."

"What do you mean?"

"I mean I haven't seen Andrew since noontime yesterday. I had to ferry the kids around early this morning, but when I got here, instead of relieving him, it didn't look as though the place had been opened up yet." She gestured in different directions. "The cash register, the answering machine, even the lights."

"Any messages on the machine?"

"Just a couple of the regulars, asking if we could do rush orders or special jobs—the usual, you know? But then the same thing today—follow-up calls, like Andrew hadn't been here yesterday afternoon? And a couple other customers stopped in during the last few hours, asking if he was sick or something because they came by earlier and we looked closed up."

"You tried calling him?"

"At home, you mean?"

"Yes."

"I tried, but no answer." Filomena gestured again, this time hopelessly.

"Tell you what," I said. "How about if I take a run over to Plymouth Willows, see if I can get anything from his neighbors?"

The gracious smile. "Thanks."

"And by the way, I don't think you're crazy."

"Huh?"

"For trying to help Mr. Dees here."

The smile got a little braver. "I'll tell my husband."

Heading south on Main Street, I crossed over the bridge, making the first right after the scenic overlook on the left. The sign Paulie Fogerty had been replacing now hung from its post at the front driveway for Plymouth Willows, and I turned into it.

Cruising the access road, I checked the clusters of townhouses in each leaf of the shamrock circuit. No brown Corolla hatchback, no orange Porsche 911. I did pass Fogerty near the tennis courts, still wearing the faded green maintenance outfit. He was on his hands and knees, carefully weeding around a lightpole. The rest of the grounds looked as good as they had two days earlier.

Parking in front of the yellow-trimmed cluster, I went up the path to the townhouse second from the end and pushed the buzzer over DEES. I heard the "bong" inside, but nobody came to the door. I tried again. Still nothing.

I considered the possibility of slipping around back and forcing the sliding glass door, but I didn't want to surprise a neighbor lounging on his or her rear deck in the late afternoon sunshine. I also thought I might get a little more mileage from my cover story, maybe enough to find out when the last time was that anybody had seen Andrew Dees.

"Yes?"

The man standing behind the opened door of the last unit on the left was Steven Stepanian, who looked even more like his wife in real life than he had in the photo she'd shown me. Tall and lanky, he wore gray slacks and a conservative tie with a short-sleeved dress shirt that revealed long, hairy forearms.

"Mr. Stepanian, my name's John Cuddy. I spoke with your wife on Wednesday?"

A brooding expression, and I remembered thinking from the portrait that he might not smile much. "Well, she's upstairs getting dressed. We're due at a school committee meeting shortly."

"This won't take long, and maybe you can help me."

Stepanian seemed to weigh something, then said, "All right, but just a few minutes."

He let me in, then closed the front door and moved to the living room. "Dear?"

A muted voice from the second level. "Almost ready, Steven."

"There's a Mr. Cuddy here to see you?"

"Oh, I'll be right down."

Stepanian turned, motioning toward one of the plushy chairs. I sank deeply into it, the thing nearly swallowing me again.

He perched on the matching sofa, much as his wife had done on my first visit. "What's this all about?"

"I'm talking to people in the complex about the Hendrix Management Company."

"Oh, yes. Lana mentioned that somebody had been doing a survey. You're representing another condo association, right?"

"That's right."

"Well, I'm sure Lana told you everything Wednesday that I could now. She's really the expert on Plymouth Willows."

Stepanian nearly smiled. A small beginning.

"Actually, I was hoping you might be able to tell me if you'd seen Andrew Dees lately."

"Andrew?"

"Yes. He's the only neighbor in this cluster that I haven't been able to interview, and I like to be thorough."

The brooding expression returned. "Well, I'm—"

"Hello, Mr. Cuddy." Lana Stepanian came down the steps

in a light wool dress, wearing one-inch heels instead of flats tonight. "I didn't expect to see you again."

I stood as her husband said, "Dear, Mr. Cuddy wants to see Andrew Dees about his survey."

Reaching the living room level, she looked from him to me. "You didn't catch him the last time?"

"Afraid not."

"Oh, that's too bad. I'm not sure when he'll be back."

"Back?"

"Yes." She looked to her husband again. "Didn't Steven tell you?"

"Lana, do you really think it's appropriate?"

I said, "Is what appropriate?"

"Oh." She seemed to concentrate. "I think it'd be all right. We saw Andrew—actually, Steven you're the one who really noticed him doing it."

I turned toward the sofa. "Noticed him doing what?"

Stepanian shrugged. "I was here in the living room last night, just turning out the lights on my way to bed, when I saw Andrew down by the curb, loading some suitcases into a car."

"Suitcases? Plural?"

"Well, some sort of luggage, but, yes, more than one piece."

"And you said *a* car, not *his* car?"

"Yes. Andrew drives a Toyota. This was a Porsche. Yellow or orange, quite flashy."

Olga's. "About what time was this?"

"Time? Oh, I don't know. Maybe eight, eight-fifteen?"

"And you go to bed that early?"

Lana Stepanian said, "We read to each other sometimes. It's very soothing and helps us fall asleep."

She said it in the neutral way I'd picked up before, no double meaning or sarcasm in her voice.

I looked to Steven. "Was Dees alone?"

He cocked his head, just like Lana had done when I'd asked her odd questions from my "survey" form. "I didn't see anyone else, but we did—"

"Steven?"

Stepanian stopped. His wife said, "Don't you think that might be . . . gossiping?"

"You're right, dear." He turned to me. "Let's just say we heard some loud voices through the wall last night."

"Before you saw Dees at his car."

"Yes."

"Could you tell if it was a man or a woman?"

"Andrew and a woman, I think."

"Mr. Cuddy," said Lana Stepanian in her neutral voice, "what possible difference could this make to your client?"

She had a point. "Probably none. It just seems a little strange, don't you think?"

"Well, perhaps. But it *is* Andrew's business, after all."

Steven Stepanian checked his watch. "Mr. Cuddy, we really have to go."

"Sure. Sorry to have kept you."

"That's all right. Good luck with the survey."

Still never smiling, he ushered me to the door.

From the old print couch, the gravelly voice said, "You're surprised I'm downstairs, right?"

"A little. Last time I was here—"

"You had to climb up to my bedroom. Well, I may feel like dogshit afterwards, but," Norman Elmendorf ticked the nail of an index finger off the aluminum braces leaning against his couch, "these things let me move around a little. Not great, but enough to get by while Kira's out."

I'd had to shunt some magazines off the chair across from him. The bottle—or more likely, another bottle—of Jim Beam rested on the floor, next to the rubber feet of the braces. "Will she be gone long?"

"Didn't say."

"How are things going with the VA?"

"You kidding? You were only here two, three days ago? The VA, it's like a glacier. Hasn't moved an inch in that kind of time." Elmendorf squinted at me. "What's the matter, you didn't find out what your people needed from what we told you before?"

"Some, but not enough. I never got the chance to talk with Andrew Dees."

"Dees? Huh." The expression came out as a laugh. "I think he's got lady trouble."

I stopped. "I thought you told me on Wednesday that you barely knew him?"

"That's right. But he had his back door—the sliding-glass thing?—or something open last night, because I could hear him and her going at it through my bedroom window, even with the Robinettes' unit in between us."

"An argument?"

"Yeah. Dees yelling and her half-apologizing and half-yelling back. It was a doozy, whatever the hell they were getting into."

"What time was this?"

"I don't know. Around eight, maybe?"

Pretty much what the Stepanians had said. "Could you tell what they were fighting about?"

"Not really. Just caught a couple of things, like Dees saying, 'I can't believe you hired him,' and her saying, 'What was I supposed to do?' "

"Anything else?"

"Not that comes to mind. I was kind of trying to figure them out, when all of a sudden it stopped, like they quit, or at least closed the door."

"The glass one."

"Or a window. Whatever I was hearing them through.

But it sounded to me in my bedroom like they were on the first floor of his place."

"You didn't happen to see an orange Porsche parked outside here, did you?"

"What, last night?"

"Yes."

"No, no, I didn't. But to be honest, I wasn't downstairs at all yesterday." Then Elmendorf squinted at me again. "What the hell does an orange Porsche have to do with anything?"

"Just a thought."

When the door to the Robinette unit opened, I could hear the soft strains of an R&B ballad in the background, a male vocalist whose voice I recognized but whose name I couldn't recall. James Robinette wore just baggy basketball shorts, no socks, shoes, or even a shirt. His upper body had that drawn and quartered look of the undeveloped athlete.

Frowning, he said, "What do you want?"

Cooler than the greeting I'd gotten my first time. "I wonder if we could talk a minute?"

"Mom's not here."

"That's okay. Maybe you can help me."

"Can't." Robinette inclined his head toward the living room behind him. "Busy."

"Won't take long."

"It's taken long enough, man."

He started to close the door on me. I put my foot against it, which stopped both the door and him.

Robinette said, "Yo, man, why you hassling with me?"

Less of the preppy, more of the street. "I'm not. I just need the answers to a few questions about last night."

"Last night?"

"Yes. Were you here?"

"No way. Had a band thing. 'Fall Concert,' over at Tabor."

"What time did you leave Plymouth Willows for the school?"

"I don't know. Had to be there by eight, so maybe a little after seven."

"And when did you get home?"

"Why you want to know all this, man?"

"What harm can it do to tell me?"

Robinette held up his hands. "Oh, who cares? Maybe eleven, eleven-thirty?"

"Kind of late for a band concert."

A roll of the eyes. "Yo, man, we went out with some of the other kids and their folks afterwards, all right?"

"We?"

"My mom and me. What difference does it make?"

"You happen to see an orange Porsche parked outside?"

Robinette stopped, grew determined. "No."

"You know who it belongs to?"

"I didn't see the car, man, how am I supposed to know who owns it?"

"Thought maybe you might have seen it before."

"Well, you thought wrong. You want to leave now?"

I nodded slowly. "Yeah. I think I have someplace else to go."

In the gathering dark, I went back to the Prelude and drove toward the tennis courts. No Paulie Fogerty, but then I noticed that the door to his little prefab house seemed to be open.

Getting out of my car, I was almost to the doorway when Fogerty came through it. He blinked, trembling a bit, first from surprise, then maybe from trying to place me.

"Hi, Paulie."

"Hi." The hang-jaw smile. "Did you see Mr. Eh-men-dor?"

"Yes."

"He show you how to use your camera right?"

"We talked about it. Can I talk to you?"

A blink. "We *are* talking."

"Right. Can we go inside?"

Another blink with the nod. Then he turned and I followed him into the small living room.

There was a La-Z-Boy recliner in front of the television set, a TV tray to the side of the recliner. Animal crackers were scattered on the tray, which also held a glass of milk. Videos of some Disney animated features lay jumbled next to the VCR, a cable box on top of the television itself. From hooks on the wall hung gardening equipment, like his rake, hedge clippers, and so on. Next to the gardening gear was a snow shovel, an ice scraper, and a few more winter-weather tools.

No pictures or photos, though, and no other furniture in the room, either. "Looks comfortable, Paulie."

"Yeah." Fogerty went toward the recliner, then stopped. "Wait." He bustled into another room, I assumed the bedroom. I could see a second door, probably for a bath. The galley kitchen was spotless.

Fogerty came back with a gray, metal folding chair, opening it for me. I thanked him and sat down as he took the recliner and leaned it back to the halfway position.

Then he seemed to notice the glass on his tray and started to get up. "You want some milk?"

"No, thanks."

"You sure? I got more, and it's good milk."

"No, really." I leaned forward in the chair, my elbows on my knees. "Paulie, I was wondering if you were around here last night."

"I'm around every night."

"What time did you go to bed?"

"I don't know. After dinner, I think about the tools for a while, so I know what I'm gonna do tomorrow. Then I watch TV till I get sleepy."

"But you worked on the grounds before that."

A blink. "The grounds?"

"Around the complex here?"

"Oh, yeah. I'm the super. I work for Mr. Hend'ix."

"When you were working, did you see Mr. Dees?"

A blink and a nod. "I see him all the time."

"Did you see him last night?"

Just the blink. "I don't know."

"Did you see him loading anything into a car?"

"He has a lot of papers. I help him sometimes."

I recalled Dees as I'd first seen him, carrying a box and paperwork while coming down the path of his unit. "How about suitcases?"

"No. I help him with his papers. Boxes, sometimes."

"Paulie, I mean, did you see Mr. Dees putting any suitcases in a car?"

"No. I help him with his papers in boxes."

"How about an orange car?"

The hang-jaw smile. "The nice lady."

I made myself slow down. "Yes, the nice lady. Did she come to visit Mr. Dees?"

"She comes to see him a lot."

"How about last night, Paulie?"

"Last night?"

"Yes. Did you see her last night?"

The blink. "I don't know, but she's nice. I helped her too."

"Helped her how?"

"She had a lot of bags one time, from the store. She couldn't carry them all, so I helped her."

"And she drove an orange car."

A blink and a nod. "The only orange car I ever saw."

"Did you see the car last night?"

Blink. "I don't know."

Dead end. "Paulie, how did the nice lady get into Mr. Dees' house?"

"Unit."

"I'm sorry?"

"Unit. Mr. Dees has a unit, just like Mr. Eh-men-dor and everybody. I have the house." He looked around proudly.

"Unit, right. How did the nice lady get in?"

A blink and a nod. It was hypnotic after a while. "She had a key."

I smiled. "Do you have a key too?"

"No. I'm the super. I don't need a key for the trees and the grass and the tennis courts and the—"

"Right, Paulie. Do you know if anybody else has a key to the unit Mr. Dees lives in?"

"Mr. Hend'ix. I work for him." The hang-jaw smile. "I'm the super."

I nodded this time, Paulie Fogerty gazing at me happily, molded to his chair like a seal on a rock in the sunshine.

Leaving the prefab house, I drove to the front of the complex, hoping the brown Toyota or the orange Porsche would magically appear by the yellow-trimmed cluster. Neither did.

Parking farther along the leaf-shaped access road in front of another quartet of townhouses, I walked back toward the Stepanians' door. Looking around quickly and seeing nobody, I went behind their unit. At the rear deck, I lifted a long, stiff-tined fork from their barbecue, hoping the committee meeting would keep them away for an hour or so more.

At the next deck, I climbed over the low railing belonging to Andrew Dees—or Alfonso DiRienzi, take your pick. A set of drapes was drawn across the inside of the glass door, only darkness on the floor beneath the hems. Using the fork as a jimmy, I worked on the latch for a good three minutes, breaking a sweat during the last thirty seconds. Finally a combination of jab, shimmy, and yank did the job. I eased the door only a foot or so along its track, just enough to get me in and past the drapes.

That's when something hit me from the side, behind the left ear, and I went down like snow sliding off a pitched roof.

18

They didn't bother with a blindfold, but then again, I didn't wake up until they were lifting me by the shoulders from the floor of a car's backseat. It was full dark now, and all I saw except for the rear fender and black-walled tire was a panel of light-colored bricks rising off the macadam. Just before I was part carried, part dragged through a metal door, I did catch the sugary scent of baking ovens, a smell that made me want to gag.

"Come on, asshole," said a gruff voice to my left. I recognized the voice as the man behind it grunted, him and his partner to my right hauling me up the first of many steps. We were under a weak yellowish light, the kind used on fire stairs. After they pushed and pulled me the half-flight to a landing, I raised my throbbing head enough to see the faces of the two burly guys who'd worked me over behind my office building, the one fine-featured, the other coarse. Neither had his hair slicked back anymore, and they were wearing dark pants and crewneck sweaters now. The peculiar lighting probably helped, aging Coarse twenty or so years and bringing back why Chief Pete Braverman up in Vermont had seemed so familiar.

After a second half-flight, Fine supported me while Coarse unlocked a door that led to a small, windowless room with another door on the opposite wall. There were three wooden chairs around a rectangular table big enough for a fourth. I was dumped into one of the chairs, Fine sitting catercorner from me, Coarse standing over and behind me. Rubbing my skull only made the throbbing worse, so I leaned back, my empty holster collapsing against my right hip.

Fine said, "You didn't take our advice so good, asshole."

From above, Coarse's voice. "Bad fucking idea not to."

Fine started to say, "You know what happens"—when I interrupted him with, "Get Hendrix up here."

Fine stopped and shot a look over me, toward Coarse.

I said, "When we were outside, I smelled the ovens from the bakery. We're on the second floor of the mall building in Marshfield, just above Hendrix Management. Now bring him up here."

Coarse slapped the back of my head with the palm of his hand. "You're in no position to—"

"You guys are deputy U.S. Marshals, and, speaking as a taxpayer, I'm getting pretty sick of my federal employees playing rope-a-dope with me."

Fine worked his mouth, nothing coming out.

I stared at him. *"Capisce?"*

Over my shoulder, Fine said, "Keep him here," and then went out through the door we hadn't used.

After it closed behind him, I said conversationally, "So, is Chief Braverman your father, your uncle, or what?"

No response from Coarse.

Twenty seconds later, the door Fine went through opened, and Hendrix came in alone, eyes blazing, voice no longer mellow. "Just who the hell do you think you are?"

I said, "That was going to be my question. I'd like to see some identification."

Hendrix glared up behind me, then got madder when Coarse or Braverman or whatever his name was did nothing. "Look, Cuddy, we've got you for breaking and ent—"

"Oh, please. You civil servants have fucked the duck on this from square one. And right now the only question is how badly you're going to suffer for it."

Hendrix glared some more, but without the fire he'd had coming through the door. Sitting in Fine's chair, he said, "What are you talking about?"

"I'm talking about what you or your boss decided to do here. On Wednesday, I came around to the office downstairs, asking about your operation on behalf of another condo complex."

"Which was total bullshit."

"Doesn't matter, Boyce. What matters is that you didn't even try to close the sale when you should have. If anything, the message was, 'Hey, we sell lemons, so try another car lot.' "

"What difference does that make?"

"It made me go down to Plymouth Willows with more questions than I'd have had already."

"Cuddy, just what is your stake in this?"

"Let me finish. After I knock on some doors at the complex, one Andrew Dees, who I hadn't yet seen, seems to know about me."

Hendrix looked confused. "Dees? Yeah, I think that's one of the names there. So what?"

I shook my head. "The cat's out of the bag, Boycie. Your Dees is a figment of the federal imagination. The real Dees died two days after graduating from college, up where," I thumbed toward Coarse behind me, "one of your loyal troops has a relative on the force."

Now Hendrix sat stock-still, no expression on his face.

I tried to phrase things as though I didn't know about the Milwaukee connection. "I'm guessing Chief Braverman gave you guys the idea of using a real—or 'formerly real'—identity for whoever your 'cooperating witness' was in his prior life, when he must have helped you or the FBI or somebody on a major case."

Hendrix worked his mouth, much like Fine had. "No comment."

"Terrific. Just listen, then. When I saw the guy you have as Dees, he knew I was reaching for a questionnaire before I ever showed it to him. So somebody must have put a call in to him. Maybe you, except I didn't show or even refer to my form when I was here. That tells me you've got somebody in the complex with Dees, somebody who tipped you or him about the questionnaire I'd been using with the neighbors."

Hendrix was looking a little green around the gills.

Thinking back to Robert Murphy at Boston Homicide, I said, "A watcher, maybe?"

Greener still. I could hear Coarse breathing behind me.

"Make a phone call, Boycie. We start up again when the watcher joins us."

Hendrix really didn't like the turn things had taken, but I didn't see a way out for him, and apparently he didn't, either.

His next comment was aimed above my shoulder. "Keep him here."

After Hendrix closed the inner door, Coarse rested a beefy hand on either side of my neck. I tensed, but all he did was say, "The chief's my uncle," then let go of me.

When the inner door opened again, Fine came through first, apparently to make sure Coarse was still holding the fort. Then Hendrix followed him in. Tángela Robinette appearing behind Hendrix made us a quintet.

"Ms. Robinette," I said.

"Mr. Cuddy," watching me like Coco Cocozzo had. No smile, no frown, just concentration.

I looked over at Fine. "Just so I can speak politely about everybody, what's your name?"

Fine looked to Robinette, not Hendrix, which confirmed something I'd already suspected. The woman glanced briefly to the side and then came back to me, nodding once.

Fine said, "Kourmanos."

"A pleasure. And the gentleman behind me?"

Coarse said, "Braverman."

"Thanks." Back to Robinette. "Let me catch you up on the conversation so far. After I saw Hendrix here on—"

"Boyce already filled me in, Mr. Cuddy. Who are you working for and why?"

"I'm getting to that."

"Get to it now."

"No."

We looked at each other for a while. I had the feeling that Robinette wouldn't blink first.

I said, "All right. A client came to see me. Said she was a little concerned about her boyfriend-*cum*-fiancé not seeming to have a background. She asked me to check into—"

"Jesus fucking Christ," said Hendrix. "His *girl*-friend is your client?"

Without looking away from me, Robinette said, "Boyce? Please?"

Hendrix shut up.

I said, "I come to see Boycie—"

"You say that one more time, fucker, and—"

Robinette said, "Boyce," again, this time with that steel core in her voice.

Hendrix folded his arms across his chest.

I looked at Robinette. "I come here, I visit you all at Plymouth Willows, then Dees at the photocopy shop, where he's already upset about me. I head back to Boston, and you guys check me out. Not too thoroughly, I'm thinking, just enough to make sure I'm who and what I say I am, a licensed investigator. Then Kourmanos and Braverman try to convince me as unconstitutionally as possible that Hendrix Management is mob-connected, emphasizing how I can save my butt by butting out. Whose idea was that, by the way?"

Robinette's nostrils flared a little, as they had when I'd riled her back in the condo unit. "Let us just say it was not a unanimous decision."

"Well, it might have worked, I suppose. But it didn't, because other than you all obviously being made nervous that anybody was asking any questions, you couldn't have known I was after Dees in particular. That's why I let my client know I'd been warned off, but I told her the rotten apple still might be the management company or the condo complex, not Dees himself. So I go up to the university yesterday and try to get a copy of the guy's college records with a nicely worded letter of authorization."

"Which the college notices is forged," said Hendrix.

"Because a lifer in the registrar's office knows the real Dees wouldn't be signing current correspondence. And that gets me an introduction to Deputy Marshal Braverman's—what is he, your father?"

I hoped Braverman would like the way I covered for him. Robinette's eyes went up behind me briefly, and Braverman said, "Close enough."

I returned to Robinette. "Only problem is, there had to be some failure of communication between Vermont and Marshfield yesterday too, because you guys didn't know I was interested in Dees himself after I saw the chief."

Hendrix said, "What makes you think we didn't?"

I spoke to him. "Because if you did, either you tell Dees his cover is blown, which seems to me the right thing to do, or you don't tell him squat and watch his movements, waiting to see what happens next."

Hendrix said, "Or we just have you put under surveillance."

"I don't think so. I might not have noticed right away, but I left Chief Braverman yesterday afternoon, and I've been taking precautions ever since Kourmanos and Braverman here paid me their first visit the day before. Nobody from your end's been watching me. So what happened when the chief finally got you the word that I was after Dees personally? Did you tell Dees or stay on the sidelines?"

Robinette said, "Why do you want to know?"

She seemed genuinely curious. In a very even voice, I said, "Because my client has disappeared."

Hendrix looked around at everybody. Kourmanos looked back at him, Robinette didn't, and Braverman I couldn't see.

Robinette said, "Since when?"

"Yesterday afternoon, when she left her bank."

"To do what?"

"She didn't say."

Robinette's eyes went down toward the table top, trying to work the problem through.

I said, "You didn't tell Dees anything, did you?"

No answer.

"You just let him twist in the wind after he saw me at his photocopy place on Wednesday, let the man wonder who I was and what I was doing."

Hendrix said, "And if we did? How's that any different from the scam you and your client—his *girl*-friend—were running on our witness?"

I looked at Hendrix. "We didn't know Dees wasn't who he claimed to be. You did."

Robinette raised her head. "I will tell you some things, Cuddy. I am not sure you need to know them, but it seems to me you have been ahead of us on this." She paused. "My husband was in DEA, where we met, but I took a leave of absence after getting pregnant with Jamey. My husband was killed a few years later, and they let me transfer agencies, be a watcher for the Marshals' Enforcement Operations. Specifically, witnesses cooperating with the FBI on Italian-American mob operations."

Hendrix said, a little theatrically, "Tánge, this isn't a good idea."

Robinette never looked away from me. "And sending two of our people as Mafia muscle after this citizen was?" She paused again, but Hendrix didn't reply. Then, "As a woman born in Haiti, I was a good risk. Not likely that anybody from the mob searching for a cooperating witness would see me connected to him."

I said, "And Dees, whoever he really is, cooperated with the government in an organized-crime case."

"In exchange for immunity from prosecution himself. So we did a relocation, gave him a new identity. Usually we use small towns, even rural areas, anywhere the hunters—what we call the other side, 'hunters'—are not likely to search because there are just too many such places *to* search."

"With you so far."

"A witness gets accepted into the program, he buys an all-or-nothing approach. He must give up any contact with the old 'danger zone' of hometown and people he came from, assuming his new ID completely. We give him a package of documents—birth certificate, social security card—"

"College diploma, so long as nobody looks too closely."

Robinette said, "Even letters of recommendation, though those are trickier, and we did not use any here."

"How about seed money?"

"Dees had his own."

"And you didn't wonder just a bit about the source of his stash?"

"Not our concern. That is up to the Bureau and the U.S. Attorney in the prosecuting jurisdiction."

"All right," I said. "Dees is at Plymouth Willows and in the program. Why does he leave?"

"I do not know." Robinette counted on her fingers. "You get kicked out for committing crimes, using drugs . . ."

"Not a problem here."

"No, and since we were not about to kick him out, we would have relocated him should his new ID be compromised."

"Wait a minute. Given that I—and you—might have contributed to blowing the 'Andrew Dees' cover, you'd have relocated him?"

"Yes."

"With a new identity?"

"Completely."

"And he would have known that?"

Robinette looked to Hendrix, who said, "Absolutely. Explained it to him myself."

"When?"

"When he first got relocated here."

"But he didn't turn to you for that after I spoke with him at the photocopy shop."

No response.

Robinette said, "Boyce?"

Hendrix shook his head. "No. Tángela called me about you, and I called Dees, but when he phoned me back after throwing you out of his shop, he didn't say anything about wanting to be relocated somewhere else. Dees was nervous, but that's all."

I thought about it. "You monitor a cooperating witness's bank accounts?"

Hendrix said, "Not as a regular practice."

"Why not?"

"It could alert somebody at the bank that the customer was in our program."

"But have you checked since you noticed Dees is gone?"

Hendrix said, "We don't know for sure that he is gone."

I looked back to Robinette. "Have you checked with his bank?"

"Yes," she said. "He spent most of yesterday afternoon cleaning out his money."

Which meant Dees had waited a day after I'd spoken with him. "And how about last night?"

Robinette said, "I was at a band recital, watching Jamey at his school."

"Instead of watching Dees at the complex."

A slight flare of the nostrils. "Yes."

"So, what do you think? Did Dees just turn rabbit and run?"

"We think it is possible."

"With my client?"

"Also possible."

"Have you followed up at all?"

Hendrix said, "Followed up?"

"Yes, Boyce. Airlines, charge-card companies, that kind of thing."

His face told me he didn't like my tone, but all he said was, "No, we didn't."

I thought about it some more.

Robinette said, "So, Mr. Cuddy, if you find out anything you think can help us, I would—"

"You don't care what happened to Andrew Dees, do you?"

She stopped. "What are you talking about?"

Again I tried to speak blind of the Milwaukee connection. "Dees was relocated from somewhere. You're not going to relocate a cooperating witness before he or she comes through with testimony for you, am I right?"

No answer from anybody.

I said, "You don't know whether Dees just panicked and ran, with or without my client, and you don't really care. Oh, you'd like to believe it, because then you don't have to investigate anything, follow up on whether a 'hunter' got to one of your protected people. That kind of investigation might get noticed by some criminal defense lawyers, send a little tremor through the program and maybe the hearts of other folks you'd like to see cooperate in the future."

Robinette said, "Mr. Cuddy—"

"You'd rather have Dees be gone than have it get out that somebody under your protection was discovered and killed, because potential witnesses might be less than confident about your program in the future."

Hendrix smirked, which bothered me, but Robinette couldn't see him as she spoke. "Mr. Cuddy, the cooperating witness program is just an option that witness has. If he or she decides to leave the program, there is not much we can do about it."

"In other words, it's a free country."

Hendrix said, "Exactly."

I looked over to him. "Wrong note, Boycie."

The glare.

I said, "Your smiling just now when I said you guys were worried about other witnesses finding out. You shouldn't have found that funny, unless I was a little off the mark."

Hendrix just stared now.

I said, "What am I missing?"

Robinette turned for the door. "I do not see any purpose in going further with this."

To her back I said, "No, I wasn't being specific enough, was I? You've been at Plymouth Willows for two years, yet 'Andrew Dees' moved in just over a year ago. Hendrix has this management cover for longer than that, and here in Marshfield, instead of down in Plymouth Mills. Why?"

Hendrix and Kourmanos looked quickly toward Robinette's profile. Braverman shuffled his feet behind me, the first thing he'd done for a while.

Leaning back in my chair, I said, "Bet I know why."

Robinette turned around. "All right, let us in on it."

"Plymouth Willows was a complex in trouble. Lana Stepanian told me that. Some of the people were pioneers, and others came later, but when the developer went belly up, a real estate trust bailed out the operation, kept it viable. The 'C.W. Realty Trust,' only Stepanian didn't know much about the trust itself because the documents are confidential. The initials stand for 'Cooperating Witness,' don't they?"

Going green around the gills again, Hendrix started to say something, but Robinette held up her hand, and he swallowed his comment instead.

I said, "When the developer of the complex had problems, the FDIC had to step in. There's an auction of properties, and your outfit—another federal agency, but one that needs 'housing,' so to speak— raises its hand as the C.W. Realty Trust and buys up all the distressed units you want. At Plymouth Willows, and given Boycie's operation here, probably elsewhere in the area as well. It's perfect, really. You send your witnesses, one each, to East Jibib or North Moosejaw, somebody has to babysit them one each as well, or at least drive a few hours to drop in and take their temperatures from time to time. Instead, Ms. Robinette can watch over a whole bunch at Plymouth Willows, and her counterparts the others elsewhere on the South Shore, while Mr. Hendrix sits in his management office here and oversees everything efficiently. The oversight includes hiring superintendents like Paulie Fogerty, somebody who'll do a fine job of maintaining the grounds but probably not ask awkward questions about the residents. By having the witnesses 'buy' their hideouts, they're more encouraged to stay in them, not walk away from any equity they might have built up. You even had Dees file a homestead exemption on his unit to protect that equity from future creditors. Tell me, Boycie, is that how I could find the other protected witnesses, just by cross-referencing the complexes you manage and the registry of deeds for any homestead exemptions over the last few years?"

Hendrix looked worse than green. Robinette's eyes were shooting lightning bolts at me.

I said, "But for all that to work, somebody like Dees can't know that other people at Plymouth Willows are in the program too. And that probably means he can't know that you're a watcher, am I right?"

Robinette said, "I really wish you had not stuck your nose into this, Mr. Cuddy."

"Ms. Robinette, I don't give one of your 'rat's' asses about what you wish. You answer my next question, though, and I'll be out of your hair and not share my thoughts with anybody else."

She didn't like the situation any more than Hendrix had earlier. "What is your question?"

I'd been remembering how vague Lana Stepanian had seemed about her husband's hometown, Norman Elmendorf the same about his duty station in the Gulf War. "Is either of the Stepanians in the program?"

Robinette took a moment to say, "No. They bought at Plymouth Willows before we established there."

"Is the same true for the Elmendorfs?"

"You already had your next question, Mr. Cuddy."

"Be generous, Ms. Robinette."

It took an effort, but she said, "They are not in the program, either."

"Thank you. Now, this last one's a toss-up question for any team member who wants to take it. What the hell has happened to my client?"

Nobody answered.

"All right, I think I believe you." I stood up slowly. "Where's my gun?"

Kourmanos handed me the Chief's Special and its bullets separately.

Without reloading, I put the revolver back in the holster. "How about a lift from somebody back to my car at Plymouth Willows?"

Robinette almost smiled. "I am going that way myself."

We'd been riding for maybe five of the twenty minutes to Plymouth Mills when Tángela Robinette said, "This goes in a report, lots of people could be hurt."

"My client may already be hurt."

"Self-inflicted wound."

I looked at her. "That's pretty harsh, don't you think?"

A glance to me, then, like Primo Zuppone, she checked all the mirrors before speaking. "If your client believes in love, she does not hire a private investigator, and you never disturb the hornets' nest."

"Ms. Robinette, my client told me she was crazy about Andrew Dees, told me by word and body language both. She's an intelligent, aware businesswoman. What was she supposed to do, ignore that her lover seems to have been dropped as an adult from a spaceship?"

Robinette started to say something, then deflected herself. "What are you going to do about your client?"

"Try to find her. Or at least, find out what happened to her."

"You think she is with Dees?"

"On the level?"

"Yes."

"I'm afraid to think."

Robinette glanced over again. "I do not understand."

"You've been part of the marshals' program long enough to have had some contact with the mob by now?"

"Some," she said dryly.

"You ever know them to be subtle about the body of a guy who flipped on them?"

A moment before, "No."

"They make a statement, some splashy kind of taboo warning to others who might be so inclined."

Some steel came into Robinette's voice again. "We pronounce it 'voodoo,' Mr. Cuddy."

"Don't get you."

"I am Haitian. You think I missed your 'taboo' comment?"

"I hadn't thought of it that way."

A third glance.

Looking toward her, I said, "Truly. I was picturing some old movie, the skull on a stake at the entrance to the valley. 'Walk no farther.' "

" 'Said the savage black native to the civilized white explorer.' "

"If that's the way you want to take it."

Another moment before she said, "I am sorry. You really were not trying to be insulting, were you?"

"No, I wasn't."

We passed through Plymouth Mills, the sidewalks downtown as quiet as if someone had rolled them up. Just before the bridge, I turned to Robinette. "Straight answer to a straight question?"

"Try it and see."

"You people really don't know whether my client and this Dees guy hit the silk together, do you?"

"Straight answer: we really do not. And you were right back there at Boyce's place. We almost do not care. Our job is to protect the people in the program. As far as we know, Andrew Dees left it voluntarily, there being no evidence the other way."

"Before they slugged me a couple of hours ago, Braverman and Kourmanos went through his unit?"

231

"Yes. Not forensically, of course, but a thorough search. Some gaps in the closet where clothes would have hung, and in the bureau, for socks, underwear. No suitcase when I am sure he had at least one. No wallet, no checkbook."

"You talk to the neighbors?"

"On what grounds? That another neighbor, named Andrew Dees, who I had little to do with, might not have been around for a day or so?"

Staying sidesaddle, facing Robinette, I said, "There're still a few things I don't understand."

"Probably always will be."

"First off, Hendrix is an idiot."

"No comment."

"Why do you put up with him?"

A glance, away from the road but not quite to me. "He is my superior."

"That's not how it played back in the interrogation room."

"What do you mean?"

"Everybody—including Hendrix himself—took their cues from you."

A smile. "We did run a check on you. Military Police, correct?"

"For a time."

"And overseas. Back then, did you ever notice how some superior officers yield to others when things are going into the toilet?"

I saw her point. "Yet, Hendrix still outranks you."

The smile flew away. "There are statistics on women serving in the federal law enforcement agencies, Mr. Cuddy. We have been 'allowed' to be field agents for over twenty years now, but the FBI is less than ten percent female, ATF less than five percent. And the Secret Service? Worse than that."

"How about the U.S. Marshals?"

"No comment."

I shifted a little on the seat. "Second thing bothering me, I don't see you going off to a school concert with Jamey if you thought a cooperating witness you were watching was in any kind of jeopardy."

Robinette didn't say anything.

"I also don't see Chief Braverman up in Vermont failing to get word to his relative on your team that this private investigator who visited Plymouth Willows, ostensibly to talk about Hendrix Management, was at Dees' alma mater the next day, obviously tracing the background of the witness himself and not how well Boycie's company ran your condo complex."

"We already talked about this back in that room."

"Yeah, and you nicely brought me off the subject once I said I was sure Braverman and Kourmanos weren't trailing me. But that leaves us with a dilemma, don't you think?"

No response, not even a glance.

"The dilemma," I said, "is this. If you got left out of the loop by Hendrix regarding my trip to Vermont, then I can see you going off to the concert with Jamey. But I can't see Boycie not keeping an eye on Dees, using Braverman or Kourmanos or both."

If Robinette didn't have to move the steering wheel, you'd have thought her a statue.

"And that says to me that Hendrix made a bad call, a decision to have Kourmanos and Braverman *try* to find and follow me last night."

Robinette spoke very precisely. "They went to your office, assuming that you would come back there from Vermont. Then, when you did not, they went to your apartment, but your car was nowhere in the lot."

Which meant the marshals didn't know about Primo Zuppone picking me up at my condo building on Thursday night and taking me to the airport to welcome the

Milwaukee contingent. Kourmanos and Braverman would have missed me at Fairfield Street, because by the time they got there, I was already over at Nancy's, and they would have been back in Plymouth Willows by the time Primo brought Ianella and Cocozzo to my office earlier on Friday.

Which also meant that nobody from the marshals' service was watching Andrew Dees on Thursday night. And therefore they couldn't know what happened with or to him after Norman Elmendorf and the Stepanians heard him arguing with a woman in his condo and Steven Stepanian saw him loading luggage into Olga Evorova's orange Porsche.

I turned back toward the dashboard as we came up the front driveway to the complex and headed for my car. Reaching it, Robinette stopped, leaving her engine running.

Looking out the windshield, she said, "I am hoping you meant what you said at Boyce's tonight."

"About?"

"About keeping whatever we have going here at the Willows to yourself."

"You can count on it. I don't want to see anybody else get killed."

"You do not know Dees and your client are dead. In fact, you argued against it."

Not mentioning the Milwaukee boys, I said, "It's not that I think the mob did anything. I'm more worried about Dees himself."

"Dees himself?"

"He runs away from the equity he has in the condo, taking just the money from his bank, maybe realizing my client was responsible for his identity being—what did you call it, 'compromised'?"

Robinette set her jaw. "Mr. Cuddy, I have no reason to

believe Mr. Dees could turn violent. When he was in . . . Let us just say his history would be to the contrary."

"It's not his history I'm worried about. More his current affair."

I opened the door and got out. Tángela Robinette drove off toward her unit before I could thank her for the lift.

19

Once in the Prelude, I looked down at the passenger seat. Nancy's rose was standing tall against the door, but about half the water seemed to be gone from the tube. It was a good reminder of where I should go next.

"Am I lucky to catch you home on a Friday night?"

"I guess so," said Nancy, wearing loose-fitting sweat-clothes and holding the front door to the three-decker open with a soxed foot. The bulge from her Smith & Wesson Bodyguard barely showed under the towel in her right hand. "What's behind your back?"

I said, "You'll see when we get upstairs."

Just before Nancy reached the second landing, Drew Lynch's door closed discreetly. At the third, she turned the unlocked knob of her own, Renfield trundling out and in and out again. Something smelled awfully good in the kitchen.

Laying the towel and gun on the shelf by her telephone, Nancy moved to the counter by the sink. "Homemade soup in the crockpot. I stopped at the market on the way home."

"Ingredients?"

"Chicken tenders, lightly fried, then cut up with fresh mushrooms, baby corn, carrots, onions, and a few spices. Mrs. Lynch gave me some of her special broth for stock." A shifting of stance, a canting of head. "So, what's behind the back, chardonnay or cabernet?"

I brought out the rose. Nancy blinked twice, her mouth forming a little "O." Then she came toward me. Taking the flower from me, she held the bud to her nose. "John, it's beautiful."

"Mrs. Feeney said be sure to give the stem a fresh cut. With a knife, not scissors, so the 'pores' stay open for absorbing water."

Nancy raised her chin. "Mrs. Feeney."

"The woman who runs the florist—"

"I know who she is. It's just that you've never. . ." Nancy shook her head, then closed her eyes, taking another breath over the rose.

"You okay?" I said.

"Yes. I'm making a memory." She looked up at me. "The blossom hasn't opened yet."

"That's why I asked for this one. I thought we could kind of watch it open together."

"I'd like that, John Francis Cuddy." She paused. "I'd also like just some cuddling again tonight."

"Probably be too full after the soup for anything more strenuous, anyway."

A smile without showing her teeth. "Maybe an old movie on the VCR too?"

"From your extensive collection, or do I call the video store?"

"We can talk about it over dinner." Nancy rotated the rose in her hand like a wineglass. "One more thing, John?"

"Name it."

"Can we have a normal day tomorrow?"

"Normal?"

"I'll have to go into the office on Sunday to prep some more for this trial, make up the time I lost Thursday at the doctor's. But tomorrow, no work, no talk of tests. Just a nice, simple Saturday, okay?"

I thought about it. On the one hand, Olga Evorova was missing, which made me want to do something positive toward finding her. On the other hand, I didn't have any more cards to play in that direction, and another get-together with the hitters from Milwaukee didn't seem wise until I had something tangible to prove I wasn't hiding Andrew Dees from them. And there were my memories of Beth just after we'd found out she was sick, and how much time with her then had meant to both of us.

"John?" Nancy was looking at me, her eyebrows forming a worry line.

Cupping my palms, I rested one on each of her shoulders. "A normal Saturday sounds great to me, kid."

In the morning, we ate muffins and drank hot chocolate at a little hole-in-the-wall near Anthony's Pier Four that used to cater exclusively to the men who worked the sea, a Fisherman's Prayer still nailed above a roster of those who could no longer say it for themselves. After that, Nancy and I hopped a bus to Back Bay and the Institute of Contemporary Art, taking in the Elvis and Marilyn exhibit, goofing on the crucified Las Vegas lounge suit and gold-painted shrines but lingering over some of the affecting portraits and candid photos. We had a pub lunch at Charley's on Newbury Street, then spent the afternoon walking hand-in-hand along the river, all the way to the Larz Anderson Bridge and up into Harvard Square, shopping the shops without buying the buys.

Dinner was at Grendel's Den, a large restaurant of surprisingly intimate little tables and superb food priced for grad students and assistant professors. Across the alley is the

House of Blues. Passing the tourists clucking over T-shirts on the first floor, Nancy and I climbed to the second level. The cathedral ceiling has skylights, each a silhouette of a seminal blues artist with names and places of birth underneath. Rick Russell's band played wonderful riffs, from guitar to brass, and while it wasn't exactly dance music, we found ourselves doing a modest bump, hip against hip, here and there.

By eleven-thirty, I was hailing a cab that delivered us back to Southie twenty minutes later. Inside her apartment, Nancy gave Renfield a midnight snack.

Then she turned to me. "That ought to keep him diverted." Winking, Nancy took my hand and led me into the bedroom. "Only thing is, I want to leave my bra on while we make love."

"Nance—"

"Please. We can talk about it afterwards, but not before, okay?"

"Okay."

I lay on my back, spent.

Nancy leaned over me in the near-dark, her lips just brushing the right side of my nose. "Sailor, you sure know how to show a girl a good time."

The past half-hour had been intense, each of us moving with the other for reasons selfish and sharing. Nancy had spoken first.

I lifted my right arm, and she cuddled frontways against my side. Using my right hand, I stroked her gently along the spine, up and down below the bra strap.

"That feels so good."

"Nance?"

"Yes?"

"I thought you said last night that until we heard from the doctor, you wanted to lead your life as normally as possible."

"Just like today."

Fingering the strap, I said, "Do you think keeping this on when we make love is 'normal?' "

She burrowed a cheek into my chest. "Probably not."

"Then why do it?"

"I just don't want you to see me ... wounded, I guess."

"What, from the biopsy?"

"Yes."

"Nancy, I've seen you after this," I said, tapping lightly on the slight, puckering scar at her shoulder, from a bullet she took right after we first met. "And it didn't make a difference."

"I know."

"Well?"

"Not the same, John. This isn't some bump or bruise—"

"—a bullet hole's not exactly—"

"—this is almost a mutilation, and I have to be careful with it."

"Careful how?"

"In the way I deal with you about it. Me staying focused at work helps a little, by keeping my mind off everything else. But if the doctor ... If the news isn't good, then ..."

"Then what?"

"Then I want you to remember me as beautiful, the way you once told me I was."

I shifted carefully, so as not to jar or even irritate whatever was beneath the bra cup. Now I was facing her, just enough light for me to make out the bone structure under the whites of her eyes. "Nance, the beauty doesn't come from what's on you, but from what's in you."

"Easy to say."

"I've been there, remember?"

"And I don't ever want you to go through with me what you went through with Beth."

"Nancy, whether that comes to pass or not, neither of us can say. But meanwhile, how about we both act normal?"

Silence, then a playful tone. "Meaning you're going to unhook the strap?"

"Unfortunately my Catholic upbringing makes me incapable of such a thing."

"The snap's in front. Try it."

I did, the fabric coming away in my hands. I touched her cross-hatched Band-Aids gently with just my left index finger, then ran the finger, gentler still, over the surrounding flesh. "Doesn't make a difference, Nance."

She brought her hand behind my head and drew me toward her for a kiss.

On Sunday morning, I used Nancy's living room phone to check my answering service. Mingled with messages from Primo Zuppone ("My friends would like to know how you're doing") were three from Claude Loiselle, all the same: Call me, urgent. She left her number at the bank.

I dialed it, figuring to get the voice-mail system, but instead drew Loiselle herself.

"Where are you now?" she said.

"Why?"

"How soon can you get here?"

"To the bank?"

"Yes."

"Claude, what's happened?"

"I think you'd better see for yourself."

Loiselle hung up.

Behind me, Nancy said, "Problem?"

I turned to her, standing in the fuzzy mauve robe. "Not sure. You still interested in going to your office for a while?"

"At least until one or so."

"How about if I drive us both downtown, then pick you up at two?"

"Sounds good. Let me just brush my hair."

To the downstairs security guard at the scimitar counter I said, "John Cuddy. Ms. Loiselle's expecting me."

A nod, and he hit some buttons on his telephone. After whispering into the receiver, he nodded again before hanging up. "She'll be waiting at fifty-four. You know which elevators to use?"

"Yes. Thanks."

"You came quickly. Good."

I followed Loiselle through the eerily empty reception area and corridors. It was as though some foreign power had dropped a neutron bomb that eliminated all the people but left the workstations standing. In her office. Loiselle went behind the utilitarian desk. Everything looked the same as when I'd been there on Friday, two mornings before.

She said, "Have a seat."

I took one of the chairs. "All right, what am I supposed to 'see for myself?' "

Loiselle said, "Me."

I stared at her. "Claude—"

"I called the police about Olga. I even went over there, to the Missing Persons Unit."

"And they told you . . . ?"

"What you said they would. She's an adult, there's no sign of 'misadventure'—is that a real word?"

"It is to them."

"They also told me she wasn't missing long enough, and no indication that she'd crossed a state line. It was all very frustrating."

I could picture Loiselle showing some poor report-taker

just how frustrating she thought it was. "Look, Claude, why didn't you just tell me this over the phone?"

"Because I want to hire you."

"Hire me."

"To find Olga."

I stopped. "Olga's already my client."

"So, now I will be too."

"Claude, I'm basically out of ideas for finding her."

"That's what I mean." Loiselle squared her shoulders, fixing me with an almost pleasant smile. "You've been trying to help her, both before and after she disappeared. I understand that. But there's only so much you can do without serious money to do it with. And I'm prepared to help."

"Bankroll me to look for Olga."

"Exactly. Given what the police said they weren't going to do, I have to hire somebody. And you're already up to speed on everything." The smile got conspiratorial. "In fact, I'm sure you know things I don't know."

"That might be the problem, Claude."

A puzzled expression. "I don't understand."

"Conflict of interest. There are things I learned working for Olga that maybe I shouldn't share with you."

Loiselle seemed to look within herself. "All right, I accept that. I don't really care about what you know. What I care about is finding Olga."

"Or just making sure she's safe?"

Again puzzled. "What do you mean?"

I chose my words carefully. "From what I've found out, it's at least possible that Olga and Andrew Dees have taken off together."

"Taken off where?"

"I don't know."

Another inward look. "No. No, Olga wouldn't have left without her PDA, without packing things at her apartment."

"Maybe she didn't think she had time."

From puzzled to exasperated. "Now what do you mean?"

"It may be that Dees and Olga had to leave suddenly on Thursday night."

Loiselle said, "Thursday? Why?"

"One of the things I can't share with you."

A shaking of the head, slowly at first. "Olga would have called me."

Basically what Uncle Ivan had said, too. "Maybe she didn't want to give anything away."

"Give anything . . . ?" Loiselle crossed her arms, hugging herself. "And here I thought hiring you would make me feel better about all this."

"I'm sorry, but while there are some things I can't tell you, I don't want to lie to you, either."

She watched me for a moment, then turned to her computer. "Where would they have gone?"

"No idea."

"How?"

"How?"

"Yes," said Loiselle. "How would they get wherever they were going?"

"Car's the most anonymous, plane's the fastest."

Nodding, she began punching buttons quickly. "Plane would mean airport, and the closest with the most flights is Logan."

"Not necessarily."

Loiselle stopped. "Explain?"

"If they left from Plymouth Mills, Providence or Hartford might have been faster for them."

Back to the computer. "It shouldn't matter for what I'm checking."

"Claude, they probably wouldn't have used their own names."

Studying her monitor. "What?"

"If you're checking the airlines somehow, they probably used different names."

"Not for the ATM. Olga may have been in love with that jerk, but I can't believe she wouldn't have hit up an automatic teller some place to have cash before she went anywhere with him."

It was a good point. "You can check that on a Sunday?"

Loiselle gave me a withering look, then went back to her screen. "Motherfucker!"

"What's the matter?"

"Blocked out."

"Can you call that guy for the password again?"

"Different. Hold a minute, let me try . . . Yes!"

"You found it?"

"Olga uses the same code I do, to keep prying eyes at the bank from getting into her account. I think . . . there we go." Smiling triumphantly, Loiselle rotated the monitor so we both could see the screen.

A series of chartreuse ledger sheets on a black background. I said, "Nothing since Tuesday, right?"

Realizing what that might mean, Loiselle stopped smiling. "And even before that, basically just lunch-money level of withdrawal."

We sat in silence for a moment. Then Loiselle swung the monitor toward her, attacking the keyboard again.

"Now what?" I said.

"I'm breaking the law."

"How?"

"By violating the commercial privacy of one Horse's Ass."

After a moment, she said. "Andrew Dees pulled six thousand six-fifty out of a business account on Thursday afternoon at three-forty-five."

Consistent with what Tángela Robinette had told me.

Loiselle clacked some more. "And another nine thousand

five out of a personal account at . . ." She lowered her voice. "Fifteen minutes later."

"Cleaned out both accounts?"

"The business one, yes. Still a few thousand in the personal one."

"Why would he leave any?"

"Banking regulations. He goes over ten thousand cash withdrawal, there'd be a paper trail."

"But you found a trail anyway."

Loiselle looked at me. "Yeah, but only because I'm searching for it, and illegally at that. The over-ten trail would go to the federal government, tip them to . . ." She hardened the look. "Is that why Dees is running, he's in trouble with the feds?"

"I can't say."

"Or with those guys who roughed you up?"

"Same answer."

The harder look got stony. "Is hiring you going to be worse than dealing with the police?"

"There are all kinds of frustration, Claude."

"Yeah, tell me about it." She turned away from the computer. "Okay now what?"

"Can you check on Olga's bank accounts every few hours?"

Loiselle just snapped her fingers. Then, "Dees would be tougher."

"If he's running, he's not going to risk giving away his new location by trying to access a few thousand in a bank account."

"Makes sense. So what are you going to do?"

"Drive out to Logan."

"But I thought you said—"

"That they'd have used phony names. Right. If they're smart, they even took different airlines to different hubs, planning to match up again in a day or so at another airport."

The lowered voice. "Assuming they're still together."

"Yes."

Puzzled once more, Loiselle said, "But then why are you going to Logan at all?"

"Because it's the closest to where I am now, and they had to get to any airport somehow."

She looked inward. "Their car."

"His or hers, but maybe at least one of them."

"And if you find it?"

"Then maybe it'll tell me something. Or maybe somebody will remember seeing them."

"Do you need any money now?"

I told her how much, and how many days of my time it would buy.

As Loiselle was writing out a check the old-fashioned way, I said, "You wouldn't happen to know Olga's license plate, would you?"

"Of course not, but the computer will."

"The computer's tied into the Registry of Motor Vehicles too?"

"We make car loans, so it's a convenience to be able to access their records. Even on a Sunday," the last a little sarcastic.

"While you're at it, get the tag for the brown Toyota Dees drives as well."

Handing me the check, Claude Loiselle snapped her fingers again.

At Logan International Airport, there's short-term parking closer to the terminals and long-term parking farther away. The short-term is exorbitantly expensive, but I figured that people in a hurry would choose closer, especially if they weren't expecting to come back for their car. Starting at the first terminal after the airport on-ramp, I pushed the self-service button for a time-logged ticket, the Prelude going under the rising bar and over the tire treadles. Five minutes later, I was out again, paying the exit attendant for an hour's worth.

I repeated the sequence twice more before reaching the fourth lot, waving to the slim, Latino attendant as I drove by him. He didn't wave back.

I'd gone down only one row before spotting it, tucked into a corner space near the terminal. I checked the plate against the registration Claude Loiselle had printed out for me, but I almost didn't have to.

How many orange Porsches have you ever seen?

I parked behind it and got out. The lock buttons on both doors were down, a decal on the vent window advertising an alarm system. From outside the vehicle, I couldn't tell if the system was activated.

"Hey, man?"

I turned to the attendant walking toward me. He wore a maintenance jumpsuit—something like Paulie Fogerty's, only brown—the name ELMER stitched on the flap of the left breast pocket.

He said, "Plenty spaces, two rows over."

"I'm more interested in this one, Elmer."

"My name is pronounce '*El*-mare.' " A confident grin, like he'd been in this situation before and knew how to handle it. "Plenty people is interest in this car, man. Real hot, you know it?"

"Kind of stands out."

"Definitely."

I showed him my ID. "Mind telling me who's been interested in it?"

"Oh, everybody. Kids, couple middle-aged guys, think they have all the young chicks, they get a hot car like this one."

"Sounds like you're kind of watching over it."

"Me?" Elmer looked defensive. "No, man. Just keep an eye on the lot, don't want nobody break no windows, steal the radios."

I nodded. "You wouldn't have been here when this one came in?"

"Yeah, I was here."

Bingo. "When was that?"

"Thursday night, maybe nine, nine-thirty. I work nights, weekends. Need the money, you know it?"

"You see who was in the car?"

The confident grin. "That is worth something to you, man?"

I took out my wallet and held up a twenty.

The grin broadened. "There two people in it, that is forty, no?"

I brought out another twenty. "Description?"

Elmer took the bills, put them in his chest pocket. "Guy and his woman."

"What did the guy look like?"

"I don't know, man. Dark hair." A shrug.

"White, black?"

"Not black, I don't think."

I gave him one of my photos of Andrew Dees. "Could this be the guy?"

Elmer held it up, moving his hand back and forth like a trombone player, and I felt a little twinge.

"Could be, man. Dark hair, and your guy here, he is tall, no?"

"How do you know that?"

"I don't see him too good when the car go past my booth. You don't need me to get in, just to get out, you know it?"

"Yes."

"So I counting the money in my drawer, and I see this

Porsche come in. I watch the guy take it to the space too, hot car like this.''

"The man was behind the wheel?''

"Like I said.''

That didn't sound right. When I first met Olga Evorova in my office, she told me no one drove the Porsche but her. "You're sure?''

"Sure I'm sure. He park the car over here, then they get out, with some luggage. The guy look over to me, and he wave.''

"He what?''

"He wave to me, like you did before, man.''

That didn't sound right, either. "The woman wave, too?''

"No. I don't really see her too good. It is dark, and she is behind the other cars, walking.''

"Walking?''

"With one of the suitcases. To the terminal.''

I looked around. "So he was over here when he waved to you.''

"By his door.''

I gestured toward the lot entrance, a hundred feet away. "And it was dark, and you were at your booth.''

"Like I tell you, man.''

"Elmer, tell me something else.''

"What?''

"You need glasses?''

A sheepish grin. "Kind of.'' He tapped his chest pocket. "What I maybe use your forty for, you know it?''

Inside the terminal, I showed my photo from Plymouth Willows to skycaps, ticket agents, and custodians. Unlike Elmer, most of them hadn't been working Thursday night, but even those who had said they didn't recognized Dees/ DiRienzi. On the way out, though, I noticed a mailbox next to a coin-operated stamp dispenser.

I stopped in my tracks. If Evorova was running with "Andrew Dees," he probably would have told her that he was really Alfonso DiRienzi. He also might have warned her against using any telephones. But maybe, just maybe, she would have mailed me something from the airport, something that wouldn't arrive till long after they were gone but still let me know that she was all right. Thursday night mail from Logan could have arrived at my office on Friday, but Saturday was more likely. And I hadn't been there since late Friday afternoon.

I walked out to redeem my car from Elmer's lot.

Driving back through the Sumner Tunnel, I went over what I had so far. Alfonso DiRienzi fears his cover might be blown after I pay him a visit Wednesday at the photocopy shop. He doesn't run that night, but he's nervous enough the next day to leave work in the afternoon and withdraw most of his money. About the same time, I'm telling Olga Evorova from Vermont that "her Andrew" isn't on the level. According to Filomena, DiRienzi doesn't come back to work Thursday afternoon. That night, when the Robinettes are off at a band concert, a woman argues with DiRienzi in his townhouse at Plymouth Willows loudly enough for both the Stepanians and Norman Elmendorf to hear. Probably the woman is Olga, since Steven Stepanian notices "Dees" loading luggage into a car like hers around eight o'clock. Between nine and nine-thirty—or about driving time from Plymouth Mills to Logan that late at night—Elmer the attendant sees the orange Porsche arrive, a man and a woman getting out. He can't see well enough to really identify the man as DiRienzi, and the "tall" is probably more reliable than the "not black" and "dark hair." Elmer says the guy was driving, which doesn't sound like something Olga would allow, and the man waves to Elmer, which doesn't sound like something anybody on the run would do. Also, if DiRienzi and Evorova are taking off together, why leave the more conspicuous Porsche at the airport rather than the drab Toyota?

I looked through my windshield, maybe twenty cars ahead. It was a little brighter at the far end of the tunnel, but somehow that didn't make anything clearer.

20

Stopped at a traffic light back downtown, I checked my watch. Only 1:00 P.M. Still an hour before picking up Nancy, and plenty of time to visit the office for any mail Olga Evorova might have sent me. From what Rick Ianella had said the first time I met him, he and Cocozzo were more likely to be camped outside the condo, where there was some parking, than outside the office, where there was none. Even so, rather than put the Prelude in the space next to the dumpster off Tremont, I left it three blocks away and walked the rest.

At my building's entrance, I looked around. The trolley ticket guy, with nobody at his booth across the street, was the only person paying any attention to me. Upstairs, I stood outside the pebbled-glass door for a full minute, hearing nothing. Using my key on the lock, I went inside, skimming the mail that had come through my slot. All but one envelope had a return address on it, and the exception proved to be from a former client whose daughter I'd tracked down a year before, the letter thanking me again, because the girl was still at home and now doing well in school.

Facing the windows, I called my condo number, got Primo Zuppone's voice twice on the tape machine, and hung up. Next was my answering service, with two more messages from him. Nothing else.

I was returning the receiver to its cradle as my door opened. Coco Cocozzo came in first, wearing the same suit, a semiautomatic nearly lost in his right hand. Close behind was Rick Ianella, a different suit but the same expression on his face.

Cocozzo said to me, "Up, and real slow."

I did what he wanted.

"Assume the position against the wall."

I went over to it, legs spread apart, palms leaning into the plaster above Junior's punched holes. Cocozzo planted the outside of his left shoe against the instep of my left foot and began to frisk me.

I said, "This come kind of natural to you?"

The balding man brought the barrel of the gun up hard between my thighs, but not as hard as he could have. I bit back what was in my throat.

Cocozzo found the Smith & Wesson Chief's Special on my right hip and pulled it free carefully. Finishing the search, he stepped back.

Ianella said, "Turn around and look at me, dickhead."

I turned. "The trolley guy, right? You paid him to watch for me."

Cocozzo said, "We paid four shifts of them, just in case you decided to show up when we weren't around."

The scar through Junior's eyebrow was twitching like a rabbit's nose. "Coco and me, we been waiting since Friday for you to fucking call us, and that fucking Primo says you ain't been answering your phones again. I been in touch with Milwaukee, telling them, 'Let my father know, it's gonna be any time now.' Only you been letting us down, shit-for-brains. How come?"

"I didn't have anything to tell you, until now."

Ianella moved closer to me. "Until now?"

"Yes. I found out some things, but I want Primo here when I tell you about them."

Junior contorted his features like a chimpanzee's, nodding elaborately but not sincerely. I figured I knew what was coming.

Ianella made the quick effort to cuff me on the chin, the way he had with Zuppone. I parried it, the edge of my left hand slashing into the fleshy part of his right forearm.

Junior bent at the waist, his left hand clawing at the place I'd hit him, the mottling coming over his cheeks. "You little fuck, I'm gonna—"

"Boss?"

The younger man turned toward Cocozzo. "What?"

"Probably be easier, we just call Primo on his car phone, get him over here."

A look of disbelief. "You don't think I can handle this piece of shit?"

Softly, patiently, Cocozzo said, "I know you can handle him, Boss. It's just you might not want to handle him here, and Primo's the one with the car and maybe a place we can take him."

Junior brought himself under control, then jerked his head toward the telephone. "Do it."

From the floor of the Lincoln's backseat, I could hear Primo Zuppone say, "Mr. Ianella, I don't think—"

"You don't got to think." Junior was in the front, on the passenger's side. "You just got to find us a place, so's we can have a talk with dickhead here."

Cocozzo sat on the leather upholstery above me, one shoe resting lightly on the back of my neck, the muzzle of his weapon just under my earlobe. He said, "A quiet place, Primo."

We were in the car for about half an hour before I could feel the suspension leaving a good road for a potholed one, my nose bouncing off the floor mat, the transmission hump compressing my ribs. Then Zuppone braked very gradually, killing the engine.

Junior said, "This looks good. Your people control it?"

"Yes, Mr. Ianella. But—"

"Let's go."

I heard and felt the doors of the Lincoln open.

Primo pulled on my right shoe. "All right, Cuddy. Back out, real slow."

Once my feet were on the ground, Cocozzo said, "Hands behind your neck."

With Zuppone leading, the others trailed me toward a derelict industrial building, windowpanes rock-broken on the first two floors. At the main entrance, Primo keyed a huge padlock, the door swinging inward, the way they were built before the Coconut Grove fire in 1942. A wave of dank air greeted us as we moved inside, the pang of old blood hanging heavy between the stone walls and above the stone floor.

Junior said, "Fucking place smells like a slaughterhouse."

Primo shrugged. "That's what it was, Mr. Ianella."

Cocozzo said, "Lights work?"

"We got a utility thing, down the hall."

"Why don't you go put it on," said the balding man.

Zuppone faded into the darkness, his steps even, like a sentry marching along his castle's battlement. At the end of the hall, one of those hooked and caged lamps with a rubber handle came on. Hanging from a nail in the crossbeam, it spotlighted Primo's head and torso.

Cocozzo nudged me between the shoulder blades, but

with the off-hand, not the gun one. A careful guy, Coco. Not exactly a good sign for my future.

I walked toward Zuppone, Ianella saying behind me, "Fucking slimy stones, gonna ruin these loafers."

Primo said, "Hey-ey-ey, I'm sorry, but this was the best place I could—"

"Shut up and let's get to it."

I could see Zuppone's cheeks whiten in anger around his acne scars as he unhooked the light from its nail, giving himself plenty of slack in the long extension cord. We moved down the corridor, almost a torch-lit processional.

Primo stopped at a solid oak door with an oversized, icebox handle. He yanked on it, and the door groaned on rusty hinges. A while since anyone else had been through it.

"Hey," said Ianella, "we gonna find a guy wearing a hockey mask in there?"

Cocozzo said, "With a chainsaw, maybe."

"No, Coco. You're thinking of a different fucking movie altogether," said Junior.

"Actually, Boss, I was thinking of Cuddy here."

Ianella grinned and nodded. "That's good, Coco. I like that, yeah."

The interior of the locker spread before us, twenty feet square, the big meat hooks still embedded in reinforced beams running the width of the room. A couple of gouged and stained oak benches occupied the center of the space, some cobwebbed cutlery like cleavers and long-handled knives on an old oak stand against one wall.

Junior looked around once, returning to the old cutlery. "Perfect." Then, to Primo, "Pull one of those fucking benches over here."

Zuppone hung the lamp from one of the meat hooks, then did what he was told.

Ianella put his right foot atop the bench, a football coach

about to diagram a play for the defense. "Cuddy, you go sit on the other one."

I went over to it, turning and lowering myself, the old oak feeling as cold as the old stone had looked in the corridor.

Cocozzo picked a wall and tested it with the pads of his fingers before deciding not to lean against it. Primo moved to the other side of where I was sitting. If you'd had a compass, Junior and I would have been north and south, Cocozzo and Zuppone east and west.

Ianella spoke to me from ten feet. "Okay, dickhead, we did this like you wanted. Now talk to us."

"Can I put my hands down?"

He looked at Cocozzo, who said, "Yeah."

I brought them to my lap. "Here's what happened, as straight as I know it. A woman comes to me, says she wants her boyfriend investigated. I find out he isn't what—"

Junior said, "We heard all this shit. Cut to where Di-Rienzi's at, or"—glancing meaningfully toward the old oak stand—"we start cutting you."

I just watched Ianella. "When I told the client what I'd found out, that your bookkeeper wasn't who he claimed to be, I think she went down to see him at his condo unit. There's some indication they took off together."

The mottled look. "What's this 'some indication' shit?"

"His neighbors overheard an argument. One of them saw your guy loading suitcases into her car the night he cleaned out his bank accounts."

"What night's this?" said Cocozzo.

I still addressed Ianella. "Thursday."

"The night we got here," said the balding man.

"Right. Only thing is, my client never touched her own money, and when I went around to the parking lots at Logan—"

"Where?" said Junior.

To my left, Zuppone's voice said, "That's our airport, Mr. Ianella."

"When I checked the lots, I found my client's car, a flashy Porsche."

"There another kind?" said Cocozzo.

"Which didn't strike me right, since your bookkeeper was driving a much quieter car for dumping. And the parking attendant said the male was driving, when my client told me she never let anybody else touch the car. And the driver waved to the attendant."

Junior said, "Waved to him?"

"Yes."

Shake of the head. "That Judas fuck DiRienzi never waved to anybody in his life."

Cocozzo said, "He was a cold guy that way, Cuddy. No personality, you know?"

I said, "Even if DiRienzi was Mr. Congeniality, he wants to ditch the car and disappear. Why would he try to make an impression by waving to anybody?"

Cocozzo didn't reply.

I went back to Ianella. "Which is what I meant before by 'some indication.' I think it's possible they took off together, but those things seem wrong."

Junior looked over at Cocozzo, who said to me, "You been sticking your nose into DiRienzi's cover, the feds running the witness program should have been on to you."

"They are. They say they don't know where he is, and they don't care."

Ianella said, "The fuck does that mean?"

"I think it means he's already given them what they wanted, which was testimony against your father, and now they'd just as soon he did disappear as have to be accounted for."

"Accounted for?"

Cocozzo said, "Like if we got to him, Boss. Only we

259

didn't." The balding man turned to me. "You say the neighbors where he lives told you that DiRienzi and his girlfriend were arguing on Thursday night, right?"

"Right."

"Seems to me, they were lovey-dovey before, now they're not, it's gotta be because the girlfriend tells him she hired you."

"Probably."

"Yeah, but that means DiRienzi oughta know his cover ain't blown, except to you and her, right?"

Cocozzo's point was a conversation-stopper. I hadn't thought about it that way.

Junior looked lost. "The fuck you saying here, Coco?"

The patient voice. "What I'm saying, Boss, is that DiRienzi knows the only one on to him is his own girlfriend and Cuddy here, then his new ID is still just fine, account of we don't get into town ourselves till Thursday night and Cuddy don't know who his 'client's boyfriend' really is till we see him at his office on Friday."

I didn't like where this was leading.

Cocozzo said, "Which means that Thursday night, Di-Rienzi's got no reason to run. He just calls his keepers, and they straighten things out, and he gets to stay Mr. Whoever-he-is." From ten feet away, the muzzle of the semiautomatic hovered about heart-high on my chest. "If Cuddy's been telling us the truth, that is."

Primo Zuppone stepped toward Ianella. "Cuddy don't lie."

Junior looked at him, astonished. "The fuck you saying, he don't lie?"

"I seen him in a bad situation before, Mr. Ianella. I grant you, the guy might have more balls than brains, but he don't lie."

Junior glared, the mottling spreading upward and breaking like a wave over his features. "Primo, this dickhead knows he's gonna die here he don't tell us what we want, and you say, 'He don't lie, Mr. Ianella?' What's the matter, all those pimples spoil your brain too?"

The rage ran visibly through Zuppone. "Mr. Ianella—"

"Shut the fuck up, pizza-face."

Cocozzo said, "Boss . . ."

"You too, Coco, for chrissake. Give me his piece."

"His piece?"

"His gun, the one you took off him. I ruined my loafers in this fucking pigsty, I don't want to wreck the suit too, playing butcher boy with those fucking knives."

Cocozzo reached into a jacket pocket, sending the revolver to the younger man in an easy, underhand toss.

When Junior caught it, he moved toward my bench, hefting the gun rather than pointing it. Cocozzo shifted with him, so as to have a clear field of fire toward me.

Ianella said, "Coco thinks you're lying, I think you're lying, no matter what this fucking stooge here believes."

Primo made a noise, deep inside.

Junior turned to him. "You got something to say, pizza-face?"

Cocozzo said again, "Boss . . ."

"Shut up! Answer me, pizza-face, you got something to say?"

"Mr. Ian—"

The quick cuff to the chin, rocking Zuppone a little this time. "When I ask you that question, and you know I don't want to fucking hear nothing from you, you just shake your head, you understand? You keep your mouth closed and you just shake your fucking head, you got it?"

Primo's whole body was shaking as he just nodded this time, once and decisively.

Now Junior turned back to me, glowering down. "Your story don't add up, Cuddy, and I think you're running some kind of game on us. But even if you ain't, even if you're just stone fucking stupid and DiRienzi outsmarted you, the fact is, you lost him, and you don't have a single fucking clue where he went. And that makes me very fucking mad."

Speed-talking, Zuppone said, "Mr. Ianella, DiRienzi ran before Cuddy here even met you, so—"

This time not a cuff, but a backhanded clout that knocked Primo sideways. "Shut the fuck up, you fucking pimple-freak, or you'll get the first slug! And you, Cuddy, you make me fucking sick. My father's rotting away in a cell because some Judas fuck set him up and sent him up, and then you lose the piece a shit who should have paid for it. Which means you get to pay for it. One part of you at a time."

Junior cocked the revolver and pointed it at my crotch, a step too far away for me to lunge for it. I was still going to try when Cocozzo made the only mistake I'd seen him commit.

He stepped toward his boss, blocking his line of sight on Primo.

Zuppone drew the Beretta from its shoulder holster and shot Rick Ianella twice. Junior lurched against his bodyguard as the balding man was trying to elevate his own gun hand. Then Primo emptied the rest of the Beretta's clip into Cocozzo, who fired his weapon three times, reflexively but harmlessly, into the ceiling. Dust from above began wafting slowly downward as the two Milwaukee mobsters, clutching each other like clumsy dancers, fell to the floor.

I looked at Zuppone, the Beretta jacked open and empty, the trembling of his right hand scattering the smoke curling up from the chamber.

"Primo—"

"No! No." His voice was raspy. "Don't say a fucking word till I tell you." Then he seemed to notice how the gun was moving in his hand and lowered it. Something short and harsh in Italian was followed by, "The fuck did I do here?"

We were coming over the Charlestown Bridge into the Boston Garden area of the North End when Zuppone stuck a fresh toothpick in his mouth and said, "All right, talk."

"Thanks."

Zuppone glanced over to me, then at each of the Lincoln's mirrors. "For letting you talk?"

"No, for saving my life."

A movement of his head that was more shudder than simple shake. "Maybe only temporary, for both of us."

"How long can you leave the bodies there?"

"After I drop you, I make a couple, three calls from a pay phone, handle it the same way as last time."

Which meant a no-questions-asked team from the friendly funeral home. "And the death certificates?"

"Dr. T.—the guy helped us out before?—he'll put down anything I want. Only thing is . . ."

"The people in Milwaukee will expect the bodies back for burial, right?"

"Right. And our coordinator here—the one who called them out there in the first fucking place—he's gotta be satisfied that this didn't happen the way you and me know it did."

"Which means?"

"Which means that I gotta fucking account for a clip full of bullets in two organization guys. And that means I gotta give Milwaukee and our coordinator somebody who pulled the fucking trigger."

"Some somebody."

"Yeah, but preferably not me."

Zuppone couldn't quite make the tone light enough.

I said, "DiRienzi is the only candidate who comes to mind."

"Even that's gonna be a tough sell, he was only a paperwork guy, not muscle."

"And why weren't you around when he was shooting your out-of-town guests, who ought to be checking in with their people in Milwaukee soon."

Zuppone made a careful left turn. "I'm glad you appreciate my situation."

"It gets worse. I wasn't going to hand DiRienzi over to Junior, I'm not going to help you bundle him on a plane back to the Midwest."

"Even if you knew where DiRienzi is, right?"

"That's right."

Another glance. "You really don't fucking know?"

"Primo, you just killed two guys proving it."

Zuppone brought the Lincoln slowly to the curb outside a furniture store shuttered for the night. Always the careful driver, he seemed to be concentrating even more on the little tasks, something I remembered doing after having to take a life. Or lives.

He left the engine running. "Cuddy, I never done anything like this before."

I looked at him.

Primo shook his head. "No, I don't mean whacking somebody, for chrissake. Or even somebody in the organization, for that matter. I mean doing a hit on my own, something that wasn't authorized."

"Especially if it was somebody you were told to protect."

"That's right. That's exactly right. Those guys, they were my responsibility. Ianella, he might have been the worst prick I met in ten years, but him and Coco were my responsibility, and I didn't ... Aw, shit."

He rubbed his right palm over his eyes, like he was trying to wake up from a dream. A bad one. "What I'm saying here, I never did anything I wasn't told to. I always been faithful to my oath, the one I took when they made me a member. You read in the papers about how the ceremony is all mumbo jumbo, like some kind of witch-doctor shit. But it's real, Cuddy, the realest thing I ever went through. I'm a made fucking member of our organization, and for twenty-two fucking years I always stood up for it. And now I'm so fucking bummed out, I can't even think straight."

"Primo?"

"Yeah?"

"Just one question."

"What is it?"

"There any doubt in your mind that you did the right thing today?"

Zuppone looked at me steadily, the eyes moist but not filling with tears. "No. No fucking doubt whatsoever. You were telling them the truth, and Ianella was going to kill you for it, and Coco couldn't have stopped him."

"Well, then, you shouldn't feel bad about that."

"I won't, you can explain to me one thing."

"What's that?"

"How you going to get us off the hook with my people and Milwaukee?"

Primo dropped me at my car in downtown, and I drove toward the condo, nagged by what Cocozzo had said back in the slaughterhouse. "Andrew Dees" really didn't have any reason to run on Thursday night. He might have been madder than hell at Olga Evorova for having me check into his background, but that didn't explain his leaving the Witness Protection Program, with or without her. Especially since DiRienzi knew the marshals' service would have relocated him again if he had any real reason to fear that his current identity had been compromised. It just didn't make sense.

I thought about what I'd been told by Norman Elmendorf and the Stepanians, the argument from unit 42 they all overheard, Steven Stepanian seeing "Dees" loading luggage into the Porsche. If Stepanian was lying about what he saw, then he and his wife could have been the couple dropping off Olga's car in Elmer's lot at the airport. But why would the Stepanians want to impersonate DiRienzi and Evorova? To help with some escape plan that a neighbor they hardly knew didn't really need?

And if Steven Stepanian was telling the truth, then did somebody else hijack DiRienzi and Evorova before they got to Logan? Most of the other males I'd seen were probably "tall" enough for Elmer's description of the driver. But none had any motive I knew about, and besides, Boyce Hendrix was part of the cooperating witness program, Norman Elmendorf wasn't very mobile, and Jamey Robinette was attending a band concert with his mother on Thursday night.

Things were making even less sense to me as I parked the Prelude behind the brownstone. Upstairs, the window of my tape machine was blinking a single message. I played it back. Nancy, saying she'd waited until two-thirty before taking a cab home and what the hell had happened to me?

When I was connected to her number, the outgoing announcement clicked on, but as I started my own message after the beep, Nancy broke in. "John, where are you?"

"Home."

"What—"

"It's a long story, Nance."

A pause. "John, is something wrong?"

"What do you mean?"

"I mean your voice. It doesn't sound right."

I cleared my throat. "How's this?"

"Uh-oh. Something bad happened, didn't it?"

"This mean I can't fool you even over the telephone anymore?"

"It must. What's wrong?"

"How about if I drive to your place and we talk there?"

"I don't have anything much for us to eat."

I suddenly noticed the scent of the slaughterhouse coming off my clothes. "I'm not very hungry."

"There's still some of that chicken soup left over from Friday night?"

"That'd be fine. See you in thirty minutes."

"Thirty? It shouldn't take you fifteen without traffic."

I was already out of my suit jacket. "I need to shower and change first."

Inside the kitchen, I could smell the soup simmering in the crockpot. Renfield kept his distance, sensing something the shower hadn't washed away. Nancy first looked up at me, then laid the right side of her head against my chest, arms around my waist.

"You seem sound of wind and limb."

I said, "Just barely."

Nancy tilted her head back, then broke the hug. "Meaning, you're the one who could use some cuddling tonight."

"I came close this afternoon, Nance. Real close."

Her eyes grew troubled, then she smiled without showing her teeth. "The soup can wait. Let's bring some wine into the living room, and you can tell me about it."

I said I thought that would be a very good start.

21

After I told Nancy as much as I could about what had happened, we made our way to the bedroom. A few hours later, while she dozed, I got up and went quietly into the kitchen for some water. The phone rang, startling me, and I answered it instinctively. "Hello?"

"Cuddy, that you?"

"Primo, what're you doing, calling me here?"

"Look, I been burning the fucking wires to your condo there and getting squat. If your girlfriend answered, I would've hung up."

"That doesn't—"

"Besides, I figured we still had kind of an emergency on our hands, you know?"

No question there. "Okay. So tell me."

"Things suck, but I'm still alive." The whooshing sound as he breathed. "After my guys took care of the cleanup, I figured I oughta let this friend of ours—the coordinator?—know that everything hit the fan."

"And?"

"And he's bullshit, what do you think, but he believes what I told him because he wants to believe it."

"What did you tell him?"

"That Rick and Coco found a lead on their own and left me a fucking message. When I picked it up, I went straight to the slaughterhouse and found what I found."

"Primo, how would they know to go there in the first place?"

"Account of they asked me in advance to show it to them, give Coco a door key, in case they wanted to use the meat locker for entertaining somebody."

Smart. "Somebody like Alfonso DiRienzi?"

"I had a brainstorm there, I think. I told this coordinator that it was just possible the fucking feds had made Rick and Coco somehow and decided to send our organization a message by whacking them, so we were going to have to be real careful, here on out."

"Only the feds wouldn't do that."

"Hey-ey-ey, some other time I'll tell you about these former friends of mine would argue the point, they were still alive to speak their piece."

"And you think the rogue-cop story sounds better than what we came up with?"

"Yeah, but it's not gonna buy you and me much time. I was able to convince our coordinator that Rick and Coco oughta stay on ice for a while at the funeral home, till we could hand the Milwaukee people a better result."

"Primo—"

"Look, don't say it again, all right? You ain't gonna give up DiRienzi even if you do find him. Fine. You fucking spook that rat from wherever he is, though, and it's open fucking season on him, far as I'm concerned."

I didn't much like what I was about to suggest, but I couldn't see any other way to be in two places at the same time. "Primo, I'm going to ask you to do something else."

"Now what?"

"I've got to run around tomorrow, trying to trace a couple of things. I need you to get a pair of binoculars, some kind of writing pad, and a rent-a-car."

"A rent-a-car?"

"Yes."

"What the fuck for?"

I told him.

He said, "And you think that if DiRienzi and your client didn't take off on their own, one of his neighbors had something to do with it?"

"Go back to what Cocozzo said in the slaughterhouse. DiRienzi had no reason to run if my client tells him she's the one who hired me. And the neighbors are basically the only other people I talked with about him."

"You got a reason why one of them should have a hard-on for DiRienzi?"

"No, but I'm out of better ideas. You?"

About ten seconds went by before Primo Zuppone said, "All right. How am I supposed to recognize these assholes?"

After a teeth-pulling hour with my word-processing wonder at the copy center, I rode the Green Line trolley to Boston University. The transcript department is on the second floor of 881 Commonwealth Avenue. It reminded me a lot of the registrar's office at the University of Central Vermont, except that I had to wait on a growing line of seniors earnestly hoping their BU grades could get them into the graduate school of their (parents') choice.

When my turn came, I walked up to a young, red-haired man.

"Can I help you?"

"Hope so. I need a former student's transcript." I handed him the authorization letter for "Andrew Dees," modified to "Lana Stepanian."

He scanned it quickly, barely glancing at the signature I'd forged from Stepanian's "Hendrix Management" questionnaire. "There's no Social Security or student ID number on here."

"She didn't give those to me."

"Or date of graduation."

"Sorry, but isn't 'Stepanian' unusual enough—"

"We require all that stuff, plus date of birth, any former name used, and—"

"Lopez."

"Lopez?"

"Her maiden name."

The red-haired guy sighed, writing "Lopez" on the letter. "Well, I'll have to do some checking. If I find her, I'll mail the transcript out to you this afternoon."

"Can I come back and pick it up instead?"

He looked behind me, probably at the growing line. "This place'll be a zoo the rest of today and tomorrow. You're better off with me mailing it."

I didn't want to push my thinning luck. "Okay."

He wrote down the Tremont Street address. "That'll be three dollars, please."

Same as the university in Vermont. Even registrar's offices have a going rate.

"What, you again?"

"Sorry to disturb you, Mo."

"Well, you already have, so the harm's done. Come in, close the door."

I took a chair across the cluttered desk. Mo Katzen was in the vest and trousers of the usual gray suit today, some strands of his white, wavy hair spit-curled onto his forehead. Between index and middle fingers he held a lit cigar.

"Find your wicks, Mo?"

"My . . . ? Oh, yeah. The ASN's thought they got them all,

but they didn't." He gestured with the cigar toward the desk top. "You know anything about the organ market, John?"

"You mean human organs?"

"Yeah, human. What, you think they transplant for kittens and bunnies?"

"No, Mo, but—"

"Well, Freddie's funeral—Freddie Norton, I told you about him, last time you wrecked my train of thought—it got me thinking. He had this organ-donor card in his wallet. Now Freddie's own equipment, it wasn't what you'd call fresh off the shelf, if you see my point. But I asked myself, what's the business itself like? Life gives you lemons, you make lemonade, right?"

"Sorry, you lost me."

"John." A baleful look. "Concentrate, okay?"

"I'll try, Mo."

He spoke very deliberately, as though I was block-printing notes. "Freddie gets clocked by a truck, he's a good friend, I'm at his funeral. That's the lemon, get it? Only the organ-donor card gives me the idea to research the market for human organs, the basis for a newspaper article. My business, John. That's the lemonade, see?"

"A friend's death is a sad thing, but it inspires an article for you, which is making the best of a bad situation."

"Move to the head of the class. Anyway, I start looking into this 'market,' and it's fascinating."

After the slaughterhouse the day before, I wasn't in the mood for that kind of fascination. "Mo—"

"One of the computer Nazis got me some of the laws on this." He picked up a densely printed Xerox. "It seems some doctor got the idea of buying organs from living donors, then selling them on the open market. That made Congress pass the National Organ Transplant Act of 1984, which kind of regulated things. But," picking up another Xerox, "every state in the Union passed this Uniform Anatomical Gift

Act—which, I got to tell you, doesn't seem all that 'uniform' to me. Anyway, under the state law, the families of people killed kind of 'quickly and cleanly' can donate the decedent's organs. Only guess what, John?"

"No organ-donor card, no organ donation."

"What?"

"Without a card from the donor, the families can't—"

"Oh. Huh, never thought about that." Shaking one Xerox like a rattle at the other, Mo said, "Have to read these over again, dammit. No, what I meant was, the families won't receive a dime for the organs, but something called a 'transplant agency'—that's a nice touch, don't you think? A transplant *agency*, like they're selling insurance or real estate. Anyway, this agency gets something from the hospital, and the hospital gets fifteen, twenty thousand for each major organ, and so the old joke, it doesn't hold up anymore."

I had to bite. "Which old joke?"

This look was more disappointed than baleful. "Holy Cross would be—you went to the Cross, right?"

"Right, Mo."

"The good priests would be ashamed, your lack of chemistry culture."

"Chemistry?"

"Yeah, The old joke, that every human body is worth only about a dollar forty-nine in chemicals. Well, I'll tell you, John, if my computer Nazis are right," reaching for a pencil and touching the sharpened tip to his tongue, "the price went up to around . . . let's see . . . fifteen and change for a kidney, times two, plus twenty for the liver, times—no, just one per customer on—"

"Mo, speaking of computers."

He looked up. "What?"

"Speaking of the computers, could you loan me one of your people to do a little more research?"

"Research? They already got all I can use on the organ market."

"I meant for me, on something else."

"Will it get you out of my hair?"

"Cross my heart."

Waving at his Xeroxed statutes, Mo Katzen said, "That supposed to be funny?" and then reached for the telephone.

The computer researcher who came to Mo's door this time was a young African-American woman named Giselle with dreadlocked hair and a Lauren Hutton gap between her two front teeth. Giselle led me back through the rabbit warren of cubicles to her carrel, and she turned out to be much faster than the first helper had been.

We ran "Steven Stepanian" through the search commands. Just a couple of isolated references to his being on the Plymouth Mills School Committee. Then Lana Stepanian. Nothing. We tried Lana Lopez. Nothing again.

Next was Norman Elmendorf. A couple of photo credits on pictures he'd taken for his Brockton paper years ago that apparently the *Herald* had gotten permission to use as well. Nothing about his military service, despite the exhaustive media coverage the Gulf War had received.

Giselle and I tried Kira Elmendorf too. No entries.

Tángela Robinette. Three stories—one main, two much briefer follow-ups—on her husband being killed and her own previous federal service. Son Jamey was listed as another survivor in each article.

For the hell of it, I asked Giselle to run Paul or Paulie Fogerty through. Zip, but that's what I expected anyway.

Giselle looked up, the gap somehow making her smile seem more helpful. "Anyone else?"

"Yes," even though it was really scraping rock bottom. "Try the names Yale Quentin and Plymouth Willows."

"That's Y-A-L-E and Q-U-E-N-T-I-N?"

"I think so."

"And Willows, like the tree?"

"Yes."

"You want them linked?"

"Linked?"

"Yes. 'Plymouth Willows' within so many words of 'Yale Quentin' as the search command."

"No. Run his name on its own first."

The computer found a few articles from the early eighties about Quentin doing some smaller developments elsewhere on the South Shore. Later articles overlapped in discussing him and the Plymouth Willows project: the initial optimism, the unfolding difficulties, the eventual financial and personal tragedy. There was even a grainy photo of Quentin's widow, a flight attendant, at the cemetery ceremony following his suicide four years earlier. The story and caption gave her first name as "Edith," but she wore no veil, and the photo captured her lower lip curling as she concentrated on something at the graveside.

Just the way Edie did, drawing a beer behind the bar at The Tides.

Aware of my concentration on the screen, Giselle said, "Would you like a printout of this one?"

"Please."

"Mo?"

"Now what?"

The cigar was in his mouth but dead again. "I just wanted to thank you for all the help."

"Don't mention it."

"One more thing?"

He made a ritual of taking the cigar out of his mouth. "John, maybe you ought to put me on the payroll, you know?"

"Last one, promise."

"What is it?"

"You know anybody on the Brockton paper?"

Mo Katzen turned the cigar to stare at its unlit end, as if seeing it for the first time. "Not since Chester Snedeker died. It's an interesting story, though. You got a minute to hear about Chet?"

22

An hour later, I left the *Herald*'s building, the air temperature feeling like seventy and still putting the lie to October on the calendar. Brockton being closer than Plymouth Mills, I got on the Southeast Expressway to Route 128 and eventually Route 24. Three miles after taking the second Brockton exit, I found the newspaper where Norman Elmendorf had worked, housed in an old granite elephant that could pass for a public library.

Locking the Prelude, I stuck under my arm the portfolio briefcase I'd been using. Inside the building's front doors was a fiftyish guy wearing a blue security uniform who couldn't have looked more bored if he'd been snoring. I showed him my identification, saying I was there to do a routine check on a former employee now applying for a job with a client of mine.

The guard picked up a telephone, dialed three digits, and passed my information on to somebody named "Betty." Nodding and hanging up, he said, "Take a seat. Somebody'll be right with you."

"Thanks."

"Hot as blazes for October, isn't it?"

"Global warming," I said.

"What?"

"Never mind."

A middle-aged woman in a hound's-tooth suit came through the door to the right of the guard and introduced herself as Betty without giving a last name. She asked me to follow her.

On the other side of the door, the city room wasn't exactly bedlam because it wasn't exactly populated. Three college-aged kids huddled around a single computer monitor, the cables twisting and lifting up through the ceiling like Jack's beanstalk. One woman Betty's age played hunt-and-peck at another terminal, muttering under her breath. A dozen more computer stations were empty, four of them apparently cleaned out.

At the back of the city room, Betty knocked once under a brown plastic plaque that said MANAGING EDITOR, then opened the door for me without getting an answer from inside. I went through, she closing behind me.

The man at the desk swung around from another computer screen, some henscratched notes in a small spiral notebook next to the keyboard. "And you'd be?"

"John Cuddy." As he stood, I extended my right hand to shake.

Taking it, he said, "Mike Yoder. Sit."

Yoder was about five-eight and shaped like a pear, the sloping shoulders under a V-neck sweater a good foot narrower than the middle of him. His thinning hair was gray and his hands were heavily veined, but he had a twinkle in the eye that made him seem younger than the sixty or so I'd have estimated.

Dipping into the portfolio, I took out the PERSONNEL RECORD REQUEST—also thanks to my wizard from the copy center—with a version of Norman Elmendorf's signature at the bottom. "I'm looking into the work background of a former employee here."

I passed the request to Yoder. He glanced at the signature area before reading the rest of it. Then he reached over to the telephone next to him and pressed a button. The door opened almost immediately, and Yoder said, "Betty, get me Norm Elmendorf's personnel file, will you?"

A hesitation, then, "Right away," and the door closed again.

Yoder said, "Mind if I ask what this is all about?"

"Mr. Elmendorf's applied for a job with a client of mine."

"I got that much from security via Betty."

"Not quite. I didn't give the guard or Betty Mr. Elmendorf's name."

"No," said Yoder. "No, you didn't. Who's your client?"

"I'm not at liberty to say."

Yoder was taking that equably as Betty knocked and entered. She gave him a red manila folder and left without looking at me.

As the door closed, Yoder began fussing around in the file, scouting for something, then held my form close to a document, glancing back and forth. Putting my request at the front of the folder, he left it open on his desk. "I'm no expert, of course, but that looks like Norm's signature. Can you tell me what sort of job he's applying for?"

"Photography work, on assignment."

Yoder seemed to gauge something. "He's getting around better, then?"

"The braces help, he told us."

"Us."

"My client."

Like a perplexed kid, Yoder tugged on his earlobe. "Mr. Cuddy, I know damned well Norm isn't applying for a newspaper job, because if he were, you wouldn't be sitting in front of me."

"Really?"

"Really. Some old hand like me would be on my phone there, getting what was needed without wasting gas and tires."

"My client's a little more formal. Plus, this way they have me to sue if I screw up."

Yoder seemed to gauge something again. "What is it you want to know?"

"Anything you can tell me about how he was as an employee."

"How he was?"

"You were his boss, right?"

Yoder didn't nod or shake his head.

I said, "He's been upfront with us about the drinking."

"He has."

"Yes. In a program for some time, now."

"I'm glad."

I leaned forward, lathering my hands with invisible soap. "Look, Mr. Yoder, it's like this. You can tell me about Mr. Elmendorf, and I can go back to my client with a report that says it's okay to hire the guy. Or, you can not tell me about him, in which case I give my client that instead, and I'm guessing Elmendorf loses out on a job he could really use." I leaned back. "Your call."

Yoder watched me some. "You've met Norm, then."

"I have."

"And his daughter?"

"Kira."

A little softening. "That girl's had to put up with more than most."

"Mr. Elmendorf told me his wife went south just as he got back from overseas."

The softening stopped, like a seized movie reel. "And you've checked on that?"

"On his wife leaving him?"

"No. The military stuff."

"Not yet. This kind of thing, I generally start with previous civilian employers."

The managing editor fussed some more with the file in front of him. "I could show you this, but I can tell you straight out that Norm was never overseas."

I felt my eyes closing for longer than a blink. "No Persian Gulf."

"Not for us, not for the Army." Then a different tone of voice, almost nostalgic. "Norm was a damned good photographer, Mr. Cuddy. Lots of people can work the equipment, learn the technical side. Norm, though, he had the eye. Could pull up to a fire or accident scene, and before he was out of the car, he'd be framing a shot in his head. And damned if his first photo didn't turn out better than anybody else's three rolls. Then the troubles started at home."

"What kind of troubles?"

Yoder stopped, and I was afraid I'd pushed him too far. After a moment, though, he said, "Norm's wife got tired of the crazy hours he kept. You have to understand, Norm wanted to be the first one on the scene every time out, so he didn't mind us calling him, day or night. Eventually it got to his marriage, and when she started packing, Norm started drinking."

"And all this was ...?"

"About the time of Desert Storm in late ninety, early ninety-one. It was half my fault, I suppose. Publisher wanted us to cover the hell out of the homefront, kind of a miniature W-W-Two—clear enemy, real heroes—a 'good war,' to paraphrase Studs Terkel."

"How was it your fault, though?"

"I kind of gave Norm his head, let him shoot to his heart's

content. He had a pager, so we could always reach him wherever he was, and I guess the worse hours made the marriage break up a little sooner than it would have otherwise."

"But only a little sooner."

"Yeah, probably." Yoder tugged on the earlobe again. "But her finally leaving sent Norm well over the edge and deep into the bottle. The man got the notion that he'd served in the Gulf. Norm had covered enough of the guys—and women—going over there, had seen the letters and videos to the families. Point is, he knew enough about the war to talk a good game, so long as the people buying him drinks didn't require too many details."

"And that cost him the job?"

"Pretty directly. Almost crashed the newspaper's car into a school bus rushing off somewhere half-crocked. I had to fire him, Norm sitting right in that chair where you are when I told him."

"What brought on the physical disability?"

"A fall. Kira contacted us about it, but his health benefits here had long since expired, and he hadn't used COBRA."

"COBRA?"

"Acronym, as in the snake. It's a way you can extend your health coverage from your most recent employer, but it's expensive as hell."

"Have you seen Elmendorf himself lately?"

"Heard from him on and off since . . . since he was sitting in that chair. Always by telephone, usually more than half-crocked." Yoder stared at me. "I'm glad to hear Norm's on the wagon now, but it doesn't sound like he's aware the Desert Storm stuff wasn't reality for him."

"From what I know, you're right."

A final tug on the earlobe. "Mr. Cuddy, I probably haven't sounded like much of a recommendation for Norm, but he really was great with the camera, one of the best I've ever seen. If you can see your way clear to make your client understand that, then I won't feel as though I've wasted my breath on you."

"Mr. Yoder, believe me. You've been a big help."

At the forlorn mall north of Plymouth Mills, I cruised the haphazard rows of parking until I heard someone tap a car horn twice. Then I took the next available space, got out of the Prelude, and looked around me.

It was a different vehicle all right, but another Lincoln Continental. Yellow, with Florida plates.

I went to the passenger side and slid in, the upholstery as supple as Primo's own model. "What's the matter, you don't believe in experimentation?"

The toothpick rolled from one corner of his mouth to the other. "You told me, rent a car. I'm used to the way these here handle."

"It sticks out like a sore thumb."

"That's where you're wrong, Cuddy. You were right about not taking mine, though. No place to sit at that fucking condo complex except inside what you're driving, and no place to park it except on one of those little—what did you call them?"

"Leaf roads?"

"Yeah, leaves." He looked down at his suit, bits and pieces of dead foliage sticking to the pants and sleeves. "Let me tell you about leaves."

"Before you do, did anybody spot you?"

"Spot me? Hell, no. That's what I mean about this Lincoln here. After I phoned you yesterday, I saw this friend of ours, has a rent-a-car agency. I tell him, 'I want a Continental.' He hits his computer thing and says, 'Only one I got has Florida plates on it.' I think, great, anybody notices the car on the street, they'll think it belongs to somebody's parents, up to visit the grandkids, you know? So I tell him, 'Fill out the paperwork.' Then this morning, I drive it down to Plymouth whatever-the-fuck and park and watch for nobody to be around before I walk up that hill you told me about. Where I sit down in the trees for about eight hours with all kinds of animal shit around me and leaves that stick to you like fucking Velcro."

I looked at his sleeves and cuffs. "Nettles, probably."

"Nettles? Is that where that word comes from, like somebody pisses you off?"

"I think so."

"Well, anyway, it's gonna take a fucking forest fire to clean this suit, so I hope I got what you need." Zuppone reached into an inside pocket and came out with a small pad. "You want to read this or have me read it to you?"

"You can read it."

Primo squared around. "All right, I'm in the trees at seven-oh-three—no, seven-thirty." I remembered Zuppone once telling me about his dyslexia. "I take out the binoculars, sight them in. It already feels like fucking July at seven-forty, when this colored kid comes out the third unit—third from the left, number 43—then walks the way I drove in till I can't see him anymore."

Jamey Robinette. "Catching a bus for school."

"Where the fuck does he go to?"

"Tabor Academy."

Zuppone looked at me in disbelief. "That's like a college-prep place, right?"

"Right."

"Can't be. This kid was done up like a gang-banger."

"Probably has a locker there, put on the blazer and old school tie before classes."

"No wonder we're losing ground to the Germans and the Japs."

"Primo . . ."

"What?"

"Skip it. Go on with what happened."

"All right, let me see ... Seven-forty-five, the door to the first unit—number 41—opens up, and this couple comes out onto the stoop there. He's kind of tall, and she's kind of short, both dark-haired. He kisses her, she hands him his lunch bag, Ozzie and fucking Harriet for the nineties."

The Stepanians. "Then what?"

"Ozzie drives off, and I notice this short guy in a gardener's uniform, who's raking the lawn like he was maybe gonna have surgery performed in the grass there."

Paulie Fogerty. "He see you?"

"Of course not. After the grass, it was the bushes. I swear, I thought the kid would shake some trees, make more work for himself, he seemed to like it so much. He turned my way once, I put the binoculars on his face. Hard to say for sure—he was wearing this baseball cap—but I think he's retarded."

"He is."

Primo shook his head. "Except for Rake-boy, it's pretty quiet till noon, when a girl comes by in a car. She goes up and knocks on the fourth unit—number 44. This other girl with hair like Madonna answers the door. From the clothes and all, both of them look like punk rockers."

Jude and Kira. "The girl in the car stay long?"

"Two minutes. Harriet from 41 comes over—doesn't cut across the grass, either. She walks all the way down the path to the sidewalk, then the sidewalk till the path to number 44. Harriet knocks, and goes in as the two girls come out and drive off." Zuppone glanced at me. "This Madonna, she got a yard-ape out of wedlock or something?"

"Sick father."

Primo looked thoughtful, then said, "The girls, they're gone for an hour. When they come back, the one with the car drops Madonna off, then Harriet comes out and goes back to her place, path-to-sidewalk-to-path again. I got the impression she's kind of repressed, you know what I mean?"

"Then what?"

"Then nothing while I'm using a dead branch to dig myself a fucking hole to take a leak in. Two-forty-five, O.J. Einstein comes walking home to number 43 from school. A colored woman leaves his place, goes out to a car's been sitting there all morning, and drives away."

Tángela Robinette.

Then Zuppone perked up a little. "Tedious shit till now, I grant you, but all of a sudden, some jungle music comes on."

"Jungle music."

Primo looked at me. "That rap shit. What do I have to do, hum a few bars?"

"How could you tell it was rap?"

"How could I tell? Hey-ey-ey, Cuddy, I might not give two cents for a truckload of the shit, but I know rap when I hear it."

"And you could hear the music all the way up the hill?"

"Fucking A. Then a minute later, it drops off. Matter of seconds after that, Madonna comes out her front door, only she's dressed different this time."

"Different how?"

"She's just got a T-shirt and shorts on, real pale legs, and two different-colored socks, blue on the right foot, red on the left."

"Where does she go?"

Zuppone grinned. "Next door to O.J.'s house, quick as she can, across the grass."

I looked at him.

Primo said, "Without knocking, his door opens, and Madonna slips inside."

"For how long?"

"I made it half an hour. Then she comes out and slips back into her place. Only thing . . ."

"What?"

The grin grew broader. "Now the blue sock's on the left foot, and the red's on the right."

I thought about it. "The music's the signal."

"That's what I'm seeing too."

"Mom is gone—"

"—and the coast is fucking clear." Zuppone stopped grinning. "So, does this multicultural soap opera shit help?"

"Maybe."

"Maybe? What's with fucking 'maybe'? I sat in nature's toilet for going on eight hours, it better be better than 'maybe.' "

I said, "You see anything else?"

"No. I left before Mom got back or Ozzie from 41 there came home from work."

"Nothing from 42?"

"Which is where I gotta figure DiRienzi was hiding, right?"

"Primo, you didn't go down there, did you?"

A hurt look. "What, you think I got rocks in my head? The feds fucking bobble the ball with the guy, they're gonna babysit the place, hoping he comes back or somebody who knows him shows up."

I resisted the temptation to rub my skull behind the ear where Kourmanos or Braverman slugged me Friday night. "And that's everything you saw?"

"Yeah." Zuppone folded over the pad, stuck it back in his jacket. "So what do I tell Milwaukee?"

"What do they know so far?"

I saw some anger rise in Primo, but he shook it off. "What they know is that number-one son and a pretty good fucking gun named Coco got on the silver bird Thursday P.M., called home twice, and ain't been heard from since early yesterday."

I said, "And your 'coordinator'?"

"He's getting nervous. Real nervous. Which ought to fucking terrify me, but I'm so numb, I don't have the sense to be scared." Zuppone glanced away from me. "Which scares me even more, tell you the truth."

The Tides was nearly empty on a Monday afternoon, and I didn't see Edith "Edie" Quentin behind the deserted bar. As I took a stool down near the end, though, she came through the kitchen door, a distracted look on her face.

"Lose something?" I said.

She started and turned, then recognized me.

I shrugged. "Or maybe you were just trying to remember something."

Edie didn't bite at that, either, before moving past the raw bar and toward the taps, using a damp towel to clean the metal posts. Sort of.

I said, "Maybe something you forgot to tell me?"

She concentrated on the towel, her lower lip curling. "I don't see what we have to talk about."

"How about a Harpoon, then."

Edie reached for a mug. "That's what I'm here for."

As she set my ale down on the bar, I said, "You prefer 'Edie' over 'Edith,' I know, but do you still go by 'Quentin'?"

She closed her eyes, let out a breath. "Look, if all this is some kind of scheme to collect on Yale's old debts—"

"—it's not—"

"—let me tell you, the estate's been bled dry already, okay? This isn't even my place. I just work here."

"Since you left the airline."

A steady "Yes."

"I didn't come in to dun you for money, Edie. I'd just like to ask a few questions about your husband and Plymouth Willows."

"And if I don't feel like answering them?"

"Then I go talk to other people, but I'd rather get the truth."

"The truth." Bitter, almost a laugh.

I said, "Your version of it, anyway."

Edie slapped the damp towel on the bar like a judge would a gavel. "Yeah, well, my version won't take too long. Yale had big dreams and a big Cadillac Coupe de Ville to carry them around in. He thought he had the touch after developing a couple of dinky subdivisions further inland, so he tried his hand—and all our money—on a condo complex that was, get this, 'Virtually oceanfront, Honey.' "

"And things didn't work out."

"Work out? Plymouth Willows sank like a stone. Oh, Yale kept telling me, 'It's not a recession, Honey. Just a bump in the road, our road to riches.' " Another almost-laugh. "Only one problem: it *was* a recession. Hell, it was a depression, and poor Yale kept trying to shovel sand against the tide he should have seen was coming at him."

"There were a lot of people with shovels back then, and most of them didn't see it coming, either."

"Yeah, I know." The bitterness left her voice. "And to give Yale credit where credit's due, he protected me all right."

" 'Protected' you?"

"We kept a little house in one of those earlier developments, took title in my name only, then did a homestead exemption on it. You know what that is?"

A very quiet "Yes, I do," from me.

"Well, when the walls came tumbling down around Plymouth Willows, the house was where we could have stayed, nice and warm, to ride out the storm."

"But you didn't?"

A labored sigh. "I thought we were. Only Yale got obsessed with saving his equity in the condo complex—which was crazy, all the prices had fallen so far, there was no equity left. That didn't stop my husband, though. No sir, he kept trying to show the mortgage lenders he was going to come out of it, prove to them his already existing buyers were solid people."

"How?"

A wave of the hand, which came to rest on the towel, kneading it a little. "Yale 'investigated' them, in his own half-assed way. He couldn't afford a real private investigator—hell, by this time, even his lawyer had bailed out on him—so Yale went to talk with the people already in the complex, get them to vouch for him."

I remembered Norman Elmendorf telling me that Quentin had asked about him at the Brockton paper. "And?"

"And I guess Yale wasn't getting what he needed. Cooperation, I mean, or enough people with the juice to convince his lenders. So, instead of weathering the storm in our safe little house, the man who dreamed big got behind the wheel of his Coupe de Ville and drove it off that scenic overlook south of town."

Elmendorf had told me that too. "Suicide."

A slight change in the tenor of Edie's voice. "That's the way it looked."

I stopped. "Meaning you weren't persuaded?"

"Meaning the lenders weren't about to kill Yale when they or the FDIC could just foreclose on him, the way they ended up doing anyway. And he sure didn't accidentally go over the cliff and down onto the rocks."

I pictured the bluff in my head; Edie sounded right about that part. "And so the incident was written off as a suicide?"

"Hey, look, what was I supposed to do, huh? Tell me, please. Yale owed over a million dollars, and if I tried to contest what the cops thought happened, who would it help?" Again the bitterness faded. "Besides, Yale was all up-and-down those last few days."

"How do you mean?"

"Like manic depressive. He'd be down in the dumps, then figure he had something that might help him, then take another nosedive when the something didn't pan out. The cops told me it sure sounded suicidal in their book."

And you couldn't really blame them. Enough people who lost everything when their own "Massachusetts Miracle" burst certainly took that way out of the problem.

I hadn't touched the Harpoon, and I didn't want to. "What do I owe you?"

The almost-laugh. "On the house. I always like to comp a guy comes in, makes me feel like shit all over again."

Yanking the towel off the bar top, Edie Quentin strode back into the kitchen.

Driving to Plymouth Willows, I tried to see a connection between Yale Quentin's "suicide" four years earlier and what Primo had told me about Kira Elmendorf and Jamey Robinette. But while the Elmendorfs had lived there before Quentin's death, the Robinettes hadn't moved into the complex until just two years ago.

Going up the front driveway, I parked near the tennis courts and walked to Paulie Fogerty's door. He opened it soon after my knock.

"Where's your camera?"

"Didn't bring it today, Paulie."

Fogerty stood in his doorway.

"Can I come in a minute?" I said.

A blink and a nod. "Oh, sure."

He left and bustled toward the bedroom again, coming back with what looked like the same chair for me. I sat down while Paulie aimed the remote at his VCR, the screen showing Bugs Bunny about to get the best of Yosemite Sam before dissolving to royal blue. Then Fogerty went to his recliner and flopped into it.

I said, "I'd like to ask you a few more questions, Paulie."

Blink and nod. "Sure."

"You work around the complex pretty much every day, right?"

"Right. I'm the super. I work for Mr. Hend'ix."

"Have you seen Mr. Dees?"

"Sure. He lives in unit . . . uh, 42."

"I mean, have you seen him lately?"

"Lately?"

A test. "Today, for example."

Fogerty just blinked. "No."

"Yesterday, maybe?"

Blink. "I don't know. He has a store too. In town."

"Right. I've been there, Paulie. How about the day before yesterday?"

"Before yesterday?"

"Yes, Saturday."

Blink. "I don't know."

Okay. "Have you seen anybody else around his unit?"

"Just his friends."

"His friends?"

"Yes. Two men."

"Can you describe them?"

Blink and nod. "Like you."

"What do you mean?"

"They were big, like you."

"When was this?"

"I don't know."

Probably Kourmanos and Braverman on Friday, when they were going in to babysit Dees' place. "Paulie, have you seen anything unusual around there?"

"Where?"

"Mr. Dees' unit."

"No. Summer's over, so the grass isn't so good. And the leaves, they blow everywhere, no matter what I do."

Fogerty pointed toward the rake hanging from a wall hook. "But it's okay."

"What's okay?"

"The leaves. I'll get them tomorrow. I work for Mr. Hend'ix." Paulie Fogerty beamed the hang-jaw smile at me. "I'm the super."

Leaving the Prelude by the tennis courts, I walked to the cluster Primo Zuppone had been watching for me that day. I put my ear against the door of the Elmendorfs' unit. Hearing nothing, I knocked softly.

The door opened, Kira standing behind it in black denim shirt and almost-matching jeans, no shoes or socks. Another change of clothes since she'd visited Jamey Robinette earlier. "Oh, hi."

"Hi, Kira. Can I come in?"

"Yeah, but my dad's, like, asleep, and I kind of hoped I wouldn't have to wake him up."

"That's okay. It's you I wanted to talk to."

A shadow passed over her eyes, then, "Why not, I'm sure not doing anything."

We walked into the living room, still awash in magazines. Kira pushed a poker hand of them onto the floor so I could have a chair.

She took the old print couch across from me, her left leg folded under her rump. "So, what's the question of the day?"

"Andrew Dees seems to be missing."

"Missing? You mean, like, gone or something?"

"Yes. Have you seen him recently?"

Kira seemed to think about it. For the first time, if she wasn't a great actress. "No, I haven't, but then, I don't get out much."

"Just with Jude, for lunch."

"Right."

"When Mrs. Stepanian comes over to keep an eye on your father."

A funny look. "Right."

"Or when Jamey Robinette blares his music."

Kira's eyes widened before she could control them. "He doesn't do that often, but it really, like, bothers my dad, so—"

"You call him, and he turns it down."

She seemed to relax a little. "Right."

"But then you can't go out the back door, even though that would be more private, because the deck's right under your father's bedroom window and he'd hear you. So you make up some excuse and slip out the front."

The widening of the eyes again. "Look, I don't know what—"

"Wearing a T-shirt and shorts today, with one red sock, one blue."

It seemed an effort to keep her voice down, but after a glance toward the loft, Kira managed. "You've been spying on me. Why?"

"Kira, I'm not spying on you. I just need some information, and I'd prefer not to use things I've found out along the way unless it's necessary."

"Blackmail?" She said the word almost as a laugh, so much like Edie Quentin that I noticed it. "You're trying to blackmail somebody who's almost homeless?"

"No blackmail, just information. What do you know about Mr. Dees?"

"Nothing." Kira could tell I wasn't buying. "Honest, nothing but what I told you last time."

"When you were next door with Jamey, did you ever hear anything?"

"From Mr. Dees' unit, you mean?"

"Yes."

"Never. Jamey and I . . . we, like, have to see each other when his mom's not around. She's real strict with him, and my dad—huh, he found out and . . ."

Kira stopped, seeming to realize she might be giving me more leverage that I already had.

I lowered my voice. "Kira, I'm just trying to find Mr. Dees. That's all I care about."

The funny look. "I thought you were here for some other condo place?"

"This is something different. Has Jamey ever said anything to you about Dees?"

"No."

I watched her.

A shake of the head, the rings through the ear clinking. "Honest, Jamey's never said a word about Mr. Dees."

"So Mr. Dees doesn't know about you and Jamey?"

"About . . . ? No. No, Mr. Dees is at his copy shop during the day, and he couldn't know."

"How about your father?"

"I already told you, he doesn't know, either."

"I talked with some people about him."

"About my dad, now?"

"Yes. His war record, for example."

Kira nearly laughed again, suddenly seeming relieved. "God, why didn't you just ask me?"

"He wasn't hurt in the Gulf."

"No."

"He wasn't even over there, was he?"

"No, of course not. That's just something he, like, made up, although he's said it so many times now, he might just believe it himself."

"It's important to his pride."

"Mr. Cuddy, it's important to him to have something. Originally, it was my mother and his job, but he lost both of them. Then it was this place, which pretty soon is going to be gone too. That'll leave him with his bottle and me, probably in that order."

Kira stopped again. "No, I'm sorry, that's wrong. My dad really does love me more than the bourbon, I think. But he got it into his head that something from Desert Storm instead of the booze makes him shaky and gives him those ucky blotches, and that's all there is to it."

"But what if somebody else found out about that?"

"You already did."

"I mean somebody from the complex. What if Andrew Dees found out your father's stories about being in the war were just that, stories?"

Kira ran a hand randomly through her platinum hair. "I don't get you."

"What if Dees confronted your father with that, threatened to expose him for—"

This time Kira did laugh, clamping a hand over her mouth to stop the sound from carrying up to the loft. Past her fingers, she said, "Mr. Cuddy, everybody, like, *knows* about my dad not being in the Gulf."

"They do?"

"Sure." She dropped her hand into her lap. "Oh, Mrs. Stepanian, she goes along with him on it, and Jamey's mom does too, the little she ever sees him. But they all know it's just so much bullshit." A look to the second floor that could break your heart. "No, the only one my dad's fooling is himself."

After leaving Kira, I walked down to the Stepanians' end unit and pressed the button at the jamb. It would be professional to actually hear Lana Stepanian confirm what I'd just been told about Norman Elmendorf, but I wasn't really sorry when no one answered the bonging sound inside the condo.

Kira's version of "everybody-knows-about-my-dad" had convinced me.

I left Plymouth Willows in the fading daylight, feeling more frustrated than ever. At the "scenic overlook," I pulled into the empty parking lot and got out of the car. Moving to the edge, I stared down at the rocks where Yale Quentin's Cadillac must have landed. Plunging nose first, the bumper would've smashed through the grille, the engine and steering column violating the front seat, crushing anybody . . .

Shaking my head, I said quietly, "Olga, Olga. Where are you?"

Then I shook my head some more.

"Does this mean we have something to celebrate?"

Nancy didn't answer as we moved through the entrance to Skipjack's, a great seafood place in the huge New England Life building. The restaurant's only a few years old, the decor aggressively Art Deco. But somehow it's welcoming too, and if I could figure out why, I'd be in a different business.

At the reception podium, Nancy shifted her briefcase from shoulder to hand and asked the hostess if they were serving outside. After a nod, the hostess asked us to follow her through the indoor dining area to the patio at the corner of Clarendon and St. James Street. The tables here were black iron and the chairs white resin, set off from the rest of the sidewalk by a black curlicue fence.

A young waiter with what they used to call a Madison Avenue haircut materialized immediately, introducing himself and asking if we'd like to start with a drink. Nancy set her briefcase on the cement next to her chair and ordered a bottle of Murphy Goode fumé blanc.

"Would you folks like to hear tonight's specials?"

"After you bring the wine," said Nancy, and he was off and running.

I reached across the table for her hand, having to go only halfway to find it. "Same question?"

"Something to celebrate? In a manner of speaking. The attempted murder trial pleaded out this morning."

"Based on your side of the case alone?"

"Plus the defendant's attorney persuading him that his version of the incident was just not going to the top of the flagpole."

"The trial the only good news?"

The waiter appeared with our wine. He opened the bottle and poured Nancy a taste. She approved it and he gave each of us a half-glass before reciting the specials in duly elaborate fashion. We decided to split a Caesar salad, anchovies on the side for me. Nancy chose the Swordfish "Skipjack's Style" and a baked potato, while I ordered the Hawaiian Moonfish special with barbecued french fries."

As he left us, Nancy raised her glass. "To a great waiter."

"I can ask around, see if he's unattached."

The Loni Anderson smile. "I'll bet you don't even remember his name."

"You're right, and they always put so much effort into saying that at the beginning."

Nancy touched her glass against mine. "To Jason."

"You remembered."

She managed to nod and sip, all in one fluid motion.

Jason brought us a bread basket, the contents wrapped in a napkin. The napkin was still warm, and the contents turned out to be rolls, spiced up something like focaccia.

After Jason moved away, I said, "So, do I finally get a real answer to my question?"

Nancy dipped into her briefcase, coming out with the rose I'd brought her Friday night.

"It's halfway open now," I said.

She extended it toward me. "And it looks like we'll get to see it—and many more—open all the way."

I felt a great sloughing deep inside my chest. "The test results."

Another nod. "Benign."

"Jesus, Nance." I stood and came around the table.

She got up as well, and we hugged long and hard for a good twenty seconds.

Into my neck, Nancy said, "What will Jason think?"

"No jokes for a minute, okay?"

"Okay."

We broke the hug and sat back in our chairs. A gentle breeze riffled the napkin, but the day's sunshine was still on it.

"You picked a good place and a better night, Nance." I watched two tourists photographing the John Hancock Tower diagonally across from us, the parallelogram skyscraper of aquamarine glass that rises sixty-some stories like an improbable special effect to dominate every long view in Back Bay.

Nancy caught my look. "It's gone from eyesore to icon in what, twenty years?"

I turned back to her. "That's pretty deep."

"I've been thinking deep thoughts lately."

"How about we postpone them till another day?"

"That sounds awfully tempting, John Francis Cuddy."

With no indication he'd seen us hugging, Jason brought the Caesar salad, and at some point the entrées, and at some point after that two slices of key lime pie with shredded coconut on top and a dollop of raspberry sauce to either side. It was one of those meals you eat one bite at a time, chewing thoughtfully and actually having an engaging, roving conversation that has nothing to do with work and everything to do with life.

Then the check arrived and Nancy paid it just as the air temperature dropped at least ten degrees. Only a cold front coming through, now not an omen of anything, and I draped my suit jacket over her shoulders for the six-block walk back to my place.

23

At the office that next Tuesday morning, there was a message with my answering service to call Claude Loiselle. I did, but the brusque Craig told me she was at a meeting outside the bank and would call back when she could. After hanging up, I didn't bother to try Primo Zuppone because he was supposed to be "in the trees" again for another surveillance of the cluster at Plymouth Willows, though I couldn't tell him what I hoped he'd see. I was about to lose my thoughts in some old paperwork when five envelopes slid through my mail slot and onto the floor.

Picking them up, I saw that one was from Boston University. Three sheets were folded inside. The first page was a BU transcript for Lana Stepanian, the second a form explaining what the grades on the transcript meant. The third sheet was a puzzler, though: an earlier, abbreviated transcript from the University of Idaho, in a town named Moscow, showing that Lana Stepanian had spent a full year there before transferring to BU, where she received her degree, a bachelor's in Spanish.

I put the pages down, then pulled my Plymouth Willows questionnaire file to check Stepanian's form. I'd noted only Boston University for her, husband Steven having the University of Idaho connection. Lana had been vague about his hometown and generally reluctant to discuss a lot of their background, but I was sure that she'd told me they met at a party while she was attending BU. Yet the Idaho transcript showed her as Lana Stepanian, not Lopez, with a mailing address in Cedar Bend, Idaho, not Solvang, California, the hometown she'd given me.

My telephone rang. "John Cuddy."

"Claude Loiselle."

"Back from the meeting already?"

"No. I told Craig to call me on the cellular if he heard from you. But I am a little pressed for time right now."

"Understood. Have you been checking on Olga's ATM activity?"

"Every few hours. No transactions." Her voice became hopeful. "Anything from your end?"

Without identifying Primo, I rapidly summarized what he'd seen at Plymouth Willows, then mentioned Stepanian's school records.

Now Loiselle sounded disappointed. "None of that's much help, is it?"

"No, but these transcript discrepancies are the only things I've found that I can't explain."

"So what are you going to do about them?"

I told her what I wanted to do.

"You can't just call for that?" she said.

"Remember Olga getting me that check of hers that Andrew Dees endorsed?"

"Because without written authorization, universities keep their information pretty close to the vest?"

"Exactly."

A huffing breath. "Well, why do I make money if not to

spend some on a wild-goose chase? You're the investigator. If you think the trip makes sense, I'm good for it."

"I'll contact you when I get back."

My travel agent was able to arrange the bookings. Then I tried the DA's office. Nancy was in conference, so I left a detailed message, saying I'd call her that night if I could.

I locked up the office and headed home to pack.

Both my flight to Denver and the connection to Spokane were on United Airlines. The Denver leg was long, but Libby, the woman sitting next to me, turned out to be both pleasant and talkative. A student at a Baptist college in southern Colorado, she was returning from a monthlong "mission" in Spain and shared with me the charm of a foreign country as seen through the unjaded eyes of a twenty-year-old.

When the flight attendant served us lunch, my seatmate bent at the waist toward her tray and closed her eyes. A minute later, Libby opened her eyes again and reached for the plastic bag of utensils.

"Were you saying grace?"

"Yessir."

I thought, "Usually I pray *after* eating airline food," but kept it to myself.

The leg to Spokane was shorter, but by now I'd been sitting cramped for longer than anyone could be comfortable. The guy next to me, "western states sales manager" for an appliance company, said our destination was pronounced "Spo-*ken*."

As the plane started its approach to the airport, the senior flight attendant came on the PA system, speaking in a whisper. "Today's the captain's birthday, so when we arrive at the gate, I sure would appreciate it if you all could sing 'Happy Birthday, Don,' on my count of three."

After the laughter died down, my seatmate said, "See what happens when employees take over the company?" But ten minutes later, on the attendant's signal, he joined in with the rest of us.

At the Spokane terminal, I stopped in the men's room. On a wall of the stall, somebody had used a honed point to scratch:

> *Got no paper,*
> *Got no towel.*
> *Wipe your ass*
> *With a Spotted Owl.*

which made me remember I might be approaching logging country.

From the restroom, I headed toward baggage claim. Killing time waiting for the carousel to start, I stood near a glass case. Its caption read: EVERYTHING IN THIS CASE WAS TAKEN AT THIS AIRPORT. The case itself contained revolvers, semiautomatics, switchblades, boot knives, brass knuckles, even ninja throwing stars and a hand grenade. The poem on the men's-room wall seemed less out of place, somehow.

After picking up my suitcase, I found the rent-a-car booths. A young woman with sunny hair and a "We're No. 1" smile asked if she could help me.

"About how far to Moscow?"

The smile got wider. "If you really mean 'Moss-*cow*,' about fifteen thousand miles. If you mean '*Moss*-co,' about ninety."

I returned the smile. "Thanks. Any other tips?"

"It's a real pretty drive, but only one lane a lot of places, so be patient if you get stuck behind a tractor or stock truck."

"What would you recommend for a vehicle?"

"Business or pleasure?"

"Business."

"Too bad," she said, starting the paperwork on a four-door sedan. "There's just the most beautiful lake at Coeur d'Alene. Named after the Indian tribe. The French called them 'Heart of an Awl' because they were tough bargainers in the fur-trading days. Now there's this big resort with speedboats for hire and a golf course that even has one hole on an island in the water."

"In the lake, you mean?"

"Uh-huh. If you like golf, I guess it's a real kick. If not, there's companies that run Jetboats up the Snake River south to Hells Canyon."

"South *up* the river?"

"Yessir. The Snake runs south to north—as the border between Oregon and Idaho down there—and those Jetboats just fly around and over the rapids. You get to see bighorn sheep, mule deer, maybe even a cougar if you're lucky."

"I don't think I'll have time. Any place to stay in 'Moss-co'?"

"Only one I know is the Best Western University Inn, but that's where everybody seems to stay anyway."

I wasn't sure about the logic of that sentence, and I decided to pass on any other questions.

The sedan came with a good map of the area, the best route appearing to be 195 South. It was fairly wide for five or ten miles, and I drove past large contemporary homes clinging to the ridges, more modest trailer parks sprawling in the flats. Pretty soon the road narrowed, though, and I could appreciate the booth woman's advice about being patient. But at least the slower speed gave me time to sightsee.

The views would make you realize why eastern Washington is part of "Big Sky Country." White, puffy clouds couldn't quite cover the stretch from horizon to horizon, letting the sunshine through in gauzy cascades, like a series of bridal veils. The topography below was hilly but contoured, all swells and curves, almost feminine. The colors were shades of brown, green, and gold, the stubbled remnants of last summer's crops, with dust devils kicking up tan funnels fifty feet high. Farmhouses painted gray and barns red dotted occasional oases of spindly pines and broader deciduous trees, curling tracks of driveways bringing pickup trucks toward access roads.

Every twenty miles or so I passed big, silvery silos like the Tin Man's head from *The Wizard of Oz*, the superstructures over them probably grain elevators. There were a few herds of beef cattle too, and when the highway veered near or through the towns, you could see men in straw cowboy hats and tooled leather boots, a motel marquee advertising an "Ice Cream Social." The rolling wheat can sure smell sweet.

Closer to Moscow, I went by a big, bare mountain to the east with signs saying "Steptoe Butte State Park." After the downtown of Colfax, I hit Pullman, then turned east onto Route 270 and crossed into Idaho.

There seemed to be more trees, and bigger ones. Ponderosa pines, long-needled and almost bulbous. Douglas firs with that disheveled, "Bill the Cat" look to them. Tamaracks sprouting golden needles that I remembered somebody once telling me fell off the "evergreen" come winter.

Even gaining three hours by flying west, it was nearly 5:00 P.M. when I found the University of Idaho on a hillside in Moscow, the campus dominated by what looked like an airplane hangar in gray, brown, and gold mosaics—the "Kibbee Dome." The rest of the buildings were mostly Gothic stonework, though, which surprised me, I guess because I suffer from the easterner's prejudice that only we have "older" architecture. Leaving the car in a visitors' lot,

I started up one of the tree-lined, crisscrossing walkways, little markers identifying this spruce or that cedar as being planted by President Howard Taft or Eleanor Roosevelt.

After asking directions from a strolling undergraduate wearing a "Lady Vandals" sweatshirt, I finally located the registrar's office in a red-brick annex to the main Administration Building. There were peach-colored tiles climbing halfway up the walls from yellow granite floors, a set of interior windows showing one woman still toiling away at her computer. A sign read: TRANSCRIPT REQUEST TAKES 3 TO 4 DAYS.

As I reached into my jacket pocket, the woman looked up from her keyboard. "Can I help you, sir?"

"Actually, I'm just glad to find you still open."

A warm smile as she stood and came to the window. "My husband doesn't get off his job till five-thirty, so I kind of flex-time it here."

"I need to see a former student's file."

"You mean transcript?" she said, glancing toward the sign.

"No, I already have that." I handed her my stock letter with the forged "Lana Stepanian" at the bottom. "I'd like the file itself."

The woman went through the letter quickly, then slowly. "Well, we don't have our own form for that, but this seems more than fine." She appeared a little pained. "Of course, the photocopying would be awfully expensive, and I'd have to mail the package to you after we received your check."

"Actually, I'm in kind of a bind, timewise. I really have to see the file today, though I shouldn't need any copies."

The woman looked at me differently. "Where're you from?"

"You don't get many Boston accents out here?"

"No, but I thought that's what I heard. My husband and I had a great vacation there—oh, it must be three years ago now. Paul Revere's House, Faneuil Hall, the wonderful churches along the Freedom Trail."

"Plus you get to walk it instead of driving two hours south from Spokane."

"Oh my, you didn't come all the way to Moscow just for this, did you?"

I nodded.

The woman's face broke into the warm smile again. "Well, we can't turn you away 'hungry,' so to speak. One minute."

I didn't hold her to the minute, and in fact it was five before she came back to me. "Oh, I'm afraid this student transferred."

"To Boston University?"

"Yes. But we still have her application to us. State resident back then."

I read through the pages. "Lana Stepanian" gave as an address "121 Nez Perce Street, Cedar Bend, Idaho," the same as on the transcript I'd already seen. Listed as next of kin were "Nibur and Ellen Stepanian." Her personal statement was an essay about how she wanted "to study Spanish and become a teacher in a big city like Boise." None of it made any sense.

"Something else I can do for you?"

I looked up. "Yes. Where's Cedar Bend?"

"Down by Lusston."

"Lusston?

"L-E-W-I-S-T-O-N. Lusston. It's across the Snake from Clarkston. Get it?"

"Lewis and Clark?"

The warm smile.

Her directions took me south of Moscow on Route 95 and eventually to the crest of an incredibly steep grade with a big sign saying LEWISTON HILL: THE FIRST CAPITOL. On the downslope, smaller signs indicated spurs functioning as RUNAWAY TRUCK RAMPs. At the bottom of the grade was a broad, slow river that might have been the Snake.

Turning here and there, I saw the CEDAR BEND arrow the registrar woman said I would. The town itself was small and dusty, middle-aged men appearing to be Native American standing next to dinged and rusting pickup trucks, talking and laughing quietly. They were tall, with husky upper bodies running flabby at the belt, their legs both skinny and bowed in blue jeans.

I pulled up to a man with a wispy moustache under a broad, sun-scarred nose and a cowboy hat tilted back on his head, the shaggy black hair tumbling onto his shoulders. He was talking to a kid of sixteen or so who looked enough like him to be a cousin. Despite the chill in the evening air, the younger one was dressed in baggy jeans and a basketball singlet, his hair shorter and pulled back into a ponytail.

"I wonder if you can help me."

The older man said, "Might be."

"I'm looking for 'Nez Perce Street.'"

The younger one said, "We're called 'Ness *Purz.'*"

My day for being corrected. "Sorry."

The older man pointed with a tattooed index finger. "Southeast."

"How far?"

A shrug. "Guesstimation, mile or so."

"There a sign?"

Deadpan. "I can't remember, right offhand."

The kid grinned, but said, "You'll see an old filling station, just a pump sitting all by itself. Another fifty yards, on your left."

"Thanks."

I drove southeast, saw the shell of a filling station with the pump as described, and shortly thereafter a left. No sign, but I took it.

In the growing darkness, it was hard to make out numbers, but one soul kept a light on above the doorway of 97, so at least I knew which side of the street to watch. After a few more internally lit houses and a vacant lot, I saw 125 and pulled over. Backing up slowly, I tried to find a number on the home before the lot. It looked like 117. Which would make the empty space 121, the address on Lana Stepanian's application and transcript. Not great news.

Leaving the sedan, I walked up the path to the house—more a bungalow, really—before the lot. A dog started barking, and I was almost at the porch steps when my eyes focused well enough to be sure I'd seen correctly from the car. The numerals next to the screened door were 1-1-7, no question.

A man's silhouette appeared behind the screen, his head turning to hush the dog, who stood down to a low, throaty growl. "Whatever you're selling, we don't need it."

"I'm not selling anything, but I would appreciate talking with you."

"About what?"

"The vacant lot. Number 121, right?"

"Not for sale."

I moved up to the door, the dog going from the low growl to a woofing. "I'm not interested in buying, either."

The man, maybe sixty-five or so, with sharp features, hushed the dog again. "What's your business, then?"

"My name's John Cuddy. I was looking for some people named Stepanian."

"Oh." He shook his head, slowly and sadly. "Well, that's too bad. Maybe you'd best come in, sit a while."

He'd shaken my hand as Vern Whitt, then bade me take a chair that wasn't covered by dog hair. In better light, Whitt's own hair was still sandy, but it didn't change my impression of his age at the door. He wore a chamois shirt, faded and patched, over corduroy pants and old hiking boots. His wiry body gave off that faint, musty odor of a man who doesn't have a woman reminding him to change his shirt every day. The dog by his side was a mutt, the German shepherd in him trying hard to push past three or four other bloodlines.

Whitt said, "Beer?"

"Please."

The living room was small and fitted with a woodstove that took some kind of pellets stored in a nearby aluminum feed bin, a big scoop stuck in the center of the pellet mound. The furniture was sturdy but old, wedding photos from the same vintage on top of the television and copycat Remington prints covering the walls. The prints depicted cavalry mounted on chestnuts and roans being ambushed by war-painted Indians on Appaloosa horses.

Whitt came back with two cans of Hamm's beer, the dog trailing closely. Giving me one of the cans, my host sat in the opposite chair, the dog now slumping over the front of his boots.

"Thanks, Mr. Whitt."

"Vern, please. We're both well past being young."

'Then John, too."

"All right, John, what brings you after the Stepanians?"

Whitt might be warming up, but the sharp features discouraged lying. "I'm looking into a disappearance in Boston. I thought talking to the Stepanians might help."

"Boston." Another slow, sad shake. "I'm afraid you've come a long way for naught."

"How do you mean, Vern?"

He sipped his beer. "Nibur and Ellen, they're gone to glory."

I stopped with the Hamm's halfway to my mouth. "Dead?"

"Killed by the fire that destroyed their place." Whitt gestured with his can toward the empty lot. "Next door."

"When?"

"When. Let's see, it was about seven—no, my Katie was still alive," the beer toward the wedding photos, "so it's at least ten years ago, maybe eleven. Yes, eleven." He looked at me. "I lost Katie to a heart attack."

"I'm sorry."

Whitt nudged his dog with the toe of a boot. "We got Chief Joseph here the year before she died. Katie named him after the Nez Perce chief who stood off all those cavalry so long." He gestured toward the prints this time. "Admired that Indian, Katie did—she always liked it when I said that. 'Katie did,' made her think of a cricket sound, summer things." He coughed. "Anyway, Katie named the pup after Chief Joseph, and when she died, he just followed me around everywhere, like he'd lost track of her and didn't want the same to happen with me." Whitt looked toward the wedding shots again. "Don't think I'm going senile, but somehow the years since she's been gone kind of, I don't know, run together."

I took a little beer. "You said the fire was eleven years ago?"

Back to me. "What? Oh, right. Tragedy. Katie was better friends with Nibur and Ellen than I was, being off working all the time. But they were fine people, and when the flames took them, well, we had some money set aside, and Katie said, 'Wouldn't it make sense to buy their lot rather than see somebody else build on it?' So we did." The slow, sad shake. "Hit the daughter real hard, especially after what happened to her roommate up at the university."

"The daughter?"

"Yes. She wasn't up there a year I don't believe, when her roommate died."

I leaned forward. "Died how, Vern?"

"In a fall. Terrible thing. Broken neck, I think it was."

"Do you remember the roommate's name?"

"No. No, I don't, but it was the brother who found her."

"The roommate's brother?"

"No. Lana's. Steven was up there too. His senior year, if I'm remembering the spread right."

I stared at Whitt. "Steven Stepanian is Lana's brother?"

"And devoted to her, he was. Always taking her places, even when they were in their early teens, then him coming home from the university when he was up there and she was still in high school down here. A nicer pair of youngsters you couldn't have wanted. Katie and me weren't able to have kids, but I'll tell you something. I can't imagine being prouder of my own than I was of them, handling all that tragedy piled one on top of the other."

My voice sounded hollow to me as I said, "Handled it how, Vern?"

"Well, at Nibur and Ellen's funeral, big brother looked crushed every time he was alone, but by his sister's side, he stood tall, arm around her shoulders or holding her hand, just being strong for her and their parents' sake."

"The children weren't hurt in the fire, then."

"No. I was working the night shift—twelve to eight for Republic over in Clarkston—but Katie told me all about it when I got home. She had the good sense to spray the garden hose on the side of our place nearest them. By the time the fire engines arrived, the flames next door were shooting a hundred feet in the air. Started in the kitchen, they figured afterwards, right below the parents' bedroom. Steven got himself and his sister out in time, but the parents—well, I guess that was God's plan."

"God's plan?"

"Sparing the younger generation. Letting the children live while taking Nibur and Ellen."

"And this happened after Lana's roommate died."

A strange look from Whitt. "Yes, like I told you. Then

Katie and I made the offer to Lana and Steven, and you could tell they were relieved by it."

"Relieved."

"I told them I'd take care of the demolition and the carting, so they needn't have any worse dreams about the place than the fire'd already caused. I didn't say that last part out loud, of course, but Katie did to me." A small smile. " 'Katie did'—there I go again."

"Vern, what happened after that?"

"After we bought, you mean?"

"Yes."

"Well, like I said, Katie passed on pretty suddenly, and that left me—"

"I'm sorry. I meant, what happened with the Stepanian children."

Whitt scratched his head, which stirred Chief Joseph some, and his owner reached down and scratched the dog's head too. "I heard they used the money from the estate to move back east."

"You mean the money you paid for the land?"

"And the insurance on the house, since they didn't rebuild. I believe Katie also told me once that Nibur and Ellen had some life insurance on themselves. It'd make sense."

"What would?"

"Well, having the beneficiaries be the children if the mother and father both died together, right?"

After the parents stumbled on what they might have suspected themselves but refused to believe, would have wanted not to believe. The existence of the relationship that got their daughter's roommate killed in the first place.

I drove back to Moscow and found the Best Western University Inn on a main road near its intersection with a street named "War Bonnet." I checked in and asked the desk clerk if the restaurant was still serving. He looked at his watch and said politely that it was, but I might want to hurry.

Inside, I ordered the prime rib, but I don't remember much else about the meal or the wine I had with it. I do remember thinking about the Stepanians of Plymouth Willows. How much they resembled each other in appearance and mannerisms. How determinedly "normal" Lana projected herself to be the first time we met, not wanting to seem like a "gossip" about other people's personal lives. How her answers to my questionnaire were off just enough to finesse me, including mentioning the developer's bankruptcy but not his "suicide" or his "background checks" on the original purchasers. How carefully both Stepanians acted that second time, telling me only a little bit about the argument coming from the unit of the man they knew as Andrew Dees. But not nearly everything about what they must have heard said by the man and the woman arguing with him. Nor what Lana and Steven might have feared threatened their "normal" existence, and what they might have done about it.

After dinner, the polite clerk at the front desk hailed me. "Mr. Cuddy, did you get one of these?"

A printed, mustard-colored card. "What is it?" I said.

"Just a little survey we do. Don't worry, you can read it in your room. Have a good evening, now."

My room turned out to be only a few doors down the corridor. Once inside, I took off my watch, realizing how late it was back in Boston. I tried Nancy's number, anyway. Her answering machine clicked on immediately, giving me a chance to leave a message.

"Just calling from Idaho to say I love you."

When she didn't pick up, I hung up. After showering, I was trying to decide whether to postpone bed long enough to let my hair dry when I noticed the mustard-colored thing I'd laid on the night table.

It was a WARM & FUZZY CARD, the management wanting me to share any "great guest moment" a member of the hotel "team" had created during my stay. A nice touch from awfully nice people, but the way things had gone so far in Big Sky Country, I didn't expect to be completing it.

24

Outside the United terminal at Logan, Primo Zuppone said, "Cuddy, you look like shit warmed over."

"Thanks. How about some music?"

He checked all the mirrors of his rented Lincoln as we moved onto the loop road. "I'm not into music right now, you don't mind. I'm more into survival. Where the fuck you been?"

"Studying the effects of jet lag."

"What?"

As we took the back way toward the tunnel, and eventually the city, I told Zuppone about the trip to Idaho and what I'd discovered.

"You're saying that Ozzie and Harriet turn out to be . . ." Primo shook his head, as though he were trying to clear it. "So, it's them?"

"Probably."

"What's with 'probably'? We gotta know for sure, right?"

"Right."

"Well, how do we do that?"
"I've had seven hours in the air to think about it."

"Hello?"
"Mrs. Stepanian?"
"Yes?"
"This is John Cuddy. I interviewed you and your husband at Plymouth Willows regarding Hendrix Management?"
"Oh. Oh, yes."
"I was wondering if the two of you would be home tonight."
"Tonight?"
"Yes. I have some information that you might like to hear before anyone else does."
"Information? What kind of—"
"Let's say seven-thirty at your place?"
"I don't know if Steven can—"
"See you then."

I hung up the pay phone outside the grocery store in East Boston. Thankfully, too, given how much colder the air had gotten in just the thirty-some hours I'd been away.

From the driver's window of the Lincoln, Primo said, "We set?"
"Just one more call."

I dialed Nancy's number in Southie, leaving a message on the answering machine that I was back in Boston and would call her later.

After I got in the passenger's side, Zuppone put the gearshift into drive, and we pulled slowly away from the curb.
"Where to now, Cuddy?"
"My place."
"To pick up your Honda?"
I looked at him. "Among other things."
Primo said, "Good idea," then checked all his mirrors.

* * *

Opening the front door of unit 41, Lana Stepanian angled her head and shoulders to peer around me. "I don't see your car."

"I wanted to talk with Paulie Fogerty first, so I parked over by his house. It was such a nice night, I decided to walk from there."

I brushed past her then, moving into the living room with its marshmallow furniture. We seemed to be alone. "Your husband couldn't make it?"

Lana Stepanian joined me, perching on the arm of an easy chair. Alert. "Steven had a meeting for the School Committee that he just couldn't reschedule."

"I know how that can be." Going by the closet and downstairs bath to the sliding glass door, I looked through it onto the rear deck, then tried the handle. Locked. I slipped the latch and slid the door open.

Stepanian stayed where she was but twisted her torso toward me. "What are you doing?"

I made a ceremony of sliding the door shut solidly, then clicking at the lock. "Just making sure he hadn't come back unexpectedly."

"Steven?"

I returned to the living room, Stepanian turning again as I took the chair across from her. It swallowed me, but then I wasn't banking on being able to get up quickly. "Steven."

"But, Mr. Cuddy, I told you he's at a meeting."

"So you did. Meaning he's not upstairs or hiding in the closet, either."

She just watched me.

"Right?" I said.

Stepanian folded her arms irritably across her chest. "I think you'd better tell me what you came to tell us, and then leave."

I liked that she wanted to hear what I knew first. "Mrs.—

can I call you Lana, by the way? It'll make the rest of this flow a lot more easily."

Carefully enunciating each syllable, Stepanian said, "Whatever will be quickest."

"We have to start some years back, when you were still a teenager, maybe even early teens. You fell in love, and, dream of dreams, the love was reciprocated. You were very happy, but also very worried, because the two of you weren't supposed to be in love. Not that kind of love, anyway, and so you had to be very careful as well."

No reaction.

"But I guess you were also a terrific actress, and your lover an actor, because while perhaps one or both of the elders suspected, the neighbors didn't, and probably when you were able to be together at college, you must have thought, 'Now we can live a little more' . . . what, Lana, 'normally'?"

Still just a stony look.

"But then that darned roommate of yours. Did she come back to the dorm unexpectedly? I'm guessing it would have been something like that. And you couldn't explain it away, not what she saw. So, you two had to kill her, but make it look like an accident, a fall. Tell me, Lana, was she the first?"

"I don't know what you're talking about."

"Well, she's the first I can identify, anyway. So you're obviously distraught, or putting on a good act of it, and the next time you and the lover come home, the elders maybe have started sounding out the word, and they don't like what it seems to spell. They confront the both of you, and a second 'accident' becomes necessary. Only you have the good sense to realize that another fall, especially *two* other falls, would look awfully peculiar, so this time it's a fire, one that nearly takes you too, but for the heroism of your lover."

Stepanian's cheeks flushed, almost as if the flames from

that night were in front of her still. "Steven's parents died—"

"—in a fire that conveniently wiped out not just the elders, but also all kinds of family photos and potentially embarrassing other stuff that would show the idyllic lovers started life as brother and sister."

Her lower lip trembled. "You're saying crazy things."

"I don't think so, Lana. You and Steven sell the devastated house and lot to sympathetic neighbors, nice little bonus on top of the insurance policies. Combined, a nest egg for the new couple to start a 'normal' life in the East, about as far as one can get from Idaho. Big university here, nobody likely to pay much attention to a 'married' woman studying Spanish—a good choice of major, too, so she could pass as somebody with Latino roots. Then settling down afterwards, Steven with the more demanding job that might require a background investigation, you content with a simpler career of temping. Shallow maybe, but no risky credentials checks, either. The normal life of a normal couple, something that seems very important to both of you. No children, of course, given concerns of what a union of such close blood might produce. Tell me, Lana, which of you had the operation?"

A flinch.

"Even without kids, though, a couple could learn how to—'compensate,' I think, was the word you used when we first talked. Dedicated School Committee for him, lower-profile condo trustee for her, plus some charity-begins-at-home stuff like helping Kira Elmendorf with her father. Your unit here may have lost a lot of its resale value, 'trapping' you at the Willows, but everyday life was so natural, so normal. Until the developer who built this place began to have financial problems."

"Yale Quentin committed suicide."

"Only by trying to save his little empire through looking into the backgrounds of his original purchasers, to show his bank what solid citizens they all were. Did Quentin come to you directly, or did he just nose around Steven at work?"

No response.

"Whichever. You and your husband decide old Yale has to go too, and the 'scenic overlook' provides a perfect setting. You probably held your breath for a while after his death, but when nobody kicked the sleeping dog, it was time to relax and get back to normal again. At least until Andrew Dees moved in next door."

"Andrew was nothing to us."

"But something of a mystery, nonetheless. A loner, the man ran his own business, yet didn't try to be part of the community toward encouraging customers. He acquired a ladyfriend over the summer, which probably reassured Steven and you somewhat. Even though you were a little leery of Dees, you didn't see how he was any threat to you, the way your roommate and your parents and even Yale Quentin had been. Then I came on the scene."

The lower lip trembled some more.

"I showed up here with my 'questionnaire,' supposedly interested in how the Hendrix company managed Plymouth Willows but asking about things that couldn't have much to do with the complex itself. Personal questions, even probing ones. I have to tell you, Lana, my little survey wasn't designed to find out about you and Steven. It was just meant to give me cover for asking the same questions about Andrew Dees. But you couldn't know my intentions. All you knew was that something about me felt wrong. So up went your antennae, testing the wind for what it could tell you."

Stepanian started to speak, then stopped.

"Something to add, Lana?"

A shake of the head.

"Anyway, after my first visit, you and Steven probably began paying more attention to what was going on around the 'cluster.' Noticing Dees acting more strangely, maybe overhearing him on the phone or in person in his unit, yelling things. Things you might have caught only bits and pieces of, maybe while sitting out on the rear deck, reading in your lounge chair. Things that troubled you, because you couldn't understand the context in which he was saying them."

Stepanian just watched me.

I said, "Then last Thursday night, you and your 'husband'—"

"Don't say it like that!"

"What, Lana? The word, 'husband'?"

She didn't reply.

"Last Thursday, you and . . . Steven became aware of an argument next door. Not just one-sided, either. Dees and his ladyfriend, from what you could hear. Only you couldn't hear that well. Tell me, did you try to improve the acoustics? Did you maybe take a kitchen glass and put it up against your party wall? Did you hear something that set you and Steven off?"

Stepanian flinched again.

"I'm guessing you did. I'm guessing Dees was yelling something about his ladyfriend retaining a private investigator. Maybe, 'You hired somebody to investigate me and my *neigh*-bors?' Outraged, he would have said that loudly enough for you to hear it. And you both sensed another problem, another threat to 'normal' life as you lived it. The 'we-met-at-BU' cover you weaved was credible, but a little flimsy. Tug on the string, get on a plane, and the fabric of your and Steven's life together starts to unravel fast. Intolerably so, just like it would have when Yale Quentin started nosing around."

Stepanian gnawed on her lower lip.

"And so you must have decided pretty quickly what to do. Based on what happened next, I'm thinking that Dees also yelled something on Thursday night about worrying that he'd have to take a quick trip, even including ladyfriend coming with him. That gave you and Steven all the inspiration you needed. The roommate fell, the parents burned, the developer crashed his car into the sea. The newest threat would just . . . disappear."

Stepanian's lip lost some more skin.

"The only thing was, you had to deflect attention from Plymouth Willows. It couldn't look like they disappeared suspiciously, because then somebody might start poking around here after them. So you and Steven took ladyfriend's Porsche to the airport, carrying what were probably the suitcases missing from Dees' unit. Steven is close enough in size and coloring to pass for Dees at a distance, especially with a stranger, but you gilded the lily a bit by having Steven wave to the parking attendant. That was a mistake, Lana, since Dees himself would never have done that. And his ladyfriend would have insisted on driving her own car. Which brings us to why you used the Porsche. Because it was more conspicuous, easier for somebody to find at the airport and start the trail there instead of here?"

Suddenly one of the marshmallow back cushions on the sofa fell forward, the upper body of Steven Stepanian facing me, leveling and cocking a revolver from about ten feet away. He raised the index finger of his other hand perpendicular to his pursed lips. I didn't say anything.

Lana Stepanian moved behind my chair, pushing me gently at the shoulders as she felt around my back and sides for a wire or weapons. I had on the same suit I'd been wearing at Nancy's the previous Friday morning, and Lana found the Scottish fiddle tape in my jacket pocket, putting it back once she saw what it was.

After as thorough a search as she could manage without risking my grabbing her, she said, "Nothing," and then perched back on the armchair.

Steven Stepanian used his free hand to flip the seat cushion in front of him off the sofa, stretching his long legs out from a yoga-style, ankles-crossed position. "Ah, that's better. I was afraid I'd cramp up before you told us everything we ought to hear."

I inclined my head toward the loft. "I figured you to be upstairs."

"You'll appreciate why I'm not in a minute. To answer your earlier question, though, we needed Andrew's car for the bodies."

Until those words, I'd hoped I was wrong about that part.

Stepanian wiggled his right foot, as if he had a kink in the ankle. "Your version of what happened was really quite accurate. Very impressive, but also very . . . threatening to us, as you said before. After Lana told me about your first visit here and your peculiar questions, we were concerned. And then when we heard Andrew ranting and raving about being 'investigated,' we knew that he and his 'ladyfriend,' as you called her, had to take a 'trip.' Unfortunately, Lana can't drive a stick shift, so that left it to me to take the Porsche. Quite a machine, actually. I'm sorry I couldn't have enjoyed the experience a little more.

Lana said, "I followed Steven to Boston, where I parked our car and rode with him to the airport. Then, after we left the Porsche in the terminal lot, like you said, we took a cab back to our car and drove home."

Like a den mother, explaining the logistics for her troop's last scout trip.

I needed more than wanted the answer to my next question. "How did you kill them?"

"It was rather easy, actually," said Steven. "We keep a gun here—Lana, show him our gun, would you?"

She reached under the cushion on her chair, coming up with a small semiautomatic in her hand.

Steven nodded toward it. "Nothing showy, just for home defense. But effective enough. On Thursday night, Lana went knocking next door, supposedly with a question about the condo association. Andrew answered her knock and started to say he didn't really have time just then. The sight of me behind Lana, pointing our gun at his head, seemed to change his mind. With the four of us in the living room, his ladyfriend became quite nervous. Fortunately, I thought to search Andrew, much as Lana just did you. And what did I find but this revolver? Andrew wasn't very coherent— I imagine the stress of the situation was wearing on him— but he tried to talk us out of killing the two of them, offering us cash. It turned out to be . . . Lana?"

"More than sixteen thousand dollars, dear."

Steven's expression was almost rueful. "When the money didn't do the trick, the poor devil even trotted out some cock-and-bull story about being in the Witness Protection Program."

"He was telling you the truth."

Steven squinted at me. "No."

"Yes. Dees was planted here." I turned to Lana. "Your C.W. Realty Trust stands for 'Cooperating Witness.' Basically, the feds own the complex."

Lana looked to her husband, who was frowning at first, then smiling. The first I'd seen of it, his teeth tiny, like his sister's and at the same time like a child's.

Steven's head wagged slowly. "Ironic, isn't it?"

"Ironic?"

"Yes. All the time we lived next door to him, Andrew was lying, and we believed him. Then, as we're about to kill him, the man tells us the truth, and we think he's lying."

Very quietly, I said, "The killings happened in Dees' unit, then?"

"Yes. Oh, we made up our own cock-and-bull story, telling them we had to 'get away,' so would you both please just go upstairs into the bathroom and we'll lock the door and then give us an hour . . ." More head wagging.

I said, "What did you tell them you had to get away from?"

Lana broke in. "They never asked."

I turned to her.

She shrugged. "I think they were so frightened—and also so relieved, from what you've told us, that we weren't whoever Andrew 'cooperated' against—that they believed us without really caring about our reasons."

Steven said, "They wanted to believe us. You could see it in their eyes. They wanted so very much to believe that once they were in the bathroom, we were going to let them live."

Quietly again. "But you didn't."

He got indignant. "We've never killed anyone we didn't have to. For whatever reason, that ladyfriend started you investigating about us, invading our privacy."

Lana said, "We're not monsters, Mr. Cuddy. We simply love each other." An affectionate glance toward her brother. "We always have." Then back to me with, "Only people wouldn't think we were normal if they knew. They'd report us, like my roommate or our parents were going to."

"Or just discover the truth," I said, "like Yale Quentin, and maybe try to . . . use it?"

Steven shook his head. "He never got that far. We don't gossip or pry into anyone else's life. Why can't people like you respect our privacy as well?" Stepanian reverted to the matter-of-fact tone. "Anyway, we sent ladyfriend into the bathroom first, then I hit Andrew from behind with the butt of my gun, and he stumbled against her. They both fell, Andrew unconscious. I was on the woman before she could scream." His fingers flexed. "I choked her. She thrashed around some, but it didn't take long. Then I did the same to Andrew. He never even woke up."

Lana said, "And there was very little mess."

I just looked at her. If Olga Evorova hadn't retained me,

if I hadn't thought to use the "questionnaire" as cover, if Olga hadn't confronted DiRienzi with what—

Steven said, "Are you wondering why we didn't kill you as well?"

I turned to him. "No. You wanted to make it look like Dees left town, and you didn't believe him about being in the witness program. So you had every reason to think it would look odd to have me turn up dead right after they took their 'trip.' But that still means you had to do something with the bodies."

"Correct. Can you guess?"

"No."

"Think about it. We have to dispose of Andrew and ladyfriend, but we don't want to go very far with them, either. We drove the Porsche to the airport, but why not use Andrew's car for that?"

Steven was giving me hints, so I'd play the game. "Because the Porsche stands out."

"Yes, but you're looking at the right hand instead of the left."

"Because the Toyota hatchback can take the bodies more easily?"

Steven grew impatient. "*And?*"

The left hand, not the . . . "And because the Toyota doesn't stand out."

The tiny-toothed smile.

I said, "You used the Porsche for the airport because you needed a drab car like the brown Toyota for the bodies."

Still the smile.

It came to me. "The bog."

The loving wife said, "And there's plenty more room in it, too."

I looked at her. "Won't wash, Lana. You try to sell me on going peacefully 'to the bathroom,' I'm not going to believe it, and the neighbors will hear any shooting."

Steven said, "I've been thinking about that, actually. It seems that your fingerprints are nicely on our sliding glass door. What if you slipped in because we accidentally left it unlocked, then found you here and shot you for a burglar?"

"Sitting in your chair?"

"You slumped there after I fired, but before I realized the intruder was you."

Given Kourmanos and Braverman finding me breaking in next door, Boyce Hendrix and Tángela Robinette might believe that. Because, like Dees' "running away," they'd "want" to believe it. And they might sell the Plymouth Mills police on it, too.

I said, "One problem, Steven."

"What's that?"

"You're holding the wrong gun."

"Wrong?"

"The revolver belonged to Dees, may be traceable. Lana would have to be the shooter."

"Oh, that's not a problem." She came off the arm of the chair. "I don't enjoy killing, Mr. Cuddy, but it is my turn." Now backing toward the staircase, glancing toward her brother, "Would this be far enough, dear?"

Raising my voice and speaking sharply, I said, "Primo."

The sliding glass door, which I'd unlocked, whistled open. Shots blazed from the muzzle of my Chief's Special in Zuppone's hand as I hurled a throw pillow at Steven. Lana being closer to the door, Primo took her first, the weapon flying from her grasp and somersaulting through the air. Rising, Steven got off two shots, but my pillow hitting his wrist sent them high and wild as Primo's next bullets nailed him to the sofa like spikes driven by a sledgehammer.

My ears were ringing from the gunfire. "You hear what they said?"

"About the swamp and all? Yeah. Look, I gotta get out of here." Zuppone tossed the Chief's Special to me.

"Primo, thanks."

"Don't mention it." He went back to the glass door. "And I fucking mean that."

Moving out onto the deck, he hopped over the low railing and was gone.

25

I know where you can find Andrew Dees."

Tángela Robinette stared at me from the front stoop of the Stepanians' unit. Empty-handed and arms raised, I was standing in the entrance foyer after having answered her pounding on the door. You could see the adrenaline surge in the whites of her eyes around the irises, and in the way she gripped her weapon, combat stance and chest high.

Robinette said, "Lace your fingers behind your head and turn around. Slowly."

I complied.

"All right, now walk forward till I tell you to stop."

Again.

"Jesus Lord," said Robinette behind me.

"They're both dead as far as I can tell from a pulse. The revolver on the dinner table is mine."

"Sit in that chair there, hands where they are."

Taking a seat, I saw her going toward the telephone. "You might want to hear me out before calling the locals."

Robinette hesitated. Then she moved toward my chair, stepping carefully around Steven Stepanian's splayed legs in front of the sofa. "Short and sweet, Cuddy."

The police chief of Plymouth Mills was named Niebuhr, a human bowling ball in flannel shirt, uniform pants, and anorak, hood down. A reed-thin detective named Hertel wore a turtleneck sweater and khaki slacks the way a scarecrow wears its waistcoat. I stood with them at the edge of the bog. Behind us, both Robinettes, Kira Elmendorf, and Paulie Fogerty were among maybe twenty other people from the complex and town. The two patrol officers who had initially responded to the scene in the Stepanians' unit held the rubberneckers back from the action.

A big tow truck with four rear wheels was parked nose to road, the driver playing out metal cable from the winch in the bed of it. A town diver and a State Police one in scuba gear buddied up on parallel ropes to enter the chocolaty water.

Niebuhr said, "I don't envy those boys this one."

Hertel spoke from the corner of his mouth. "Cuddy, let's have your story for the chief, huh?"

I began the version Hertel already had heard, the one Robinette and I had agreed upon in the Stepanians' townhouse. "A banker from Boston named Olga Evorova hired me to look into the background of her almost-fiancé, Andrew Dees."

Niebuhr said, "Whatever happened to romance?" then spat. "Go on."

"I figured a good way of investigating Dees would be to visit his neighbors, using as a cover story this fictional condo complex that was thinking of changing management companies to the outfit that oversees Plymouth Willows here."

Hertel spit too, not quite as well as Niebuhr. "Would have

been nice to let us in on that when you started asking around."

"I saw it as harmless at the time, and it would have been, but for the two psychos who lived next door to Andrew Dees. Apparently my questions about their background—so I could do the same with Dees—pushed the wrong button in their heads, and they came to think I was investigating them somehow. So, when they overheard Dees and Evorova arguing about me questioning his neighbors, the Stepanians decided to protect themselves the only way they'd learned how."

Chief Niebuhr inclined his head toward the bog. "By killing Dees and your client."

"Right."

Hertel said, "Which the Stepanians supposedly did already to a college girl and their own parents in Idaho."

"That's what I realized from my trip out there."

"And you flew across the country on a hunch that maybe this couple wasn't kosher?"

"All I had to go on was a school transcript and the bad feeling I got talking to the Stepanians themselves."

Niebuhr said, "Bad feeling?"

"They were trying so hard to be normal, Chief, they seemed off the beam."

Hertel followed up. "And you had yourself a second client, right? This other banker who was willing to pay the freight for the trip."

"That's right."

One diver surfaced, looking like a bug stuck in the icing on a birthday cake. The town guy, I thought, but it was tough to tell.

Taking the regulator out of his mouth, he said, "We got a vehicle."

Niebuhr said, "How can you see anything down there?"

"You can't, Chief." The diver caught the clamp end of the

cable swung out to him by the truck driver. "But you can feel the bumpers and tires and stuff." Then to the driver, "When I give this three tugs, start your winch, but really baby it." Putting the regulator back in his mouth, he slid beneath the surface again.

"Alright," said Niebuhr to me. "I get why you thought the Stepanians were hinky. Off the record, I went to one of the School Committee meetings, and the guy seemed to have a rod up his ass the whole time I was there. What I want to hear real slow and clear, though, is why you had to do a *Wild Bunch* routine back there in the condo unit."

I took a breath. "All I had was a missing client that another client was paying me to find, and some odd things involving the Stepanians as brother and sister in Idaho when they were playacting at being husband and wife here. I couldn't see your department doing anything about that beyond charging them with incest. Especially when the only evidence about what had happened to Evorova was a near-sighted parking-lot attendant who saw a man and a woman leaving her neon Porsche with suitcases outside an airline terminal in Boston."

Hertel said, "So tonight you came visiting the Stepanians to—what, bluff them into making a confession or something?"

"Or to eliminate them as suspects in my client's disappearance, the same as I'd done with the other neighbors."

The chief nodded. "But instead, the Stepanians tried to eliminate you."

"As soon as I was in their unit, they got the drop on me. The wife did a quick search, but she never thought of an ankle gun."

"And after they told you their story . . ."

". . . the two of them had me get up and move to the sliding glass door, which I did. Then I faked a stumble, drew the revolver, and came up shooting."

To Hertel, Niebuhr said, "Check out?"

"Dispatch logged in calls from first an Elmendorf, K-I-R-A, then three minutes later from a Robinette, T-A-N-G-E-L-A. Both reported shots fired, and I interviewed them. They confirmed that Cuddy made the rounds last week, talking to the neighbors about all kinds of shit they thought was goofy." The detective glanced at the crowd behind us. "Elmendorf looks like a punker, but Robinette's a service widow and a steady head, far as I can tell. Both the Stepanian corpses had weapons near them, two shots discharged from the husband's. Assuming the crime-scene techies don't throw us a curve, the physical evidence I could see supports Cuddy's version."

All three of us noticed the tugging on the tow-truck cable, like a big fish had just taken the bait. The driver cranked a lever, and the winch began drawing the cable tight, then whining a little as it strained to break the inertia of something heavy on the bottom. After five seconds, the driver goosed the lever, and the cable started winding onto the reel of the winch.

Chief Niebuhr said, "I am not looking forward to this shit."

The divers surfaced before anything appeared at the bog end of the cable. They were ashore, walking backwards to accommodate their fins, just as the roofline of the hatchback broke water.

When the front doors were visible, the town diver held up his hand to the truck driver, who stopped the winch. The diver waded back into the bog, using a wet-suit glove to wipe the gunk from the driver's-side glass. Then he shook his head.

Niebuhr said, "What've we got?"

"The stuff of nightmares, Chief," the diver waving toward the truck to start the winch again.

As Hertel turned to the uniforms, asking them to keep the crowd back, I said a silent prayer for Olga Evorova.

Sitting at her kitchen counter, Tángela Robinette said, "Would you like some privacy?"

I lifted the phone receiver off the wall. "No, thanks."

Trying Nancy first, I left a message on her machine in Southie that I was fine, despite what she might hear from a news bulletin. Then I dialed Claude Loiselle's home number.

A sleepy voice answered.

"Claude?"

"Yes?"

"It's John Cuddy, Claude. I'm sorry to be calling so late, but something's happened, and I didn't want you getting—"

"John, is Olga dead?"

I gave it a beat. "Yes."

"Aw, no." Then, not into the phone from the pitch of her voice, "No, no, no."

"Claude, I'm so sorry."

Back at me, snapping. "How? How did that son of a bitch Dees kill her?"

"He didn't. A couple that lived next door was psychopathic, thought Olga had somehow hired me to look into *their* lives, and they had something to hide they thought was worth killing both Olga and Dees to protect."

"No. No, that's not fair, not fair."

"Listen, Claude. I'm sorry to impose on you, but I think Olga's uncle ought to be told too. The problem is, I'm going to be here in Plymouth Mills for a while longer, and I don't have his number with me."

"I can get it." More determined. "Let me call him. I'll be up the rest of the night anyway." Then, "This psycho couple, what's going to happen to them?"

"It already has."

A pause. "I'm glad. Glad for that, and glad I hired you."

Another pause, and I pictured Loiselle sitting up in bed, trying to cope. "Look, I appreciate your letting me know, I really do. If you're stuck with anything down there, have the cops contact me, and I'll ... I'll ..."

When I hung up, Loiselle was still crying.

Tángela Robinette took a swig of coffee from a mug, then pointed with it to a pot brewing on the stove. "Some of this might help."

"No, thanks."

She set her mug down on the counter. "I appreciate your keeping a lid on the situation here, far as the locals are concerned."

"Too many cooks."

"That is exactly right. We just cannot be cutting the town departments in on these group situations. First thing you know, somebody talks in their sleep or lets it slip in a bar. Then Geraldo and Oprah will be here next, elbowing each other out of the way to film a show on location."

" 'Anonymous turncoat felons and the women who love them.' "

"Your client." Robinette closed her eyes. "Sorry."

"I'm the one brought it up." I started to leave. "Thanks for the use of your phone."

"Cuddy?"

"Yes?"

"I truly believed that Andrew Dees had just flown the coop. If I had thought—"

"Ms. Robinette, who are we trying to convince here?"

When she didn't answer, I walked through her living room and out into the night.

"Hey-ey-ey, Cuddy, how you doing?"

Zuppone's words were right, but the tone and facial expressions belonged to a man hanging on by his fingernails. He stood at the curb outside my condo building, behind the open door of his own Lincoln. In the faint lamplight, my watch read 2:00 A.M.

I went over to the car. "Primo, I figured you'd be in bed by now."

"No way. You got a couple minutes?"

"Sure." I moved around to the passenger side, glancing into the backseat as I did. Empty.

We both entered the Lincoln at the same time. Instead of starting the engine, Zuppone hunched over the wheel, like a driver having trouble seeing out the windshield. Then he started thumping his thumb on the top of the dashboard.

I said, "Okay, where do we stand?"

"With the two organizations—mine and Milwaukee?—pretty good, considering. The funeral home here's gonna embalm Rick and Coco. Better than trying to semi-thaw the bastards so their people won't know they bought it three days ago. The way our coordinator put it over the phone tonight, Milwaukee thinks their guys were fucking heroes, done in by the Judas and his girlfriend before you and me got them."

"You and me."

"It was the only way made sense, Cuddy. We avenged Rick and Coco by putting DiRienzi and your client in his car and pushing it into the swamp there. Then we used the couple next door as the cover for it. The Milwaukee people weren't happy, but they ate up the shit about Ozzie and Harriet being brother and sister. Incest, they don't like that very much, so it appealed to their sense of morality, us icing 'the sinners' to fool the cops. Speaking of which, everything go okay on your end?"

"It didn't, I probably wouldn't be here."

"Right, right." But distant. Then, "Cuddy, you ever shoot a cop?"

"No."

"How about another soldier, then, like when you were in the Army?"

"Came close a few times overseas."

I waited for him to get to it.

Zuppone cleared his throat. "This thing . . ." He cleared it again. "This fucking thing is tearing me up."

"Shooting Ianella and Cocozzo."

Primo spoke to the windshield. "I can't eat, I can't sleep. Shit, I had to take some pills for tonight, for what we pulled off down there. Me, a fucking druggie now. It's like I told you before, I swore this oath, a blood oath to the only fucking people that ever did for me in my whole life, ever made me feel I belonged to something. And now I betrayed them."

"By killing members of another organization without orders to do it?"

"Right, right. Before, it was always . . ." Primo turned to me. " 'Sanctioned.' I looked that up, because I knew there was a word for what I was thinking, only I couldn't remember what it was. Every other time I killed a guy, it was 'sanctioned' by the people above me, thought through and decided after everybody weighed the risks and the bennies, you know, of whacking the party involved. Only this time . . ." Primo faced front again, his voice lugging like my Prelude trying to climb a hill in the wrong gear. "This time, back in that fucking slaughterhouse there . . . I wasn't acting on orders. I was freelancing. . . . Cowboying it to make things turn out the way I wanted them to. And I been lying ever since." I realized Zuppone was choking back tears. "Lying to the fucking people who made me . . . what I am today. I don't understand it, and there ain't even anybody I can talk to about it. I . . . I . . . " He gave out, sinking his chin into his forearms on top of the wheel.

I lowered my own voice. "Primo, you crossed a line. Crossed it to save me, but like you just said, you made the decision for yourself."

No reaction.

Fingering the Alasdair Fraser tape in my jacket pocket, I said, "Maybe we could ride around for a while, listen to some music."

After a moment, Zuppone lifted his chin from his arms. "Yeah." Snorting, he turned the ignition key. "Yeah, matter of fact, I wouldn't mind that, you got the time."

"I've got the time." Taking the cassette from my pocket, I handed it to him.

"What's this?"

"Scottish fiddle music."

"Scottish fiddle?"

"Kind of 'Old Age' stuff." I thought back a few nights to Nancy and me, awaiting the results of her biopsy. "It's good background for talking things out."

Primo looked over. "Tell you the truth, I wouldn't mind doing that, either. The talking part, I mean."

After popping the tape into the slot by his radio, he took a fresh toothpick from the ashtray and stuck it in his mouth. "So," clearing his throat again, "what do you want to talk about?"

Settling back into the buttery upholstery, I caught myself almost smiling. "Whatever comes to mind."

Primo Zuppone nodded once. Checking all three mirrors, he edged out into the empty street, his voice blending with the fiddle's melancholy strings.